the Mozart CODE

A Novel

RACHEL MCMILLAN

THOMAS NELSON
Since 1798

The Mozart Code

Published in Nashville, Tennessee, by Thomas Nelson. Thomas Nelson is a registered trademark of HarperCollins Christian Publishing, Inc.

Published in association with William K. Jensen Literary Agency, 119 Bampton Court, Eugene, Oregon 97404

Thomas Nelson titles may be purchased in bulk for educational, business, fundraising, or sales promotional use. For information, please e-mail SpecialMarkets@ThomasNelson.com.

Library of Congress Cataloging-in-Publication Data

Names: McMillan, Rachel, 1981- author.
Title: The mozart code: a novel / Rachel McMillan.
Description: Nashville, Tennessee: Thomas Nelson, [2022] | Summary: "From author Rachel McMillan comes a richly researched historical romance that takes place in post-World War II Europe and features espionage and a strong female lead"—Provided by publisher.
Identifiers: LCCN 2021050453 (print) | LCCN 2021050454 (ebook) | ISBN 9780785235057 (paperback) | ISBN 9780785235064 (epub) | ISBN 9780785253419 (downloadable audio)
Subjects: BISAC: FICTION / Historical / World War II | FICTION / Romance / Historical / 20th Century | LCGFT: Historical fiction.
Classification: LCC PR9199.4.M4555 M69 2022 (print) | LCC PR9199.4.M4555 (ebook) | DDC 813/.6—dc23
LC record available at https://lccn.loc.gov/2021050453
LC ebook record available at https://lccn.loc.gov/2021050454

Printed in the United States of America

22 23 24 25 26 LSC 10 9 8 7 6 5 4 3 2 1

For Kat,
The kind of friend we read about in books as
kids but we lucky few grow up to find.

*I could never recommend you to do the
frivolous type of work which is popular because
easily understood. Great matters should
be met in a great and exalted spirit.*

—LETTER FROM LEOPOLD MOZART TO HIS SON
WOLFGANG AMADEUS (NOVEMBER 1, 1777)

A NOTE FROM THE AUTHOR

HISTORICAL NOTE

There's a line in the film *A Knight's Tale* in which its fictionalized version of writer Geoffrey Chaucer admits he gives the truth *scope*. I used my scope and lens to write a book set against events rooted in truth—but given enough elasticity to serve the core of Simon and Sophie's love story.

In order to set the stage of the early days of the Cold War in a Europe bearing the scars of WWII, I implemented some fictional license. I encourage readers to look at this book as a bridge to the past and as an opportunity to be enticed by a fascinating time amidst two cities often overlooked in historical fiction.

VIENNA, PRAGUE, AND KALTER KRIEG

Post-war Vienna was a quartered city starved of electricity and petrol in the Russian quarters and overrun by German immigrants wading from one barren land to the next, and it was also plagued by record-breaking food and crop shortages. Rations were precarious and housing shortages were tragic. The once jewel of the Habsburg empire was felled only to be captured by four different allies. Die Vier im Jeep, or "Four in a Jeep," was a city-wide symbol of the split Innere Stadt of the Baroque city. The Soviet quarters did cut off Red Cross supplies as well as control petrol and electricity often in hopes of starting an uprising among their portion of a population desperate and still experiencing the trauma of war.

History leaves cracks through even the most beautiful places and histories, such as Vienna's. Communist support and leftover fervour for the National Socialist Party complicated a parliament just beginning to vote for Austrian interests after being headlocked by Hitler for so long. The city was a free-for-all in terms of philosophy, ideology . . . and spies. Vienna is still renowned as a "city of spies": the shadowed corners and coffeehouse meetings, not to mention the slow passage of messages and the dead-end trails of those killed in the line of espionage duty, have been popularized by authors such as Graham Greene, who wrote most of his book, *The Third Man*, at the Café Mozart adjacent to the Sacher Hotel where Sophie meets her contacts.

Those looking for a breakneck speed of the Hollywood version of the Cold War need only to notice the irony of its long stretches in history textbooks. Indeed, I tease with my editor that it was a "war of nerds" in many ways: using academics and artists and influential men at soirees and lectures for a slow burn infiltration of Communist ideologies spread throughout an isolated and terrified post war population desperate for a return to normal life.

The exhibits (such as those Brent and Simon visit at Moser's request) and propaganda provided by each of the four allied quarters are very real. I had an opportunity to visit several replicas at the Architekturzentrum Wien, which showed the good intentions of all four parties to rebuild the city to their specifications and meld Vienna's most beloved architectural structures to their own patriotic ideas.

The Marshall Plan

After the war, there was also the very precarious balance of allied countries who had a common enemy in Hitler and now found themselves facing an enemy they had fought alongside. One such ramification was The European Recovery Program. In its first iteration it was named The Morgenthau Plan: while this plan narrowed in on depriving Germany of its ammunition, it soon evolved in its determination to see ravaged cities such as Vienna rebuilt and American funding secured for reconstruction. Beginning with the installment of independent government, the renamed Marshall Plan accounted for much more than financial assistance as its American creators offered not only food and necessities but the "bread of life" of culture, books, and art.

BLETCHLEY PARK

Men and women from various backgrounds in academia and beyond were recruited, and debutantes or women from high social background (like Sophie) were preferred due to a belief that they would be the most trustworthy in this world of guarded secrecy. As in my companion book, *The London Restoration*, I wanted to excavate some of the more human interest aspects of Bletchley Park and the fascinating men and women who worked there. Like my fictional Simon Barrington, many men with a proficiency for chess were recruited. Perhaps the most famous was Hugh Alexander: a renowned chess master whose logical mind and codebreaking abilities appear in nearly every piece of research and memoir I read about this fascinating place.

The biggest historical liberty I took with Bletchley was in Sophie's working of the Bombe Machines. In actuality, these were worked by the Women's Royal Navy Service (or WRNS). But while visiting Bletchley Park for research, I was fascinated by how Alan Turing and Gordon Welchman preferred tall women who were able to reach the drums and rotors. It was not too far-fetched that a tall and athletic woman might be assigned to this rigorous role.

The Death Mask and Mozart

Mozart's arrangement of Handel's Der Messias is one of the many recovered artifacts still on display at the Lobkowicz Palace within Prague's Hradcany Castle. The Lobkowicz family represents many similar estates whose art and artifacts fell victim to Hitler's greed. At first poorly reviewed and still studied to be an unwelcome interpretation by some purists, Mozart's arrangement of this beautiful piece proved a complicated and beloved puzzle to musicians and audiences alike. Similarly, in Vienna, you will hear differing claims about the authenticity of Mozart's death mask. History does assert that a death mask believed to belong to Mozart did appear in a pfandhaus in Vienna in 1947—even though the composer is notoriously buried in a pauper's grave. Indeed, if you travel to Austria, you will find a replica of the mask in Michaelerkirche near the Hofburg and in the Mozarthaus Museum in Domgasse. Yet, when speaking to Viennese historians, I received alternating opinions as to its authenticity.

Civilians in Espionage

So many books speak to the amazing feats but also the great intelligence and bravery of men and women spies in the war years. In this way, Sophie and Simon's breeding and background allotted them a different war experience than many. And, in the case of The Mozart Code, they show the more human side of people untrained and often unready to be thrust into this new world.

The "Baker Street Irregulars" (the name Special Operatives Executives were given in their earliest form) proved an endlessly intriguing means of highlighting the roles women played and the sacrifices they made for the good of their country. While I played fast and loose with a few dates in order to ensure Sophie's fictional background, the coverage of that world is hopefully reflected in Sophie's indomitable spirit and her desire to make a mark on the War.

The Fall of the Iron Curtain

Throughout my research, I was shocked to learn how precariously close Vienna was to falling behind what Churchill referred to as "The Iron Curtain" in 1946. While it is still renowned as a "City of Spies," the Marshall Plan assured that any visits today offer a breathtaking step into the grandeur of its Baroque past. Prague's happy ending, however, was delayed. Even the rebuilding of some of its more beautiful war-ravaged structures was waylaid as it fell under a Soviet stronghold that lasted nearly half a century. The political tensions referred to in the book and the dwindling support of the Communist Party in the Czech political sphere would reach a breaking point with a Coup d'Etat in 1948—just one year after the events of *The Mozart Code* take place.

Yet, despite the varied shadows over both historic cities during the Second World War and thereafter, they do share a composer. To visit Vienna and Prague even today is to be shrouded by Mozart. Both cities can rightly claim Mozart, who—even through the darkest tenets of their respective histories—loans a mournfully beautiful musical backdrop to cities that have stood the scars of many wars. They are cities I will never stop exploring—in books and on foot—for the rest of my life.

CHAPTER 1

November 1946
Schloss Schönbrunn, Vienna

Simon Barre had left his best revolver back at his family estate near Wilmington, Sussex, along with the Barrington surname. He didn't miss the surname, but he did miss the expensive steel of his Webley MkVI and the smooth curve of the handle. His preference for it was one of the few things he shared with the man who gave him the name he had shrugged off.

Now, in the shadow of the moonlight, he could make out the remains of the Baroque palace's bombed gloriette, stretching over the depleted shell of once-manicured gardens and a fair distance from the twinkling champagne glasses and winking chandeliers of the party he had abandoned.

It had taken a bit of time and a rather flirtatious telephone call with his target's secretary for Simon to discover that Dieter Hofer would be here at the party in hopes of procuring the favor of an investor from like-minded individuals in attendance. Before the war, Hofer Family Industries had been a leviathan of industry, settled amid power plants and near the Aspern airfield. The Nazis had seen to its repurpose for their own munitions gains. Now, the Soviets spread out on the other side of the Danube, their influence creeping into the border between Vienna and Lower Austria.

No matter the Hofer family's political allegiances, their precarious position in the minefield of shifting ideologies made their sudden interest in uranium production stand out to the Secret Intelligence Service, given the European interest and fear in atomic warfare. The Americans had not only changed the game of war but had overseen the shift of the world's greatest threat from Nazi terror to the ability to obliterate entire populations with the press of a button.

Simon's interest was a matter of deciphering *how* the Hofers would exchange information and through what means.

Austria had enough academics, scientists, and curious minds affiliated with the Eternity spy ring committed to pursuing this new war. Simon's leads on Eternity had struck hot the moment he settled in Vienna, but they had begun to slowly dwindle after the June election.

The Communist shadow loomed large long before the war. Simon was familiar with the movement of the first half of the century when it spilled through the First Austrian Republic. Then, after the first war when the last of its monarch rule fell and the Social Democrats rose to power, Red Vienna presented many of the similar ideologies that were advancing the Soviet agenda now.

The longer Simon divided his time between Vienna and London, the more transient he felt. Even while successfully and covertly continuing the work of his small team, he had been unable to suss out how the ring could be linked to the rise of Soviet influence in the city: in political cabinets, in withholding rations, in unequal treatment of prisoners of war, in the inability to show the same compassion the other Allied counterparts attempted in providing aid from their respective countries.

When his target approached, it wasn't hard to follow the man's secretary's description. She had said Simon couldn't miss the younger Hofer son. He wore an eye patch. Simon spared only a moment of sympathy for the man's wartime scars. Hofer now served his country by aiding Eternity: a ring of prominent Soviet sympathizers spreading the Communist agenda in a far more violent way than in the political arena.

A vast difference existed between the atrocities perpetrated by the Red Army as they marched to end the war and those with political idealism that would set the next chapter of the world's history. Simon wasn't precisely sure how involved Dieter was in Eternity or in the business itself.

What he did know was how to lure him out to the gloriette and away from the party. The Eternity calling card was the infinity symbol in mathematics. He'd slipped it in a note to a man presumably part of its elite and small circle of influence. If Hofer was affiliated with Eternity, the symbol would be an immediate draw. If not, Simon hoped the man's curiosity would draw him anyway.

This man was the pawn, and perhaps the game was finally beginning. What would Dieter choose? One or two spaces? Simon had set up the board to start with the front line of his opponents. And he intended to uncover the man's business.

"I still do not understand why you are so eager to speak to me."

"Must I spell it out?" Simon widened his eyes framed by gold-rimmed glasses. He had been told that his eyes were remarkably disarming, apparently to great effect. "Well, your family owns a fuel factory in Meidling, does it not?"

"*Ja.*"

"In one of the Soviet zones. The same Soviet zone that is starving people by stealing their UN rations. And you work at the factory as a general manager. You see to all of the accounting. To the shipping and receiving. To the fact that goods that should be making their way into the hands of the general populace are not."

"There is no evidence that I—"

"You are being paid," Simon enunciated. "You are being paid or there is no other reason you would keep your fellow countrymen from basic human necessities in this drawn-and-quartered city." He drew his regulation-issue Enfield No. 2 from his coat pocket and aimed at the man's chest. "I know several of you are complicit. Men you work with. Men you never associated with before this bloody war. I want the manifest for Meidling. *Now.*" He jabbed the man's jacket lapel with the barrel.

And if I have that, maybe I'll know where to start.

The man held his hands up and swallowed hard. "How do you know I have a manifest at all . . . ?"

It was quite remarkable the information men inside the party were willing to pass along when they didn't expect Gabe Langer, professor and artifacts enthusiast, to be watching them. Simon utilized Langer to great effect and capitalized on Hofer being in over his head. Perhaps the man had begged and convinced others he was the perfect person for the job—to attend a soiree and exchange information.

Simon chose to ignore the man's question. "Who are you truly working for? And don't say your father."

"Herr Barre . . . surely you can see reason."

"My reason is this: I came to the party with the express purpose of seeking you out." Simon's casual tone belied the intensity of his grip on the revolver. "I find you and then I retrieve what I assume is inside your breast pocket, since you glance down in its direction every forty-five seconds."

And then I get one step closer to figuring out how Eternity is using this city much as it did London.

Simon narrowed his eyes. "That's a rather ill-fitting suit jacket. Droops a little at the collar, far too roomy at the elbow, don't you think?" He steadied his hand and pulled the trigger.

The bullet shot directly in the path of the man's elbow. Simon was rather proud of himself. Charles Barrington always said he was just a little off on his shot. Too passionate. Too logical. That there needed to be some heart in it.

The man skittered over a few feet. "You shot me!"

"I shot *at* you." Simon tucked the revolver back into his jacket pocket and used the man's surprise and distress to approach him. "Do you play chess? Well, *en passant*. If you had taken one step, I wouldn't have shot at you. Two and you somehow would have avoided your opponent."

Simon peeled back the man's lapel and sought the paper therein. "Ah!" He retrieved the folded manifest. *"Danke."* He tucked the paper into his pocket with flourished aplomb.

The man motioned to the graze on his elbow, the clear tear in his jacket sleeve. "You . . . you *shot* me!"

"A mere technicality. And your repetition bores me."

"You're a loathsome, heartless b—"

"Stop right there." Simon spoke over Hofer's last word. "You've suffered an egregious loss." He raked his gaze up the man and over to his arm. "And there's little your tailor can do about it."

Simon straightened his shoulders and turned from the gloriette back to the golden palace.

The grounds of Schloss Schönbrunn were Versailles-like in opulence, span, and scope and offered Simon ample opportunity to retrieve his gold cigarette case from behind the manifest he had tucked into his jacket pocket. Leaning against the stone columns underneath the outside staircase, he could see that the Great Gallery was chaos, erupted with people.

With a lighter slid from his cummerbund and the flick of his long fingers, it was but a moment before he pressed the cigarette between his lips. Simon drew in a long length of smoke. The lights from the grand, sprawling palace shone over the grass and gardens glimmering from a recent rain.

He headed inside and reached for a glass of amber liquid from a passing tray. A scene familiar to him during his thirty-five years on the planet. He recalled his father's countless insufferable parties at the family estate in Camden. The music, high-end *Schwarzmarkt* cigars, and bottomless glasses reminded him of long spring nights when Simon strolled around the room, a calm presence to compensate for his half brother Julius's intoxicated antics, already looking forward to the moment he could escape.

This party was to celebrate Viennese industry and the restoration of the economy. Many similar and somewhat vague soirees of the same were held throughout the city, each a more glaring contrast to the housing and food shortages.

The moment Simon had entered the ballroom, several eyes latched on to him. It wouldn't be the first time his regal posture and expensive tailoring led men to assume he was some dignitary or another. He sartorially met any challenge, and the face Simon Barrington presented to the world was untouchable: his armor Savile Row; his weapon his slickly pomaded ebony hair; his shrewd, ethereal blue eyes flashing confidence he didn't always feel.

Vienna's usual business of coffee and pastries and music was, on account of the war, swapped for espionage. One could cozy up and bribe people for secrets or trade, to advance the ideologies that would usher in the new war. As long as one had money and time, there were pockets to be filled and men whose allegiances were apt to turn in spite of Vienna's reputation of being a neutral zone. Ironically, the paperwork and propaganda spoke of peace, but there were always backyard deals to be made to further the Communist agenda in and out of the Soviet quarters.

Still, Simon enjoyed the old-world charm of Vienna, even after its bombing—a nostalgia tied to a gentle, elegant, and refined Europe. His privileged experience clashed with the shattered world he witnessed every day. The attendants he recognized were from such different spheres. From nearly the moment Simon had arrived, his spit-shone shoes and pinstripes authorized a quick introduction to the vital players in Vienna's new game.

Simon squashed his cigarette in a decorative dish nearby and lit another. Cigarettes were worth more than currency here. The loss of the Germans meant the loss of the Reichsmarks, which now sat worthless under the cracked soles of a city blinking its way from desecration into a new occupied regime.

Gabriel Langer approached him and stopped next to a high table. "You were gone a long while."

"I needed the air."

Gabe raised an eyebrow. "Air indeed."

An academic of history and Habsburg aficionado, Gabe had a background not unlike Simon's: descended from a long aristocratic line. And while Gabe's Austrian empire had crumbled, he still bore its influence in his noble bearing and elegant mannerisms.

"Did you get what you needed?" Gabe smoothed his slicked-back white-blond hair.

Simon clenched his jaw behind a long drag of smoke. "I got what I needed. Anything?"

Gabe inclined his head to the ornate doorway, where a man named David Moser accepted a drink from a passing servant. "I cannot get a read on Moser. He's chancellor at Leopold University and is familiar to some in my social circles."

Their highbrow heritage was not the *only* thing they had in common. They had someone else too. "Oh?"

"Sometimes he's working with his fellow Austrians, and sometimes he's using Starling to sell antiquities to Russian sympathizers on the black market. To whoever the highest bidder is. And he doesn't work alone."

Simon had a network of reliable informants in the city, and Moser's name was often mentioned among them.

"And Moser gave me this when I casually approached him about retrieving a fragment of a manuscript. Ja."

Gabe continued and Simon barely heard him. He was too interested in accepting the card Gabe gave him. Simon turned it over. It held the name *Tomas Adameck* and an address in the Staré Město quarter of Prague.

He tucked it in his pocket as their attention was momentarily drawn toward the arrival of a dignitary wearing medals, a sash, and everything that glistened of the recent war. The side unsullied by men lining up for watery coffee, with no pensions or stipends. The men who had money even as prisoners of war trudged in from the Hauptbahnhof, or train station.

Recently, author George Orwell had given name to the war of ideas and propaganda: the Cold War. *Kalter Krieg.* When a country was ripe for the picking, any ideology could find fertile soil to root and grow. And the rich would get richer. It was why Simon so preferred this new war: one of tact, diplomacy, and hopefully as little violence as possible. His corner of it was a world of affluence and influence he was bred to understand.

Marcus Brighton, his overseer at the Secret Intelligence Service, appreciated Simon's concern with the rise of Communist ideals that had crept onto the coattails of the war that just ended. What some labeled as an obsessive and unfounded pursuit of Communist influence during the Blitz, Brighton not only tolerated but appreciated.

"Tomas Adameck was wounded in the war," Gabe said. "Walks with a stick. I am still not completely sure of his influence here. But he has important contacts in Budapest and Prague. Odd man. Czech."

Simon nodded at a passing waiter and took a glass of whiskey from his tray. "Contacts you know?"

"And that Starling knows as well."

Simon swirled the dregs of whiskey in his glass. Starling was the code name of his dear friend Sophie.

"Whispers are circulating around Leopold University about . . . well, something of a higher value than most of the art and artifacts we have been working with. Considering the caliber of men pursuing it— at least insofar as my leads—" Gabriel stopped. Raised his shoulder. "There's more here, Simon. I am not sure how much more. Or what . . ."

"The war has certainly overturned a treasure chest." Simon downed the last of his drink.

"It's more than that. There's an ideology attached to it through artistry. In art and beauty. Sophie and I went to one of Moser's elegant soirees. He is so taken with Starling. She's also been spending more and more time *with* the artifacts. I go on a mission to see it to an end. Finding you information." Gabe watched Simon, as if expecting a response. "Sophie seems more interested in the value of the pieces than in who is seeking or purchasing them."

"I don't think her fascination with a few interesting objets d'art is anything of concern." Sophie liked finery. But more still, Sophie loved music. It was partly how he had coaxed her to Vienna in the first place: a city song she hadn't memorized enough to hum or play. "She's never given me any hint that she's not helping me."

But belying Simon's casual tone was a thoughtful gravity. He wanted Sophie to be of use to him, yet never go *too* far. Impossible when he considered that she was a flint ready to spark against the first stone standing in her way. He couldn't be held responsible for the connections she made or had made in the city even when he was occupied in London.

"She's *changed*, Simon. Since you've been back in Vienna . . ." He raised a shoulder. "It's different now. I don't know exactly what she is telling me or not." Gabe shook his head. "She's far more sought out now than when we first started here."

Simon patted the card in his pocket. "Well, we're far beyond finding suspects selling snuffboxes and pocket watches to fund the Soviet agenda," Simon said evasively.

"More than that." Gabe took a sip of his drink. "Money's money. Few in Austria have any, and even if you can buy a few delegates or votes, that influence doesn't last long around here. What the Communist supporters need is *ideology* that will convince those who didn't vote for them to do so now. They need to control the feelings of patriotism. Austria's history was almost taken from us at Heldenplatz the moment Hitler marched in with his tanks. The moment he addressed thousands who had shown up to hear his words."

"With no one armed to meet him," Simon said darkly.

Hitler had notoriously marched in without even a single rifle to stop him. Simon wasn't the only Brit in the city who had trouble understanding why the Austrians put up so little resistance. But he decided to consider each person as he would a player on his chessboard. Each had their advantages and faults. One could never lump them into a straight line. Not even the pawns.

Though men like Langer revolted without bullets. He was more of an ideas man. It was why Simon liked him.

Gabe nodded sadly. "There are those who want to return Austria to its former greatness, who would be well rid of Allies, and those who feel so guilty for siding with the enemy for extra rations or to keep their precious mementos that they slide their guilt under the carpet, hoping the Russians make such a mess of it, it absolves them." He tapped ashes from his cigarette and scanned the room.

Simon knew the National Socialist Party still held a strong standing at the last election. He slid his gaze in Moser's direction. "And him?"

"I'm no further in my investigation than the last time you asked. He has strong political ties and leanings and often throws parties that, to my knowledge, exist merely to show off his not inconsiderable collection of rarities repossessed after the war."

"Eternity?"

"What if there is something larger than Eternity at play here?" Gabe theorized after a moment.

"More potent than an invisible web of Soviet sympathizers?" Simon tipped his whiskey glass. "Larger than the messages they are surreptitiously passing and their quiet infiltration of entire cities?"

It wouldn't be long until Moser approached their table. He had been weaving in and out of the crowd, engaging in short conversations, and Simon could sense the man's eyes flick over at him.

"When the world is a free-for-all." Gabe's carefully measured words held a somber note. "You're seeing my city through the lens of a British man determined to stop the spread of Communism. I see my city as one who knew what it once was and what it could be again. I *know* you are highly regarded. Trusted, even. But forgive me if I remain—what is the English word?—*wary*."

Simon wasn't offended. His covert career had taken him on a long journey and to a great many parties.

A similar conversation had occurred before Simon packed the last of his custom wardrobe from his family's Georgian-era Mayfair house.

"But I'm not sure my heart's in it," Simon had told his boss, Marcus Brighton, an old friend of his father's and a man who was adamant about Simon's potential, whether at a soiree or a rickety mansion in Bletchley where Simon became a team leader for a group of code breakers during the war.

"Well, make sure it is," Brighton responded. "I've a lot riding on you."

"You're sure of an awful lot." Simon frowned. He supposed Brighton saw in him more than Simon saw in himself. It wasn't a feeling he had much experience with. Charles Barrington was determined that Simon knock himself down a peg if ever his voice was too confident in relaying his success in examinations or his acceleration in a chess match.

Gabe had every right to be wary of a man who couldn't decide whether his heart was in his position here, let alone foresee a future that would restore the city and Gabe's beloved country to what it had been before the war.

Sure enough, Moser approached their table as Gabe excused himself for a refill. Simon had just finished straightening his right cuff link and smoothing the lines of his jacket.

"They're rather wonderful." Moser gestured toward Simon's monogrammed cuff links. "Special, are they?"

"A present." There was far more to the story, of course. But Simon had learned from childhood that stories were manipulative things. After all, Charles Barrington had made up Simon's heritage as needed and wielded it as a weapon.

"You have fine taste." Moser gestured toward Simon's refilled glass. "I'm having a small soiree at my home two nights from now. If this scotch is to your liking, I have plenty more in the cellars."

Simon assessed Moser's dark brown hair and medium build. He conveyed a casual sort of handsomeness. Perhaps unremarkable on first glance but distinguished, dressed as he was now and offset by the glamour surrounding them.

"After the war, I decided never to deprive myself, to snatch at the chance for finery whenever I could find it. You strike me as a man who would appreciate that." Moser studied Simon a long moment. "You should come."

"That's very kind of you."

"I have a feeling that ours could be a symbiotic relationship." Moser didn't look directly at Simon but rather at the action around them.

"How so?"

"Gabriel Langer obviously confides in you and perhaps so should I. I have been in the city a lot longer than he has, and it is not always easy to decipher who is a prospective friend or another foe."

With a swift smoothing of his tie, Simon verified that the manifest from Hofer's was still firmly tucked inside his breast pocket. It was a reactive move common when he was in proximity to someone he couldn't get a read on. Moser didn't seem to notice.

The moment Moser was out of Simon's sight line, he relished a long exhale. Only one person knew the toll it took on Simon to convince the world that he fit. Only one person knew that while he seemed to command a room with natural ease, he was far better suited to occupying a corner with a chessboard or a shared cigarette.

Simon twisted his cuff links. A gift from a wedding that wasn't really a wedding. A marriage that wasn't really a marriage.

From a woman who knew him better than anyone else in the world.

CHAPTER 2

That same evening
Schloss Belvedere, Vienna

Lady Sophia Huntington-Villiers once imagined the code name Starling would help her deliver messages behind enemy lines for the Special Operations Executive, a division of MI6, during the war. Instead, it became a constant reminder of things she might have done before she had been rerouted to a manor house in Bletchley Park and her war effort involved turning rotors on Bombe machines that decrypted Nazi messages. So she repurposed her *nom de guerre*. Resurrected it. Now, men who dealt in high-end artifacts and antiques used *Starling* to summon her throughout the muted grandeur of a felled Vienna.

Her clients imagined they were dealing with someone elusive and mysterious, and she wielded her skill in plenty of anonymous actions. When Simon Barre learned an arrested double agent assumed to be involved with Eternity had been found with a valuable Habsburg artifact, Sophie found herself working with Gabriel Langer to help uncover other possible ties between artifacts and the Soviet threat Simon was so intently focused on.

In London, Simon had only been able to narrow in on a King's College professor with a penchant for finery. But it set something off and sparked Simon's looking into more connections between suspects and art and, fortunately for him, allowed for a role for Sophie Villiers.

She waited in the orangery for Herr Karl Haas in the moonlight. If she angled her head the right way and squinted just enough at the city, she could imagine the jewel of the former Austro-Hungarian Empire as it had once been. Not as it was now, so militant that *Die Vier im Jeep*—an army jeep boasting the flags and soldiers of the four Allied victors—was a symbol of a city quartered.

But tonight, when the hills and low mountains encased the wrecked palace like a gem and light funneled through the maze of spires and steeples unblemished by bombs, she could almost forget the ration queues and worthless bills. The wretched POWs and refugees slumping through, shoulders burrowed with the leftover war and on the brink of another one.

Sophie ensured that her ivory-handled pistol was loaded and within easy reach in her waistband. Most of the men involved in the Schwarzmarkt, or black market, she worked in were not in the business of killing or assaulting women. But Sophie could never be too careful.

She had helped men from all levels of government, art, academia, and army rank restore some of the opulence and beauty Hitler had taken when he barged into the city and claimed the art as his own. Hitler's curator, Bruno Grimschitz, had used Austrian galleries and museums to his whim and will, pilfering anything desired for the new Reich.

If someone wanted to pawn a piece or reacquire it from said pilfering, Starling's name settled easily on their lips. She could get them the best deal while at the same time discover who held the most financial influence.

The few people who still had money in Austria were often using it to restore their estates to their prewar glory, though Simon suspected some were using their affluence to bribe their way into political spheres or to further the cause of Eternity.

Fortunately for Sophie, she didn't give a hang about the money until she found a way to filter it to a food bank or an orphanage or a housing office for displaced and bombed-out citizens. If men wanted to pay her handsomely to track down a set of candlesticks bearing the Habsburg crest from the time of Maria Theresa, she was more than happy to do so. Especially since she found a sly ally in Herr Müller from a *Pfandhaus* in the Neuer Markt. A man who understood quite well that Sophie's hunting, bartering, and trading were far from her own gain.

The vantage from the orangery gave full view of the Belvedere's Upper Palace in reconstruction. The Lower Palace's famed Hall of Grotesques was badly bombed near where she stood looking over the immense grounds up to the Upper Palace on a small hill. The Marble Hall and magnificent Baroque statues were one of many casualties of war. The reparations had begun on the blasted castle but would doubtless take years.

She typically met clients at locations determined by Herr Müller, but in Karl Haas's case, she determined the meeting place, drawn to the scarred interface and architecture still bearing a shadow of beauty and imagining it in happier times.

Though she occasionally passed Simon intelligence integral to his monitoring of the rising Soviet agenda in the city, her role in Vienna was a race of adrenaline . . . especially in seeking and finding a particular rare piece. The more it related to the city's musical heritage, the more interested she was.

"Entschädigung." A voice pierced her thoughts.

"Herr Haas." At a height that startled some, Sophie was often in a position to look down at a man as she was doing now.

"Ja. And you are Starling." He gave her a polite once-over, then locked his gaze on hers. "I need you to acquire something for me. Something rumored to have been recently found."

Men like Haas often sought her out to start a hunt. "I can try."

"It's more than just a piece of art. An artifact." A grave expression settled on his handsome face. "I need to hire someone I can trust. Someone who will be sympathetic to my cause."

"Why do you think you can trust me?"

"I was at a party with Herr Moser, and he mentioned that you might be of assistance." He took in the ruined castle and grounds around them: the barren fountain and bare trees, the overrun gardens. "Austria's market is a free-for-all. A missing Klimt. Thirteen of his paintings for the Universität Wien sent for safekeeping are now incinerated because of the Nazis." He clucked his tongue. "I want the right artifacts to be returned to the right people."

"And *you're* one of the right people?"

"I'm a patriot. I want to build up my country again. I want to *recover*. So many of the original owners are heaven knows where. Many have died. Shipped out. Many were Jewish families. You comprehend."

She dug her nails into her palm. "I *do* comprehend." During her SOE training, Sophie had met a few young Jewish women who shared their stories of how they'd barely escaped Germany and Austria with their lives during the horror of the *Kristallnacht* pogrom—the "Night of Broken Glass"—while their fathers were sent to concentration camps. Thereafter, any property remaining was repurposed for the Reich. She comprehended all too well that too many rightful owners of the art and artifacts she pursued were orphans to owners long perished. And any legitimate claim was caught in the web of a country now confused by four competing Allied forces.

"It gives me no great pleasure to be working with a Briton." Haas drew her back to their discussion. "I, for one, feel we are more than ready to get our great country back. We don't need the Allies playing nanny. We can run our own government. But I have heard that you can find things. For all sides."

"I can imagine the disruption." More than that, she could empathize. War was a great equalizer: it demanded far too much of staunch patriots and forced regular people into a holding place where they weren't ever truly sure if they lived up to the standard living history had set.

"Moser said you have a deft touch when it comes to procuring that which no one else can find."

"I have contacts."

"I know. But you are not Austrian, and yet he said you worked so delicately because you *believed* the right person wanted it."

"And this is what inspired you to come to me for your precious artifact?" Sophie raised an eyebrow. "The fact that I am *not* Austrian?"

"You have no personal attachment."

"Maybe I will when you tell me what it is."

"I will pay you handsomely."

"In Reichsmarks? Cigarettes?" She smiled. "Chocolate and silk stockings, perchance?"

"Schillings. What I want is deeply important to me."

Sophie crossed her arms over her chest. "A family heirloom, perhaps?"

"I will not be the only person attempting to locate this. But it is of the utmost importance that I find it first." Just under the certainty in his voice she detected the slightest falter. "Many doubt its existence and have since before the war. But I do not. Dangerous men of immense power will stop at nothing to find and keep this rather remarkable piece of history as a bargaining chip. You would be taking a risk."

"I've taken risks before." Sophie hoped her mounting heartbeat wasn't evident through her blouse.

"I have heard that before. Yes. Your interest in Mozart will serve you well, Fräulein. There is a contact who will meet you at Minoritenkirche tomorrow evening. After mass. He will tell you where to start the search."

"I thought that would be you."

"I want an intermediary to keep as much distance between myself and your recovery as possible. I am an influential man. You are known as a woman of taste and discretion. And I like you."

"That's a by-the-way, Herr Haas."

"But an important one." He reached into his breast pocket and produced several Austrian schillings as well as a folded note. "This should see to your immediate expenses. Inside the note you will find the name of the contact and the object of your pursuit. But please burn it right after reading."

She opened her pocketbook and tucked the bills inside. She casually opened the sheet of paper with a slight laugh as soon as she read it. "This cannot be real. Cannot be authentic."

"There are rumors. Here and in Prague. But they're only whispers that this is real."

"Then why do you need a go-between? What if I just take what you've already given me and go and find it for you?"

"As I said, there is a risk. I have a wife. Children. But it is for more than just its monetary value. It is our history." He leaned into her ear even though no one was around to hear their conversation.

Sophie shuffled through her mind for something to say. From what she had learned during her time in Vienna, history was as easily bought and sold as cigarettes on the black market. Everyone felt they had a claim to history.

While the most recent election had seen the Communist Party gain only four legislative seats, Gabe told her numerous men of his acquaintance voted Communist, and the Nazi Party still had a surprising voter turnout. So even though Herr Haas had said "*our* history" with certainty, the country and its ideologies were rebuilding just as the fallen grounds around her would be.

"And what if I get a better offer?" Sophie asked on impulse. If he wouldn't take the risk, why should she?

"I'll ensure that you don't." His tone implied retribution. He tipped his fedora at her and left her.

During her time in the Austrian capital, Sophie had helped high-ranking and powerful men retrieve wedding rings and pearls, gold cigarette cases and lost love letters. She had flitted in and out of parties and withstood the advances of men who were fascinated by her beauty, height, and bearing. Soon the love letters became Klimt paintings and famed pieces of Habsburg jewelry.

Still, she had never been asked to retrieve something of this status. While her skills were stellar, were they sufficient for this job?

Sophie struck a match and burned the note before she placed the ember to a cigarette and lifted it to her lips. She didn't need to retain the instructions or the commission—they were branded on her brain.

Minoritenkirche. After mass. Tomorrow night.

Die Totenmaske von Amadeus Mozart.

Sophie folded into the back seat of the taxi. *The death mask of Mozart.* A smile tickled her lips. She played Piano Concerto no. 17 over the knees of her pressed trousers. No matter where she was—from New York to the Bombe machines in Hut Eight at Bletchley to a recital at the parish church near Ashton—Sophie recalled music. She *loved* Mozart: a composer of ineffable beauty but also logical precision. He was a language she understood when her mother's meterstick rapped on her palms after a shoddy practice session or her father spoke of her growing up to marry Julius Barrington or one of the other wealthy, titled bachelors to ensure their family's legacy continued.

To find Mozart's death mask would be to recognize the face of a friend, she was sure.

Vienna spread before her in the distance, bombed buildings marked by wear and craters, the fluttering streetlights catching the sheen of a recent rain like jewels sparkling on the pavement. She was out past the unofficial curfew, and it wouldn't be the first time. She had long since decided the easiest way to feel like she owned the city was to *act* like she owned the city. While some women might have simpered and played innocent, Sophie would straighten her shoulders, stiffen her spine, and convince herself that she belonged.

And the longer she convinced herself, the easier it was for her to believe it.

Karl Haas had engaged the beginning of her evening, but it was definitely not her last stop before home.

In the Volksgarten on the second bench adjacent to a path rimmed with trees long deprived of their leaves, she knew Frau Wagner would be waiting. They had a standing appointment here.

Sophie's high prices for her work for men like Haas became higher once Herr Müller had put her in touch with Frau Wagner. She ran a shelter for women for whom the liberation at the hands of the Red Army had resulted in far more than deprived circumstances. The women nursing illegitimate children were trying to piece together a life after brutal assaults.

At first Sophie had sent money via anonymous donations, leaving it with Herr Müller or having Gabe run the errand. But Frau Wagner wanted a touch point, someone she could trust, and Sophie had proven herself to be that person.

She paid for and dismissed the taxi. Then she slowed her steps, making out the outline of the middle-aged woman she was set to meet.

"You are very kind to be here." Frau Wagner's salt-and-pepper hair fell over her creased forehead. Her callused hands were tucked into the rehemmed sleeves of her overlong coat. "I always worry that this is too dangerous for you."

Sophie believed it necessary. Was it dangerous? Certainly. Vienna was full of moments of unspoken public tragedy. During the first wave of Soviet liberation, the desecrated buildings and lack of food, water, and police force of any sort found both Austrians and foreigners plundering to survive. With the second wave of the Red Army, discipline of any sort was replaced with utter chaos.

Candid photographs of civilians shot on park benches peppered papers in English and in German. Some snapped not far from where Sophie was now. She never let down her guard.

Sophie pressed an envelope into Frau Wagner's hand. "This way I know that you receive it personally and can do with it what you deem best. I don't trust men in this city."

Frau Wagner was rarely effusive. The slight lowering of her shoulders and a softness smoothing the rigid lines of her firm mouth were the only indicators that she appreciated Sophie.

Sophie, whose upbringing was a careful study in reading body language and facial expressions over words unspoken, understood her quite well. A lady, Sophie had learned, tucked emotional words into her handkerchief or into the smooth folds of her collar. If you mete and measure just enough for the listener to glean your meaning while leaving them wanting more, then you always had the upper hand.

A moment later Frau Wagner departed, and Sophie watched until she reached the more pedestrian-heavy Ring. On their first meeting she had told Sophie that nothing surprised her. She had seen everything. Whatever weighed her shoulders down and creased a kind, sympathetic face made her eyes far older than middle age.

Sophie had seen similar worn faces throughout the city, and each one impressed upon her the need to charge more for her services. To find more means to help. What else was she going to do? Go home and wait for her mother to shove her in the path of the next available blue-blooded bachelor? A woman didn't spend four years of the war turning her brain on only to flick it off to play hostess.

Part of her wanted to go abroad. Part of her *would* have gone abroad—if it wasn't for the pesky piece of paper she kept tucked behind her sherry decanter.

The wind whistled around her as she approached the classic Theseus Temple just behind the Hofburg Palace, where she would cross into the Innere Stadt and make her way to her flat. Sophie's ears were perked for the slightest footfall, eyes alert for the slightest moving shadow, careful to compensate for the paths not lit by streetlamps as she neared the Doric-columned temple that felt a bit like Athens in the middle of the community park in Volksgarten.

Her nerves tingled at movement behind her.

Sophie swiftly removed her revolver from her waistband.

"Which hand are you going to shoot me with?" a familiar voice said behind her. "The one you want people to *think* is your dominant hand? Or your dominant hand?"

Sophie's exhale moved through her shoulders and down her spine. "You know I could outshoot you with either. What's the term for that?"

"Ambidextrous." The shadow met her stride and bowed his head to her. "Villiers."

"Simon. Refreshing night, is it not?"

"*Tsk, tsk.* A woman out at night alone." But the seriousness in his tone belied his tease.

Lord knew how his eyes could be so piercing blue even in the darkness. She put her gun in her handbag and fastened the clasp.

"We really ought to stop meeting like this, darling," Simon said. "In the chill of autumn, the leaves a romantic shade of crumpled brown, two Soviet soldiers over there near the National Library might be waiting to shoot us for breaking curfew." He smoothed back the lines of his carefully pomaded black hair. "Or for whatever fabricated excuse they find to justify their power."

He looked her over. "You really should be careful, Villiers."

"I am careful. I was nigh prepared to shoot you. *You* should be more careful. What are you doing here?"

"Needed air. Insufferable party. Langer had some interesting information about a man in Prague." She could sense rather than see his smile. "I shot at a man."

"At a party?"

"Just outside the party. I didn't actually hit him, just his ill-tailored suit."

They walked a few steps in silence. Simon had once told her

that Dickens would walk the whole of London again and again at night, trying to find his muse in the dark streets and steeples. Simon enjoyed silence and the same walks that allowed him to stretch into the city like a familiar coat. She alone knew that after a long day in a crowded hut overseeing workers at Bletchley, he would take to the village for a long stroll before he joined the crowd at the pub, pasting on a smile and playing several rounds of chess with Fisher Carne. Listening to Diana regale her peers about church architecture.

Though Sophie's mind often roamed during these silent moments, she recalled them when she saw the devastation of Vienna around her. Her friend Diana told her to see the structures not as they were now, their beauty snubbed like a snuffed-out candle, but in the splendor they would be again. After all, the scaffolds crisscrossing over towering monuments like Stephansdom and the blockades around the Plague Column on the Graben spoke to how quickly the city was determined to restore its beauty.

"Why are you here?" Simon asked. "I saw you at Theseus Temple and confess to waiting until you had finished your business."

Sophie raised a shoulder. "The usual. *Starling.* Charged to find something." The name had often been enough to denote her meetings and transactions.

Simon shifted and turned to face her, their shoulders brushing in the darkness. "And will Starling find it?"

"I think that Starling . . . I . . ." Starling had never been charged with something so magnanimous before.

"Because I happen to think that Starling can do anything she sets her mind to." His voice grew more serious. "Though I'd prefer that she not set her mind on clandestine midnight meetings."

She felt the tension pulsing in him due to his proximity.

A rustle sounded beyond them, and a shadow emerged. A flash of metal and the length of a rifle protruded. Simon stiffened from inches away. He instinctively started to slide her behind him, but she had another idea and stalled him with a grip on his forearm.

Simon swiftly met her gaze in the moonlight. She gave an inkling of a nod. There was a quick solution that would yield an easy explanation.

He gently cupped her cheek, pulled her face forward, and lowered his mouth to hers.

CHAPTER 3

Simon felt Sophie's mouth part slightly under his. It wasn't the first time he had kissed her, but the urgency and danger around it sparked a fuse burning through him. He lingered on the sensation until the rifle barrel dug into his shoulder.

"What is the meaning of this?" Many of the Soviet soldiers were merely doing their duty, but this man clearly enjoyed his temporary authority.

It took longer than Simon wished to recover the breath he had given her in their improvised exchange.

"We have so few moments together." Sophie continued their ploy and pouted for the soldier.

"I don't know . . ." The soldier frowned.

"Please." Sophie's alto voice was as high as she could make it. "His wife will not . . ."

Simon pressed his lips together to mash down a laugh. It wasn't the first time they had evaded severer danger by kissing away suspicion. Not the first time the irony blasted through him either. If the situation wasn't so blasted threatening, Simon would have enjoyed it more.

"Spare me." The soldier backed away from Simon and waved his rifle. He said something in Russian to Sophie that they both understood far too well. Simon flared and Sophie grabbed his forearm to still him.

Aware of the rifle's proximity to his face, Simon took a step forward, thankful the soldier was closer to him than Sophie. More often than not, these instances were a show of power. But Simon didn't want to risk the rare chance when it wasn't.

"Go," the soldier eventually said.

Simon placed his hand on Sophie's back and led her away. When they were out of hearing distance, he said, "I'll walk you home."

The moonlight and streetlight mingled with shadows across Sophie's high cheekbones. She was striking: tall with long, athletic lines and ruby-red lips. But more than that, she controlled attention in whatever room she entered. Wore trousers in a city where women typically wore skirts.

Simon, more cognizant than he would wish of these traits, wondered if that was her allure to the soldier. For Simon, a result of the first chord they had struck, she was the best type of exhausting. They often played their chemistry up or down depending on the situation. They had for years. Sometimes he couldn't tell where the spark ended and Simon began. Theirs was an elaborate dance that appeased Simon's family and saw him through numerous parties, seeking her out—a safe space under spirals of shared cigarette smoke.

He often anticipated seeing her or hearing her as if by elaborate radar. At Bletchley Park it was easier: their perimeter was smaller. Here, the occasions were rarer but still occurred. He'd turn a street or cross a *Platz* to make out her long lines and the curve of her hat rim. But this homing device went two ways: She could always seek him out in a crowded room or pub. Two magnets surged by the same current and drawn into each other's field.

Simon fell into stride with her step. "Before we were so rudely interrupted, you were telling me something that Starling uncovered." He surveyed their immediate surroundings. "Eternity?"

"Starling didn't uncover anything. Not yet. But . . ." She leaned into him. "A man asked me to meet someone regarding . . ."

Simon stopped in his tracks just as the arch from the Hofburg led into Michaelerplatz. "Tell me."

"I just . . . You're giving me that look."

"Sophie . . . ," he coaxed. "It's near pitch-black." Even the brightest pedestrian walkways were devoid of their streetlights. The blackouts ushered in with the Anschluss still pervaded the city. "How can you tell what look I am giving you?"

"An annoyed one."

Just beyond, Soviet soldiers with long guns saluting the stars stood sentry not a stone's throw from Demel's famous *Konditorei*. She followed his sight line over to Kohlmarkt.

"That soldier was dangerous, Villiers."

"Aren't they all?"

"I'm serious. I'm responsible for you."

Sophie set a hand on his shoulder. "You have to trust me, darling."

"I do trust you, but I also . . ."

"You also . . . ," Sophie said after a moment when he didn't fill in the blanks.

They both looked in opposite directions. Simon, out to the ruins of Vienna, Sophie straight ahead. Simon read her frustration in the press of her lips and the slight drop of her shoulders. Sometimes he felt they were so in sync that the slightest shift in her tone or tilt of her chin was a signal just for him. Currently, he was left in silence as she took the familiar street in stride.

For all the silence exacted by Bletchley Park: the Official Secrets Act, the *Careless Talk Costs Lives* propaganda in the canteen, the paranoia that drinking too much at the Swan or even the light anesthetic needed for a tooth extraction could inadvertently lead to spilling the Crown's secrets, he missed the camaraderie in that silence.

How telling it was as she fell into his shoulder or flicked him a look under lined lashes when she was sure no one else would see. Even their earlier kiss lingered with a warm buzz on his lips. Her kiss was given with the ease and pageantry needed for the moment, but there was too fine a line between friendship and desire in Simon's case. And Simon wanted to keep his own lines firmly drawn.

Vienna was sanctioned off between the four Allies dividing the *Bezirks*, or districts, between them. On a larger scale the whole of Austria was similarly quartered. Each Allied power wielded control over a patchwork quilt of a country liberated from the Anschluss only to meet a new occupant and, in many cases, a new language and expectation. Freedom found too many accustomed to little but makeshift tarps to weather the gaps merely blocking the starlight, settled together and huddled with soleless shoes and watery coffee. Lights through ruffled curtains played mellow noughts and crosses: blacking out some shades and illuminating others.

A lone army jeep rambled over the stones, and Sophie stiffened beside him. It was understandable given the animosity between the Soviet and Western Allies. Simon, by playing the foreign-diplomat card, rarely had issues crossing freely from one of the Soviet-occupied sections of the city into the neutral First District or Innere Stadt.

Depending on which soldier was running the watches, one could whistle on his way or be subject to prolonged interrogation. No wonder thousands of refugees from Yugoslavia, Czechoslovakia, Romania, and Hungary were desperate to find reprieve in a Western Allied zone. Oftentimes, the Soviet guards were mercurial. The *Volksdeutsche*, or displaced Germans, merely took what they could find.

The jeep stopped near Sophie and Simon and a man stepped out. Soviet. His regulation Tokarev rifle was raised.

Not again. Simon cursed.

He instinctively stepped forward to guard Sophie and reached into his overcoat for his inter-allied identity card. *"Guten Abend."* Simon used German as a preferred medium in case this fellow didn't speak English.

The soldier took his card, then zoomed in on Sophie. "Papers," he said in curt English.

Sophie rummaged in her handbag. Simon's heart accelerated.

"We have every right to be here." Simon swept his gaze over the pedestrian square. Why was no one else around? "We're in the First District," he continued in German.

"Ah!" Sophie's face brightened upon retrieving her card. "Slipped to the bottom. I'm not always asked for it, I suppose, because I rarely cross zones." She smiled up at him, voice smooth as glass.

The soldier fumed a moment but eventually gave a curt nod. They were supposed to be allies, yet this was the second stop tonight. Fortunately, the soldier was satisfied with his slight abuse of authority, leaving Simon to wonder—not for the first time—what might befall her if he wasn't so close at hand.

Their walk to her flat was too long and too fast at once. His heart was pounding, and his brain matched the accelerated pace. "I need to know where you are going and who you are meeting."

"Simon. They're just showing rank." Sophie inclined her chin. "I encounter danger every day."

"You're wandering Volksgarten alone at night."

"I had business in the city. You don't always pursue Eternity in broad daylight and crowded places."

"It's different." It was different because she was a woman, and the Red Army's reputation during their sieges and raids—despite being allies—turned his stomach. As such, he couldn't help but feel a strong surge of protection every time he found her in a moment that could have had a very different outcome from the one where Sophie stood safely beside him.

He had brought her here to help with his mission. But his needing her, trusting and admiring her abilities, constantly chafed against his guilt for placing her in a situation where he might not protect her.

They neared the familiar cobbles in front of her flat. The church bells tolled, and mellow light spilled from curtained windows onto the pavement. The *Hof*, or courtyard, tucked behind a wrought-iron fence overflowed with twigs, branches, and dead leaves that would make the chief gardener at Ashton, Sophie's childhood estate, pale.

"You can tell me anything, Sophie. Anything at all. I know you don't need me to slay dragons for you, but I would anyway."

This coaxed the desired smile. It had since the first time he said it several years ago.

"I know." Sophie reached out and tugged his collar.

But even as his breath fluttered the scarf at her neck, she turned the key. "Good night, Simon."

"Night." He wished he could smooth away the feeling that there was more to say, that he wanted to know. There was something she wasn't telling him. He was always conscious, even at the height of their usual rapport, that at any moment she could slowly slip away.

For there was a part of Sophie—evident even tonight in the way she casually used *Starling* in lieu of a detailed explanation as to her activities—that was removed from him.

Once he was certain she was tucked safe inside, Simon met the path of empty, uneven cobblestones. He wove his way through streets now familiar. The British had moved their headquarters to Hotel Sacher, usurping the famed building from the Russians in the midst of the shift of Allied dominance. Simon was rich enough to rent a suite there and his role enigmatic enough that no one questioned him about it.

Rich enough . . . It struck him on numerous occasions how disparate his situation was from the city he saw around him. In his pursuit of Eternity he was comfortably settled into the Mayfair house, and while London was deep in the throes of its restitution, there was a familiarity to Marcus Brighton's office at Fifty-Four Broadway, tea at the Savoy, and a world Simon was conditioned for. Here, while he loved the history and resiliency of Vienna, he still didn't speak the language beyond the Babel-like overlap of German, French, and Russian.

And while strolling through the Western-occupied space was a boon, it made the stark contrast of the ravaged sections of the city more apparent. Especially as the Soviets were doing everything in their power to block the supplemented rations the United Nations Relief and Rehabilitation Administration provided to help and aid. To usurp the region's every last munition, agricultural output, and oil field to keep the residents in their unhappy, pseudoliberated state. Unhappiness led to uprising. Starvation led to riot.

Simon turned onto Operngasse, a large street flanked by the Staatsoper on one side and his opulent hotel on the other. Once there, he smiled at the doorman and stepped across the russet-red carpet. He meandered to the bar and ordered a whiskey neat, then checked his watch. Past midnight. Soon a barman appeared bearing a silver tray holding a glass and a newspaper. Simon lifted the glass for a long sip.

He looked around the room as he had several previous nights when the lack of patrons was as telling as a crowd. What secrets were being revealed? A flick of ash over a tray, a twinkle in one's eye telling the story one had heard time and again. A leg crossed over a knee, and a telephone call. Most were War Office men who filed paperwork and clerked, but in a city of spies, shadows met every corner and crept over every wall.

Brighton was adamant that Simon's background procured him an edge and a rare ability to assess people. After all, Simon had been silently studying men his whole life: at his father's parties, from across a chessboard, and most recently at Bletchley, attempting to find Brighton's traitor while determining who from Simon's small group would be the most help at finding Eternity when the war was officially over.

He removed his gold-rimmed glasses from his suit pocket and placed them on his nose, then reached for the newspaper. *The British Morning News*, an Allied-commissioned periodical that reminded him of the pragmatic BBC back home, was the antidote to another late night in a wrecked city. Simon shifted the page only to read of the drought of farm harvests and subsequent fail of hydroelectric genera- tion needed to help produce goods and manufacturing.

His worry for Sophie still prickled the back of his neck. His dis- traction wasn't helping.

Simon extracted the Hofer manifest he'd acquired at the Schönbrunn and tucked it into the newspaper, concealing it. Why would anyone want to waylay the efforts that would help feed, house, and warm a city bearing the scars of war? The Soviets' boom barri- ers cut off supplies. While they had certainly fought the same war as Britain, they were not in the business of restoration like the other Allied occupants.

It was this friction that turned Vienna on a knifepoint. Whoever controlled the resources had the opportunity to control everything. Simon knew Vienna could fall either way. Either it would establish itself again as a ruling empire in its own right, aligning itself with the peaceful Allied occupation slowly opening to a new era. Or it would fall to Soviet dominance.

There was a reason Churchill was wary of the Russian rise even as the Red soldiers fought against the Nazis during the war. They were another leviathan. Previously the lesser of two evils, now, perhaps, the prevailing one. For men like Hofer, the momentary inconvenience might give way to the promise of eventual affluence.

Simon could speak to the threat for hours on end. Had become obsessed with it to the point of connecting the *blitzed* bombs that nearly obliterated the city of Coventry and its now desecrated famed cathedral with a Russian spy ring to focusing in on Diana Somerville's potential as a civilian aid when she waxed on for half an hour on the dome of a Christopher Wren church.

Yet Brighton never questioned the roots of Simon's obsession. Rather, he played off it. In some cases fostered it. Did the man just chalk it up as an eccentricity of a chess player who outranked many men in

MI6 with several decades more experience? Or was Simon's interest a boon to Brighton's own orders to stall the flood of Communism as best he could?

Simon narrowed in. The Hofer manifest stipulated which shipments were allowed into the Soviet zones for delivery. Without fuel, every other needed resource from coal to wood to sustenance—food and warmth—was scarce. As he read through the ledger, something didn't add up. The revenue exceeded the rate of the transactions. And the supplemental income was not in Austrian schillings but Czech koruna.

The part of Simon's mind that enjoyed the spark of a problem entertained this new variable as a probable connection between the two cities. Perhaps Adameck, the man Gabe had mentioned, could be the connector. There were certainly similarities between the two countries: both under occupation, orphaned somewhat by war, still hosting men with fascist and socialist views, and host to men of Communist influence.

A waiter came and with a slight bow took Simon's empty whiskey glass with an air of *Gemütlichkeit*: the customary Viennese friendliness edged by curt politeness. He presented Simon with a crisp white envelope before he turned with a nod.

Simon retrieved a small silver file from his pocket and peeled open the heavily scented paper.

Herr Barre,

Did you know that chess had a significant role in the Salzburg home of the Mozart family? I suspect now that you're in Austria and so far away from many things that are familiar, you will appreciate the anecdote. And when you hear Mozart, as I am certain you will, it will not be difficult to find a common denominator. We are all a product of our heritage, are we not?

Simon shifted in his seat. He was familiar with unusual correspondence, certainly, but the mention of chess and Mozart caught his interest. That and the writer was aware that Vienna was not his home.

> Nannerl, as the composer's sister was affectionately known, was the first documented female player in Salzburg. And one of the first in all of Europe.
>
> I understand you like chess. So I propose we play. We are both serving a common purpose no matter how different you believe our roles to be. We are both on the right side: an end to war and to oppression. You can choose to accept this challenge, but even if you choose not to respond, you are already a part of this game.

The note continued in German, providing Simon with a postal box where he could send his response to the challenge if he chose to accept it.

Simon studied the notation underneath the signature initials D. F.: e4. A classic opening chess move.

Simon charged his drink to his account and crossed through the russet hallway to the lift to try out the play on his board. Mental notation was one thing, but it had been so long since he had the experience of feeling the grooves of the pieces in his controlled fingers and over the polished board. Truth was, he missed it.

Moments later in his suite, Simon approached the chessboard, untouched in the corner near the bureau and rolltop desk. One of the few personal effects he had kept with him. Sophie had given it to him for Christmas one year—back when things were simpler. When he would muse on one of her clever anecdotes and they would solidify their friendship in a synchronized look across a long table, or their mingled laughter over a pun no one else caught. And then her gift—it was the same style of board he grew up playing with.

Simon lifted a white marble pawn. He glanced at a book on the desk nearby on chess philosophy he had found tucked into Charles Barrington's esoteric leather-bound tomes in the study at his family estate. Simon recalled a chapter that spoke to the virtues of a game played from two different locations.

Simon set the white piece on the board, exactly to the position in the note.

He had a choice. He could continue the game with an immediately bold counteroffensive and show his hand quickly. Take a risk bolstered by confidence he was only just feeling. Or he could play it safe. A traditional move. A gentleman's move of quiet respect.

Choosing the former, Simon positioned the piece and moved it to c5.

So someone knew he loved chess. Simon had been mentioned in his fair share of papers for winning tournaments.

"We are both on the right side."

D. F. had made a competent first move. It was far more unsettling to Simon than the Soviet soldier who had approached Villiers and him. Here was an opponent ready to test Simon's strengths and limitations, given the lack of signature and the riddle—the mention of Mozart's sister and the start of a new game. Someone who seemed to understand him, at least insofar as choosing this specific language for their communication.

But what about another language? Encryption? Was D. F. trying to say something beyond the play? Simon scratched out a few theories as to how a play might mean something else. But he would need more than the opening move. He'd just have to wait.

Simon ensured the board was perfect: every knight faced forward, every pawn proudly displayed in the center of its square. And while all he had of his opponent was fine black lettering, his world grew smaller. Probably because he couldn't shake Sophie from his head.

From the moment she had shown him immense loyalty long ago,

every time he was confronted with a problem that placed him at odds with himself, he recalled the indomitable power that straightened her spine during times of trouble and concealed the words unspoken between them.

Her mind, where he was concerned, was still encrypted. As was her motive.

Simon eventually performed his evening routine and retired to the turndown service of eiderdown silk. He turned off the bedside lamp and waited for his eyes to adjust to the darkness. There was the ping of a chess move, a cryptic message, and a manifest from Hofer's fuel factory. Why did everything his brain stored during the day decide to parade itself across his mind just as the curtains were drawn, keeping his lids from fluttering into sleep?

The muted streetlight striping through the blinds and the tolling of the bells from a church just beyond Albertinaplatz did little to ease his mind. Just as he was beginning to drift, she showed up. Rather annoyingly. Especially because he had just kissed her. Or she had just kissed him. Pantomime, of course. Acting in a moment.

Lord, but how many times had Simon used the excuse of "acting in the moment" to dictate the decisions he made?

The loud voices of insecurity overtook the rational ones and reverberated so loudly he felt his brain was an echo chamber. He was here to do his small part to keep the world from being thrown into chaos by zooming in on men who would suavely blur the line between war and temporary peace with their interest in a new world.

He was here to determine how men like David Moser fit into the Eternity spy ring Brighton had charged him with uncovering. Further, to decipher why this anonymous chess player was so certain Simon was already part of his game.

He was not here to pursue anything with Sophie beyond a friendship that puzzled him on nights he lay awake staring at the ceiling. The difference was, the more she seemed to hide things from him, the more he felt that her conversation told him one thing while her mind turned over quite another.

Especially when he recalled that piece of paper in her flat that bound them together in sickness and health, till death did they part.

CHAPTER 4

Sophie opened the outdoor gate to her apartment building. Singerstrasse was tucked away but a moment from the Deutschordenskirche, with its arched windows and steeple that while a grand compass at night paled to the grandeur of some of the city's more opulent offerings. Sophie fancied its unassuming presence as an interruption of a narrow and otherwise mostly pedestrian street.

Months ago, Gabe Langer had approached her about something that had nothing to do with Simon's pursuit of Eternity. Rather, a church that had once belonged to the knights of the Teutonic Order and was filled with treasures. The *Schatzkammer*, or chest of imperial treasures, set beyond the church's inner courtyard, hosted everything from Gothic coins to silver goblets to armored coats of arms harking back to the fealty of fourteenth-century knights. When a few treasures not on the church's registry appeared on the black market, Gabe had asked her to retrieve them and have them appraised by Herr Müller.

It seemed that many of the treasures displaced to several corners of the city were done so by those who believed their homes were better than the mantels of the treasures' Jewish owners.

Sophie hadn't been well known to the higher set of influential men in the city back then, so it was easy for her to recover items and "trade" them to Herr Müller, who had a knack for ensuring they reached their rightful owners.

"But it is not your story to tell," Müller had reminded her. *"No one*

can know." No one. Especially not Simon, who couldn't have his work for MI6 complicated by acts of charity that had nothing to do with his purpose for sending her to Vienna.

Sophie had agreed. And for the first time since she had botched her chance at what she considered a *real* war effort, she felt she was doing something worthwhile.

———◇◇◇◇◇———

Sophie still had the taste of Simon's lips on hers and the feel of his expensive shirt collar on her fingertips as she opened the door to her flat. The wireless was on: low and melancholy, spreading music throughout. She hadn't remembered leaving it on, and she instinctively reached into her handbag to extract her revolver.

She tossed her keys onto the settee as she made out a shadow occupying the wingback chair near the window. She was quick to stretch out her arms in a shooting stance and cock the hammer, then the figure turned.

"Canary! I could have shot you!" Sophie stared at Diana, then peered around the flat. "How did you get in?" She had called her friend "Canary" since their Bletchley days, an ironic take on Diana's truly abhorrent singing voice.

"The porter let me in."

"If this is the level of safety my building possesses, I'll need to find a new flat." Sophie set her revolver on a side table. "You might have called, you know."

"I wouldn't have been half as surprised as finding this." Diana rose from her chair and handed Sophie a piece of paper. "It was sitting on the side table when I went to turn on the wireless."

Silence spread between them as Marcello's Oboe Concerto in D Minor eased out of the wireless. Diana was holding a marriage certificate.

Sophie's marriage certificate.

The concerto ended and the next piece warmed through the speakers. Serenade no. 11 in E-flat Major by Mozart. Sophie much preferred to have important conversations when Mozart was playing. She had once privately requested a chamber ensemble play the popularly nicknamed "Dissonance" quartet so she could refuse one of her parents' chosen suitors.

"Listen to that, Canary. It's the adagio movement. The clarinet and oboe are warring for the starring line." If she framed a conversation in music, she could keep the upper hand. If not, Diana was sure to lure her into answering questions her heart had no answers to, let alone her head.

Sophie snatched the certificate from her friend and tucked it into the top drawer of the bureau. "Now, tell me about my candelabra."

Diana was an architectural historian and enamored with old churches. It was here she was able to discover things Simon needed during the war in pursuit of Eternity. Many members of the spy ring were often found using churches for a twofold purpose: to pass messages covertly and to find sanctuary. They were easy drop-off spots, and few men would perform violence within their sacred walls.

"That won't work, Villiers. Stop trying to distract me with music. You're *married*."

Sophie cocked her head to peer at the faded streetlights. "Officially, yes."

"I lived with you for four years. Every time I tried to bring up your relationship, you waved me off. I see one of you almost every day. And now . . . now I wonder about *both* of you. Simon was my friend."

"I never waved you off." Sophie poured a sherry from the table hosting the wireless, then sat on the settee and tucked her legs under her. "Simon *is* your friend."

"It concerned me."

"How?"

"You're *married*. And . . . and there were other men. They bought drinks for you."

Sophie chortled for show. "Simon is *not* my keeper." She sighed. "Besides, you know I would never betray him. It was only ever a marriage in name."

Diana looped a long strand of blond hair around her finger. "While he needs Brent at the university to keep a close eye on Communist associations in academic realms, I am stuck in that flat almost every day. And now I find out one of my dearest friends is married to my other dearest friend and . . ." She stalled a moment. "He said you refused him! After he was sick. When he had pneumonia at the village hospital and . . ."

Sophie remembered all too well, and while Diana carried on, her memory lit to a night she had snuck past the Bletchley guards to see Simon at the place he was boarding not a mile away. Sophie had nearly sloshed hot tea on him from a barely steady hand once she saw how pale and wan he looked.

Before the piece of paper and the sickness-and-health vow she had recited with as much conviction as a Keats poem she had been made to memorize in school.

"I did refuse him," Sophie said after a long moment. "He asked and I almost think he *believed* it would help me avoid marriage to a less savory prospect. It was ages ago. I doubt he was serious about it. Then, I suppose about six years ago, a *far* less savory prospect for both of us and *le voilà!*" She gestured toward the drink cart. "A marriage certificate."

"Well, now both of you have secrets from me." Diana's voice grated in a register Sophie hadn't heard before.

"I don't want to have secrets from you. And I never told you because it is just a piece of paper." She was impressed at how calm she was, considering the leftover adrenaline from her meetings that evening to the desire in Simon's eyes searching hers under the sputtered streetlights.

"But Simon has a title! He stands to inherit a grand estate."

Simon didn't want the title, and the last thing Sophie wanted was for Diana's usually endearing curiosity to go and sniff them out. "Simon is precisely the man you met at Bletchley. Good at chess and fond of you. That is all you need to know."

"But—"

"Canary." Sophie cut her off.

Diana took the hint. "I got your candelabra. And I charged twice its worth as per your directive. The gentleman wasn't as forthcoming. Seemed to resent that he wasn't being seen as bartering with Starling but . . ."

Sophie grinned. "You bartered for it?"

"You told me to!"

"I know, I just didn't—never mind." She eyed Diana. While Sophie had the long, lean lines of a Katharine Hepburn, Diana's figure resembled cinema stars Jean Harlow and Veronica Lake.

"At least it was something to do." Diana looked away.

"Better than burning biscuits and making tea?" Sophie joshed, but Diana didn't laugh.

"Sometimes when I'm sitting in my flat, I have this restlessness in my being. This feeling that I should be doing something—working at Bletchley or waiting and wringing my hands for a shift to start or a decoded message to run through the correction device." Diana lowered her head for a moment, then her somber gaze met Sophie's. "I always wanted to see Vienna. To see its churches. And now I'm meeting the Austrian capital's ghostly visage."

Sophie swirled the sherry in her glass. "After the war, I know you wanted to get home to your husband and restart your life, but I miss some of the moments we had back then."

Diana picked at the pleat in her skirt. "I do, too, and then I feel guilty. Especially when I don't feel I'm doing anything but feeding Simon and you bread crumbs."

"No, *my* purpose is feeding Simon bread crumbs of intelligence." Sophie smiled. "To suss out men who might be using the Schwarzmarkt to further Eternity's cause. Yours is to wait for Brent to come home and cook for or Simon to decide that Eternity's next drop will be in a bombed church." Sophie shrugged a shoulder. "And *theoretically* it is a good reason for us both to be here."

"You never do anything without a reason, Villiers."

Sophie nodded. "True."

"So I thought your reason was Simon. That maybe . . ."

"You once told me that when people are in love, they see it in everyone else. I am sorry to disappoint you, darling, but that is simply *not* the case here. We are different people, Simon and I. We are from different worlds than yours. Where love is considered a weakness."

"You sound like Miss Havisham."

"So did my mother when I was growing up." Sophie sighed. "You knew Simon and me in a different moment." She thought back to her kiss with Simon. The . . . *performance*. It was just that. A performance. Just like the piece of paper was just a piece of paper.

When she looked up, Diana was watching her with interest. Sophie held her gaze without wavering. The slightest exhale and Sophie knew she had won. Diana would drop the Simon subject, for the moment at least.

"You also asked me to find out about that Habsburg Communion cup," Diana said. "From Votivkirche."

"Well?"

"It was missing and not because of the bombs. Votivkirche remained mostly intact."

"Go on."

"You know the Germans took what they liked, and I think this is another example."

"Those stuffed-shirt Nazi peacocks who used to filter in and out of the Metropole, I gather." After the Anschluss, the hotel that had long been a watering hole for the Gestapo had been blasted. No one shed a tear over it, though Sophie secretly delighted in any artifact or treasure she could pay dearly for and more chuffed when she could pass its earnings to Frau Wagner.

"A Herr Moser has it. Paid quite handsomely."

"Thank you, Diana."

"Do you know this man? This Moser? Brent has mentioned a Moser before in conjunction with his work at the university."

"I've heard the name," Sophie said evasively.

Diana nodded. "Well, I just wondered . . ." She pressed her finger to her lip a moment. "You know, there was a man back in London." She shifted. "Rick Mariner. Also an academic, and he was interested in artifacts to the point where he was caught up in Eternity. He died because of it. Fisher Carne killed him."

"Simon said as much. But I am not like Simon. I don't try to see Eternity everywhere. There is enough devastation in this city without espionage darkening it. Women with no protection. Beautiful art seized by the whims of men who harbor the same destructive thoughts as Hitler."

The conversation had steered Sophie from paying attention to the music on the wireless. She always found the evening program much like a rich banquet. The BBC was all well and good, but Vienna was the city of music. So inherent it was etched and carved into the architecture of Baroque palaces and dignified buildings: in the cherubs with violins and statues of composers whose lineage Hitler tried to rewrite.

Beethoven funneled through the speaker static now. The other father of Vienna's musical legacy, though not as familiar to Sophie's fingertips as Mozart. The building known as Pasqualatihaus, which Beethoven had once inhabited several blocks away, had been occupied by a Jewish family driven from their rooms so the Nazis could transform the flat into a museum.

Sophie tried to hear the composer's defiance against the liberty in the accelerating speed of the pianist's fingers as the allegro portion of Piano Concerto no. 5 crescendoed. Diana rose to leave as the music grew to a fevered pitch.

Sophie walked her to the door, pressed taxi fare into her palm, then escorted her down the stairs and to the gate to ensure she reached her black taxicab safely. They said good night, and Sophie turned only to hear Diana call out before she opened the car door. "Villiers."

"Yes, Diana."

"I only want you to be happy."

"I've never set in for wedded bliss," Sophie said dryly.

"Then maybe set in for something else. Maybe set in for at least acknowledging that you care. You care deeply. You care enough to be here, Sophie. And you care enough to try to convince me it is just a piece of paper. Start from there."

Their marriage existed only for Simon's estate, for Camden. Not for love, of course. Sophie wasn't sure she believed in it or the electricity that sparked between them whenever they occupied the same room. Not for anything else. It was safer that way.

———◦◦◇◦◦———

Once tucked under her bedsheets wearing a silk nightgown, Sophie stared at the puckered grooves in the plastered ceiling. Then she reached over to the nightstand and retrieved the card Herr Haas had given her.

Die Totenmaske von Amadeus Mozart.

The death mask of Mozart.

The composer died indebted and with a requiem whose unfinished notes drifted through Vienna's hallowed streets. A pauper's grave kept any admirer from genuflecting their respects.

Sophie, as Starling, had seen the restitution of many artifacts during her tenure in Vienna. The war unearthed relics and rediscovered paintings and manuscripts torn from the fallen Nazi coffers. But Mozart?

Over the coverlet she mimed the allegretto movement of Piano Concerto no. 17.

If Karl Haas was telling the truth, she was steps away from seeing the composer whose notes thrummed through her fingertips and crowded her brain. Something "deeply important" to Herr Haas.

Sophie picked up the card again. She supposed she merely wanted to see the request again.

Mozart's death mask.

The genius composer who wrote his sister in long tomes of philosophy and defied his prodigy status by squandering his earnings and writing a dark Faustian opera to counter the light Italian froth scrutinized by the court.

She admired the straight slashes of handwriting until something in the corner caught her eye: the faintest loop that would almost blend in the background if she hadn't recognized it.

The infinity symbol Eternity had often attached to messages that Diana decoded. It was how the ring communicated with one another.

Sophie wanted to find the mask for her own curiosity but also for the historical value it afforded. But she also knew that telling Simon she was in pursuit of it would betray what Herr Müller had requested of her. And yet—the Eternity symbol. It was so close to Simon. She had long promised him loyalty. Years before he had entrusted her with his Brighton-assigned work.

A Müller betrayal was one thing, a Simon betrayal quite another.

CHAPTER 5

Two adjacent estates sat on the patchwork quilt of Sussex Downs equidistant between London and Brighton, near the village of Wilmington. The Downs referred to fertile farmland dotted with tiny villages before the roadway led out to some of the oldest manor houses in the peerage. Camden and Ashton were century-long neighbors, with vast acreages between them.

Lady Sophia Huntington-Villiers wondered how the grounds where she learned to shoot and ride seemed smaller to her and suffocating when the estate was one of the oldest and most coveted in the county. Tonight she lingered by the refreshment table as her father hosted yet another gala benefiting a charity whose name and purpose she had forgotten. And with her two elder sisters married off, it fell to Sophie to add her own appropriate match to the family fortune.

As it was, Sophie hoped the large statue behind which she stood and the floor-length drapes from the French doors just beyond her would keep her appropriately hidden.

It was only in the piano where she found her escape. With just a bit of ornamentation, she could slow a measure or change a key. She could skip a half beat or ignore a dictation. What was music if not a series of phrases and motifs liberating their interpreter? What she would never dare speak in strong words to her parents, she pressed into the keys.

Her grandmother, a regal dowager figure who loomed larger than her staid likeness in an oil painting, had told her, "If you must rebel, Sophie darling, and you must of course, do it on the piano keys. Fall in love with music if you must, fall in love with art and the splendor of the world. But to fall in love with a person is to set an expectation that may never be fulfilled."

So music, rebellion, and love carved into her makeup the ability to interpret moments when a musical phrase swerved off course and left little room for interpretation.

It was clear these hired musicians too quickly adhered to her mother's dictation. Sophie might be expected to perform for the guests later, but for now she ate an oyster on the half shell and washed it down with champagne. She was just out of the path of a few giggling women, hovering around the buffet table like agitated bees.

"I wasn't expecting him to be here tonight," one said, smoothing her Jean Harlow hair.

"Oh just *look* at this garnish!" said another, liberally spreading foie gras onto a cracker. "He is certainly handsome."

"Better than that brute Julius. He's over there being handsy with Ethel."

"I had no idea he was coming tonight," said another.

Sophie peeked out just a little from behind the statue and searched the milling guests around the ballroom for the object of their collective swooning. Then she saw him.

Simon Barrington.

He accepted a Swarovski tumbler from a passing tray and was clearly more interested in studying it than truly making eye contact with anyone in his vicinity. Though when he crossed the room, he did so as if he owned the place—until he came face-to-face with Sophie's father. Simon nodded through a few pleasantries, then his smile vanished as quickly as it had been conjured.

The dissonance stirred something in her. Especially because he so clearly didn't want anyone to see it. A private world where his tailored clothes, distinguished smile, and bright blue eyes were pretending to belong.

"He wasn't supposed to be back from London," another young woman said.

"You heard he won another one of those chess tournaments. I signed out three books from the library and my brother has been teaching me. Don't look at me like that. Simon *loves* it, apparently. And he's brilliant. A national treasure."

"A national treasure, maybe," Harlow hair said. "But certainly not a *natural* one." Her friends joined in on her giggle.

Rumors circulated about Barrington. They waltzed around the soirees Sophie never wanted to attend. She had heard them since she was a child and in the halls of her all-girls boarding school.

He was not the legitimate spare heir to Camden Estate.

When the ladies had finished blushing over their appraisal of his physical attributes, they concentrated on how he kept to himself except for playing chess, fencing, and boxing. While Sophie was beginning to recognize it as a shyness not welcome in their world, the vocal admirers merely translated it as his being aloof. Hard to get.

Charles Barrington's marriage to Simon's late mother was well known as one of property and to a woman, not of incomparable beauty, but of significant wealth. He kept Simon near, perhaps, because it was a lesser scandal than outing his wayward wife's indiscretion.

Though Charles doted on his son Julius, his distant treatment and sometimes outward disdain for Simon did more to verify the rumors about his natural parentage.

Sophie knew exactly what it was like not to fit in. She was seen as too strong and too formidable and far too exceptional. She could outride and outshoot dozens of the men at her father's hunting weekends. She just couldn't handle when a potential suitor was spouting off on a piece of philosophy or history or religion that Sophie was more than prepared to challenge toe-to-toe.

She studied Simon. Did he also have a means of repurposing rebellion? He relaxed a little and his Adam's apple bobbed. Something crossed his face. Sadness, perhaps? Uncertainty? Yet it seemed the point he felt eyes on his profile, he straightened his spine and set his face. The contrast was startling to anyone who took the time to notice, which the ladies at the refreshment table did not.

Rumors of Charles Barrington's considerable fortune and Simon's attachment to Camden certainly helped gild the ladies' interest.

And as quickly as his bout of melancholy had surfaced, it disappeared as he flashed his white teeth and charmed them with his tenor voice. Perhaps it wasn't shyness after all. Perhaps he had built himself a mental fortress and stole into it when necessary.

Sophie inched out from behind the statue.

The women assessed Barrington as if he were a prized horse at auction.

Sophie wasn't sure what inspired her to snatch another oyster in that moment. She only knew that she set it in her palm, picked up a shucking knife, narrowed her eyes, and flicked the shellfish in the direction of Barrington's ear with the same precision that she took out partridges and badgers on one of her father's hunts.

He swerved and settled his bright gaze on her with confusion. She quirked a smile and nodded in the direction of the French doors behind her. Then, after replenishing her champagne, she slipped through to the veranda.

It was a calm night, and the moonlight teased the pond in the vast green outside her parents' sprawling estate. The stars were easily sought, their canvas a swath of navy.

"Pardon me."

"Oh good," she said to him. "They didn't eat you alive."

"Did you just fling an oyster at my ear?"

Sophie raised her thumb and index finger and simulated a quick reenactment. "I have impeccable aim."

"How did you know I wasn't enjoying myself? Wooing one of those lovely young women?"

"Wooing? Oh please, any split second alone and a shadow of *The Sorrows of Young Werther* passes over your face. You're as happy to be here as I am." She sipped her champagne.

Nonplussed, Barrington swirled the liquid in his tumbler and took a long sip, then set it on the stone partition before him. He reached into the pocket of his fancy tailed Savile Row dinner jacket and produced a pack of cigarettes.

He pulled out a cigarette and pressed it to his lips, then reached behind his black cummerbund and produced a small gold lighter. After the slightest flick, she inhaled the secondhand taste of his first long drag.

"Care for one?" He created a halo of smoke with his exhaled words.

Sophie closed the space between them. "Please." She accepted the offered cigarette and was pleasantly surprised when, rather than use his lighter, he merely pressed the end of his ignited cigarette to enflame her own.

They smoked in a silence as loud as a conversation for a moment— and easily far more pleasurable than any she had had inside. Barrington balanced his words between long puffs of smoke and sips of her father's high-quality whiskey until both vices were depleted. He tapped his cigarette ashes against the expensive Swarovski glass.

He studied her a moment. "Lady Sophia Huntington-Villiers. It has been a while, has it not?"

Sophie smiled. "Everyone's favorite Barrington son."

"Tragic, isn't it? Here." He extended his whiskey-glass ashtray to her, and she smudged the remains of her cigarette inside.

"Not according to the society pages. You're the fourth most eligible bachelor in the British Isles. And a few young ladies at the oyster table are studious chess players of late." If the rumors of his true parentage were true, that should have made the ranking nil. But it seemed the society papers would excuse many indiscretions when it came to a striking figure such as Simon's.

"Sixth, actually." He returned her smile, then ducked his chin, regarding her. "If you were so kind as to raise me a few notches, then I must have made quite an impression in the past."

"Hmm. Well, when I was ten and fell off my horse—"

"Oh yes. Nasty cut on your knee, wasn't it?" He arched an eyebrow.

"And you, ever the gentleman, used your handkerchief as a tourniquet. Then there was that time I was twelve years old and you were leaning over a chessboard. You looked up just long enough to murmur a 'how do you do' before you turned back to the game. I had never seen any boy with that level of concentration. You, sir, were a bit of a prodigy." He was five years older than her and ancient then. Now, the years narrowed the margin between them.

"Since we've shared a cigarette and I saved your life, you might just call me Simon."

"Simon."

The music inside settled into a familiar three-quarter rhythm. Sophie glanced over her shoulder.

"Simon," he repeated. "Even as you tried to kill me."

"Pardon me?"

"Oh yes, Lady Huntington-Villiers. Oysters are akin to arsenic in my world." He surveyed her reaction.

She kept her interest in check. "How so?"

"An allergy. You flicked my ear with something I might devastatingly perish from."

She cocked her head to the side. "Is that so? Well, I'll *try* not to do it again."

She momentarily lost him to the lanterns and the night: the sun tugging low, setting the horizon beyond where the Ashton grounds ended ablaze with brandished orange and gold.

She followed his gaze over the shadows of trees and manicured gardens and admired the lingering silence. It was amicable merely to watch the sun fade in time with someone who equally appreciated it.

"A shame to keep a lady as beautiful as you outside when you could be inside in the throes of a waltz," he said.

"I'm not very good at waltzing." She shrugged. "At dancing in general, to be exact."

Simon cocked his head. "My father says you are one of the best pianists he has ever heard, so you clearly have a sense of rhythm."

"Born with two left feet, I guess."

Simon extended his hand. "Well, no one will see us out here and I love Strauss. Makes me think of pastries and a blue Danube that's not really blue."

He made a casual reference to Strauss and the Wiener Blut modified for the hired chamber quartet. Sophie pressed her fingers in his and felt the light but firm steadying of his hands on her shoulder and waist.

"Ready?"

"Yes."

He nodded, his eyes on hers waiting through a few measures until the main theme returned to the melody and set the tempo. He steered her a few tentative steps. "Precisely."

The music swelled on a crescendo and Sophie preempted a step, leaning heavily into Simon, who gracefully steadied her.

"Keep your eyes on me," he said as they tentatively found the rhythm again.

"Perhaps I don't like waltzing because I don't like following anyone else's lead."

"I'm not leading you. We're merely having a conversation . . . with our feet." He smiled.

Sophie fought the urge to look at her feet. The shyness she had attributed to Simon inside had all but dissolved. He looked at her straight on, not once wavering. The more she trusted his rhythm, the more they fell in sync and achieved a deep affinity.

So different from the Simon Barrington unaware of the debutantes circling him.

Sophie was breathless from the rotation and the champagne and was almost dizzy when the quartet finally slowed and she and Simon came to a spinning halt. She barely had a chance to inhale before she heard her name.

"Sophia!"

She and Simon turned at a voice in the double door.

"Sophia, come inside." Her mother glanced from her and registered Simon, who was smoothing a damp swath of black hair from his forehead.

Sophie swished up the skirt of her emerald dress and sidestepped Simon. "Simon Barrington and I were just recalling old times."

Her mother slowly raised her nose at him in assessment, then at Sophie's disheveled collar. "You haven't been *smoking*, have you?" The euphemism wasn't lost on either of them.

"My vice, Lady Huntington-Villiers." Simon slipped his gold lighter back inside his cummerbund and gave her a slight bow.

Behind her shrewd brown eyes, Catherine Huntington-Villiers was recalling everything she could about Simon Barrington. What she settled on, Sophie never knew, for she turned and led the way to the large, shiny Bösendorfer Grand in the ballroom.

"Ladies and gentlemen, if you will join us. My daughter Sophia is more than proficient on the piano."

Sophie slid the bench over the hardwood floor and smoothed the silk of her skirt as she sat on the bench. Then, without music or an orchestra to flourish and supplement the lines of Mozart's famous piano concerto, she threw herself bodily into the piece.

—◇◇◇◇—

Simon had been half a decade older when Sophia fell off that pony, and that was the last clear memory he'd had of her. Sophia—though he had heard her referred to as Sophie, which suited her much better—had grown into her aristocratic nose and gold-rimmed brown eyes under carefully arched eyebrows, which were at prime viewing under the gleaming lights of the ballroom. He didn't know much about Mozart, but this piece had a sense of urgency to it he liked. A frantic energy matched by her attention to the piece, fingers dancing, wrists graceful and strong as she gave her whole body into the rhythm and movement of performance.

If his father had his way, Simon would marry some trophy who ornamented his arm and fulfilled the obligation of an heir or two, who would be raised by a well-referred nanny. He would argue over investments and bonds at the dinner table and withstand his father's rants about politics on Sundays.

Simon would try to forget that everything connected to his name was blemished.

He supposed his father would be pleased if he were to set his sights on Sophie. She was worth a fortune, and Charles Barrington often cast longing looks in the direction of the Ashton estate. But Simon's attentiveness had nothing to do with her breeding and estate but the fact that she was a different variety from the wallflowers he had met at similar affairs, wilting on the sidelines after a valiant attempt at flirtation.

Sophie was never more different than now, enraptured by Mozart. Her cheeks flushed and her eyes sparkled. He could almost feel her heart rate accelerating. Mozart was the end of her every sentence, the name she always wanted to bring into conversation like a schoolgirl crush.

He hoped she might look at him, given the rapport he had felt during their conversation on the veranda. But—never mind. He hadn't looked up at her during that chess game years earlier she had recalled.

"No. 17 in G Major." His father's voice was at his shoulder. But then the man was not really his father. Something he assumed all the men in coattails and women frosted with diamonds tonight didn't realize.

Simon was the natural-born son of a stranger: a visiting academic who had left little of his presence other than Simon behind. What little Simon *did* know was overheard: bread crumbs tossed in the trail of the mystery of his life.

It was far less embarrassing for Charles Barrington to merely accept Simon publicly. The family name had to be preserved—but it was also the only scrap of family Simon was likely to get. He carried the Barrington name, but Charles was as likely to consider him a Barrington as he was to demonstrate any paternal affection. And Julius, of course, being the elder and the natural son, would be the next Lord Barrington, while Simon would enjoy all of the clothes and parties and none of the recognition or affection.

"I love Mozart," Barrington said. "Bet you didn't know that."

"I'd never really thought about him," Simon said evenly. Sophie's fingers were flying over the keys, but not flippantly so. She made it look easy.

"Wolfgang Amadeus Mozart." Barrington downed a measure of expensive scotch to lubricate his suddenly gruff voice. "Amadeus means 'God's beloved.' Did you know that? For all of your first-form grades and your chess?"

"I didn't."

"To be beloved by God." Barrington swilled the dregs of amber liquid in his glass. He elbowed Simon forcefully.

Simon straightened his tie. Only Charles Barrington could twist a musical anecdote into an insult. Mozart may have been beloved; Simon was unequivocally not.

"I'd been saving her for Julius." His father waved a hand in Sophie's direction. Simon shifted. He hadn't realized he had been so obvious in his interest. "I suppose she's pretty but too severe: all angles and long lines. So you're welcome to her."

Simon straightened his spine and shoved his clenched fists into his pockets. "Welcome to her" as if she were a prime slice of veal. Or a secondhand hunting rifle. "Benevolent of you. Though I don't think Lady Huntington-Villiers is the sort who would let any man offer for her."

"I don't quite *hate* her. We could think about some kind of bargain."

Simon thought of responding but was distracted watching Sophie rise from the piano bench just as his father turned in pursuit of another expensive cigar and the company of Marcus Brighton, who, catching Simon's eye, nodded.

She fluttered out the silk skirt of her shiny green dress and flourished a little curtsy. She gracefully accepted champagne from a passing servant holding a silver tray and slowly raised her gaze to meet his over the rim of her crystal flute.

"Father said you're moon-eyed for that Huntington-Villiers woman. Too tall. Almost unnatural. Like a praying mantis," a voice said at his elbow.

Simon wanted to slug his half brother, Julius, in the face for his remark. "She's interesting." Simon appreciated that her height gave him the ability to meet her gaze straight on.

"So you like her?"

As children, if something was within Julius's reach and Simon enjoyed it, Julius would snatch it: from chess pieces to lemon cake. His mother had always turned a blind eye; his father would reprimand the competition with a patronizing tone all while encouraging Julius with a twinkle in his eye.

Simon's peripheral vision took in Lady Sophia's shoulders and backbone, exposed by the low drape of her dress. But he would play the game and level the field.

"What was that you said about a praying mantis?" Simon said nonchalantly, then drained his glass and lit a cigarette.

CHAPTER 6

November 1946
Vienna, Austria

Simon woke from a dream where he was back at Camden. The estate courted every season, and he slipped out of bed to open the blinds to a crisp autumn chased by winter chill. There had been too many dreams like that lately.

He wiped his hand over his face. Maybe it was that he had kissed her. The first time had been at Camden. Anytime he tried to taste or feel something in Sophie's kiss or touch, he was left to grapple with the fact that he *didn't* want it. Or he didn't *want* to want it.

The phone rang just as he had finished dressing for the day. Unlike usual, Marcus Brighton's voice didn't sound crackled and from faraway London. He was but several blocks away and awaiting Simon's arrival.

Brighton was unfazed by war, by bad news, by human emotion. Simon felt too much of each, despite his best efforts to tuck them into his pocket.

Simon remembered the austere figure with an expensive cigar parting his lips. Brighton most likely had put two and two together in the calculation of Simon's true parentage. But it didn't stop him from seeking Simon out at parties and sending congratulatory notes each time his Cambridge chess proficiency provided several nice paragraphs for an eager reporter's article.

Brighton had sized Simon up for something special, it seemed. He promised Simon that his bearing and breeding would allow him to slip in and out of gatherings and meetings other agents would only dream of. But Simon sometimes felt he was as suited to espionage as Sophie was to knitting.

He stepped out the revolving door of the Sacher and navigated dislodged cobblestones that had been swept to the side in small piles of barricades. Stone fountains shooting up spring water under dangling flags and propaganda: *Wieder Frei!* pronounced "free again" as scaffolds like building blocks as Simon walked in the direction of his meeting place with Brighton. Chiming streetcars lumbered along the tracks and passed him. An impromptu quartet sawed at Haydn on instruments with a pristine sheen that clashed with their owners' frayed seams and scuffed shoes.

As Simon neared his destination, his vision was assaulted by a monstrosity with long, arched columns. On the heels of the war, the Russians made the German POWs build a statue to celebrate the Russian victory off Schwarzenberg Palace: *Heldendenkmal der Roten Armee.* Its ornamented soldier high atop a pedestal to watch the city as it turned in the Third District—the traffic from Schloss Belvedere to the Ring and the numerous dignitaries in sleek black cars.

The Allies were situated nearby for their diplomatic meetings, and they couldn't ignore the gaudy Russian influence on the city or its flourished gold touches in stark contrast with the devastation around.

Brighton had commandeered an office in the former Haus der Industrie building, familiar to any Brit stationed in the city. It reminded Simon of a four-story layer cake. The sandstone facade's deft delineation of each floor used wraparound ledges.

Simon pulled back one of the heavy double doors and entered the building, his polished shoes meeting the shiny marble tile floor. He let his gaze stroke every opulent balustrade intersected by the sun preening through the windows.

A guarded wheat-haired man in uniform with gold buttons clicked his heels at Simon's approach. Simon swept his fedora from his head and tucked it under his arm. "Simon Barre," he said by way of greeting.

After a curt nod and a small bow, the man ushered Simon through double doors to Brighton's office. "Herr Barre," the attendant announced.

"Ah. Simon," Brighton said. What Marcus lacked in height, he made up for in sheer presence. Even seated, he commanded the room with broad shoulders and a bass voice that rumbled as clearly as the acoustics at the Royal Albert Hall. His silver-streaked hair was sparse now but only emphasized his aquiline profile and grim mouth.

"Good morning, Marcus."

"That will be all." Brighton nodded at the attendant and waved Simon into a seat. The door clicked shut and they were alone. "I appropriated the office. It was easy enough." He leaned back in his chair. "Simon, you've been here a long while now. You were invaluable when it came to discovering Eternity in London, and you showed great ingenuity in using someone like Diana Somerville."

Simon crossed his legs. Settled in.

"I am only here in passing." Brighton watched Simon closely. "Looking into messages that bear a close resemblance to suspicious messages found in and around Vienna."

"Oh?" Simon knew Marcus was waiting for him to offer information. Perhaps on David Moser, whose reputation according to Langer was an anomaly in terms of his respect throughout the city. Simon knew he wanted to appropriate each as pieces for his board. He just wasn't sure how to lay them.

"There seems to be a special sort of double agent," Brighton said. "Some of the intelligence is just too convenient. And if that is true, then that person would play both us and the Russians." Brighton slid a file across the desk.

"I doubt someone would use the same codes for their Soviet interactions as they would use for us." Simon opened the file and took his time with the contents. He didn't immediately see anything suspicious. "*Special*, you say?"

Brighton steepled his fingers, his elbows resting on the desk. "True. That's why this interests me. Because I cannot be sure it is a code at all. Look. It's written in—"

"Descriptive notation."

"Your wheelhouse. Not mine."

Simon studied the moves closely. Not a cipher. He was imagining the chessboard. How he would play each move. "Why were you sent this?"

"It wasn't addressed to me. I came by it. Some Soviet sympathizers mean to employ the same tactic in Prague as they are inciting here: to starve out the inhabitants and wait for revolution. Prague is still under a democracy, if a wavering one. But President Beneš is rumored to be losing control and his country will crumble. Prague is on the precipice of having no government intervention at all. Perfect climate for the Communists to overtake the city."

"And you think these messages have intelligence on Prague?"

"I am only in Vienna briefly on my way there. These messages were intercepted by someone from *our* team in Prague, but the same notation was used in a message *to* one of our team. And all we have is a ghost of a lead. The people call him *Das Flüstern*."

"The Whisper."

"Precisely. Because this man has intelligence among the higher echelons, he can silently find things of tremendous value, and yet no one knows his real name. And he sells what he wants to our side and some to the Soviets."

"Tremendous value?" Simon averted his eyes and fixated on a point just above the window.

"Antiques. Artifacts. Manuscripts. I'm led to believe that messages from Das Flüstern have been decrypted on both the British *and* Soviet sides. This man is well connected, but no one yet knows where his loyalties lie. That's why it is less important *what* artifacts he is dealing with than *whom* he is buying from and selling to." He took a beat. "You know Vienna has a long history of Communism, even before the most recent war."

"I do."

"Let's see if this man's influence spreads here, shall we?"

Simon started to push the folder across the table, but Brighton lifted a staying hand. "I know you are still working on Eternity."

"Yes, as is Sophie Villiers."

Brighton studied him closely. *Too* closely. "You have a unique perspective."

Simon adjusted his tie. "Because my father is titled? Because I'm used to fine things? Because I play chess? I got a message, too, you know. Using descriptive notation similar to the one in your note."

Brighton leaned over the borrowed desk but didn't confirm any of Simon's suppositions, nor did he seem overly surprised. "It makes sense that a man of influence would want to reach out to you. I keep you on, Barre, because you have good hunches and you are good at making people do things for you."

"Is this supposed to flatter me?" Simon said dryly. "I don't feel I have ever passed whatever test you created to weigh the worth of the men who work for you. Sometimes, Brighton, I don't know the next move."

"You'll find it," Brighton said casually. "Once you get going. Just like at Bletchley. These chess moves. This potential to find out who is trading secrets. Ideologies. If Das Flüstern's influence stretches to Vienna, I want to know."

"Is he linked with Eternity, then?"

"You'll tell me, won't you? This is why I rely on you."

"Because you're a friend of my father's and . . ." The look of disbelief Brighton gave him disclosed how far off track Simon was. "Because you *know* I don't want another war. Not like the one we had."

Brighton studied Simon. "What, pray tell, did you lose in that war?"

Simon twisted his cuff links and raised his chin. "Sometimes I sense you're baiting me, Marcus, and I am not sure how or why. Do *you* want another war? Certainly I wasn't at the front, but that doesn't mean I fancy being locked into a crowded hut like a tin of sardines straining my mind day in and day out."

"It's why I wanted you as an intelligence officer. Because someone who has everything to lose is usually unhappy with whatever *everything* is and more ripe for a mind change. And that is unlike a Barrington."

"And what, pray tell, is a Barrington like?" Simon prodded.

"For one, they have a history of listening to what I tell them to do."

Simon didn't have an immediate response. He had long reappropriated Barrington's disappointment into hopefully appeasing Brighton.

"I might be off the grid for a while, so make sure you keep in close contact with Tab Martin. Ah! Come in, come in," Brighton said to a man in passing, and Simon knew he was dismissed.

Brighton's voice met him as Simon was halfway out the door. "Keep that little team of yours on Eternity . . ." If Simon didn't know better, he might have suspected an undercurrent of patronization. "And keep this one to yourself, will you, Simon? Find out who Das Flüstern is and *how* he has influence here."

CHAPTER 7

Sophie peered out the window of her small flat and envied her friend's view of Domgasse. Diana lived across from what Mozart aficionados called Figaro House, since it was where the composer had written his beloved opera, most likely looking out at the *fiakers*, or horse-drawn carriages, clopping over the cobbles as the bells of Stephansdom rang out.

Mozart was all over every city to Sophie. He was the unspoken friend beside her when her mother made her practice for hours on end with the threat of—and sometimes use of—a meterstick over the wrist for too many fudged lines and passages.

Sophie had used the code name Starling for all of five days during a botched mission as a Special Operations Executive agent. It had been a nod to Mozart and her handler at the time, who had been as enamored with music as she was.

And now the code name had a revised purpose. Her work finding stolen artwork and artifacts used her significant education from both her father's set and her university degree with great success. But the language of music was the one she preferred. When anything in the Schwarzmarkt was related to music, her interest and passion made it more likely she'd get the highest price.

Which was why the mask interested her beyond the infinity symbol.

Sophie put the kettle on the hob and waited for its whistle. She yawned loudly. She hadn't slept well. At first she wasn't sure if it was because of Simon. Then she supposed it might be Mozart. Or perhaps Diana uncovering the secret Sophie had kept since they roomed together at Bletchley Park.

That Sophie was married.

But sometimes when Simon looked at her, she imagined she saw something that transcended a hastily scrawled signature to protect his claim on his father's estate.

The kettle shrilled and she saw to her tea.

Mozart was a safer train of thought. He was in her bloodstream. What would it be like to see a molded likeness of his face? There were paintings, of course, but a death mask? A morbid prospect, sure, but a deep impression of what the man looked like in repose those first days after his soul had slipped was unfathomable. Would it be punctured with the pockmarks left by his illness? Would his genius show through the molded and waxen lines?

The easiest way to seep into the heart and consciousness of the Austrian nation was music. A tonal change, a signature shift, a legato movement married well with a new ideology. When presented in minor chords performed under domes with splendid acoustics, a message would be internalized in eighth notes and fluid phrases.

She was *aching* for a piano. Her left fingers mimed bars of Concerto no. 17 over her kneecap, but it was never the same.

She spent the morning giving herself a manicure and thumbing through the pages of a magazine from back home, the wireless spilling forth suite after suite of Beethoven. When the second movement of his *Pathétique* sonata crackled through the speakers, she stopped. Maybe she couldn't love a person, but she could love a piece . . . *this* piece.

With the sun slinking down on the horizon, night settled in and Sophie set out to meet a Russian diplomat before picking up Diana to head to Minoritenkirche.

As a rule most Soviets steered clear of the Sacher and the surrounding Albertinaplatz. The French sidled over for the music at the neighboring Staatsoper, and the British attempted to find some semblance of a good cuppa and a paper in Cafés Sacher and Mozart attached to the opulent hotel. Pieter Sidorov had high taste for one promoting a Communist ideal that would see the even distribution of goods.

Sophie was accustomed to the monogrammed dishes and deep russet chairs of the Mozart Café as well as a menu that did its best considering heavy rations and limited imports. By the time Sidorov arrived, Sophie was already deep into a cup of mélange.

"How do you do?" He folded himself into a chair, looking up to catch the waiter's eye.

Sophie smiled. "You seemed eager to meet."

He nodded and waited, crystal-blue eyes focused on her, until the waiter had taken his order of straight espresso.

Sidorov stopped to light a cigarette. "There is a rumbling of a highly valuable commodity on the market." He offered Sophie one.

She inclined her head to accept. "How valuable?"

"Near priceless. Especially to my men. My cause." He appraised her candidly, from her brown hair pinned into victory rolls and curling just above her shoulders to the visible part of her torso. Sophie didn't shift. "If it is found, it can change things for my side."

"*Your* side. I thought we were all on the same side," she said with feigned coyness.

"It has deep significance to Vienna, and its acquisition would serve my purpose very well. I have been told that you're neutral and you'll work for the highest bidder."

"You've been told correctly." The conversation was sounding an awful lot like the one she'd had with Herr Haas.

"I will need your complete discretion."

"Of course." Sophie crossed one leg over the other under the table.

"It is a death mask."

"Oh." She arched an eyebrow.

"Of Mozart."

Sophie sipped her coffee in ruminative response. An Austrian patriot and now a Russian agent. She was always curious as to what party was interested in the different offerings on the black market. The mask seemed to bring out something beyond the promised schillings or pounds. It spoke more to the weight of Haas's response to the situation: an emblem. And for the first time since she had arrived in Vienna, Sophie realized she wasn't just responsible for a few transactions.

This was something *more*. Something dangerous.

He slid a piece of paper over the table and left it beside her saucer as he rose. "You know where to find me. But if you can procure it, that will be your commission."

Sophie nodded. "I will be in touch." But they both knew these words were just a formality. She needn't be in touch if he knew where to find her, and judging by the gravitas of his request and the ominous look he gave her just then, it was clear he knew where.

He gave a curt nod and left enough money for both of their drinks, even though his hadn't arrived yet.

Sophie waited until his tall figure crossed the Albertinaplatz before she opened the paper. The commission was a ridiculous sum. A sum that told her more was at play than just Pieter Sidorov.

Sophie was charged to find an artifact *two* separate parties wanted.

She valued her reputation and wanted to be trustworthy, but something made her want to step beyond the bounds of her self-ascribed regulations. She didn't want to pit the clients against each other, nor was she worried about securing the highest price beyond providing a donation to Frau Wagner. Rather, she was intrigued at how their certainty pitted against her disbelief that the mask existed at all.

And the two parties didn't just want to hoist it onto their mantels. Its value rested in something deeper than mere sentimentality. Some virtue or philosophy was attached to it.

Perhaps just being *seen* with it would be enough for the victor who procured it. Though certainly it could also be a bargaining chip.

Two parties would know of it.

Sophie chewed on her bottom lip. She had withheld things from Simon before. She hadn't meant to, of course. But secrets—even born of good intentions—were sewn into the tapestry of her years at Bletchley Park. Simon understood that while their social worlds might collide, her daytime activities were as hush-lipped as his own, especially until she felt she had something that was worth passing along.

She finished her coffee, so strong its aftertaste lingered on her tongue.

———⚬⚬⚬⚬⚬———

Minoritenkirche stood out just beyond the Rathaus town hall. Unlike the latter or the opulent churches with steeples and spires or columns supporting an ellipsoid roof, such as Karlskirche, Minoritenkirche had seen numerous iterations.

Diana had once told Sophie that its mismatched facade was the subject of one of Adolf Hitler's first sketches in his rudimentary art days. Before his reign of terror and years sporting Socialist agendas in beer halls. Still, it had existed centuries before his unwanted influence.

Now they stood before it, and with Diana's reverence looking up and around it, Sophie felt a hallowed hush.

It was easy to move in and out of churches. And while many of Vienna's were bombed and cratered, people still attended mass and private prayer. They even lit candles in *Der Steffl*—what the Viennese called their most famous cathedral Stephansdom—even though a neighboring fire had caused its wounding and near demise.

Sophie's knowledge of churches wasn't quite as academically bent. She associated them with Simon's pursuit of Eternity and Diana's presence in Vienna: you could conjure up a reason for being in one even if the person you were meeting stood you up or you no longer wanted to keep a standing appointment. There were pews and statues, candles to light and altars where you could bow your head and remain undetected. Starling could easily meet a man who wanted to discuss the price of a piece of jewelry or silver goblet, the likelihood of a Klimt painting finding its way back to its city home.

But to Sophie there was an added appeal rooted in the verse Diana's theology-professor husband often mentioned about storing not your treasures on earth. Hitler had pillaged churches for altarpieces and relics much as his Nazis pilfered everything else in the name of God's purpose. Churches were a literal treasure trove.

The November night was falling harsher with winter on its heels. The sanctuary wasn't much warmer, but it was a nice reprieve from the icy breeze.

"Its foundation stone was laid by the king of Bohemia in the thirteenth century." Diana's whisper was faint. "It bears some French influence, but the *hochaltar* is Gothic." She stepped around Sophie.

Sophie assessed her friend's careful attribution to the panels and columns, stone sculptures and stained glass.

After mass the last parishioners made their solemn way outside, and Sophie and Diana lingered in the vestibule before they entered. An echoed chill welcomed her over harsh tiles of the stone-slatted sanctuary and into its heart of crisscrossed arches, wooden pews, chipped tombstones, and art.

Sophie removed her dark green hat. "So, why would my contact want to meet at this of all churches? Something about Mozart? Or perhaps because it is a little out of the way?"

Diana led Sophie to the far side of the sanctuary and a monument etched into the strong fortress of the church's wall. Diana was being, well, Diana. Her rambling of historical details settled over Sophie's shoulders like a blanket. Sure, it was partly annoying, but her passion was infectious.

"Look at this." Diana waved. "There is Pope Pius blessing the dying poet . . . see? Pietro Metastasio was Vienna's poet laureate. Here, Salieri, Haydn, and, of course, Mozart look on."

Sophie leaned in to inspect the engraved scene. She couldn't match her friend's knowledge when it involved columns and arches, but upon seeing Mozart's likeness, she felt close to him here. As close as she felt to him when she passed the Michaelerkirche near the Hofburg and Stephansdom, where his funeral was conducted before his body was taken to an unmarked pauper's grave.

After several moments, just as a custodian was dimming the last of the candles and night washed through the still-open sanctuary door, they were joined by a man.

Diana immediately pretended to be a solo visitor, glancing up and around the choir and roof before she made her way through the sanctuary.

"*Guten Abend*," a stranger said, just as Diana ensured she was several pews away. Sophie only made out the back of her hat.

"Hello." She didn't turn to watch him slide in next to her. It was clear given the serious slant of this man's homburg that he didn't fancy his visage being identified. But he did nod in acknowledgment.

As with so many men she worked with, he pressed through a few lines of small talk. Did they use pleasantries when doing business with another man, or was this reserved for interactions with her sex?

"This is a beautiful church, ja?"

"Yes," Sophie said too quickly. "I understand from Karl Haas that you have information for me."

"You know your music."

"I try," Sophie said. "Again, Herr Haas said—"

"You are familiar with our father of music?" His eyes glittered from the moonlight alighting the stained-glass figure she had passed.

"I thought that was Bach." Sophie supposed he was testing her.

"Very, very clever. Bach is the father of the German *Lieder*, but Mozart? Mozart! He is Austrian. It is important that our musical heritage is restored in Austria."

"So I understand from Herr Haas. But what you want me to find is very expensive and I am assuming very dangerous, given how until recently I, like most of the world's population, didn't know it existed."

"There is a man who runs a Pfandhaus in the Neuer Markt. Do you know Seilergasse off the Kärntnerstrasse?"

"Yes." She kept her tone matter-of-fact. As if she merely did business with Müller as she might anyone else.

"Herr Haas wants to be once removed from this."

"So he'd said." It made little sense, but Sophie would take what she could get. There was, after all, now the recent inclusion of Sidorov. If she were pursuing something of equal interest to a Soviet, she would want a middleman too. "But he left me little but a card with *your* name. So you're my dead end. Unless I should just work with the Pfandhaus proprietor? He's a jittery bunny. Do I go back to him? What do you provide?"

"I am paid well. I sit in a pew."

Sophie let out a low whistle. "So you're not an intermediary?"

"A messenger."

"Haas must have paid you well." She pressed her lips together in a hard line.

"This is so valuable that everyone wants it, but no one wants to be directly connected to it."

"So I've gathered." Sophie smirked. "I'm assuming because with great value comes great danger. But perhaps the danger is more in the rumor than in the actuality of the piece? I mean, not that you would *know*. You're just the messenger."

He ignored her facetious tone. "If it is true, then we need it here in Vienna. There are whispers that it might be over the border in Czechoslovakia. Or what *was* Czechoslovakia. A country that is no longer a country . . ." His voice trailed off a little wistfully.

He clearly didn't want that to happen to Austria. Perhaps that was why he charmed his way into a soft question: "If it does exist, wouldn't you want to know?"

"So you concur it might be a rumor." She wasn't surprised when he didn't answer. "Who is the man who must trust me?"

"See to the Pfandhaus, Starling." He rose and bowed slightly, tipping his homburg to her before he crossed himself and turned in the direction of the exit.

Diana was still roaming near the altar. A chill rippled up Sophie's spine. Why would a man send her to meet another man about something that didn't exist?

She wandered to the north end of the chapel where she took a closer look at the monument to the poet laureate. It was an interesting piece—Haydn turned to the pope while Mozart averted his gaze downward and his contemporary composer Salieri peered subtly to the side.

"Well?" Diana slid up beside her.

She meant to tell Müller about this Mozart mask anyway. At the very least he might be able to ascertain if there were any other interested parties. Any whispers. "We have one more stop tonight," Sophie said.

It wasn't that Sophie didn't trust Diana to care for herself. Rather, she assumed responsibility on behalf of Simon, who was very protective of Diana and Brent. The latter would hunt Sophie to the ends of the earth were something to happen to his wife.

So Sophie linked her arm through Diana's as they walked through the Innere Stadt. "For someplace that is supposed to be neutral territory, it is so deeply biased toward the Soviets." Sophie gritted her teeth. She beheld the men standing sentry with guns and insignia much like she had encountered with Simon the previous night. "You have your papers with you?"

Diana merely tilted her chin up and walked ahead. Soldiers were everywhere, guarding against some perceivable threat and keeping order between each zone.

Sophie pretended it was a usual stroll between two friends even as her mind attempted to process the interaction she had with the man at Minoritenkirche. Haas, who was pulling the strings of this search, felt so strongly about keeping his anonymity that he made her jump through hoops.

She kept her eyes straight ahead and her arm looped tightly with Diana's as they crossed through the arch of the Hofburg near where she and Simon had been approached. From there she felt a little more comfortable, the lights of Kohlmarkt winking and the familiar Julius Meinl Café under its reconstruction signaling they had reached the Graben. Her hold on Diana relaxed somewhat as they neared their destination.

The Pfandhaus on Seilergasse was tucked into a street off the pedestrian-busy Kärntnerstrasse, overrun by barricades and blockades. Telephone wires draped low over the uneven cobblestones on which Sophie's and Diana's heels clacked out a staccato rhythm. The door they approached was not numbered. The name "Müller" was engraved in a clear, bold font.

No light spilled through the windows, but Sophie knocked anyway. She waved at Diana to get behind her as she made out a shadow behind the door.

"*Guten Abend*," Sophie said as he opened the door.

That was certainly *not* Herr Müller.

"Starling, I presume?" The man nodded at Sophie before he regarded Diana behind her.

"Indeed," she said curtly, not enjoying being so quickly recognized by a stranger. She looked over his shoulder. "I am here to see Herr Müller."

He stepped into the doorway blocking her sight line and her access. "Wait here."

"Is this usual?" Diana whispered without looking at Sophie. "Leaving us out here on the doorstep?"

Sophie shook her head. "I don't know what is usual. Everything about this is my playing it by ear."

Diana nodded. "And you can't tell me what the object is you're seeking?"

"Not until I can read what's truly happening. It's safer."

The man returned a moment later and handed a carefully sealed envelope to Sophie. "This will tell you everything you need to know. Herr Müller says he is busy tonight."

He tipped his hat at them and set in the opposite direction.

Sophie's hand twirled the pearls around her neck to calm her nerves and to keep her voice in check. "Now, Diana, I—"

But Sophie's sentence was truncated when footsteps sounded from behind them.

And when the streetlight's glow glinted off a gun, she straightened and instinctively tucked Diana behind her, holding her fast and still with a steady grip.

"Sophie . . ."

"It's fine." She was rarely followed. "Just let me take care of it."

The shadow closed in. Sophie's brain filed through a dozen possibilities. The danger Karl Haas had spoken of. Her affiliation with Simon. Had they been followed from the church? Was she too conspicuous with Diana?

A grip on her shoulder tightened, then pulled her back before the figure struck Diana with an object Sophie couldn't see in the darkness.

Sophie bit out a curse, and the intensity of her SOE training spiraled through nerves shot through with adrenaline.

The man had hurt Diana.

Her lithe lines and tall frame proved advantageous, not only in the assailant's initial surprise and recoil, but in Sophie's ability to wrest the weapon from him.

He compensated with his not inconsiderable weight.

Sophie moved as through memory: weeks of exercises and training, not to mention muscles defined by years of riding and shooting to good use. He might have the weight advantage, but she had the height, movement, and anger coursing from the abuse of her friend.

In defense mode Sophie found reserves of strength that propelled her into fighting stance. Sophie huffed. She fashioned her long fingers sculpted by years of piano training into a blade and centered her strike just right of his Adam's apple.

She watched him falter and fall over. He'd survive, but it would take him a while to catch his breath. She kicked the rifle that had fallen with his surprise across the damp pavement.

Sophie blew out a long line of air and steadied her shoulders. Diana, coming to, held the back of her head and blinked over the prostrate figure, then gazed back up at Sophie.

"Oh." Sophie studied Diana's stunned face frantically a moment to ensure she was all right. Then she peered over her neck and assessed her head wound. "Well, little Canary, incredible what one can accomplish when the moment calls for it, wouldn't you say?"

She looped Diana's arm in hers to steady her. "Serves him right," she added as they left the figure—wounded but likely to soon stir—and set off hurriedly in the direction of Diana's flat.

CHAPTER 8

U nlike a Barrington." It was the last thing of note Brighton had said, but it crossed with Simon over the Ring.

How much did Brighton suppose about Simon? Was it merely a throwaway line to help him remember his lineage and how he was? A sort of backhanded entreaty to act his part? Or was it a subtle reminder that Simon's time in Vienna was at the behest of someone who thought highly of Simon's heritage?

Simon glanced left and right before he crossed the road, a streetcar rambling beyond him and the usual rhythm of traffic circling. When a black car accelerated, Simon picked up his pace, but it was of little help. The car swerved toward him at an odd angle, the tires screeching.

Simon hopped up on the curb as the car sped away. A quick look back revealed a silver head in the driver's seat.

That swerve seemed deliberate. Too deliberate.

Simon caught his breath, swallowed, and continued in the direction of the hotel. No one, from the construction workers outside the bombed Staatsoper to the usual pedestrian traffic of the Albertinaplatz, seemed to have noticed the car's erratic path or paid Simon any particular attention.

He raked his fingers through his hair, trying to focus on the parallels between the folder Brighton had given him and the chess game in progress in his room. But he was still unsettled somehow. And rightly so, it seemed.

Was the folder the reason for Simon nearly getting hit by a car?

Simon rolled his shoulders and smoothed his steps. Brighton was in Prague now, leaving Simon with the impression that he was king of a teetering castle. That Vienna was his responsibility. *Some* king he was.

Once inside the hotel, Simon took the lift up to his floor and was met with the empty stretch of hallway: russet walls and carpet, carefully spaced doors adorned with gold numbers. He turned the key and was welcomed into his temporary home as he had been a hundred times before. It seemed so impersonal he sometimes wistfully listened to the foot traffic on the street below or appreciated the racket from the other Brits on the floor below: crammed together, most likely envious of his space.

Simon shrugged out of his overcoat and took a long look at the folder from Brighton's office. Then he retrieved the message from the man who had begun the chess game, now sitting in midgame on the side table.

He consulted the missive in the folder. He was familiar with men exchanging descriptive notation and messages to play a game from afar, but his opponent took it a step further. To an uninitiated player, it might have seemed just a second move, but to a skilled player, it exemplified a great deal of planning. Indeed, Simon could almost imagine himself in the man's position taking his time, sipping a drink, crooking his finger under his chin in rumination.

Sure, his responses were sent to an unnamed postal box in the Old Quarter of Prague—Staré Město—where the clock towers chimed and the church steeples stabbed the skies like pitchforks. But when Simon was playing, each notation allowed him to imagine a real, breathing figure across from him.

He was still at the board until the early winter night settled over the city like a blanket and swallowed the pink blush of sunset from behind the spires outside his window.

Nc3 was an interesting move. He tried his best to anticipate the next move in any game, but this one—especially this early in the game—seemed to set up his opponent for a losing piece.

He glanced at the board until he settled on a move confident and risky at once.

A Closed Sicilian defense.

Simon turned back to the notation. He had spent the better part of four years with eyes glazed behind his glasses, attempting to read more than what a few numbers or letters offered. There was a calculation to the message Brighton had given him. Something in the slight strokes and spaces that *tried* to give off the impression of an amateur or enthusiast. The play might have suggested the same had Simon not had a penchant for reading too far into what might well have been left alone and a propensity to add several lines to a complicated equation when a quick jot of numbers might have achieved the same calculation.

Simon picked up the discarded chess piece. He still held it when the phone on the bureau rang with a very irate Brent Somerville on the other line.

"I've *just* seen Diana. She showed up injured with a rather irate Sophie."

"And a good evening to you."

"Barre! I swear!"

"You swear? I hope there are not ladies present."

"Put down the receiver and come to my flat and *fix things*."

"Is anyone hurt? Diana?"

But Brent had already clicked off.

Simon squeezed the chess piece in his palm until it left an indent. As he grabbed his coat and fedora, he gave a cursory glance over a game in midplay.

A silent opponent.

Brighton's opponent.

Simon was playing chess with a traitor and a double agent.

When Simon arrived at the Somervilles' flat, he jogged up the steps to a door cracked open even as soft music from the wireless funneled out. "What happened?" Simon strode inside, catching his breath.

Diana was sitting by the fire with a cloth pressed to her head. "It's not as bad as it looks!" she said, as Sophie said, "If I suspected that it would be dangerous . . ."

Sophie. Simon smoothed his hair from his damp forehead, then quickly assessed her profile. Her chin was raised a little in defiance. She never let on if she was worse for wear, but he assessed her face just the same.

"But it was dangerous, wasn't it?" Brent said from the direction of the kitchen. A moment later he arrived with a pot of tea. He poured a cup for Diana, then gingerly combed her long blond hair back from her cheek. Then he looked up at him. No one could glower at Simon the way Brent did. No derision, just . . . well-founded annoyance.

"I don't know why Brent called you," Diana said to Simon. "It all turned out all right." Her face was pale, but not so much as to hide a proud gleam. "Because Villiers was there. Simon!" Diana nearly bounced. "She was remarkable! She knew exactly how . . . It was unlike anything . . . Villiers leveled him! A man who had several stone on her. Oh, Simon." Her eyes brightened. "You should have seen it."

He could only imagine, of course. But what he imagined was the capable woman standing beside him—drawing on reserves of strength and finesse well known to him. He cleared his throat in hopes of cracking some of the tension creeping over his shoulders and neck at the vision of a Sophie he had never seen in action. How resplendent she must have been. How he would have wanted to jump to her defense. How she would have railed against it.

"Why were you there at all?" Simon narrowed in on Sophie's face, piecing together the few fragments of sentences involving a pawnshop and a church. For one thing, he hadn't required Diana to do anything for him in several days.

"I asked her to come with me." Sophie waved off a cup of tea. "It was at a church I knew she'd love, and I didn't fancy going alone."

"A church? But you were at a Pfandhaus," Brent said.

"Well, yes, but that was *after*." A flush crept up Sophie's cheeks. "First we went to a church. I've been commissioned to find something extremely valuable."

"Everything you find is extremely valuable." Simon frowned.

"True. But this is almost priceless."

"Priceless enough that someone would follow you and attack Diana?" Brent asked.

"Sophie, you know better," Simon said when she didn't respond and the wireless filled the mounting silence. "What are you looking into?"

Sophie glared at him. "I don't need you chiding me in front of our friends," she said in a low voice.

"And I don't need you running around with Diana when she might get hurt," Simon said, perhaps too shortly, but he was tired and his nerves were jangled.

"Where was *this* concerned Simon when we were in London?" Sophie said.

"Enough!" Brent said. "Di, what were you and Sophie looking for?"

"I . . ." Diana traced the rim of her teacup with her forefinger.

Watching Diana and Brent, Simon felt a peculiar tightening behind his carefully pressed pocket square. They were so in sync. So suited to each other. Diana cherished Brent's worry for her.

Simon glanced at Sophie only to see her spine stiffen and her breath tickle the scarf around her neck. Sophie was ready to demand swords or pistols. He almost laughed at the contrast before his lips smoothed into a line. Brent was holding a conversation with his wife using only his eyes and the room was getting smaller.

"If it is that priceless, perhaps you and I should talk privately." Simon motioned Sophie toward the door. "We'll let you get some sleep," he said to the Somervilles.

Once outside, he turned to her. "Why are you dragging Diana out with Starling?"

"She's bored, Simon."

"Starling or Diana?"

But she didn't acknowledge the jest. "Diana is not your plaything."

He raked his hand through his hair. "She's *my* responsibility."

"She's *Brent's* responsibility," Sophie said. "She's her *own* responsibility. You brought her here, and now she often sits at home burning biscuits with spotty electricity in a bombed-out city. She needs something to do."

"I'm well aware of what I asked Diana to do, Sophie."

She sniffed. "Diana lived through the same part of the war that you and I did. She deserves a role in helping you."

"If you're seen with Diana, that could compromise her." He flicked a look at her. "And you. You were hurt."

"How selfless of you." Rain was beginning to mist rather than fall, and the encroaching chill made Sophie cross her arms over her chest. "And me?"

"Well, you don't listen to me, do you? Diana, at least, heeds my warnings."

"Simon, listen to yourself." They walked a few moments in silence. "The man who hurt Diana tonight is the same man we saw the other night in Volksgarten."

Simon startled. "The Soviet soldier?"

"He takes his job very seriously it seems."

Simon ignored her snarky tone. "I've half a mind to send you both home."

"You aren't her keeper, Simon."

"I know that." But he also knew Sophie well enough to infer what she was thinking. That perhaps what made him so protective with Diana was merely his attempt to exercise the control he wished he could wield with Sophie: to keep her safe.

But if he truly wanted to keep her safe, why had he tugged her here in the first place?

To keep her near.

He wanted to share a look with her that conveyed a dozen words much like Brent and Diana in their shoddy flat, sharing a cup of tea and Brent's worry.

He wanted to keep her near, but didn't that just smack of control?

Control intimated that Sophie was a pawn or a piece on his chessboard. Rather, what Simon was feeling was helpless. And it helped them little if he was possessive. His immediate need to jump in and overtake the situation was what Charles Barrington would do, when what Simon really wanted was reassurance. That together he and Sophie could do anything.

He could just tell her everything he was thinking, of course. Yet neither of them was primed for that level of blunt honesty.

So while his throat tickled with everything he wanted to say— words about protecting her and wanting to be the person she turned to and that he lov—he straightened his shoulders.

"You're a smarter woman than that, Villiers. You know better than to drag Diana into danger." He was worried about Diana. That was why his world tilted a little.

He blinked away the sudden burn in his eyes.

———⬥———

Simon was too silent and a little too attractively disheveled. Sophie noted how his ebony hair fell onto his forehead and that he had loosened his collar. Even that pristine pocket square wilted, on full display since his overcoat was slung over his arm.

"You'd keep secrets from me," he said after a long moment.

"You'd keep secrets from *me*?"

"This isn't a game. This isn't us trying to outshoot each other at Camden."

"What's gotten into you tonight?" She shook her head. "I saw Diana home. It was *her husband* who called you."

"Diana is not like you. She can't shoot perfectly using either her left or right hand."

"She can take care of herself. You have always known that or you wouldn't have chosen her to help you in the first place. You saw her grow up a little at Bletchley. I did too. Or is it that you're all right with *my* throwing myself in danger but not Diana?"

"You know that's not true."

"Do I? Tonight you rushed over to make sure Diana was all right. The other night I was near accosted at the Hofburg and all you said to me at my doorstep was good night."

"Villiers." His voice was soft despite its resonant tenor. "All you said to *me* was good night. And we had just . . . we had . . ." His eyes were fixed straight ahead, and their blue glare was so intense that she could feel the wheels in his mind turning.

"Sometimes I think you're just imagining the world as you always do. Like a chess game."

He ducked his chin. "And you're the pesky pawn I can't figure out what to do with."

She hoped he was hiding a smile. But she wasn't sure. "A pawn?" She nudged his shoulder with hers. She usually loved these moments of affinity between them. It was easy to forget that the world was crumbling around them. And that she was following the trail of something so valuable men would kill for it.

Yes, that wasn't too drastic an assumption. Men *would* kill for it. They had killed for far less. And if Simon knew, would he . . . ?

"On the other side of the board, the pawn can be anything," Simon said stoically, almost as if he were reciting something. "Even a queen."

"Your flattery gets you nowhere," she said, hoping to lighten his tone.

"You want a drink?" she asked as they neared her flat.

Simon shook his head. "But thank you."

"You're preoccupied."

"Am I?" He raised an eyebrow.

"I can tell by your fedora. When you tug it down low over your forehead, you're in espionage mode." She waited for his smile to spread. "When you're feeling confident, you tilt it to the side so everyone can read your face. See what's behind those bright eyes."

"My, my, Villiers. I'd almost think you were flirting with me."

Several silent steps. But not comfortable ones. With no falling into rhythm or slight touch or banter like similar nights when she fell into him like the exhale of taking your pinched shoes off at the end of a long night of dancing. Or pulling the bench up to the Bösendorfer Grand, hands on keys, ready to fall into a favorite piece: the notes dancing on the page, heart and memory already ten measures ahead of them.

"Good night." Simon set his fedora back on his head.

Two words. Sometimes alluring, sometimes dismissive: as they were now. A reprise of the other evening.

"Let me into your secret world, Simon," she said softly. "No competition. No shooting party."

"I never want you to have to answer for me. Or be accountable." Just by watching the shadow filming his eyes, she could remember a night, years ago, when he returned to find her at his Mayfair house. After her confidence and hunches had led her into a precarious situation and her forehead and lip were tattooed by the consequences of her decision.

She had gone to a safe space then. Much as she had assumed she was approaching a similarly safe space tonight. Müller would *never* turn her away.

"I took the risk when I came here," she said, swallowing her worry.

"I know." He tilted his head to look at her more intently. "Sophie, we are well beyond that. You don't have the luxury of keeping things from me."

"This is different."

He exhaled a long breath. "Is it dangerous if you tell me? Is that it? I want to give you the benefit of the doubt. But . . ." He sighed. "Does Diana know?"

Sophie shook her head. "She just knows that it's important."

"She's here for *me*, Villiers."

"And what am I here for?" She waited to no avail.

"You say it was the same Soviet soldier who bothered us the other night?" He pressed on.

"Yes."

"He must have followed you then."

She could feel his eyes wash over her but knew it wasn't a compliment. Sophie shrugged. "But it won't be the first time I'm stopped and, heaven forbid, have Diana with me. And it won't be the last." She squeezed his elbow. "Simon . . . you're not even looking at me."

"Take care, Sophie."

CHAPTER 9

October 1938
Camden, Sussex

Y our move." Simon had moved a knight. He took a long drag of his cigarette, the smell mingling with the dark mahogany paneling, books and leather, scotch and cigar smoke in the den.

Lady Sophia tapped a finger against her crimson lips. "This is a gorgeous set."

"Isn't it?" He held a piece up to the light. "It's Biedermeier. An antique. Franz Josef of Austria himself might have held the queen." Simon inclined his head toward her empty glass. "May I?"

She answered with a sound that was almost a word but not quite.

He returned with a snifter of scotch, refilled her glass, and they continued the game. Lady Sophia spoke even in silence, through the stretch of her neck, the movement of her left fingers over her kneecap, recalling a phantom line of what he was sure was Mozart while she was deep in thought, her teeth worrying her bottom lip, her right hand stroking her pearl necklace like a rosary.

He was so caught up in her leaning over the board that her next move was almost sleight of hand. When he finally focused, she had taken his queen and was leaning back, a smile of triumph on her face.

Simon wiped the back of his hand over his mouth and the earth shifted. "You beat me at chess."

"You speak of it as if I had just removed the Excalibur sword from the stone."

He lost a chess game. Yes, she was smart and tactical. But for the first time the squares on the board were secondary to the company he was keeping.

Sophie took a puff of her cigarette. Her presence relaxed him. It allowed him time to remember when his mother had told him about his father. His *real* father. Not Charles Barrington puffed out like a peacock strutting in the next room.

"We were playing chess," his mother said. "And it wasn't as if I was anticipating his movements or nearly as proficient as he was. Rather, I drew the attention he usually focused on the board up to me. And the few skills he had taught me sufficed. Because he was daydreaming or lost in thought or perhaps just comfortable with me, and I took advantage and won."

Up until his mother's death when Simon was seventeen, he always had to share her. Her radiant light was eclipsed by his father and Julius, and she so often looked to Simon, pale and dismayed, as a constant reminder of the mistake she had made that resulted in his being here at all.

He had tucked that story in his pocket and fashioned his chess skill until he was sharp, calculated, and remarkably talented. He won competitions. He skipped grades in school. His chess game was amplified by his brain.

"Not vanity." He plucked a discarded pawn from the board and worked it in and out of his fingers. "Just surprise."

Sophie had truly thrown off his guard. The barometer of his mother's winning of a chess game set the precedent for love, he supposed. Because it was how he measured the impact she must have had on his real father.

He shifted. Through his memories Simon was wading in dangerous territory. "I liked the piece you played. At the party. When you tossed shellfish at my ear."

Sophie's grin warmed his blood. "Ah yes. The Starling Concerto. Well, that's what I call it anyhow." She flicked a few ashes onto a tray. "Mozart kept a starling as a pet. They are magnificent birds! They can embed sounds from their own surroundings into their calls—a siren, a whistle—and yet still be wholly true to their own voice. In the last concerto movement, the allegretto, you can hear a bit of its song." She hummed a trill. "He even wrote an ode to it when it died."

"That makes me sad." He watched the firelight a moment. "It was his muse, wasn't it? Then *poof*, gone. I wonder what music he might have written if the bird had still been around."

"It makes me think that you can find inspiration in anything," Sophie countered. "Here I am beating you at chess, and it might just up your game. Now you'll move a piece, say, and remember me. Just like . . . just like Mozart and the bird's legacy."

Simon chuckled. "A legacy."

Lady Sophia crossed her arms over her chest. "*You* have a rather remarkable legacy. Do you truly fancy being called Lord Barrington?"

"Heavens, no." He was always being reminded that he wasn't truly a Barrington, so wearing the name was an albatross. "And I'm not Lord Barrington yet. And likely never will be, not with my father and Julius in place."

"I am as much a Lady Sophia as you are a Lord Barrington." She studied a pawn in the firelight. "And I'd soon as be done with the whole Huntington-Villiers nonsense. See there?" She pointed to an oil portrait, staid and static above the mantel. "*That* reminds me of a very similar portrait in my father's study. Representing the Huntington part of my dismal name. And he was a right brute. The Villiers part, on the other hand . . ." She nudged another chess piece without making a sure move. "It dates back to the time of the Norman Conquest. There was a Countess Barbara Palmer-Villiers. Countess of Castlemaine." Sophie stopped for a long, relaxed smile. "Described as the 'Curse of the Nation.'"

"And you identify with this? The Curse of the Nation?"

"Ha!" Lady Sophia elongated her spine in a stretch. She was thin and athletic, and he could make out the sinews of her long muscles as she crossed her legs. She reached for her pearls around her neck. "These pearls have been in the Villiers family for generations," she said, noting his eyes on them. "There is speculation that they belonged to the great lady herself. They've, of course, been refashioned into a less ornate necklace." She tilted her chin a little. "My nana once told me that they were all I would need. If the estate fell through or I was married off to some cad like a horse at market, I would always have my pearls as collateral for my freedom."

"They're beautiful." They clearly symbolized how deeply she cherished her free spirit, but they also shimmered with delicate grace.

"Tell me a secret, Simon Barrington." Her lips teased into a half smile.

"Why would I tell you a secret?" He kept his voice in check, because he was dangerously close to being so far gone that not falling in love with her would require a decided effort.

Simon assessed the board. "My mother and I would play chess. She was magnificent—though no one knew." He smoothed his pocket square: a refined gesture as he spilled the estate's secrets. "We would play in my room or the servants' quarters. If Charles Barrington knew . . ." Simon took in the pieces on the board before him. Each contrasting square had become their entire world. Many a silent conversation where a sleight of hand and a confident starting move replaced the need for words.

He hoped Sophie didn't see him begin to falter. "We would go on adventures. She would shrug off her mink and wrap herself in worn tweed, and we would drive into Brighton for tea. Or to see the beach. But as I got older . . . the adventures stopped. And I think I became *too* good. I never knew why."

Sophie leaned back, her pearls falling over the distracting dip between her collarbones. She smiled warmly. "Well, if I were to meet you away from here, I would extend my hand and say, 'Nice to meet you. I'm Sophie Villiers.'"

Lady Sophia Huntington-Villiers had made a wonderful impression on him, but *Sophie Villiers* crawled into his heart and stayed. It had nothing to do with this lightness, with the scotch, and the wavering light.

"Someplace where we haven't been preconditioned by our illustrious names," Simon said. "I would look across at you"—from her delicate facial features to her lovely full lips and long limbs, perhaps while she sipped sherry and Gershwin was interpreted by a pianist in the corner—"And no longer be Simon Barrington and ask you for a drink." He raised his eyebrow, waiting for her to pick up on his obvious flirtation.

"*Barrington. Barrington*," she singsonged. "Oh yes!" She clasped her hands. "Simon *Barre*! Sounds vaguely French. Softens those r's a little. One syllable. Trims it a bit. Like you're a dashing rogue from the Continent. I mean, even if you were primed to be the Barrington heir, what good would that do you?"

"Maybe acres and acres of land, a hermitage . . ." Simon stared into his glass. An elixir, perhaps, that made him blurt things before he'd wrung them through the filter of his mind. For a moment, stupidly, he wanted to kiss the cranberry shade of her lips that were tilted up a little. He wanted to run his fingers over the indent of her collarbone.

"Positively dull." Sophie laughed.

Simon felt a new sensation tuck under his collar. One far deeper than initial attraction or a stolen kiss or a flustered night. A word previously impervious. Foreign.

Vulnerable.

CHAPTER 10

November 1946
Innere Stadt, Vienna

Sipping mélange from a monogrammed cup in his hotel room, Simon revisited the board. He was playing chess with a traitor. It had started with the Closed Sicilian defense chosen in response to his assumption that his opponent might play as he did: not for immediate gratification but for a long, sure win. Simon guessed his opponent, who had already proven proficient at meeting his plays, was slowly building up his defenses.

The game was new.

The pursuit of a traitor was not.

Simon blinked at his espresso. Sophie had a secret.

Simon was bred on secrets: first at Camden and then in the war when Brighton recruited him. He didn't want secrets from Sophie. Ultimately, he was already breaking Brighton's request that he keep the knowledge of Das Flüstern to himself. But that was before Diana and Villiers had been accosted by a soldier outside of the Pfandhaus.

He left the hotel and headed to Domgasse—once home to Mozart—to the Somervilles' flat. Yesterday a man had tried to run him over, so Simon kept a keen eye out when crossing the streets. At Diana's building, he ascended to the second floor and knocked on the door of the flat. From inside, the wireless played and the smell of something burning wafted, likely one of Diana's latest baking efforts.

He knocked three more times, and when Diana opened the door, her blond hair was tied in a kerchief. Flour on her nose. "Simon!"

"Smells terrible." He smirked.

"It's bread."

"Is that what it is?"

She welcomed him in and he sat on a settee with mismatched cushions while she procured tea. As always, he was struck by how Diana created a *home*. Some of Brent's sketches were framed and hung: London churches with interesting steeples, detailing Christopher Wren's masterpieces before Jerry bombed them to smithereens. Even a wedding photo of their day against the rubble of the church that had once been All Hallows by the Tower.

The flat cracked his heart. His upbringing might have trained him to look derisively at the dust-speckled mantel and worn cushions, yet what others might write off as *homespun*, he appraised as *loved*.

She set the tea in front of him and smoothed her skirt under her on the armchair adjacent to the settee. He supposed she must be lonely. With Brent teaching all day and with fewer and fewer tasks for her to do for Simon.

"I need a key. I need to encrypt highly classified information." He reached into his pocket for a folded piece of paper he was never without and then Hofer's manifest and set both on the table. "Names of businesses, politicians, wealthy men, addresses. How they connect despite their political leanings. I don't want anyone else to connect my dots."

Diana nodded. "Playfair?"

Playfair ciphers required deeply seeded secrets into a grid pattern a little like a crossword puzzle developed to uncover the Eternity ring network in London. It required a key so the receiver of the message could decode it. "A little déjà vu couldn't hurt," he said. "We're both familiar with it."

"That Köchel Catalogue, perhaps?"

"Those old Mozart compositions." Simon had been so impressed when she had first mentioned it. When he needed to pursue leads in London, he'd called Brighton not long after, assuring him of his choice in Diana. Diana noticed things.

"*Köchelverzeichnis*," she recited. "In the nineteenth century, a man named Köchel painstakingly catalogued all of Mozart's works numerically, including fragments and lost compositions. To give it a Viennese flair."

She drew a grid on the piece of paper and then listed a few of the pieces she recalled. "We need a concerto to use for the key. Pick your fancy." She showed him a list.

"K. 453." He didn't miss a beat. They didn't need an entire book of Mozart, but a casual knowledge of his pieces might serve well.

She consulted the list. "Piano Concerto no. 17 in G Major. The Starling Concerto, as Villiers calls it."

Diana played with a few variations, working them into a new language. Only the person with the master key would have the Playfair cipher.

But this master key was his. Diana would know how it was created but not what it meant so she couldn't ever be questioned about Adameck, Das Flüstern, and his Prague and Vienna connections. If ever decrypted, there was a part of the story only he held.

An hour later Diana had transferred his manifest and names he suspected and ledgers—the places he had been and the companies he was sure were deep in Soviet pockets—into encrypted grids. Simon took the notebook he had been safeguarding with numerous lists in his own slanted hand and tossed it into the fireplace, struck a match, and watched it burn.

"The master key." Diana gave him a mock salute and proffered the sheet containing her work. Her fingers appeared to have a brain of their own before her mind caught up.

"This is marvelous." He accepted the paper from her. He leaned back on the settee and appraised her: blue eyes glistening, cheeks flushed, smile wide. She was in her element. "I'll have a master copy, but I'll need you to keep the key safe."

He sipped the last of his tea. The burnt smell from the kitchen had faded. "I should go. You're the only other person who knows about this."

"Simon." She rose.

He stopped midway to the door with his hat in hand. "Yes?"

"Sophie told me about you. And her. You're married."

"It's just paperwork, Diana." Simon touched her elbow. "It's nothing. There was never any sense in getting into it. Paperwork."

"You keep saying that."

"You know everything that is important to know about me." He gestured toward the table they had just occupied as she helped him. "I trust you more than anyone."

"But there's this mental wall in front of you, and I always wanted to peer around it. Try to break it, and I think I came close. Especially late at night at Bletchley after Fisher had done his best to beat you at chess. But I never could."

Simon raked his fingers through his hair. "I don't want you to have to face a wall, Diana."

"I know."

"But maybe I don't know how to project anything *but* a wall."

"Oh, I don't know about that." Her grin reappeared. "I know your deepest secret now." She paused. "Out of all of the hundreds of possible Mozart codes you could have chosen as your key, it was the Starling Concerto." She smiled. "You won't be able to do *anything* without thinking about Sophie."

CHAPTER 11

December 1946
Neuer Markt, Vienna

Karl Haas was dead.

Sophie had learned via Müller's telegram marked *urgent*, and the moment she realized why, she felt as if she had been slapped in the face. She made the brisk walk to Müller's Pfandhaus in mere moments. The chime from above the door stopped ringing only when Müller pulled her inside. It made the attack on Diana seem even more ominous. A threat.

"Look at this." Müller handed her the note.

Tell Starling Haas has been killed.

"Our association has been known in the past," Sophie defended. "They probably knew I would check in. Who sent this?"

"It was tucked under the door when I arrived." He adjusted his glasses. "I searched the papers." Müller showed her a series of news periodicals on his desk. "Just to see if there were any details . . . No report yet."

"No *official* report."

"Poison. The *unofficial* report. I know nothing further."

"I don't want you dragged into anything."

"I was already dragged in. Besides, I could say the same for you." Müller opened his desk drawer with a pointed look at Sophie, then the drawer. "I have this for protection."

"That firearm's not protection." She released a sad smile. "That's an antique."

But he didn't return her smile. "You should be careful too."

Sophie took the ivory-handled gun out of her waistband and held it out to him. "I can at the very least show you how to use it."

She placed his hand over the barrel and demonstrated how to easily expel a bullet. "If the time comes where you'll need it, you'll be nervous enough as it is, so the less time you have to think in the moment, the more it will all turn tickety-boo."

He opened his mouth, likely to have her translate, when they both jolted at a shot at the front of the store. Sophie's face drained of heat. She ran to the front window and looked out.

Only a car backfiring.

Sophie slowed her breathing. "I'm a little on edge."

"You perhaps do not take what care you should." Müller looked at the pistol he had set on the table. "It is one thing to fire a gun, Starling. It is quite another to put yourself in a position where you need to."

"We are both in that position."

"Let us make sure it is not in vain, then."

She nodded.

Sophie left the shop tugging the brim of her hat down, as rain shimmered under the glare of half-lit streetlamps. Austria was the land of *Stille Nacht*: the carol that, even now, trilled slightly from the vibrato of a violin bow on the Graben.

The irony was, Sophie felt the harrowed weight of that silence too strongly. She had taken the ease in which she moved in and out of the city for granted and a man was dead.

The makeshift Christmas markets—far from their previous splendor displaying woodcrafts and artistry, looped with garlands, so closely built together almost as if they were holding hands—dotted the pedestrian thoroughfares.

As Sophie neared her flat, her hand instinctively moved to her weapon upon seeing a silhouette near the streetlamp. As the figure closed the distance, relief released through the muscles of her neck and arms.

"Gabe." She accepted a kiss on each cheek as was his custom. "Would you like to come up for a drink?"

He shook his head. "I got a message at university today. Someone is trying to find Starling and thought I could help."

"An interesting way to seek me out." She accepted the note he gave her.

"You'd best get inside."

The city curfews didn't extend to the area of Sophie's flat in the Innere Stadt, but Gabe had a ways to travel. At the base of the stairs outside her building, she stared at the note. Did everyone in this infernal city use intermediaries?

Sophie shuddered at the failed protection of Karl Haas's protocol. And immediately thought of her own willingness to be involved in the hunt for the mask that had ended the life of another.

Gabe clearly sensed her shifting emotions. "Why are you still in Vienna, Sophie?"

She pursed her lips and tossed her hair. "I told you, darling, the moment I go home is the moment my mother will find me some insipid fool to marry."

"Lucky, insipid fool." He chuckled.

She liked how his teasing came through in his Viennese accent. "Thank you." She clasped the note and stopped on the stoop to retrieve her key.

"Sophie."

She startled at the change in his voice. "Yes?"

"Insipid fools are a lot safer than this city. Take care."

She nodded, entered her building, and slowly ascended the inside stairway with the weight of Gabe's words on her heels.

In her flat, she struck a match on the side of the mantel to watch kindling spark in the fireplace grate. Then she poured a sherry and opened the note. It was a request for a meeting the next morning for Starling with a man named Adameck, working on behalf of a client in Prague. Except he had used the Czech word for "Starling," *Špaček*, instead.

So when the telephone jangled and Diana asked if she might call round the next day, Sophie declined and mentioned the meeting in an abbey in Wienerwald.

The prospect of an excursion buzzed through her fingers even as she returned the receiver to its cradle.

She'd need a car.

———◦◦◦◦◦———

"Absolutely not," Simon said in response to her request to borrow his Bentley.

Sophie had walked to the Sacher, smiled at the concierge, and spoke to Simon in the neighboring café. "You look dashing today."

"Diana was just attacked, Sophie."

"It's broad daylight. In an abbey." She twinkled at him. "I'll have a getaway car."

"You're not going." He stepped closer.

"I don't believe you've rendered my left eardrum *completely* deaf." She rotated her pearl earring.

He lowered his voice. "Don't . . ."

"Darling, monosyllabic responses tend to go in one deaf ear and out the other."

"*Sophie.* I will not be the man who refuses to let you go."

"Good. I don't associate with those sorts of high-handed men. More still, if I can't have *your* car, I'll just—"

"But I *will* be the man who refuses use of his car. This way, my dear, I am not *forbidding* you, rather throwing a wrench in your plan." He ended the conversation with a little nod and strolled away.

Sophie would not be summarily dismissed. "I could, of course, find myself in the precarious position in which I would have to *owe* someone a favor."

His eyes flashed blue steel. He wouldn't want her borrowing or bartering.

"It's safer this way." Her grin widened as he placed the keys in her palm. She leaned up and kissed his cheek, nearly knocking his fedora off with the swift movement. "Thank you, Simon."

She watched him walk away. Moments later, she went outside and the parking valet brought Simon's Bentley around. He opened the driver's door for her.

Buoyant with her small triumph, she settled onto the leather seat. An unexpected figure beside her nearly sent her jumping through the roof.

Diana.

Sophie leveled her breathing. "Lovely morning, Canary." She tugged at the knot holding her silk scarf in place. Doubtless Diana had put two and two together: Sophie needing to go to an abbey and not possessing a car of her own. So Sophie put the car in reverse and began driving.

The sky was sleet gray and the clouds heavy with promised rain: a harbinger not unlike her still-unsteady feeling of taking Diana with her.

———◇◇◇◇———

Sophie was always uneasy when she left the traditional British or commonly occupied districts and meandered into Soviet territory. The remaining steeples and unbombed palaces garishly shadowed by the flak towers the Nazis had erected—grotesque cement fortresses-cum-watchtowers—blighting the skyline.

Tolls and checkpoints existed outside the city districts as they swerved onto the motorway leaving Vienna. It wasn't long before the city grew smaller in the rearview mirror. Soon Sophie turned onto a side road, and the first vestiges of the medieval abbey came into view. Stift Heiligenkreuz, or Abbey of the Holy Cross, was tucked away from the road. The sext bells chimed as Sophie steered the car over the stones. Here, hidden from war, it was almost as if she had stepped back centuries into a world preserved in time.

Sophie parked the Bentley and dropped the keys into her handbag. There was a stillness here contrasting Vienna: the abbey shrouded by trees, the whisper of the wind, and the slightest drizzle of rain that might soon be snow.

Diana and Sophie walked toward the arched entrance. Sophie watched her friend's countenance as she drank in every ancient line and crevice. Not three steps through a drafty open corridor they were joined by a tall man with harsh features leaning on a walking stick.

"Starling?"

"Indeed." Sophie accepted his outstretched hand.

"And this is?" His eyes swept over Diana's curves and beautiful face.

"My friend is an architectural historian and colleague." Sophie hoped this would snap his near-gaping jaw shut.

Diana's brilliant brain seemed at odds with her hourglass figure and striking features, and Sophie couldn't help but enjoy when she was given opportunity to prove how grossly underestimated she was.

Adameck's arm swept toward the beautiful Cistercian monastery. "The abbey comes from a fantastic financial legacy. From the Babenberg dynasty. The Holy Cross speaks to its relic. A slice of wood from the cross of Christ."

Sophie took in the relics and ornamental Baroque augmentations while listening to Adameck's discussion of the rich musical history of the Gregorian chants found centuries after. She also took in the man himself. He was nondescript save for the intense, watery blue of his eyes, of which one was glass, and the walking stick that seemed to be more ornamental than necessary.

Cloistered halls and arched windows looked out on stubbled courtyards. Russet roofs punctuated by copper onion-domed steeples drew her eyes up to clocks and bell towers. Inside, stone cloisters welcomed them, and other than a monk passing on the way to prayers, they were alone.

Adameck led them to a closed chapter house where an unassuming high grave was elevated above stones grooved with time. "I'd like a moment alone with Starling, please," he said to Diana.

Sophie gave a quick nod, and her friend retreated into the sun-filled arches. "You can trust her."

"I'm sure, but it is not she who I came to see. There is a high-profile client in Prague interested in a Biedermeier-era chess set."

"And you work for him? How does he know my name if he resides in Prague?"

"Your reputation precedes you." He glanced over at her. "Some are wary of you. A British woman rather new to this enterprise."

Sophie stalled. "If you were *so* wary of me, then why are you here?"

"I go where I am paid to. The client said you would be able to find the chess set relatively easily here in Vienna. That you will know a good Pfandhaus that has all the pieces. He is especially adamant about the Slope Bishops." He handed her a piece of paper. "These are the specifications."

Sophie tucked the paper into her pocket. She recognized the term from several conversations with Simon. "You came from Prague and met me at an abbey to discuss a chess set?"

"My client prides himself on being a good judge of character." There was the slightest bit of defiance in his tone. "And while he is in Prague, he keeps a close eye on artifacts here. If you are able to procure this, he assures me that he will be in touch with you again."

Through Gabe Langer, then this fellow? "And you came all the way here from Prague? There are telegrams, telephones."

"I had other business." Adameck tugged at his tie. "I wasn't expecting you to be so . . ."

"Forthright? Demanding? Intelligent?" Sophie leaned onto the balls of her feet, which only made her not inconsiderable height more pronounced.

"Brave enough to come and meet a stranger in the middle of an abbey."

"My friend has an affinity for churches." Sophie shrugged.

"The client is an associate of Das Flüstern," Adameck said in a tone Sophie read as meaning to level her.

She folded her arms. "An overly dramatic name."

"He is the most influential man in Prague."

Sophie refused to give in to the way he leaned decidedly on his stick. "According to whom?"

He cast a look out to the cloister. "I didn't suppose you would come alone, but no one should know we have talked."

"And why do you suppose I would agree to that?"

He patted his pocket. "How much would you like as a retainer?"

"It's not about money."

"I think you'll agree because I hear you are enthusiastic."

"From whom?"

"You're a tall British woman living in a foreign city. You stand out. My associate would like someone who is not directly involved in the, how shall I say it, political tension."

"If your associate is so taken with a tall British woman living in a foreign city, perhaps he should have come himself." She tilted her head to the side. "And I have a feeling that whether we like it or not, we are all victims of political tension."

He raised his chin. "To be seen employing Starling is the quintessence of affluence these days."

"You mean influence."

"Only the best can afford you, it seems."

Sophie smiled. The higher her price, the more money she could funnel into Frau Wagner's pockets.

"But with your reputation comes a growing caveat. You might want to think twice about the company you keep."

Sophie withheld her response, stroking the pearls at her neck. "War makes strange bedfellows of us all, does it not?"

"I thought the war was over." He tipped his fedora and she listened to his shoes and walking stick clacking down the heavy stones, then he stopped and looked back over his shoulder.

"Careful, you might turn into stone."

She smoothed her trousers. He didn't mean Diana, of course. And she doubted Gabe was of seminal interest. That left Simon.

"Get what you needed?" Diana asked when Sophie found her.

"Indeed. Let's head back, shall we?" They returned to the Bentley and got inside. Sophie turned the key in the ignition and steered away from the abbey.

"Did you see the stained glass?" Diana said. "And the windows . . . so simple. Reflective of the Trinity."

Her enthusiasm was natural, but Sophie assumed her friend's curiosity about the man Sophie conversed with bubbled underneath. "Do you never wonder what I do, Canary?" Sophie gently cut off her rapture about the historic abbey.

"I was your flatmate for four years. You were on one side of Bletchley and I on the other, and we never intersected. I *still* don't know what you did every day."

"What fun would there be if I were an open book?" Sophie winked at her.

The corner of Diana's mouth turned up. "Not a lot of fun. I wouldn't have had to find out about your marriage on my own."

Sophie kept her gaze ahead. Talking about everything with Diana had always come so easily to her. But her marriage? *A piece of paper.* Just like the piece of paper announcing Haas's death. Sophie tightened her hold on the steering wheel.

The road was flanked by deep woods dotted by little cottages with accordion shutters and overspilling window boxes. The flak towers and tall buildings of Vienna drew nearer, and soon they were past the tollbooth and smoothly on their way back to the Innere Stadt.

Just a piece of paper.

Sophie couldn't drive directly to Diana's flat in Domgasse, given the barriers and roadwork prevalent in the patched-up city, but she barely missed the curb.

Diana didn't look at Sophie directly. "Villiers, are you here to work with Simon or merely because Simon is here?"

And Sophie was left with nothing to say.

CHAPTER 12

August 1939
London, England

Dear Simon,

    This wretched war had to go and make it impossible to find silk stockings. I have no idea where you disappeared to. I tried ringing Mayfair House, but your man said you had been preoccupied. It's not an amour, is it? I figure it will happen at some point and then our alliance or rapport or what have you from our first meeting will have to shift somewhat. I had half an inkling to head over to Ashton this weekend because I am positively desperate to ride Shelby, and I was hoping you might be there?

Yours,
Villiers

Villiers,

    I've been rather preoccupied in London. But I did manage to find these. Perhaps I shouldn't be sending you silk stockings as you are not, how did you put it, my amour? But it's far more preferable than your having to use the garish stain they're selling in bottles. If you will be at Ashton over the weekend, it would be unneighborly of me not to follow. I suppose a visit to Camden is in order. Shall we meet for a ride then? Friday at noonish? My father will want you to join us for dinner, and I can guarantee you it will be an aching bore. But at least we'll have each other.

Yours always,

S. B.

Simon was late for the weekend and the horseback ride at Camden he had promised Sophie, so he rang over to the manor to let Barton know. Simon couldn't leave the city fast enough as traffic moved at a snail's pace over Putney Bridge. Would he miss their ride altogether?

He hadn't seen Sophie in so long and had a million things to tell her. Finally, on the motorway, barrage balloons and urban spires replaced with long spans of blue sky.

The prospect of seeing Sophie was enticing; the prospect of seeing his father not as much so. Simon believed Julius shipped out next week so he could beat the Huns and bring glory to the Barrington name. The prospect of Simon going to Bletchley kept him from saying little more than he was working at the Foreign Office.

Charles's own pursuit of guts and glory and raising the Union Jack high for king and country in the previous war made Simon, in his father's view, little more than a coward despite anything he would do for Brighton.

The final stretch through the Downs toward Wilmington was idyllic, the midafternoon bleeding over the landscape. Then the estate assaulted the horizon: overblown and strangely Gothic. An afterthought of a Brontë novel.

Simon let the new valet see to the car and his case and strode up to the front door. "Barton," he said genially as the butler opened the door.

"Sir." The word held urgency.

"Barton, what is it?"

"Lady Sophia is here, sir."

"Oh, she came for dinner." Simon took off his fedora and overcoat and handed them to Barton.

"Sir . . . she's with Master Julius. I tried to . . . Sir, you'd better . . ."

Simon's heart lurched. "Where?"

"The library. It's none of my business but . . ."

"Of course." Simon sprinted and swung open the library door.

Every nerve and tendon in Simon's body surged with primitive fury.

Sophie's arm was pinned above her head, and his brother had her pressed against the wall. Sophie was strong, but not strong enough to withstand the fact that Julius's bulk was almost twice her size as she struggled.

"Get away from her!" Simon lunged at Julius, ripped Sophie from him, and set her behind him. He drove his fist straight into his brother's nose and rammed him up against the wall.

Simon blinked perspiration from his eyes and cocked his arm to drive his fist into Julius's face again when he caught Sophie attempting to fix her torn sleeve from the corner of his vision.

Simon drove in again before his father's voice belted from the French doors.

He cursed. "Simon!"

From his periphery Simon saw a shaken Sophie start to fly at Julius.

"Claws in, vixen!" His father grabbed her arm and wrung it behind her back.

Simon lunged. Sophie rubbed her wrist and fell away from him, heaving. She raised her hand to turn the pearls at her neck. A nervous habit, he supposed. One he rarely saw because she was so often in complete control.

"When the *bastard* said he was running late"—Julius's word drained the heat from Simon's face—"I thought I would have a little fun." His nose was most likely broken, and he dabbed at it with a handkerchief.

"He is the only gentleman in this room," Sophie spat. "I might not be a lady in many respects, but out of affection and respect for Simon, I will not use that vulgar language in his vicinity." By the erect lines of her thin frame, Simon could tell she was railing for another round.

"It's not worth it." Simon was floored by her defending him so passionately and physically. She had thrown herself in between Simon and his father and brother, staring them down.

"I haven't had the opportunity to use the word *shrew* too often lately," Charles said.

"Father, Julius assaulted Lady Sophia."

"And what, Simon, you demand satisfaction?" Julius snarled. "Allow me to get my dueling pistols."

"If it takes that to defend her honor, yes."

"She's fair game. I don't see her locked down with a ring." Julius raked his gaze over her and then slid a challenging look to Simon.

"I know you only hurt her to hurt me. If you want to take it out on me, so be it. I will fight you. Leave her alone."

"Little minx probably wanted to be cornered by Julius. Look, she's flushed and bothered." Charles sniffed.

"I am not little and I am not a minx!" Sophie hissed. "Julius, you are a mindless brute with horse lips. No wonder you must ensnare unwilling ladies in order to satisfy your ardor. You brainless lout. And you . . ." She spun to Charles. "My father might cut me off, but I will not stand here a moment longer and watch you treat Simon like rubbish."

Sophie adjusted her blouse with tenured grace. "Your estate is a sham. Your eldest son is a Neanderthal, while Simon is the only one worthy of the Barrington name. He, not Julius, is lauded in the papers for his charm and his significant chess wins. He is the only thing keeping your name from being trampled in the mud. This oversized buffoon drags it behind him like a lame-horsed carriage."

She speared Charles with another glare. "You would do well to put your stakes and your investment in Simon. Your family name will be a laughingstock, and you can bet to heaven I will throw in my patronage to its demise as long as you favor the man who attacked me."

Her eyes were bright as she heaved in a needed breath. His heart blazed.

He had failed at any attempt to uphold his mother's name and legacy, despite the love he felt for her in stolen glances and chess plays behind closed doors. He hadn't dreamed or imagined he could inspire such deep respect and affection—especially from the person he most admired in the world.

Charles assessed Sophie with dead eyes. "You, mademoiselle, are nothing more than a common—"

"Stop!" Simon shouted.

"You are a Barrington!" His father lashed out. "You will do well not to stand by and let this woman insult your family honor."

"You remind me near daily that I am not a Barrington. I don't want the name. Oh, I won't shame or degrade my mother and her choice in marrying you by running off like a simpering schoolboy and revealing the truth. That's how I threatened you, wasn't it? You were nervous I might take some of what they'd said at school or in your social set and run with it.

"I will move permanently to the Mayfair house. I'll keep out of your way. I only came to the ancestral home to see Lady Sophia. You've never given me *anything* to believe that I was even partly of the family other than your money. And yet I am more than your payoffs and allowance. Half of me is. But the other half of me is *her*."

Simon motioned to the portrait of his mother on the wall. "And you hate that because you loved her, and she broke your heart. This war with Nazi Germany will shake our world beyond this little microcosm, the estate and the spats. And I mean to wield my mind to defeat them, and you and Julius can go hang!"

Simon spun on his heel. "After you," he said to Sophie, breathlessly, and together they set in the direction of the door.

"I wish you had never been born, Simon," Barrington said after him. "Every day of my life."

Simon stalled a moment to get his bearings. He'd heard it often enough before. When he was younger, he waited for the calendar to display the next party. On those nights Charles's arm was around Simon's shoulder, and he was introduced by his surname. But then on Sunday, Charles nursed a headache and yelled at his wife and hated Simon again.

Simon adjusted the bridge of his glasses on his nose, then closed his eyes a moment without turning back.

"Fortunately for me, I no longer care about your opinion." With the very last scrap of dignity and drive Simon could muster, he set his pace out the door. He strode past the servants in the foyer and out into the yard, with Sophie close behind. He quickened his step until he was across the yard and in the wooded area that stretched gradually into a forest.

"Simon."

"Well, now you know. He as much as said it in front of you. I'm a worthless bastard. He doesn't usually parade it in front of company. In fact, you're the first guest that—"

"Oh for heaven's sake!" she bellowed. "How are you . . . ?"

He shook his head. "I don't know who I am."

"They're so unbearably cruel to you." She softened, took a breath. "I didn't know your mother well, but I remember Lady Margaret. How did she put up with that?" Sophie looked in the direction of the main house.

"Sophie, I need something to believe in and that I can live and die for. All my life I've had to barter for loyalty! If I wanted compassion or even friendship, I had to trade for it."

"Not with me," Sophie said resolutely. "Never once with me."

"My father is a history professor from the Continent. Did you know that? My real father. He was visiting Camden to research the feudal system. He played chess too. I am good at *one* thing because of him, but that's all I have. I am serving a name I feel nothing for. And if I could just know that something about me is worthwhile, that I am not just a mistake."

"You are not a mistake!" Sophie didn't even try to hold back her fury.

He hung on by a thread, turning toward a tree and trying to wave Sophie away.

"I don't know what you visualize of yourself, Simon. I don't know what way—"

"I just need to know that all we're doing here—all *I* am doing—is worthwhile."

She inched closer. "Simon."

"I need to belong somewhere." He turned and looked at her, sentence abandoned, her eyes glistening in concert with his own.

He cleared his throat and gently touched her shoulder. "Are you much hurt? I haven't asked. I'm a fool." His knuckles still bleeding, he stroked her cheek and inwardly shuddered at her ripped sleeve.

"I'm more angry than hurt."

"I am sorry he used you so terribly. I wanted to shove him through the wall."

"Pity. That would have ruined the wall."

"You're none of the things they said about you."

"I know that." Her voice was low and tender, balm enough so Simon could begin to get himself together.

"Forgive me." He smoothed his tie.

"There you are, all lord of the manor again at the slightest show that you're human. Just like with those girls circling the oyster table."

"Maybe I can't afford to be human."

"I like it when you are."

Sophie leaned in, unexpected, and pressed her lips to his cheek, holding tightly to his shoulders. A charge blazed from his neck down through every nerve to smolder in his stomach.

"You have my loyalty, Simon Barrington." Her eyes were bright.

She reached into the pocket of her jodhpurs and extracted a long silver cigarette case. "Perhaps you haven't taken the time to worry about honoring your mother's name in the past. But you can now. By being exactly the opposite of what they are, you are already headed in the right direction."

She struck a match on the side of the tree trunk and lit it, then took a long inhale and slow exhale before she held it out to him.

He accepted it, uncaring of the red lipstick line around the rim. "Sophie, no one's ever spoken about me the way you just did." He lowered the cigarette and took her hand. "They've taken from me what they wanted, and I was stupid enough to keep giving it to them."

She retrieved the cigarette from him and pressed it to her lips. "Well, it's about time someone believed in you just for you." She smiled. "And not for what they could take in return."

——◦◦◦◦——

Sophie held the cigarette out in front of her. "Part of the reason I came this weekend is I wanted to tell you something." She tossed the cigarette onto the grass and ground it under her heel. "My parents have found me a husband."

"A husband?" His stare of disbelief was framed behind gold-rimmed glasses.

"I can bear three heirs and oversee the prolongation of our estate as the world starts to crumble."

She breathed in his citrusy sandalwood cologne. She had never seen a man so close to tears before, and it softened something in her heart, as if she was finding another layer or depth.

A lock of his ebony hair was liberated from its usual swath of pomade. And his eyes—one could drown in them if she got close enough—the perfect light blue.

They always spoke more in gestures and looks: his hand on the reins of her horse, the pass of a cigarette that had touched her lips, his gaze snagging hers from across a crowded room as if she were implanted with a homing device that informed him exactly where to find her.

To actually touch Simon, to explore his lips with her own, threatened to bind them tightly together. And Sophie wanted control beyond the many expectations and demands of a romantic relationship of . . . of *love*.

But with Simon she began to imagine the life her grandmother and mother had warned her against. Was it because he had given her the first few numbers to unlock the combination of who he *truly* was? Beyond the custom-made clothes and the checked smiles?

Or was it because she recognized how lost he looked . . . like a deer encountering the business end of a hunting rifle?

The surge of feeling she felt toward him was disconcerting and hovered on the edge of her boundaries—everything she was taught not to give. The most one could give was loyalty. It allowed you to give up dividends of yourself while keeping the tenderest parts of yourself stored away for a rainy day.

Never let anyone see your weakness.

"You don't want to get married, Villiers, do you?"

Sophie blew out a line of smoke. "I'm not certain I have a choice." She leaned forward, grabbed his lapels, and pressed her lips to his.

———◦◇◦———

Back away. Don't be daft, man. Back away.

But her strong fingers were over his shoulders and down the curve of his spine as if she were lost in the throes of a Mozart movement and all coherent thought drained. Part of him was aware this was Sophie: his friend, his ally. Another did away with thought and reason altogether the more the kiss deepened.

Finally she broke away. Her eyes, glazed and blinking, sought and held his hostage.

He tried his best to untangle his brain. She had been assaulted by Julius. His upbringing, for better or worse, inspired him to ensure her comfort. His heart demanded it. He searched her face, hoping to read the concern or fear or surprise that would dictate his next move or word. But before he could collect his voice, she spoke.

"Do you want to hear a terrible secret?"

"What?"

"I even found myself wishing for war. Isn't that dreadful? It was the one way I could see myself out of this predicament. Out of my parents' control and Ashton's jail. I came here thinking that you might be able to break me out."

Simon brushed a loose lock of dark hair away from her face. "How could I do that?"

She raised a shoulder. "I just thought if I could see you . . ." She stopped and squeezed his arms. Then she took a few steps in the direction of the estate, her spine erect as if in preparation for the inevitable awkwardness of walking back in to collect her things and arrange transportation home. "You can't apologize for Julius, Simon. Just as you can't control what will happen next."

"If you don't want to marry whomever your father has in mind, you could marry me."

She stalled. "I won't drag you down with me. I'll find a way out." She glanced down at her shoes a moment. "I should go."

"You don't have to leave." He memorized the lines and angles of her face, the swan-like curve of her neck, her figure's contours exposed by the outline of her smart jodhpurs.

"You should too. Don't stay here just to sit through an insufferable meal with them. Draw your line in the sand, Simon. You don't need them."

Then who do I have? Simon buried his thought before he said it aloud.

After she turned toward the house, it took several seconds for him to coax breath into his lungs and out of his throat. He couldn't *breathe* without her.

Later, he avoided his father and brother as a valet helped Simon pack and arrange his cases to move into the Mayfair house. He rang over to have everything arranged—the drapes aired, the furniture coverings removed, and Simon's favorite wines stocked in the cellar.

Not a week later, Simon stood in front of the full-length mirror at his tailor's on Oxford Street having shed one skin to step into another. He kept all that his mother had instilled in him too: class and grace and a little of his father's shrewdness. His real father's identity rippled through gossip as long as Simon's family lineage, driving him further from the stand-in father who preferred Julius to himself. Lady Margaret had confirmed it. Simon wondered at every quirk or habit he couldn't ascribe to Charles Barrington.

Was it his father—his *real* father—who was responsible for the way Simon inherently saw the world through the squares of a chessboard? Through his propensity to loiter on the sidelines of a party or reception until sought out?

But *Sophie* had sought him out. She was to be married, and Simon had severed his ties with home, where he was most likely to cross paths with her. But some part of him knew they would find their way back to each other.

When London failed to drain thoughts of her, he had stopped putting off Marcus Brighton's messages.

After leaving his tailor, he found his way to Broadway Street, the Thames twinkling beside him as he walked. The sun slanted over the opulent silver of the Savoy, the bells and double-decker buses, and the bustle of London's circuses and squares.

When he reached Brighton's office, he asserted his change of heart to the man. "Sure I'll be recognized here and there by those who follow those rummy society pages closely. But it'll yield more than just a double take if I use my real name."

"It's a help."

"It is a hindrance." Simon would assume the name Sophie had created. The one that kept her close even as it separated him from his world.

"Fine then, Simon Barre it is."

CHAPTER 13

November 1946
Vienna, Austria

N*ever go to the party for the host,*" Charles Barrington had once
slurred, "*but to see which bees said host can attract to his hive.*"

Simon hoped David Moser's hive attracted important bees.

Simon adjusted his bow tie and smoothed the lines of his jacket
as he set out from his room at the Sacher. Downstairs, an apologetic
concierge said the retrieval of his car might be several moments due
to the popularity of events in the city so close to the holiday. Simon
went out into the street to wait. He wasn't two feet from the red-
coated doorman when he was confronted by a man with a sharp
profile.

"You! I have seen her with you!" The man had a thick Russian
accent. "Do not let her think that I cannot find her."

Simon held in his surprise. "Forgive me, but—"

Judging by his lunge forward, the man clearly intended to ram
Simon against the brick facade of the hotel, but Simon was faster.

He drove his fist into his assailant's mouth. Not too hard since his
goal was surprise. In the desired interim, Simon retrieved the man's
wallet for a quick inspection. It held an identity card, one that would
allow ease throughout the four quarters. Sidorov. Simon's head thud-
ded more from the mention of *her*—of Sophie—than the altercation.

The doorman bellowed, "*Polizei,*" but Simon waved him off,

shoved the wallet back into the man's coat pocket, then allowed him to slump to the pavement. "He'll come to in a moment."

Simon caught his breath, straightened his bow tie, and welcomed the appearance of his Bentley.

———◇◇◇◇◇———

Moser's town house, just at the edge of the Josefstadt District, was in the heart of the city and in proximity to Leopold University—where he served as chancellor when he wasn't showing off his impressive art collection—but also tucked into the American zone.

University students leaned against crosswalk poles advocating for unified politics even as dusk dipped low over the Baroque spires of the Piaristenkirche.

Simon strolled the last steps to Moser's place and ascended the stairs to the double doors. He was ushered into the *mise-en-scène* set with candles and marble, chandeliers and silver trays so like the melodramatic soirees at Camden. David Moser lit up when he saw him, crossing the floor from his residence near a shiny grand piano where the buoyant sounds of a Mozart movement were a complicated dance for trained fingers.

The tension and movement on the keys by a pianist he would recognize anywhere: as distinctive to him as Sophie's confident footfall.

"I am so delighted you came. I feel that half the university is acquainted with you but me. Even my theology professor knows you."

"Somerville," Simon said.

"He speaks highly of your skill at a chessboard." Moser watched Simon closely. He swept the vicinity with his brown eyes. "And it seems quite fashionable to have your presence at soirees, Herr Barre."

Moser's walls were a gallery showcasing art and artifacts Simon guessed were only recently recovered from after the war.

The melody from the piano in the corner trailed to a light pianissimo before it faded out. The melody . . . *her* melody.

Moser set his glass down on a side table and gave a quick round of applause. And Simon was graced with the prospect of an unanticipated meeting with Sophie Villiers.

"Come, come, Fräulein!" Moser waved an arm. "Stand up and let us thank you properly."

Sophie rose from the piano in a sleek, backless black gown. She bowed her head to the side, acknowledging the room's applause, before she locked eyes with him.

Simon raised the glass Moser had just pressed into his hand. Then set it down and lifted Sophie's hand in the Viennese custom so it was almost brushing his lips. "You were quite wonderful. Concerto no. 21 was it?"

"How well you remember."

She didn't seem surprised to see him. Their paths had crossed unexpectedly on previous occasions. Perhaps not occasions following a Russian man accosting Simon in the street outside his hotel, but Vienna was full of surprises.

"A Mozart lover!" Moser proclaimed. "You can feel it in her passion of the piece." He turned and nodded at a guest who sought his attention, then left Sophie and Simon alone.

She accepted a glass of champagne from a passing server and swerved to face Simon. "Like old times."

"It seems I'm here because I'm fashionable." He smiled.

"A party favor! Moser famously allows his guests to explore his home with little interruption." She leaned a little on the balls of her feet. "Shall we?"

He followed her down the corridor, and she stalled him at the door of the study filled with mahogany and smoke to turn on the light.

"You certainly know your way around here."

"Thinking you'll have to fight Moser in a duel?" She winked. "If you do, please make it swords. Fisticuffs are *so* dull, and it would be a shame to mar that handsome face of yours. What was it Catherine in Hut Five said? Your face shone with the intensity of a blue-eyed Valentino? I'm more of a Gable girl myself."

"You're flirting with me."

"I'd rather flirt with you than any of the other offerings out there, just eager for Moser's canapés."

"And his politics?"

"I've made several transactions for Herr Moser. Surprisingly *everyone* wants to work with him."

Simon alerted to this. "Everyone?"

"I've always admired men who treat royalty and waiters with the same panache." She looked around the room, perhaps for said royalty or waiters.

Even in a quick sweep Simon realized that every part of the divided city was represented here. "How well liked?"

"Even the Americans like him." Sophie ran her long fingers over the back of a leather chair. "They want his advice on the early development of a recovery plan. Where they would help far more than through the Red Cross to help establish a sure path for ravaged European cities. Education. Books, even. The Americans are rich and idealistic. It makes for a wonderful savior complex."

Simon smirked. As chancellor of the university, Moser was connected to numerous committees and political affiliations. Why not include the Americans?

Sophie strolled to a bureau at the far end of the room and motioned him over. "Look at this."

"It's similar to the set at Camden." He inspected a marble chessboard. "Biedermeier era."

Sophie beamed. "Exactly." She turned a queen in her palm. "I thought of you when I saw it. Because it's so unique from the standard Staunton." She looked at him for approval.

"You *do* listen to me." He smiled.

The set was beautiful and unique with a hint of Selenus styling. They were common in Northern Europe but not in Britain, which was why Simon had always been puzzled by Charles Barrington's possession of it.

"I have a lot of chess in my life these days, Simon. Even a request from a man in Prague!"

Simon shifted. In his too. Gabriel Langer had mentioned Prague. Brighton was certain of a double agent connection to Prague. Simon's chess notation messages came from Prague.

"Can't he just find a Biedemeier set there?"

"I find more and more that I never know clients' exact names from their intermediaries. I'm always one step removed."

Simon was one step removed from *her*. He was used to it at Bletchley Park, when they had sewn their secrets tightly into their seams and kept the conversations about the war in general and not the specific ways in which they contributed to it.

Simon sidled next to Sophie. "What side do you think he is on?"

"Moser? He's more than just someone who serves whoever pays him the most," she said. "He strikes me as an idealist. Just like you."

Already Simon could see how David Moser could be attributed a name and letter sequence in alignment with his encrypted Köchel code.

The air crackled with electricity. Was it the cut of her ebony dress and red lips or her proximity to a man who might be what he needed to link the chain between the man writing him chess moves?

Sophie leaned over the table to return the queen to the chessboard. The curve of her back affected him like so many of her moves and mannerisms.

She looked up suddenly and Simon felt such a surge he almost fell back.

He forced his voice into an even tone. "Have you seen anything in your messages, even from these intermediaries, in descriptive notation?"

Sophie was mock-playing the piano over her thigh. The trait always made him want to clasp her hand in his own.

"This room reminds me of the study at Camden." Her eyes met his. "Lord, what's gotten into me." She bit down on her cranberry-stained lower lip. "Nostalgic. That's it."

At her avoidance in answering, Simon's patience was drifting too far from his control. He stared down at the pawn in his slightly trembling fingers and set it on the board. Then, to avoid her gaze, he wandered to the opposite side of the study. "Anything resembling chess notation?"

"An Eternity symbol."

"Ah." The room was drained of personality: fine, upscale adornments with no style that spoke to the man or his specific tastes.

Sophie wasn't saying much and he wasn't certain what she felt she could relay or not. There was doubtless an element of danger in what she had disclosed and who knew how thin the walls were, even as the music and laughter from outside provided a barrier.

So he offered something in hopeful exchange of more. "There is a man that Brighton has me looking for."

"Connected to Eternity?"

Simon raised a shoulder. "He is very dangerous but also surprisingly . . ." What descriptive suited the invisible man on the other side of the imagined chessboard? "Elegant."

"You love elegant," Sophie mused.

"I suppose I do."

Simon caught the edge of a telegram out of the corner of his eye, half hidden near a stack of unread newspapers. He inched closer to see a date stamp and address from Prague. As well as the name *Adameck*.

Brighton had told him to keep information to himself. Simon had let Diana in . . . to a degree. But Sophie was a highly sought-after individual in art and artifacts acquisition according to Gabe and his own suppositions.

"If you hear of a Das Flüstern . . . ," he began.

"The Whisper?"

"Rather dramatic name."

Laughter outside of the ajar study door drew her attention, and Simon moved to follow her out the corridor and back to the soiree.

———◇◇◇◇◇———

She felt guilty. A part of her was near bubbling over to tell Simon about the abbey and the strange man she had met there. Was Adameck this Whisper fellow on Simon's radar? He was telling her about Brighton and a dangerous whisper, and she was withholding her pursuit of the mask.

At the parlor doorway Simon straightened. Sophie recognized many dignitaries and their wives as easily as the polished crystal and jewels offsetting lined faces and lean figures wearing fabric rehemmed and refurbished.

"There you are, Starling." David Moser's words were slurred by champagne. "Are you and Herr Barre here well acquainted?"

"We swam in similar circles before the war." She pressed a vague smile.

"She's a real wonder," Moser said to Simon. "There's so many pilfered antiquities out there trying to find their way to the right homes, and Starling can help secure their places in Austria."

"No matter how they got here?" Simon infused his words with a placating charm.

Moser inclined his glass to them both and gave Simon a lingering look, then spun on his heel to rejoin the party.

"You're a real wonder," Simon said dryly to Sophie. "And yet you deal with the black market. Why would the chancellor of the university invite you here?"

She smiled at a passing acquaintance but kept her voice low. "Remember that with the Allied influence anyone can just sweep their wartime activities under the carpet or shift allegiances."

"Moser, you mean." Simon cleared his throat when a passing guest stepped too close to overhear their discussion. "Listen, darling," he said through his teeth. "You know as well as I that it's better if we're seen as casual acquaintances."

"Funny from the man who kissed me on a park bench." She smirked and reached out and tugged on the lapel of Simon's war uniform: his bespoke Savile Row jacket. "The tie suits you." In a world fraying at the seams, Simon was sewn up perfectly.

"Everything suits me." A twinkle glimmered in his eyes.

Simon set his empty glass on a passing tray when David Moser approached him for a private word.

Moser gave a slight bow at Simon's acquiescence, inclining his head to the side. The Viennese were naturally welcoming, determined to ensure every visitor was treated warmly. But as quickly as the charm came, it faded.

"Follow me. I've an excellent scotch that wasn't on the menu tonight." Moser gestured to the corridor, and Simon followed him into the study.

"Before Schönbrunn I couldn't decipher who you were." Moser handed Simon a Swarovski tumbler. "If you were a diplomat or a journalist. I let my imagination run wild. And came up with several theories. I think I am close to the truth."

"I have investments here. Personal interests."

"That's not why you're here." Moser rubbed his chin. "And I am not sure what your connection is to Starling."

"And I can't understand why a wealthy, influential man doesn't hide working with the black market."

"People from all four quarters of my occupied city were here tonight." Moser set down his glass, and with the movement Simon recalled the telegram from Adameck, which Moser casually swept under the blotter.

"I don't like what is happening to my city, and while I don't have all of the specifics, I think you are trying to stop it." Moser took a ruminative sip of scotch. "You're trying to figure out who is tightening the vise to starve us out. I am trying to find a way to use my influence to ensure that Vienna is given the opportunity to find its best path forward."

Moser set his palms down on the desk. "My country could turn either way. We can either use this transition to adopt the ideals you well-meaning Allies have in place, or we can fall to Communism. No matter your *actual* role here, I know what you want."

"Who's to say I want anything? Maybe I'm just well paid."

Moser sighed. "My city has many flaws and many people ended up on the wrong side of the war. But I do not want Austria to end up on the wrong side of *this* war. For it is a war, is it not? Your people—you Britons—have been quietly training a military here for several years. What is it your Mr. Churchill said? A steel curtain?"

"An iron curtain."

"It will divide East and West. I want us to be on the right side of that curtain."

"And how do you propose to do this?" Simon swirled the scotch in his glass.

"Sometimes it is not the loudest voices that are heard but the most influential ones." Moser handed Simon a pamphlet that advertised an exhibition near Freyung Square, tucked into one of the oldest crevices of the city.

Simon took a moment, weighing Moser's influence and connections. "Academics?"

"Everyone has an idea of what we should be," Moser said. "The French, the Americans, the Soviets, and even you. But the people who will steer what we *are* might speak in whispers rather than behind a lectern."

It was an interesting choice of word. Intentional?

"Our government is provisional and easily swayed. The Communist Party is a legitimate political affiliation. Even after the Red Army stomped over our city and erected that eyesore of a Soviet statue, they still managed to gain four seats in our first postwar election. You understand how disparaging it is, Herr Barre. It's fine and well to believe that Austria will act democratically, but seeds are being planted."

Moser stared pointedly at Simon. "I can hardly tell you how to do your job, but chasing businessmen like Hofer around Schönbrunn parties is not where I would start." He inclined his head toward the pamphlet Simon held.

"Men like Hofer are the ones with the financial incentive to start a revolution."

"As far as the men I meet know, I keep my affiliations to myself. I can be anything to anyone."

"You have to choose a side eventually," Simon mused. "It's a rather uneven foundation to merely follow wherever the strongest voice is leading."

"Perhaps. But all of you are here—occupying us—our victors. Convincing yourselves you are doing good. The Brits with the military so we can defend ourselves, the Americans with their plans for charity, even the French. It is merely another occupation."

The telephone in the study rang, and Simon was met with a dismissive smile. "I will see you again, Herr Barre. Thank you for coming to my soiree."

Simon set his scotch on the table and closed the door behind him, just slowly enough that he could make out the name *Adameck* in Moser's crisp German accent just as he clicked it shut.

Simon and Moser's conversation raised far more questions than it answered.

Judging by the way Moser was renowned across the upper set, it stood to reason that Moser could use them to wine and dine myriad guests from different political and social leanings. It wasn't the first time Simon had heard the name. Adameck was from Czechoslovakia and yet clearly his influence here bled in different circles. Moser, with his political ties, being one of them.

Simon was invited here only *after* his encounter with Moser at Schönbrunn. Did the man mean to recruit him? Use him for information or perhaps a doorway into the Allied British side?

What Simon did know was that Adameck was sewing together many of the different pieces of Simon's world in Vienna. And there was an Eternity symbol. His mind cast out to Das Flüstern as a possible connector.

The party had dispersed, with a small stream of people moving in a river toward the front door. Simon accepted his overcoat and fedora from a maid and stepped into the night.

CHAPTER 14

As Sophie passed Müller's Pfandhaus on Seilergasse en route home, she saw the light was on. She glanced left and right. A cat skittered across the Platz, and the few streetlights flickered. She knew every alley and bombed doorway to duck into should she be pursued, and her grip on her revolver was tight.

Often Müller invited her in for strong Turkish coffee he assembled in a little pot. Often he gave her the best deal on whatever she was selling and threw in a little bit of extra wisdom on a piece she was hired to procure. Inside the shop, Sophie took in the hodgepodge of history and music.

"Something for Špaček?" Herr Müller said. "Coffee?"

"I shouldn't stay." It was late and she still savored the buzz from Moser's champagne and the thrill of the piano keys. "Špaček?"

Müller shoved his spectacles up his nose, moving a pile of invoices from a chair so she could take a seat. "That's what you've been called, isn't it?"

"So the Biedermeier chess set with Sloped Bishops. The client was pleased?"

"Very."

"What about the other item?"

He furtively peered around the empty shop. "There is nothing like that. That mask does not exist."

"But there are whispers about it." Sophie thought of the moniker Simon mentioned at the party. "I was approached by two different interested buyers."

"And they were wrong," he snapped. "You *know* what happened. One of them was killed."

"But if it exists, if there is a chance . . ."

"You already do so much here. For Frau Wagner. For Herr Moser, and for myself. You think that is in vain?"

"I want to do more."

"You feel responsible for Herr Haas."

"I feel *confused*." She'd feel more responsible if anyone else came to harm on account of her feeling around in the dark in pursuit of a rumored piece.

He closed the conversation with a restraining hand on her arm. "You may look at this." He changed the subject and opened a small cabinet near his overrun desk.

"The Starling Concerto," Sophie said.

"Piano Concerto no. 17 in G Major." Müller read aloud the handwritten inscription at the top of the manuscript.

"Not an original." She tilted her head to assess the details.

"From around the time it was first performed at the Theater am Kärntnertor. Where the Hotel Sacher stands now."

"Why are you showing me this?" Sophie asked.

"Every day new treasures arrive. They seem miraculous after being scattered by war. You need to sharpen your skills, ja? Like a honing steel against a knife. Sharpen your mind."

Was he telling her she needed to see beyond her possibilities in Vienna, to anticipate a time when she would slice through invaluable pieces? Or was he merely warning her?

—◇◇◇◇—

Two days later, Sophie sat at the Café Mozart overlooking the scarred Albertinaplatz and casually read a newspaper while men nursed cups of mélange or Turkish coffee with whipped cream or, if their shillings were few, without.

They would read newspapers for hours while stirring and restirring their coffees with small monogrammed spoons, talking in whispers.

Sophie was tucked away enough that she could provide discretion but visible enough to be approachable. But now the stakes were higher and her pulse with them.

A man had died. A warning had been issued.

She knew the city's true black market dealt in back alleys and bullets, men at the ends of their ropes who opened their pockets and wallets to find nothing inside, willing to do anything to replenish their coffers. But that was the risk she gladly took. She wouldn't risk Simon. She wouldn't risk anyone.

She had provided Adameck's client with a Biedemeier chess set with Sloped Bishops from an earlier era, adding to the value of the piece given the circumstances. The prospect of making it to the next level or opening a door for a new opportunity—no matter how perplexing or dangerous—was at least something *new*.

Adameck found her at her table. She noted the way he smoothed the folds of his jacket, glanced furtively over his right shoulder with his good eye, and joined her without asking.

How had he found her?

"Going forward, I think you'll want to work exclusively for my client," he said.

"So the first time we meet is far away at an abbey in Wienerwald. And now you are risking being seen by the intellectual set of Vienna?" She emphatically swept the café with a pointed gaze.

"When was the last time you *truly* heard live music?" Adameck was unmoved.

Sophie's mind spiraled to the upright piano at Bletchley trying to produce Mozart from its tinny keys. "A long while ago."

"Good. Then you'll appreciate it more. You're passing your test." He appraised her with his good eye. "And then I'm sure my client will want to meet with you. You're almost there."

CHAPTER 15

While Sophie hadn't outright committed to working exclusively for Adameck's client, the magnet of the Staatsoper certainly drew in his favor. If she was being wooed, this was one way to secure her interest. She did, however, pick Diana up along the way. Sophie hoped her friend would see the opera house much as she did her cathedrals: as a relic of historical beauty waiting to be reignited.

"I can't believe the Soviets are making the opera house a point of political contention." Diana looked up and around the partially bombed-out Staatsoper with awe. "Brent just told me that there are lectures about it on campus, exhibits showing the best of urban plans and prospective developments. Everyone has an idea."

Sophie looped her arm through Diana's as they took the battered city in stride. She enjoyed the company.

"You're quite protective these days." Diana laughed.

"Women out at night in a chaotic city requires it."

"It's more than that."

Sophie loosened her hold. Her brain was turning as fast as the rotors in Hut Eight. Three different men had approached her for something invaluable, and she bore the responsibility of their requests. So where Sophie had previously been attuned to the prospect of being followed, she now took each step with the expectation of it.

The ravaged Staatsoper's roof was still its own casualty of war with a wide, gaping yawn to the blue sky above, and the famed acoustics of the grand hall little but a crater waiting to be filled with brick, sound, and an audience, the building was still majestic. It had been one of the first buildings commissioned for reconstruction. Walking past, Sophie imagined one-time director and famed composer Gustav Mahler drawing inspiration from the fountains prominent in front of its grand facade.

Sophie hoped there would be safety in an open public forum with a group touring the building. Diana of course took in the architectural skeleton, enraptured.

"The opera house opened with *Don Giovanni*," the lecturer began. "Mozart's masterpiece, while Emperor Franz Joseph and Empress Elisabeth were in attendance. The reconstruction must reflect this formidable influence."

Diana and Sophie wandered through models and diagrams on triangular pedestals, standing in stark contrast to the devastation beyond. The federal chancellor was adamant that a working opera house would be in full use by '49, but Sophie was skeptical.

"*Di rider finirai pria dell'aurora.* 'By tomorrow your laughter will have faded,'" the lecturer said, quoting the libretto of *Don Giovanni*.

"A theater." Diana smiled. "Shows the power of architecture because it's not just the experience of sitting here. It's taking in the *story* of the world created to enhance the audience's enjoyment."

Sophie could imagine music linked to Vienna: from Bach, Beethoven, Mozart, and Strauss, filling in the cracks the bombs had made.

"Just like old times, Canary," Sophie said. Diana had read codes through music in the war and, thereafter, attended recitals and church concerts to help Simon.

"Starling." A man approached her with a clipped mustache and matching blond hair. His eyes were serious under arched brows. One eye was rimmed by bruising from a precisely planted fist. It hit right at the intersection of the bridge of his nose. His assailant knew exactly what he was doing.

"Herr Sidorov. What a surprise to see you here." Sophie didn't pretend pleasantries. "This is my friend Diana," Sophie said casually.

Sidorov gave a slight bow before he turned back to Sophie. "I was hoping you might have sent word by now. About your progress on what I asked of you."

Sophie thought her words through carefully. "Unfortunately, it seems a bit of an apparition."

Sidorov didn't visibly respond to her intentional mention of a phantom or a ghost, which was odd considering how doing so could assert his power. Why was there no indirect acknowledgment of Haas's death? After all, Haas was his competitor when it came to retrieving the mask. Or was Sidorov here simply to dismiss her now that some time had clearly elapsed?

"I don't deal in apparitions."

"My, my." Sophie kept Diana in her peripheral vision and tempered her voice. "I recognize that you want a tête-à-tête, Mr. Sidorov, but you're almost on my shoe."

She hoped her voice defused the undercurrent of tension. She assumed he wasn't daft enough to assault her with so many witnesses present. But she was very aware he *could* assault her, more still something in his face let her believe that he *might*.

Sidorov slowly fell back, but not before his stale breath lingered in her nostrils.

Did he truly expect her to be threatened by his half-answered questions and suppositions? It took everything within her not to rise up and blast him with a dozen questions of her own!

Sophie forced a smile and mentally assessed maneuvers if it became necessary—first on his person: a heel to his kneecap, an elbow to his abdomen. Then, a parting of the milling crowd for an exit.

He straightened his tie in an attempt at control, and she used the opportunity to pull Diana away and into a sea of people.

Diana squeezed Sophie's elbow. "Progress on what?"

"Just something I am trying to find." Sophie scanned the room, hoping they had temporarily lost him.

"I didn't like the look of him," Diana said. "He leered a little. The way he leaned into you."

Sophie hadn't liked it either. She pasted on a smile, then looked out to the night and the traffic swerving onto the nearby Ringstrasse before joining the carousel of the city. "You seem tired, Canary. Let's get you home."

—◦◦◦◦◦—

Once Diana was safely inside her flat, Sophie felt at her waistband for her revolver. The grand shadow of Stephansdom cathedral was a leviathan, swallowing streets and stretching out as Sophie decided to prolong her stroll homeward for a stop at Müller's in hope Adameck left word for her there.

When she arrived at the Pfandhaus, rationed lamplight, candles, and lanterns flashed across several windows like a hurried game of tic-tac-toe illuminating the empty pawnshop. The bell clanged above the door and Müller once again proved how little he slept.

"I have a message for you," he said by way of greeting.

Sophie's breath rose above her stiff collar and fashionably tied neck scarf. "I thought you might." She followed him to the back office.

"Here."

The message was indeed from Adameck's client. There were a few lines about how she would have carte blanche in Prague since she was invaluable to his enterprise. He would make it worth her while. She merely had to catch the morning train, and a ticket to an orchestral performance the next evening awaited her.

To glorious Mozart in the city where his *Don Giovanni* had sprung to life.

Sophie studied the note until the intensity of Müller's gaze drove her eyes back up to his. "Carte blanche. I can go to Prague and make a very nice sum of money. For Frau Wagner."

Karl Haas was dead. Pieter Sidorov was nipping at her heels . . . Prague turned the page on the next chapter of this adventure. Prague had as much of a stake on Mozart as Vienna did. Two cities that desperately wanted ownership. To claim the composer as their son.

Müller walked her to the frosted front door. As she wished him a *Gruss Gott*, the Viennese blessing long fashioned into a greeting as typical as a "good day" in her home country, Sophie stepped into the frigid night, shoving down the portentous feeling of his door closing behind her. The lock clicking into place.

Nearby, the Kapuzinerkirche bells tolled. Sophie looked in the direction of the unassuming house of worship. Not as magnificent as the ornamented structures Diana favored but invaluable on account of its hosting the Habsburg crypts. Men and women who had ruled and possessed fortunes and whose graves were inlaid with gold roses and marble statues: the only earthly treasures they had left. It was ominous.

Your risk is your risk, Sophie. She wasn't just going to Prague for her own gain. With Sidorov's appearance and Adameck's ease at finding her, she was less likely to embroil Simon if she was somewhere else. Her conscience pricked enough thinking about Haas. It wouldn't allow her to complicate Simon's life any more than she already had.

CHAPTER 16

September 1939
London, England

Simon's war effort, as did his work with the Secret Intelligence Service, started close to home. Ironic considering how much he wanted to use it as an opportunity to step as far away from Camden as possible.

Marcus Brighton settled across from Simon in the passenger seat of the sleek hired car as they made their way back to London. "You've an ideal profile for many of the men I am looking for. Not only for as long as this blasted war is looming but after. Intelligent and distinguished."

So Simon had attended Captain Ridley's "shooting party" far from the smoke and headlines in London up at a sprawling, old Victorian estate near Milton Keynes.

"You're the whole package." Brighton appraised him with a raised brow. Especially when the higher-ups at the meeting talked about the need for logical and precise thought. Men who saw a problem and knew how to creatively and patiently solve it.

"Put me in front of a chessboard, and I know how to use it." Simon flicked ash from a much-deserved cigarette.

"You fit in *everywhere* because you carry yourself like a man who belongs everywhere. No one would dare second-guess your place."

Brighton lit his own cigarette. "Whatever Charles taught you, I know he taught you well."

By the end of the gathering, about one hundred fifty people all had been briefed on a new secret war station and a new location for the Government Code and Cipher School. With war looming, the need to anticipate having to crack codes and intelligence—such as the un-breakable German Enigma machine—was a very real possibility. A secret war association of the brightest minds in the country might very well stave off disaster.

The sleek black car dropped Simon near Charing Cross as in-structed. He wanted to taste London again, slip into the Savoy for a drink, and slide into the city away from Brighton. Simon had just tipped the driver, stepped out of the car, then was accosted by a grip on his arm.

"My, my. Someone's just come from Savile Row." Simon felt the in-tensity of Sophie's scrutiny. "New name, new threads." Her gaze swept appreciatively from his black fedora to his double-breasted pin-striped suit, down to his two-toned shoes. "It is a new name, isn't it?"

"Actually I've just come from a country manor." Surprised that she wore her casual greeting like a cavalier embrace, he was immediately taken back to another country manor. One where he confronted his brother and stepped away from his name.

"I thought we'd have acclimated you to city life by now."

She wore higher heels so he was not quite as tall as she was. So striking. Her curled brunette hair under her hat was shorter than he recalled and brushed near her collarbone. Her long lines were clothed in a knit dress that showed off the lean athleticism of her limbs but also gave her a silhouette that drew his attention to the slight swell that distinguished her hips from her narrow waist. He moved his gaze upward when he noticed her right eyebrow cocked.

"Enjoying the view?"

Simon shoved his glasses up on his nose. He was very much enjoying the view.

Yet seeing her forced a question into his brain that had resided along with the sizzle of attraction every time he remembered their kiss. Was he truly falling for Sophie, his ally and friend, or was he remembering how she had stood by him at Camden?

"I was on my way to the Savoy to find a stiff drink," he said.

Sophie looped her arm through his. "I suppose I am too."

"I'm buying." He couldn't shake the feeling that he owed her. For crying on her shoulder. For the abhorrent way his brother had manhandled her. For the way his father had talked to her. Simon wouldn't have been surprised if Sophie never wanted to associate with a Barrington again.

When they finally reached the art deco–style opening of the hotel and the iconic stainless-steel *Savoy* sign that ran the width of Savoy Court, she leaned in. "Funny how I missed your face, Simon Barre, since last we've met."

Simon swallowed. "I don't want to talk about the last time we met." They approached the monogrammed doors. A bellboy bowed, and Sophie and Simon were ushered to the cocktail bar.

"You know how to hurt a lady's feelings."

Simon didn't speak again until they were seated. He ordered a Manhattan, anticipating her request for a sherry. Instead, she ordered a French 75.

He inclined his head. "Not your usual."

"A lady must live on the edge. I'm in the city, not cozily tucked away in the country."

"What are you doing in the city?"

"Trying to woo a husband." Their drinks arrived before Simon registered her statement. She waved her glass. "Wooing. Securing. Buying." She shook her head. "I'm doing none of those things, of course. I'm drinking a far-too-expensive cocktail and bossing people around and contemplating getting a Siamese cat. I'm staying abed till noon, lunching at the Ritz on my father's farthing, and wasting my life far from those I hold dear."

She gave Simon a knowing look. "Well, not *all* those I hold dear." With a half smile she stretched, taking in the surroundings. "How's your brute of a brother?"

Simon rotated his crystal glass. "That day when I walked out, I came here as I threatened." Simon chuckled. "Can you threaten someone who doesn't care if they're threatened?"

"Hmm."

"I came to London. To the town house, and I started a new job. No one calls me anything but Simon Barre now."

"A new job?"

"An official . . . government position."

"Perhaps deeply classified and the slightest mention of it would brand me a traitor for knowing?" She raised an eyebrow, then elaborately held her hands over her heart. "Cross my heart, Simon *Barre*. I know all of your secrets."

"Not all."

"No? *Dommage.* Too bad because you know you have my loyalty."

"You said that. Before." He attempted to keep his voice vague. Distant. *"Avant."*

"Did I?" Her shoulder crept up. "And did I mean it?"

"Are you suggesting that I know when you mean something you say?"

Sophie didn't take a beat. "Of course. I bested you at chess. Our entire acquaintance is founded on saying exactly what we need to."

"Still . . ."

"I know that tone. I *bested you at chess*."

"I don't think you comprehend how significant that was. A Barrington is not merely beaten at chess."

"You'll try to make up for your family, for . . . Well, I won't have it. It's dull."

"Yes."

"And I meant it, didn't I?"

Simon rolled the word *loyalty* around in his brain. In most instances loyalty would equate a feeling of power or certainty, but not here.

He wanted her more than he had ever wanted anything in his life. The feelings that had rattled around since she chucked shellfish at him and threw herself in front of Julius carved something deeper within Simon.

He would win her.

The game he would play would be strategic: the slow, solemn crawl of a diagonal on a chessboard. Simon Barre didn't need to win quick or dirty. Oh no. He wanted to acknowledge every angle. To observe every instinct. To respect every move. Sophie was a complicated strategy. He didn't know all of the moves. Blast! He didn't know half of them. He merely observed.

A new name . . . a name she had given him, as a matter of fact, should have come with a new confidence. Yet the Simon Barre he wanted to be in the moment so inconveniently resembled the Simon Barrington he had once been.

She had aligned herself with him.

"Why didn't you look me up when you got here?" he asked.

Sophie picked at her napkin. "I didn't want to lead you on."

"We're friends, Sophie."

"The last time I saw you . . ." She met his gaze head-on without a flinch or blush.

The last time he saw her, she had been in his arms. "So your choice was to just avoid me?"

"Clearly not forever." She sighed. "You're not in love with me, you know."

Simon straightened. "I don't recall telling you I was in love with you." He had long since determined that the word would send her far from his orbit.

"Just a look there. You got all misty and far away. We'll make it a rule. Never say it to me and I won't say it to you."

Simon tried to keep casual, looking up at her through his eyelashes. "Were you going to say it to me?"

She set down her drink, then raised a cigarette to her lips and lit it. She flicked her eyes and lingered on the piano. She could always find music in the middle of a scene. To break her own tension.

A pianist plucked the first chords of a Gershwin tune. Writing songs of love and lucky stars but not for the singer. Just another fool scraping his feet across a sorry world.

She tapped the cigarette and handed it to him. He pressed it to his lips.

"Sometimes it's a kiss. Sometimes a reassurance or an unspoken commitment. And you'll want me to say that I love you someday."

Simon puffed out smoke. "How do you know I'll say it?"

Sophie mused on this a moment. "It might be easier to marry someone. Let him go off to fight for king and country."

"You don't want to just *marry* someone." Simon stripped bills from his money clip and set them on the table, then he followed her through the grand foyer to find her a cab.

He thought of a man who wanted to exact things from her. Who offered her a piano and got her parents off her back. It rammed into his chest. "Don't do anything . . ."

"Stupid?" She raised her brows.

He gently took her elbow and led her away from the lights, the sleek cars, and the monogrammed art deco awnings. "I know you don't want to go back to your parents. That you don't want to be caught in a whirlwind of spineless men who will bore you to death."

"And . . . ?" She was amused.

He searched her face. "Many women are becoming part of the war. In dangerous ways." He knew she wouldn't settle for knitting for the Red Cross or delivering blankets. She'd cock her rifle and take on Jerry single-handedly if she could.

She shook her head. "You're allowed to throw all in for the cause, but I can't?"

"Don't marry someone, Sophie."

"Simon . . ."

"It's selfish, I know. I wouldn't care if the whole bloody empire crumbled. If the Nazis—" A man turned and Simon lowered his voice. He swept off his hat and touched her elbow. "If it's just to appease your parents and to find somewhere to tuck yourself away in London rather than Ashton, then marry me."

It wasn't the first time he had proposed—but her smile stayed strong, her eyes twinkled, and her voice was soft. "Simon, I don't love you. It wouldn't be fair."

"Love . . ."

"My mother instilled in me a fear of love, yes. Said that it was a bargaining chip for a woman of property and inheritance. But you know I rarely listen to my mother. But Simon . . . my grandmother told me love could be my downfall. She made me promise."

Simon knew a direct answer would send her reeling. So he opted for a softer response. "I don't want the war to touch you. I don't want you to feel you have to fulfill an obligation. So stay in the Mayfair house."

"I was made for war, Simon. I want to make a difference for something. I don't want to find a suitable husband and wither away at the town house or host tea parties or sit as a chair of a charitable committee that fronts for an excuse to eat petit fours on a manicured lawn."

"I know that."

"Then why do you possibly want to marry me?"

"Because what is the alternative? Your family marrying you off to some stuffed shirt you can't stand? At least we like each other."

"You just want the girl you can't get."

"You're not a game to me."

"An unsolvable problem then."

"I know you better than you know yourself."

"You think I am someone to revere or to chase or to lo—" Sophie stopped, perhaps before she took the sentence too far. "Because your entire life is void of it. And it's an awful truth and one I want to spare you from. But, darling, you're looking in the wrong place. There's always some current sparking between us. From the moment you joined me on the veranda. When I beat you at chess. It could flare up at any moment."

"It's called passion, Sophia," he said hoarsely.

"It's called flustered infatuation." She laughed. "We'd fight. We're so alike. Same background. Same hatred of the customs and our families."

"That's not the reason you don't want to marry me. It's because you're scared any connection with someone equates giving all of yourself. I wouldn't demand anything of you, and it's better than spouse hunting and feeling sorry for someone and marrying them because they—"

Her brown eyes flashed. "Trust me, instead of entertaining these ridiculous scenarios."

Her lips slid into a Cheshire grin, which soon smoothed into her natural smile. She ran her hand over the back of his neck. "I know you are independent and probably won't ever need me, but I'd fight for you, Simon. In whatever way I could." She brushed her lips over his cheek. "Bye, darling."

A long day stretched even longer when Simon stopped to think about how it had turned out.

He was keeper of her first kiss. He could still feel the soft tremble of her lips and the way she fell into him. Was his attraction just because they had an allegiance? Because no one had ever stood up for him before?

CHAPTER 17

December 1946
Neuer Markt, Vienna

A homing device, that's what she thought of given their propensity to find each other anywhere. Even in the Neuer Markt cut through by the lights at Müller's and—not a stone's throw away—the glow of Albertinaplatz.

"Simon." Her heart thrummed. She had swerved and pressed the barrel of her revolver at the level of his breast pocket, but she quickly lowered it.

"What are you doing here?" he seethed.

It took her a moment to realize the pulse throbbing in her forearm was the squeeze of his grip. "You're hurting me," she said, and his grip loosened.

"I'm sorry." He looked positively mortified. "I didn't mean to hurt you." He blew out a long string of air. Simon's glasses fogged with the chill against the acceleration of his breath. He took them off and folded them into his pocket.

He had clearly been in a rush to find her. "Are you all right?"

"Right as rain!" She pocketed her gun. "You look a little worse for wear, however."

"I was worried."

"You needn't have been. Just as quick on the draw as I've ever been, eh?"

But he wasn't in a playful mood. "Brighton told me that a young woman who was *involved* in . . ." He shook his head. "A young woman was found by a river."

"I don't need you to water things down through a bedtime story."

"Fine. She's dead. She was found at the foot of the Vltava River. In Prague."

"Oh."

"Strangled," he added in a somber voice.

"Wretched business. But it is our business, Simon." Even in the darkness she could sense his eyes were intense on her profile.

"So I was worried. At least here, you have me."

Sophie nodded. "We always pretend we're invincible, don't we?" She folded her arms over her chest.

She loved how Simon energized every last nerve and line down to the soles of her shoes and squashed any attempts to appear rigid and in control. Why was she empowered by being at odds with him? And yet there was little else to explain how the last of her apprehension was allayed.

She ironed out her voice. "I had an important meeting. That's why I am out."

"Müller?"

She nodded. "I'm off to Prague in the morning."

"You're *what*?"

"A rather *influential* client needs me." She emphasized the key word, hoping he might take the bait.

"Influential?"

"Perhaps."

Simon had slowed his steps and Sophie fell in stride. They were so close to her flat and he clearly wanted to prolong their time. "After what I just told you, you cannot possibly think of going to Prague."

"I can."

He leaned forward a little—in direct contrast with her stepping back. An instinct, perhaps, once she heard the word *cannot*.

But as quickly as her defiance appeared, it dissolved, and though her mind still beat against being told what to do, her body couldn't help but exhale at his care for her.

Her grandmother said her rebellion could emerge from a piano keyboard. Would the real test be when she was forced into independence?

But independent from Simon? He was looking at her in a way that blasted *goodbye*.

Something sparked her nerves. She couldn't kiss him, though it was so often the translation for goodbye when words were stuck in someone's throat—as they were in Sophie's just now. She couldn't use the word *love*. She wasn't even sure if she felt love. But she felt *something* pressing inconveniently close, especially as she remembered why she was going.

One less dead body. One less threat from Sidorov.

But they could be as honest with each other as they could.

And for all of her vehemence at his attempt to control her next step, the vulnerability glistening in his striking blue eyes kept her heels on the ground and her eyes locked with his.

———◦◦◦◦◦◦———

Simon didn't want to lose her. The words to that effect were on the tip of his tongue. What was it Brighton had said? A civilian woman he had temporarily used at the suggestion of a contact in Prague? Used much as Simon was using Sophie: almost unofficially and in the shadows.

Brighton had said, "*She held on as long as she could.*" Well, what in the blazes was worth putting an innocent woman in harm's way, anyway?

Simon was acting like a boor because he had impressed Sophie's visage on his image of that poor, nameless young woman. Like Sophie, she might have fancied herself invincible. But Sophie's invincibility ran out the moment she was recognized, back when she had told him of her brief stint in the Baker Street Irregulars: the Special Operations Executive.

She might unknowingly be inching closer than he was to uncovering the identity of Brighton's ghost.

No. This was just about Sophie slipping away from him. And dangerously so. "I can't let you go to Prague, Sophia."

She stopped and braced her hands on her hips. "I'm not certain you have the power to stop me."

"Well, don't go just to prove that point."

"I'm not." Her fingers moved to her pearls. "You know I'm not. I'm going for me."

"What is it you hope to find there?"

"I want one part of my life that's just for me." Sophie pressed her finger to her lip, and he wondered what she pressed down with the motion. "I'm not sure if you have a better chance of protecting me than I have of protecting myself."

"Villiers."

She rocked back a little on her heels. "I miss the war," she blurted out. "Isn't it horrid? Who *misses* war? Starving and blackouts and *you* keep finding new wars, but . . . I miss what we were there."

The war allowed them to be anything. The war allowed Simon to be close to Sophie without the interference of his failed proposals. "Like we could finally be ourselves."

"You know what I'm feeling, Simon." She pressed her index finger into his chest. "Because you feel the same. It's why you're here."

"I don't know what you're feeling because you never say it. Not truly. Maybe because you're worried it would spill out in the way that would let me know what you really feel for me, Sophie. But instead you speak and it transforms into something almost like resentment or confusion or, in this moment, flight."

Sophie crossed her arms over her chest. "I shouldn't have told you. I should have just left. But that's what we do, isn't it? Wrap each other up in the other's life. Besides, maybe I'll surprise you and find that Das Flüstern you spoke of in Moser's office. Or what David Moser's ulterior motives are, if he has any." Sophie paused. "Promise me you won't find me in Prague." She set her hand on the door knocker at her flat entrance.

"Entreating me?" He clicked his tongue.

"It's working, isn't it?"

"You just told me I had no choice." He shook his head. "I don't know what happened between us, Sophie. Sometimes it's as if there's a . . . crack. But I know that I won't last. I *don't* crack. And I won't charm you into agreeing with me."

"Simon," she said softly.

"We have a history, and yet . . ." He lingered. Perhaps she would say something and close the space between them.

And while she turned her shoulders away from him as she sought the door to her flat, he was met with all he wanted her to be to compensate for all he never had. He stopped himself from following her. "Sophia."

Odd that he used her given name. Odd how he could be in control of the labels he gave her when they left his lips and yet they still struck something that set him off course: Villiers when he was nostalgic for Bletchley, Sophie for everyday, Sophia when the past nipped at their heels.

"Please, *please* be careful. If you must run away." *From me.*

As she turned to face him, the moonlight contoured her striking face. "If I must run away, Simon"—she looked him straight on—"it will never be because of you."

CHAPTER 18

With Sophie in Prague, the city was dull to Simon. He couldn't anticipate turning and finding her in Vienna, and much of the energy that had steered his steps since he had arrived was drained.

Simon strode alongside the green shrubbery and manicured lawns of the Hofburg between the two museums flanking the grand statue of the monarch Maria Theresia, taking in the palatial Kunsthistorisches Museum and the Naturhistorisches Museum mirroring it from the other side. Hoarfrost feathered the shrubs and a glistening of snow glazed the verdigris statue. If he walked too quickly, he might draw attention from the city's many eyes. Just like the ones that found Sophie and him on the bench at Volksgarten before she had left.

She had said she might find Das Flüstern before he did, which made him want to prove her wrong. Not out of a competitive sense, but because she was alone without backup. Most likely meeting the man he was still playing chess with while she carved out her corner of the world. A corner he desperately wanted to meet her in.

Gabe Langer was seated on a bench just beyond the statue and Simon joined him, sweeping his coat underneath him. The man's white-blond hair was in disarray as if he had just combed his fingers through it, and his ice-blue eyes seemed blurry from what Simon assumed was a lack of sleep.

A historian who divided his time between the Kunsthistorisches Museum and Leopold University, Gabe had a view of the world of restoration and relics Simon appropriated through Sophie.

Gabe's living situation was a temporary flat in the Wieden District of the city, occupied by the Soviets, where he saw firsthand the devastation of all withheld from its rebuilding efforts. He experienced any cutoff donated food, the lack of fuel and electricity. And while many manufacturers and laborers had begun inching their way toward restoration, everything seemed slower there and, as Simon knew, purposefully so.

"The propaganda from the Soviets is getting worse. It's moved from liberation to some sort of frantic war cry." Gabe reached into his pocket and presented Simon with a pamphlet.

Simon was familiar with some of its sentiment, *Wieder Frei*: a free, liberated Vienna—promised by several Soviet posters throughout the city. The pamphlet spoke to a prosperous rebuilding and showed how the Communist agenda could further it by ensuring that prosperity was shared. It also spoke to similar sympathies in previous years, Simon supposed, in an aim of prewar nostalgia.

"And supplies?"

"None. They're starving us out. People are trying to hole up with friends and family in the British and American districts, but the housing shortage is making it near impossible. Money for aid is coming in from many of the Allies to make my district more habitable. There are, of course, independent donors as well. But the Soviet zones give nothing, and they block the aid from getting to their quarters."

"Independent donors?" Simon mulled this over a moment.

David Moser was a mainstay in political briefs and liberal papers draped on racks at the front of cafés. He sponsored scholarships and donated to many causes: the exhibitions and opportunities for each of the Allies to produce their idealization of the city. Could Moser be one of Gabe's anonymous donors?

Simon tugged at his silk tie and suddenly felt extremely conscious about the leather of his spit-shone shoes and the cut of his Savile Row jacket in comparison to the mended material in Gabe's jacket. There was no shame in making do with fabric shortages and rehemmed material. But he did want to provide what he could beyond the bulwark of Gabe's pride.

The man didn't have a wife or children, but he did have a mother and two small nieces whose pictures had been proudly shown to Simon on more than one occasion. "Do *you* need money?"

Gabriel held up a hand. "I don't want your pity, Simon."

"It's not pity. You're helping me stop the Eternity ring in Vienna. I have money. If you need it, it is yours."

"Perhaps."

"What do you mean *perhaps*?"

Gabe took a moment. "I didn't want to worry you."

"I know that tone."

"There was a message waiting for me."

Simon straightened his glasses. "Oh?"

"For you." Gabe reached into his inside jacket pocket, brought out a piece of paper, and handed it to Simon.

Simon quickly surveyed the note from Das Flüstern: *But you are an agent, so I anticipate you would be smarter than anyone.*

So the double agent knew who Simon associated with. Simon was easy to reach. With this note, his world closed in.

A few moments later, Simon tucked his glasses into his front pocket.

"Anything I should know about?" Gabe asked.

"Just someone showing off."

"It was so peculiar, a message awaiting me at my new flat."

Simon rocked back. "There's a lot peculiar these days."

"No." Gabe looked over. "Is it Eternity?"

He turned the message to Gabe. "It's chess notation. Pawn to g3."

"That's new."

"Not to me." Simon tilted the brim of his fedora forward. "Thanks for this, Gabe. He clearly wants to show me that he can find me through anyone. Including you."

—◦◦◦◦◦—

Later in his hotel room, Simon tugged at the chain of the green barrister's lamp overlooking the monogrammed Sacher paper on his bureau. He rolled up his sleeves and reached for a pen to write his response to the note.

Over the past several days, the plays and notes had sent him on a wild-goose chase but always underscored by a portentous sense. What he really wanted to write was his supposition that Das Flüstern could be a part of Eternity. When you've spent an entire war programmed to assume everything means something else, then even moves on an invisible chessboard can lead you to wonder about any tenuous connection.

Then he put pen to paper:

> I don't know if I am smarter than anyone, but I appreciate your confidence. And your new address. If I tell you my flaws, you may think that they will give you an open door into my weaknesses. Or maybe, if you are playing on my side, they will.
>
> You're formidable even from afar, and I am used to Vienna being a puzzle. What I am not used to is someone apparently seeing the city as a puzzle.
>
> Perhaps I'm daft because I haven't caught the first train to Prague to find you. Yet something about you lingers in Vienna. On men's names. With associates. So maybe you are here after all . . .
>
> Or maybe not.
>
> You clearly know I am a chess player. What you cannot possibly

know is that few things accelerate my confidence like an opponent who does not know his next move.

Pawn to g6

That evening, as he stared at the ceiling and trained his mind against worrying about Sophie, he conjured up the confidence of his response to Das Flüstern. This man—whatever his real name was—knew enough about Simon to play beyond the moves that were given him in bold strokes of notation. Which meant he probably knew Sophie was in Prague. Perhaps he anticipated Simon would exchange a placement on the board to a visit to Prague.

Simon would train his fingers to steady over the pieces and his mind to focus on Vienna. He would keep to his side of the board. And perhaps, with enough calculated practice, he would trust Sophie to be safe and well.

CHAPTER 19

January 1947
Staré Město District, Prague

There were no New Year parties. Just as there had been no Christmas celebration. Sophie accepted both as par for the course. There were bells, however, and a lone cellist sawing at a Bach suite in the Alcron Hotel's foyer.

In her room Sophie had dressed elaborately in a green silk that would have been considered dated had the war not made fashion far more sustainable. She toyed with the Villiers pearls at her neck. Her eyes were lined with kohl, her face powdered, and her lips a deep cranberry.

Now, as she walked across the theater's lobby, she felt men's eyes move over the neckline that accentuated the indents of her collarbone and the backless cut that showed off her thin, muscled shoulders and spine.

"This way," Adameck said.

Sophie lifted her skirt slightly above her black peep-toe pumps and stepped across the sleek tiled floors. The chandelier lights sparkled off medals on dignitaries' chests and jewels around the necks of women whose dresses had no doubt been taken in a few times on account of the city's lean war years.

Sophie was no stranger to opulent places, but the stroll from Václavské náměstí, or Wenceslas Square, to the Železná Theatre was like a hidden secret of the Staré Město District and moved her far more than many antiques she had traded in her role as Starling.

Tomas Adameck led her to a man standing in front of a tall arched mirror. "*Dobrý večer*, Pan Novak."

"Dobrý večer." Novak turned to face them, then dismissed Adameck with a nod. "Good evening." He focused on Sophie. "*Špaček.*"

Starling. She held out her hand so Mr. Novak could lightly brush her fingers with his lips. There was an evasiveness about him. He was not as old as she had anticipated and certainly more distinguished. Something in the way he looked at her made her think they had crossed paths before.

Rather than release her hand, he tucked it into the crook of his elbow just as the bell announcing the curtain chimed. They inched their way into the grand hall: the Železná horseshoe design a graceful rest that curved from the stage in gilded columned boxes and rows like an ornate layer cake. A different beauty than the Staatsoper and an homage to *Don Giovanni*, where the opera was famously first performed.

It was just off one of these boxes in the third tier where Novak led her to their seats. "This is a very special performance," he said after they had settled.

Sophie rolled her program over her knee. "Mozart's arrangement of *Der Messias* by Handel. Many think it is too exhibitive and steals from the beautiful simplicity by adding too many instruments and notes. But I look at it as an example of how things can change for the better."

It was rare that Sophie could draw herself to earth when listening to Mozart, but perhaps it was because of the company or the ornate opera house or that it wasn't Mozart's original composition, rather borrowed from another.

"Can you imagine the first time it was performed at Esterházy Palace? An oratorio strange yet familiar all the same."

Sophie tried to focus on Mozart's reinvented piece throughout the first half of the program.

At intermission Novak pressed a glass of champagne into her hand. "The politicians and dignitaries are here. The new world will start here. People think revolutions begin out on the streets, but those revolutions are only furthered by those inside sipping champagne and deciding the next steps."

"Doesn't Marxist ideology suppose revolution to be led by the people and not the elite?"

"Indeed." Novak's eyes sparkled. "But war has an uncanny way of blurring the lines between the two. Especially when the elite have long been deprived of their status, treasures, and affluence."

Sophie had just asked him to expand when the lights blinked on and off and they were called to return to their seats.

After the concert, he took her for a late supper at the Alcron Hotel, where she had taken a room. A smile and an extension of his hand secured them a table.

Sophie folded her hands on the pristine white tablecloth to keep from playing her left fingers over her knee. A *snap* and sputter of a near-burnt streetlight outside and the history embracing her nearest vantage settled in her chest. She felt a bit of premonition, most likely on account of the city's hallowed history, but also as she stood at the precipice of a new assignment.

According to Adameck, she was in the company of a man with remarkable influence and, subsequently, in possession of remarkable artifacts beyond a few chessboards or a Meissen porcelain acquired by Moser.

There was a slight twitch in Novak's jaw in response to her careful regard. Perhaps he wasn't as suavely confident as she'd assumed.

The server set down their drinks.

"Tell me why I am really here." She took a long sip of sherry and anticipated he would mention the mask. "Did I pass your test?"

"Is the sherry your preferred brand? I like to know what my associates' tastes are."

"It's the best I am sure they have here."

Novak nodded. "If you tell me your brand, I will make sure that it is served everywhere you will be in the city."

"Are you trying to woo me, Mr. Novak?" But the rapport between them so far made the suggestion seem preposterous.

She was relieved when he laughed. Their waiter took their orders and she followed his lead and asked for a dish that Novak translated as dumplings and pork knuckle.

"Is that what men usually do, Špaček?"

"Lately I am not sure." She shrugged. "Everyone wants to use an intermediary. Just like your sending Adameck." She traced her nail around the rim of her glass. "These are secretive times, of course. But this was like one of those games of telephone."

"Das Flüstern."

Sophie straightened. "'The Whisper'?"

"It takes so little to establish influence here with a name."

"So you're saying that perhaps this Whisper isn't so influential after all? Adameck said he is the most powerful man in Prague."

"I am saying that it takes a brave person, man or *woman*"—he inclined his glass—"To pursue a rumor. A name."

Sophie took another sip. "How are you so certain that I want to work for you? Just because you are well connected in Vienna? Because we happen to have some similar connections? Other men are interested in my pursuing their interests who can offer a price rivaling yours."

"You haven't heard my offer yet."

"Do you suppose I am *so* mercenary that I would be drawn into working with this Das Flüstern fellow who scares everyone to death just for the money?"

Confusion clouded his features. "Why not? You spoke of these other men."

"Only to stir an honest answer from you. I am not lacking for money, Mr. Novak."

"The game then. You certainly came to Prague quickly enough."

Their dishes were set before them.

Sophie had stabbed a bite of knudel and paused the fork midway to her mouth. "Pardon?"

"Because your reputation interests me. And your time during the war absolutely baffles me. Then there is the fact that you've hidden half your name."

"You are thorough." Sophie pressed her lips into a tight smile. She wasn't sure if he knew more than he was saying. "But anyone could find this information."

She took a slow bite with a reaction that delighted Novak as much as it would have horrified her mother.

He chuckled. "I like a woman who enjoys things, and not just the *finer* things either."

They chewed in silence a few moments. "You enjoy the finer things, too, Mr. Novak."

He pierced her with his bright blue eyes. "Do you work for the Secret Intelligence Service?"

"If I did, do you imagine I would confess it here and now to you?"

Sophie had the unsettling feeling his answering stare saw right through her weaknesses and vulnerabilities. Her exhilaration at being here in the first place.

The waiter approached to refill his wine glass. "It is by sheer luck that we were able to hear the performance of *Der Messias* tonight."

"Why is that?"

"Because until recently, the arrangement they played from was one of many treasures missing from the Horacek collection. The Horacek family was one of the oldest established Bohemian families from the time of the Habsburg dynasty and Emperor Maximilian. They owned a palace in Hradčany for centuries. Hitler and his men came and stole their treasures, plundered them like the Vikings of old. But they are slowly trickling back."

"I've heard of them. My Viennese clients want restitution of their treasures too. What do you want?"

"Mozart's *imprint* is on Prague. Vienna didn't appreciate him like Prague did. Not his masterpiece. Not *Giovanni*. They buried him in a pauper's grave. Here, they *truly* mourned him."

Moments later outside the hotel, night stark and falling coldly, Novak's breath was pronounced above the knot of his carefully tied scarf. "It is the philosophy. And we need a bridge between Vienna and Prague to ensure that the right pieces are finding their way to the right homes. There is more than just that Mozart arrangement. There is a collection of manuscripts that were displaced during the war." He took out a folder from inside his jacket and handed it to her.

Sophie perused the partial age-old musical score of long strokes and neat time signature, the even bars and familiar notation found within.

Novak watched her. "There. That look on your face. You appreciate Mozart. You truly cherish this."

"You should know that you are not the only man who has approached me to find something related to Mozart. You're sure you are only interested in this manuscript? Or is this another one of your tests?"

It is not a test.

The words pricked her skull as she settled into her room at the Alcron, the moonlight striping the touch points she had set out to assure that no one had been in her space. A trick Simon had taught her years before in a casual conversation about how he protected his boyhood treasures by laying his room in a certain order with one slight abnormality to ensure he knew if Julius had gone through his things.

Satisfied that no one had been in her room, she lay back fully clothed on the bed after turning on the wireless and falling into the familiar strands of Shostakovich: a composer under siege until the tide turned for the victorious Red Army. Fitting music as she felt a slow, coiling panic increase with the triumph of the final movement until she felt it pulse in her fingers.

Each time a piece of Novak's complicated puzzle spread across her mind with the minimal knowledge she had, it moved at a pace that contrasted his desire to immerse her in the city and usher her into retrieving his manuscript. Was he indeed Das Flüstern? This whisper that chilled over her as easily as the haunting stories circulating through the city? Or merely connected to him?

Perhaps this was where Adameck came in. Karl Haas had wanted a middleman to separate him from his antiquities broker, and it seemed Novak wanted the same. Did that mean he, too, wanted Mozart's death mask? Perhaps for a different purpose than Haas's professed patriotism and Sidorov's . . . greed?

Perhaps Novak was responsible for Haas's death. But Adameck was his man in Vienna. Did that mean that Pieter Sidorov was next to die?

If Sophie failed to do what Novak required or, alternatively, excel at it, where would that place her in the plan? Would she even be needed at all?

Shostakovich's piece crescendoed. There was something thrilling about being here. No Simon. No bombed-out buildings en route to her flat in Singerstrasse. Prague had a different character. It was harrowing still but alive. At least it had been at the concert.

Then there was the music in Novak's folder. Lines and notes that immediately burst into sound the moment her eyes pored over them. Fragments of the manuscript that needed to find cohesion with pages still missing. Sophie wanted to see this Mozart piece whole again.

Novak had said good night and donned his hat, which hid the

silver at his temples, and smiled. "You'll have opportunities to meet with other clients in the city as you act as my assistant. I am a busy man, and finding the last pieces of this manuscript is something I cannot make time for."

But he didn't elaborate on what was keeping his time.

She kicked off the coverlet and padded to the lavatory. Sophie assessed herself in the mirror before she splashed water on her face. She had told Simon they were just running away. But wasn't that exactly what she was doing: using this strange, new Europe as their hide-and-seek from their lives and their estates and obligations? In this she felt a lot like Simon. Displaced.

———◦◦◦×◦◦◦———

It hadn't seemed like a week had passed, and yet she had fallen into a routine. Even with the knowledge of Novak's connection to Das Flüstern, she was at a loss to fully understand the magnitude of that knowledge and how it played into her finding missing pieces of the manuscript.

There was a graceful melancholy to the city that Novak taught her daily. If she focused on the stones and structures, the steeples and arched windows of houses crammed so closely they almost seemed positioned to embrace, and not on the blemishes of its past, she could almost imagine it as Mozart had seen it.

Novak's commission gave her an immense sense of fascination. Simon had needed her for the intel she could bring him. Novak needed her eye and expertise to begin to return artifacts and art to the original owners. This task would take her through channels that would pass under the surveillance of Nazi sympathizers still hovering over the city and Soviet soldiers silently shoving the Czech soldiers who had fought with the Western Allied offensive to the sidelines. But Novak's quiet passion for music mirrored her own.

And while Sophie had followed leads in nearby Hradčany in small shops and cobbled courtyards, in the depths of a cellar at the Strahov Monastery where the monks grew ale, and above the library where ancient tomes wove semicircles around ancient globes, she still sensed that a clash existed: between the Prague etched by history and that appropriated by the Nazis.

The city itself was on the verge of something that would change its course, she supposed. There was no other path for it when she considered the daily headlines and the friction encroaching. After all, Prague was situated in a country primed to fall on either side of a tightening political threat augmented by the very obvious lingering shadow of the Gestapo and its Nazi occupants. She could almost hear the jackboot rhythm in Wenceslas Square or imagine the interrogations that had happened over the hill in Prague Castle: a fortress peering down on Na Kampě and Novak's house.

She didn't pretend to understand all of the political theories, but she knew that, like Vienna, other European cities were at the mercy of a palpable energy that swept through fairs and rallies and celebrations of the anniversary of the end of the war and Nazi occupation. She always felt a wave of relief when she was back in the Old Quarter with Novak or at her hotel. With those certainties—those *touch points*—the city seemed less like a stranger.

What she *didn't* have was a touch point to Simon. She wasn't willing to admit how deeply his lack of approval weighed on her. Funny, she had turned the rotors of the Bombe machines in Hut Eight without him, had joined the Baker Street Irregulars and the SOE without him.

When she had settled enough into her association with Novak, she listened for when Das Flüstern might be mentioned. After all, Novak was quite fond of another legend: golem. Novak's rich voice spoke of the pogroms in the sixteenth century when a rabbi was able to conjure a force from clay to protect his people from devastation.

"If you want to understand Prague," he said, as they walked to the Jewish Quarter, "then you must start in its past. It is a city that can conjure magic and saints—for good or ill—at the turn of a tale."

Maybe that was what Das Flüstern was doing: hoping to conjure magic and saints through Mozart and music.

"It can also turn dark and dangerous, though, can it not? Turn on a farthing in terms of loyalties? Si—a friend of mine suspects so."

He looked at her a moment.

Novak's words were so carefully chosen they seemed a tapestry of scholars and poets, history and song. In her father's circle it might have manifested in a poor attempt at a Renaissance man, but with Novak she felt every word. Felt it as she explored a city that had sewn itself as deeply into him as London had her friend Diana. As if each city had chosen human portals through which to whisper their secrets.

Sophie was lured into the city in the moments he didn't require her attention. There was no hint of a mask. No suggestion of anything of political importance.

As she and Novak arrived to see the upturned grave markers repurposed to pave the streets or the uneven tombstones yawning toward the filmy wintry light, she wished the golem had been resurrected to witness the atrocities of the recent war.

The golem's legend prickled over her neck as if at any moment it might rise again to reclaim the parts of a city dangerously close to falling into another type of war. "This city's history is nipping at its heels and yet it could fall beneath more occupation," she told him. "If the Soviets win . . ."

"Liberation," Novak corrected. "Liberation comes with equality." A shadow hovered over his tone. "Not something I assume preoccupied your mind back at Ashton."

Sophie walked silently beside him, yet something was percolating. Had she told him about her ancestral home?

She was certain she had not.

CHAPTER 20

November 1940
London, England

It was rare that Simon took a day off for any reason, so the train into London was a treat. Bletchley Park kept him constantly busy with shifts at odd hours and a mind to continue to fine-tune processes for the team under his lead. Even on his days without shifts in Hut Three, he felt as if he was working.

People listened to him. Brighton was right in this much: Simon had grown up in an atmosphere of delegation. Had learned how to demand. How to tweak his tone in order to get something more quickly.

But the part of him he assumed was from his mother, or at least his real father, tried to balance the demands with a kind tone and a level gaze.

No one at Bletchley knew of his ties to Fifty-Four Broadway, except for the higher echelons, so Simon sometimes slipped away on a weekend to stay at his family's house in Mayfair and visit Marcus Brighton. And for a few splendid days he would dispose of his vests and cotton and replace them with silk and cashmere, sip good whiskey, and try to ignore the shrill whistle of encroaching bombs.

Mayfair House was still standing, but someday it might not be. What with the wreckage he had seen as the train chugged through the city. New carnage from his last trip to London had erupted in moats of rubble and felled buildings. He was almost surprised.

Before he'd left Bletchley, Diana clung to his sleeve and begged, "Make sure you see if it's still there."

"We'd have heard in *The Times* if St. Paul's had fallen to pieces, Diana." He squeezed her elbow and promised. He genuinely liked Diana. She was just delighted to be part of a team: be it in the shared jubilation of a solved code, good news of a sunken convoy in Britain's victory, or even someone's birthday celebrated with a bottle of warm Spitfire ale and a treacle cake.

Would she talk to him differently if he was Lord Simon Barrington with his slick car and high-end town house and not just a compatriot in tweed and glasses, leaning over a typewriter or a chessboard at the pub? Would her initial surprise lead to a new formality? Simon had such little experience with actual friends.

As a taxi drove him to Mayfair, he saw Wren's crowning glory—the dome of the cathedral ominous amid flits of smoke from a recent bombing and the chilled weather. Diana would be pleased.

He arrived at his destination and stepped out into a curtain of mist that sparkled the pavement and made the parked cars glisten. He tugged his collar up around his neck, removed his fogged glasses, and transferred them to his pocket.

The Mayfair town house was tucked into a long row of London houses—a leftover from the Victorian era when space was optimal. Dusk was falling and candles pierced filmy windows much as they must have the previous century when Dickens rallied for orphans and widows.

Simon wasn't sure if any of the staff would be here. He had kept them on, but there was no need for them. Yet as soon as he opened the front door, he saw a light on in a back room and sensed movement.

Simon reached for the gun tucked in his waistband holster just as a tall figure pounced from the shadows.

Before he could collect his senses or draw his firearm, lean limbs and an athletic stride near toppled him.

In a disarming move he stayed the vehement slice set on striking the torso with a counterattack of his own. He twisted the attacker's arm until he heard a decidedly feminine yelp.

"Sophia!" He immediately loosened his hold, though he could feel her shudder ripple through him.

"Are you still drinking your whiskey neat?" The breathless voice was unmistakable as she relinquished control, arms falling from him to her side.

"Are you still drinking sherry that would fund a munitions convoy?" He arched an eyebrow.

She stayed in the shadow, but he could feel her smile.

"How did you get in?"

"Hairpin. Side door." Her spine was erect, and the light through the shades caught the long, lean line of her back and shoulders. "I thought you were at the Foreign Office." She slowly approached him and handed him a tumbler of whiskey.

He made out a dark bruise above her left eyebrow and cheek, and her lip was swollen and had to be sore. His heart raced and his fingertips thrummed to stroke her face. Simon wanted to annihilate the man who had done this to her.

"My mother said if I could be smart and charming enough and straighten my spine when at the piano and keep mindful of my inheritance, men wouldn't notice . . ."

"Notice what?" She was exactly his height. He loved that about her.

"That I was tall. And none of what she taught me stuck. Including that I should never love anyone. Do you remember when you asked me to marry you? It seems a million lifetimes ago. Most flattering offer I've ever received." She was rambling.

"Have you seen a doctor?" he asked softly to steady her.

"No."

"What happened?"

"I can't tell you."

Simon touched her elbow. "Sit down, Villiers." He cleared his throat. "Well." He turned on the lamp on the side table. He saw her injuries in full view and darted his gaze to her hands as Dvořák faded and Mozart filtered through the wireless. The overture of *Figaro*. She was playing her left hand frenetically over her kneecap.

"They say Mozart never made copies." He could tell she was trying to find a safe, normal place in the span of an imagined piano keyboard, and Mozart would do.

She winced and pressed her fingers to her side. He felt a jolt of sympathy pain. "Besides . . . um, have you been well?"

She seemed lost in thought, listening to the piece. "You know that scholars say Mozart wrote under conscious control? His compositions were an active process. There was nothing stale or stoic about it. He was aware of his output. Studying. Reflecting." She swallowed. "It was all in his head. Mapped out. A blend of intelligent strategy and intuition. A *hunch*. An experiment."

He knew what she was doing. When Sophie felt vulnerable, she fell on her upbringing. Composing the situation with slight movement and well-considered words. Simon wanted to smash through her convention, allow her to improvise. "I want to ensure you're well."

"Of course I'm well." Her voice was steel. "I just don't know what to say to you. I'm not accustomed to you . . . like this." She looked him over and he felt every movement of her eyes.

"Like what?"

"Not dressed to the nines, for one."

Simon tugged at the rim of the knit vest he wore to blend in at Bletchley. "Well, it's not like I'm primed for a night at the Savoy."

Sophie fussed with her hair. "I must look dreadful."

"You look hurt. I'll ring the doctor."

"Let them focus on someone who *actually* needs it. I'll survive. There wasn't time to go home. I'm headed to Buckinghamshire next week."

"Are you indeed?" Simon tried to keep his voice in check.

"The Foreign Office," she said pointedly.

She knew. Brighton, probably. Did Brighton just sweep over Wilmington and recruit for his cause?

He smiled. "You look tired. I should let you get some rest." He strode toward her and gently touched her shoulder. "Take care."

"Simon." She spoke in a light tone he hadn't heard before.

"Yes?"

"You're not leaving?"

"No. I don't go till morning."

Her face softened. "Good."

He moved to see to his luggage and the upstairs lavatory.

"Wait!" She closed the space between them in a long stride and grabbed his arm. "Will you . . . ?"

"Anything."

"Will you stay with me?" Her eyes were wide and she was working her teeth over her bruised lip. "Here. I can stay here, can't I?"

"Of course." He exhaled. "But there's one thing, Soph. Very important."

"What?" Was it just him, or did her shoulders creep up toward her chin?

"I'm starving."

"Oh." She smiled again. Winced. Touched her finger to her lip.

"There's a chippy round the corner. Shall I?"

Sophie was ravenous, but it hurt to chew so she took it slowly. Once he had returned home with their evening fare and a box of powdered eggs and a loaf of coarse bread for the morning, Simon had shrugged out of his jacket and trench and rolled up his sleeves. She could make out the sinewy muscles in his forearms.

He was stronger than people first thought on account of the pin-stripes and carefully tailored lean suits he wore. His ebony hair fell over his forehead a little, and he had loosened his tie and collar. He had even taken his shoes off but kept his glasses on. It was endearing. Gold-rimmed armor.

She tucked her stockinged feet under her and watched him casually inspect a chip before he popped it in his mouth. She was one of the few people who would ever see Simon unguarded: without his walls up.

"I bet no chippy shop has ever seen to the sustenance of a resident of this grand house." She let down her guard a moment. "I feel safe here."

Simon rotated the cuff link on his left sleeve. "You could use a bit of safe, I fancy."

It was funny how his face came to her mind just at the moment when she had been found out. She had reported to the Baker Street Irregulars when approached by a man affiliated with Marcus Brighton: whose name was familiar to Sophie from her youth. She had begun training and was even certain that a mission in France would find her finally able to accomplish something worthwhile.

It had been a routine training exercise with an important objective. She would courier documents to a gentleman disembarking at Paddington Station—a known agent rumored to be smuggling integral documents on German surveillance of British railways.

But when she arrived, the agent recognized her from the society papers. His cohort roughed her up and took the folder she had tucked under her arm. Her cover was blown. And her supervisor recognized that a Huntington-Villiers who couldn't even undergo a routine hand-off at Paddington would be killed the moment she set foot in France.

The cohort had threatened to break her fingers.

Now, she fanned them out on the table. And for a moment she knew she had been close to spilling all the king's secrets. It was one thing to do your bit for the war effort, quite another to imagine never playing the *Appassionata* again.

When she looked up, she saw Simon's eyes glistening with worry.

And she didn't *truly* have a chance to be tested.

Were other young ladies like herself set up to believe they were primed for encountering danger and glory but never truly released into the fray?

When she closed her eyes and imagined her failure against the contrast of her life at Ashton, at the prospect of turning a tide in the war, she thrilled with it. Which was why the fall back to earth hit so hard.

She was Sophia Huntington-Villiers and she didn't deliver her message or get to France. Instead she was being sent off to Buckinghamshire, tucked away. She would be useful and the Special Operations Executive could go on without the mar of the one young lady who was found out before she could do *anything*.

Sophie turned a fork over on the pristine tablecloth. "Tell me something. Tell me a secret. Tell me *anything*." Anything to keep her from rotating what a failure she was in her head again and again.

He leaned over with a mock whisper, "Charles Barrington isn't *actually* my father."

Sophie smirked. "I said a secret."

"Being here doesn't feel like home. Maybe nowhere feels like home to me."

The reason she didn't check in to a hotel or go back to Ashton was that some part of her had hoped he would show up.

"I'd love to know who my actual father is. Barrington said that's a weakness. That I should be thankful no one demanded it and I wasn't shoved to the curb or made to muck out the stables after my worthless mother betrayed him." Simon looked around at the scalloped plaster and brocade curtains, up, up to the chandelier that had withstood the nightly Jerry bombings. She followed his sight trail. Maybe he was imagining himself as an impostor here.

"I said a *secret*," she repeated.

Simon was silent a moment. "My mother loved me. She told me when I was a little boy that we would have a secret language. Without words. She would glance at me or smile when Barrington wasn't looking. It wasn't until I was grown that I realized it was to hide from him." Simon said it like a curse. No wonder he so easily fell into being Simon Barre.

"She'd leave me a new crossword puzzle or slip an algebra problem under my door. She'd never come and tuck me in. Except when Barrington was away on business in London and Julius was at school."

Sophie noticed his jaw ticking. He was so used to swallowing the words down.

"As I grew older, I learned that he didn't mean to punish me so deeply as he meant to punish *her*. He prevented her from loving her illegitimate son. I was a threat. A pawn. If she so much as gave an inch, she must have supposed he would cut me off or expose me. She wouldn't have been bothered by his abuse of her as much as what she assumed would have happened to me."

"Do you ever wish you had a different life, Simon?"

He studied her a long moment. "Not right now. Not sitting across from you."

"Even to know your real father?"

"He must fill in all of the blanks that she couldn't, mustn't he? And part of me would give my entire life to understand how she could have . . ." He swallowed. "He's the last move. In an unfinished chess game. I *despise* an unfinished game."

Had he ever told as much to anyone else? Did his real father continue to love Margaret Barrington through Simon?

Then Sophie's thoughts shifted. Could he hear the words that settled between them? That she needed him but didn't want to tell him? That she would go to her grave convincing herself that she found the Mayfair flat because even if he wasn't here, she'd sense him and feel safe?

Simon rose to see their wrappers to the rubbish bin. She rose, too, and just as he turned from discarding their waste, their eyes met.

"You're a strong, capable woman and you probably won't ever need me." He nudged his glasses up his nose.

Sophie smiled. "You need a new line, Simon."

How had he known that she so needed to be validated in that way?

———◇◇◇◇◇———

Simon followed her into one of the many second-floor guest rooms where she had tossed what little luggage she had.

Sophie seemed like a little girl. Shivering a little and adamant that he keep a light on beyond the blackout restrictions. So since the chandeliers were snuffed, he lit a few candles.

"Don't go, Simon," she said in a tone of voice he hadn't heard before.

"All right."

"You'd never hurt me." She meant it as a statement, but it came out more of a question. She was overtired.

"Never."

After Sophie took care of her ablutions in the lavatory, he spread out on top of the coverlet, while she tucked herself under. She looked over at him, smelling of mint tooth powder and her rosewater hand cream, her brown hair loose around her face. He was already propping his eyes open despite the lure of exhaustion so he could slip out the moment she fell asleep.

She slowly stretched and moved to her side. He could nearly taste her breath.

"You're okay," he whispered.

She nodded, then let her head fall to his shoulder. "Don't tell anyone you saw me like this."

"Like what? Almost drooling on my shoulder?"

She shook her head, and strands of her hair tickled his neck. "Thank you for staying, Simon." She burrowed deeper.

"See, if you had married me like I asked, you could drool on my shoulder every night." He waited for her laughter that didn't come.

"Would you ever really love me, Simon?" Her voice was distant. Soft. At the precipice of sleep. "Or would you just love the girl who stood up for you once because no one else did?"

It took him a while to come up with a response. By the time he opened his mouth, her breathing had evened and she had fallen asleep. Simon stared at the ceiling and tucked his arm behind his neck.

Sophie was a quiet sleeper. She barely moved. So moments later when he felt her shift, it startled him. Even though all she did was rest her head on his chest and pull her knees up into her chest in a ball. Taking up as little space as a woman of her height could. It surprised him how vulnerable she seemed in this moment.

Simon gently moved her off his shoulder and tucked the blanket up to right where her hand was folded under her chin. Then he snuffed the last flick of light from the candle and quietly left the room, careful to close the door silently behind him.

With Sophie sleeping safe in a guest room, for the first time Mayfair House had the whispers of being a home.

CHAPTER 21

January 1947
Staré Město District, Prague

In the Church of St. Giles tucked deep into unassuming Husova in Staré Město, Sophie peered through the grille as a few patrons genuflected in front of a carved crèche and crucifix. Baroque columns and vignettes rimmed with gold bolstered the verse Brent Somerville had mentioned to her once. For as much as one must not store their treasures on earth rather in heaven, it seemed that heaven had the capital in consecrated places pledged to its purpose.

She breathed her awe until a man she was set to meet passed her a folder with a slight nod and a hidden air. Was it enough that what she wasn't achieving in the reconnaissance of Mozart's death mask, she was finding in snatches of a manuscript's genius? Sure, her head was turned at the prospect of fitting these pieces of a puzzle together, even while the biggest puzzle evaded her.

She opened the folder. The bars of music lined up. The notation was accurate. A quick assessment and Sophie tamped down her usual giddy excitement at procuring a slice of history given the solemnity of the church atmosphere.

And far from Novak across the city's iconic bridge, she was due for another meeting.

The crisp air fortified her lungs for her long walk ahead. Sophie began to see the churches in Prague as more than portals for artistry, but rather as a map. She could find her way on either side of the divid-ing Karlův most by the steeples. Though she preferred to wrap her voice around the English translation of the Charles Bridge. They were better than a compass. Diana would be proud.

Novak hadn't let her admiration for them go to waste. As many im-promptu concerts and recitals took place under the high chilled domes and over their sleek tiles, Sophie was surrounded by music. As much as she had been in Vienna.

She often met Novak for breakfast at a café tucked behind the forked spires of Our Lady before Týn. The church caught the sunlight in its parallel steeples so that whatever was left trickled out onto the stones of the Old Town Square, leaving it in perpetual shadow.

As she approached the café she noticed how distinguished Novak appeared. How the murky morning light etched his sculpted cheek-bones and the fine lines around his set mouth. Soon they were seated, and dark coffee, rolls, fruit, and sliced meats were presented by a server who spoke no English or German. The woman smiled at Sophie before she took her leave.

The café itself was buried in a slanted wall so close to the church that the toll of the bells on the hour rumbled through Sophie where she sat, her case at a reachable distance beside her.

"And it didn't take long to convince you to come. Who are these men you are working for? The ones you mentioned when we shared that wonderful dinner?"

Sophie blew on her hot coffee and pressed it gingerly to her lips. "I can't tell you."

Novak smiled. "Here you are in this new city, keeping a few se-crets. Can you not see how easy it would be just to turn them over to me?"

"You speak impeccable English, you're clearly a man of taste, and yet here you are in a city that could fall at any moment."

"Whereas you are more of an open book than I assume you would like to be. You are too conspicuous in Vienna for your own good. Men believe there is some virtue and class in being associated with Starling. The name. The elusive way in which you can appraise things. I find that an asset." He tilted his head to the side and folded his hands on the table. "You will probably never understand why I am here, but that is not why you're here. Do you play chess?"

"No," she said. Then Novak raised his eyebrow. "Okay, a little. A friend of mine has tried to teach me."

"Well, in chess you need an escape square. To ensure that your king will never be captured."

"So I am your escape square?"

He shook his head. *"Ne.* But I am not sure I fancy sharing you with other people."

"I'm not an object to be shared." At his responding glare, she reached into her case and provided the manuscript piece she had retrieved at the church. "But this is."

He took the folder and studied the paper inside. "You seem trustworthy, Starling. And some of my associates here are getting too political and running headfirst into stupid situations." His gaze darted toward an open newspaper on top of which he had placed the music.

It didn't matter that she didn't read Czech: the body of a woman was found in the Vltava. Hadn't Simon mentioned something about that the night he entreated her to stay? Too many negative headlines of late—the execution of journalists. The horror of people found dead in the street as peace slunk over the city bearing the weight of a war it hadn't truly won was pronounced in the headlines in any language.

Novak didn't fancy sharing her, but perhaps he didn't fancy sharing other people either. Was it possible this young dead woman was in a similar position as Sophie was now? Sitting across from a powerful man while attempting to glean information about music and walking dangerously close to a similar fate?

Sophie's fingers tightened into her palm. "How did Adameck

know to come get me? Surely you have facilitators in Prague who are just as, if not more, qualified. Whom you know better than some English woman who has long overstayed her welcome."

"I wanted you." With a dismissive wave of his hand, the conversation was over.

———◇◇◇◇———

But the conversation began again—and quickly—over the course of the next several days as Novak welcomed her into his world. His town house on Kampa Island was a lot like the man himself—refined and reflecting a veneer of class. In small salons he hosted get-togethers away from the watering holes of the upper echelons. Where wine and vol-au-vents were replaced with schnapps and Shostakovich on the wireless. Sherry too. Just for her.

Sophie felt freer in Prague than in Vienna. Novak gave her run of the place as she was wont to spend hours while seeing in musical fragments what he could not. While he fielded phone calls or entertained men with hats with the brims tugged low over their faces, she examined cases full of retrieved manuscripts.

Looking through his preference in musical manuscripts, she had found a kindred spirit. He was very fond of Mozart's concertos and of Beethoven, but he also enjoyed pieces so Baroque, they reflected the architecture and ornamented facades framing the cobbles in hilly Malá Strana. He was somehow in possession of a piece by Corelli but also of a few priceless letters tucked under protective glass. From Nanerl, Mozart's sister, to her famed brother. One was a recollection of a chess game.

She liked Novak because he was everything she enjoyed about her background: the intelligence, the music, and the conversations about Mozart and Shostakovich without the burden of her father's expectations.

When she worked with Simon, she truly had camaraderie, despite the hiccups in their relationship of late. The heat from those last moments with him before she had left for Prague prickled up her neck. No matter how well meaning he was, when Simon didn't trust her, it hurt. Especially now that her pride and stubbornness had worn off a little bit.

She wasn't sure why she was comparing her association with Novak to that of Simon, other than in both men's company she felt like she could breathe. That she wouldn't be required to aspire to her name or history.

She couldn't place Novak's need to impress her. He didn't mention Mozart's death mask, which seemed odd to Sophie considering his obvious love of music and his influence in the city, but Simon had once told her that men spoke as loudly in the things they didn't say as with the things they did.

One afternoon as ice glistened against the banks of the river and the bells chimed over the bridge, he offered her another emblem of trust. "Take a look in my study. There should be a list of names in the far corner of my desk," he said. "I am not sure they will be willing to part with any information about the manuscript, but there is no harm in trying. Find me someone who works out of the Klementinum."

The library he spoke of towered over the Vltava in the oldest part of the city and possessed some of the rarest manuscripts in Europe. It stood to reason that all of its mysteries were yet to be explored and perhaps even untouched by the war that had scattered the Mozart manuscript.

"And see if you recognize anyone from your time in Vienna." He started walking for the study door. "I need to make a phone call."

Sophie nodded as he left the room. She appreciated the measure of trust he was giving her to be in his study unaccompanied when she had found it locked on more than one occasion during small soirees over the past few weeks.

On a small lawyer's bureau near the window, Sophie saw a book on chess philosophy she recognized from her time with Simon. Novak's library was filled not merely with gold-embossed volumes to portray power and affluence but carefully selected volumes. The tomes left her with no further doubt about his loyalties. He clearly believed the Western Allies were a detriment to the Soviet power he wanted to see in charge.

She filed this away. It was one of the instances when there was a disconnect in their rapport. While the rest of the town house bore only traces of his high-end taste, a sweep of her gaze around the study revealed a small treasure chest—the perfect, dusty balance of rich artifacts against an otherwise humble room.

Sophie continued onward. She found the ledger with names: many she recognized from Novak's conversations with Adameck and a few even from when she was in Vienna. Sidorov's name was there. Haas's too.

Novak was playing his cards right. But silently, at least where she was concerned.

Sophie smoothed her hand over the names. All men in pursuit of the mask. And here she was in pursuit of a piece of music. Diana and Simon had a penchant for seeing things where there was seemingly nothing to see. Was this list a code? A map?

"Well?" His voice from the doorway drove her gaze up to him. She almost dropped the list as if caught in the act. He eyed her closely and clearly misinterpreted her careful study. "Money is not an issue, Starling." He peeled off several bills from a money clip. Not koruna but pounds. "Have your friend Müller in Seilergasse authenticate these." He handed her a folder.

She took a quick peek inside. The Mozart manuscript of *Der Messias*. Judging by the thickness of the folder, Novak was well ahead of putting the pieces of the puzzle together, and the piece she had retrieved at St. Giles fit well.

"I didn't know you were familiar with Herr Müller's expertise."
She chose her words carefully. "Considering that there are men here
who would probably be as qualified in its study."

"You thought I would find you at his Pfandhaus for fun?"

"No. I just—"

"Bars eighty-nine to ninety-nine." He gestured to the manuscript.
Novak squinted over the music: notes and measures even now her
mind could make into melody. "I cannot tell if it is an original or a
copy. And it is hard to tell with Mozart, as you know, because scholars
suspect he made few copies at all." His study stopped at a particularly
intricate phrase. "Herr Müller's proficiency in these matters is unpar-
alleled. Especially when it comes to Mozart. It is not that I do not acknowledge your abilities, but Vienna was the composer's home too."

Her childhood tutor had said something similar. Wolfgang
Amadeus, *God's Beloved*. So beloved by the Almighty it was almost as
if he had no need to make corrections?

Novak appraised the music before them. She wasn't sure if he read
music, but he clearly appreciated it. It made her think of something
her grandmother had said, "*Some of us, dearest Sophia, were made to
interpret it for those equally as talented. Oh yes. They may not play a note,
but they were gifted with the appreciation of every nuance and phrase.*"

This joint study was a peculiar way to end their interaction, when
he suddenly rang for a driver to take Sophie to the Alcron Hotel to
collect her things for a night or two in Austria.

"Take your time, if need be. But ensure you return with Herr
Müller's opinion. Some things are too delicate for a quick telephone
call, are they not?"

"But I am still searching for . . . I told you. You are not the only man
who has hired me."

"Let them wait. Drive up your prices, then."

"That isn't . . ."

She kept waiting for Novak to say that he knew about the mask, that he knew where it was, and that she was to find it for him as much as for Haas and Sidorov. Most likely he was only allowing her to see dimly so he could keep the upper hand. If so, she came close to blurting out her suppositions.

"The funny thing about loyalty, Starling, is that you cannot paint it evenly. Instinctively you know from the start who will have the lion's share of it." His blue eyes locked with hers and their intensity turned something over in her chest. A flicker. As if she was being seen by someone so clearly . . . so . . .

She blinked the odd familiarity away. "I'll take it to Müller. And—"

"Car's here," Novak said, before she could get a last word in. "See if he can see what we cannot."

By the time the driver deposited her at the Alcron, Sophie was filled with expectation for her return to her transient flat in Vienna. Still, she was stricken by the portentous end to her conversation with Novak and her realization that she might have missed something.

In her room, she immediately looked for touch points beyond a maid tending to the daily cleaning of the room. Jewelry in place. Lipstick by the mirror. A half decanter of sherry and a half-smoked cigarette.

Sophie hadn't poured sherry, nor had she lit a cigarette. Someone had been in her room.

The telephone in the corner rang. "What did you forget?" she said in lieu of greeting. No one but Novak knew she was staying here. She hadn't even told Simon.

"Starling." It was a decidedly Russian accent. Clipped and impatient.

"Sidorov." The identification tugged tightly over her shoulder blades.

"Any progress?"

"No."

"But you're in Prague searching for what I asked."

"Of course."

"And for no other reason?" His voice was a tight wire drawing her back to the moment at the Staatsoper.

"I have other business, of course."

"You might do a better job of prioritizing if I were you."

"How did you know where I was staying?"

But he had clicked off, leaving Sophie to wonder if Das Flüstern was really the man of whom she should be most wary after all.

CHAPTER 22

January 1947
Innere Stadt, Vienna

Simon expected a letter from Das Flüstern, but the one accompanying it on a silver tray delivered to his hotel room was another tug unraveling the Adameck thread. This time from Tab Martin, Simon's contact since Brighton had gone off the grid.

> Thanks to your earlier correspondence and your address, I've been keeping as close an eye on Adameck as possible. Yet there is something still evasive about the man. But I can tell you this: Adameck was a registered member of the National Socialist Party as early as the thirties and that he purchased a Škoda car on credit.

The letter went on to describe a black car Simon knew well. It had swerved and tried to run him over in the Ring. He tried to loosen the tension in his neck with a tug of his necktie, then focused on the other message.

The fourth play was an unexpected one. It surprised him enough that he double-checked the notation on the message—Bg2—and, in turn, studied the stranger's handwriting. There was an artistry to it, almost as if he was trying to appear casual, but the broad, even strokes showed otherwise.

Simon moved the player's white bishop and then focused on his side of the board. He had enough practice opposite a live player to know the little quirks and tells that Brighton later cited as one of the reasons he had recruited him. But Simon couldn't read an empty chair. As usual there was a note.

I often wonder if men do not revel in the carnage of war because it allows them to rebuild the world to suit whatever utopia they imagine. They can ascribe their own traits and philosophies in the reconstruction of devastation. They can compose, as it were. Did you know Mozart—the composer beloved by both Prague and Vienna—kept a bird as a pet?

There, on Das Flüstern's side, Simon imagined Prague from a trip in university borne of his desire to impress a girl. When he had dressed in black to match the strong coffee he intended to drink and read a lot of Kafka. Was this what Das Flüstern was trying to rebuild?

Simon remembered Staré Město (the Old Quarter—home to the Old Town Square and dozens of clocks tucked into the ancient town square) and then Karlův most, or Charles Bridge, flanked by statues and crossing the Vltava River. He tried to imagine Sophie there now. *"A bird as a pet."* This nameless, faceless opponent didn't know the half of it.

Not knowing where she was or what she was doing unnerved him. And the fact that more of his self-made defenses were beginning to crumble startled him.

He moved his black bishop to g7.

———◦◦◦◦◦———

Patriotic students stood at the edge of Albertinaplatz and outside the Burgtheatre on the Ring, holding out nationalistic papers promising to stake a claim in their own government again. Simon never felt more like an interloper, a foreigner, than he did smiling and tipping his hat to them.

Simon found his way to the exhibition near Freyung Square mentioned in the pamphlet Moser had given him at his soiree, and walked past displays boasting opportunities for Austrians to visit how their new occupants would reshape their economy, attempt to preserve their culture, and keep them from falling behind a Soviet curtain. Simon wanted to understand and see how his own country was represented in the many offered viewpoints. Britain, he soon learned, asserted itself as safe, reasonable, and domestic.

The exhibitions spread out with opulent model buildings: imaginative ideas of what the city could be under the guided influence of the hosting Allied powers—a blend of Austrian's cultures and traditions with idealism and how they might best receive help.

The displays were popularly attended by men eager to see to the rebuilding effort, to weigh their opinions on which Allied influences would best suit what Vienna would become. He stopped at a model of London, where the bustling metropolis was tentacled to suburban centers featuring uniform houses and cozy sitting rooms. The industry would stay in the city rebuilding from its destruction, and the country would provide an easy commute home for the working provider.

Real pictures spread broad and wide. Large maps and diagrams spelled out new urban developments and civic centers. Life-sized models of rooms from happy homes rimmed the floor. A mimicked world. Simon picked up a French picture book featuring little blond girls and boys in dirndls and lederhosen, happily spinning amid the edelweiss on the Alps. A children's picture-book take on a culture and its history. None of it, of course, captured the German language or the history of the country.

He found Brent Somerville standing not far away in a small group of men similarly dressed. Brent was smiling at a conversation but must have made out Simon in his peripheral vision. He turned.

Simon adjusted his glasses and his gaze caught a familiar figure. *Moser.* Simon kept a wide berth while matching the pace and rhythm of the man's steps. Simon had to give him credit. He took intense interest in everything.

"Herr Moser," Simon said cordially.

The answering smile he gave Simon didn't reach his eyes. "You came. I was hoping we could continue our conversation from the other evening."

"Quite exciting, isn't it?" Simon chose his words with care. "To see how so many people are so invested in assuring Austria makes it through this uncertain time."

Moser assessed a replica model of an urban development that bore a striking resemblance to similar housing Simon had seen in the British papers.

"I am glad you are here. It does well for my countrymen to see a British man like yourself taking an interest in our display here." Moser gave a courteous nod, which landed—pointedly—at a group of men congregating not far away. Then he bid *"Auf Wiedersehen"* and sauntered away.

Dignitaries and politicians assessed each demonstration with aplomb. A few women strolled by a replica of a rather British-looking sitting room, complete with a worn sofa cover like the one from the Somerville's second-floor flat back in Clerkenwell.

"So what is worse?" Brent approached from behind his shoulder. "Hitler or a complete overhaul of their culture?"

Simon grimaced and passed the illustrated book to Brent. "The culture is right here. With a few tweaks and changes."

"Language for one." Brent assessed, easily reading the French.

"Who are those men?" Simon said under his breath. They approached a large map of a new plan for London featuring uniform housing with easy access to central Tube lines.

"Judging by their accents, they're American," Brent said. "And they're keen on all of this. That one fellow has been taking copious notes."

Simon sensed a pair of eyes on them and focused on the nearest display of a prospective new London. "Diana would hate the homogenized architecture of this." He imagined the prefab houses of the model as they might look in an Austrian setting.

Brent chuckled, then his expression sobered. "Eternity?" he whispered. "Is Moser involved?"

"I still don't know."

Munitions, Sophie's artifacts, these new displays—Eternity could slowly be infiltrating every part of the city.

There was a quite lifelike replica of the Innere Stadt as well: a sequence of buildings in Baroque splendor with large cobbled boulevards and greenery. A miniature of what Simon hoped the city could be again when the bomb craters and rubble had been cleared.

The glass above was smudged with fingerprints, and it took all that was within him not to extract his handkerchief and swipe the smudges away. He slightly turned to a different angle and removed his glasses. The majority of fingerprints on the glass box were around a large building Simon recognized from his walks in the city. When he looked up, Brent was studying him carefully, and Simon smoothed the consternation from his face.

"Anything of interest?"

"You know this building?"

Brent squinted. "Esterházy Palace, isn't it? In Wallnerstrasse. Look at the little coat of arms."

Simon cleared his throat and Brent straightened. They were being watched.

"They're traveling like an amoeba, aren't they?" Simon said. Were they friends of Moser's? Guests? "You stay here. I could use your observation skills more than your eavesdropping." Simon flicked a second look at the group.

"And you'd think this was a May Day fair judging by their enthu-siasm." Simon didn't like to generalize academic or diplomatic sorts, but rarely were they this effusive. Especially when not plied with the type of libations that were provided the night he had attended the Schönbrunn party.

"Americans are always effusive, though, aren't they? At least in films," Brent surmised.

Simon closed in so that flits of conversations tuned in like the wireless on a stormy night in myriad languages but predominantly in English.

"Moser is very influential on the hiring board at the university." Brent raked his fingers through his red hair. He tucked his hand into his pocket for a list, gave a furtive look around, then held it out for Simon to read. "Look at these names."

Simon pored over a faculty memo in German. "They don't mean anything to me. Are they all instructors here?"

"Not yet. But Moser means to use them. They mean a lot to a narrow-minded, patriotic faculty. It was under my door when I dropped off a few books before coming here. He means to reflect what he's doing here within his halls. More people like me . . . foreigners. But ones who hold political influence. They publish papers that are widely acknowledged and revered. Not just my dusty, old tomes on St. Paul.

"These men were invited care of Moser, Simon, and it's why he pointed them out to you. This fellow, late of the University of Paris before the war. Tapping into the young, vibrant culture our French allies are bringing to the city."

Simon followed Brent's finger to another name. "And this man. I researched him. I used a few King's College connections. He's a master at urban development. And see . . . here . . . American. Four Americans."

Simon followed. "But no Soviet influence."

"Precisely. I mean insofar as their credentials, but you know as well as I do that you can't tell where a man's loyalty lies just by what he teaches." Brent tucked the paper back into his pocket. "It might be an incidental thing, but it clangs as loud as a bell. Moser's showing what side he is on. And it weighs heavily with Americans. This fellow used to work in munitions. And this one is a chemical engineer."

Moser was an established and prominent figure, not only in the city but with control of lecterns, and he'd completely disappeared from the exhibition.

———◦◦◇◇◦◦———

With Brent's help, Simon easily found Moser's office. It was as impeccable as his flat, yet without any distinctive taste other than expensive. Just like the study at his town house.

He recalled Rick Mariner's office at King's College, a professor colleague of Brent's who had ties to Eternity. It was more about showing affluence than personal taste. Brent was right: what people taught and what they believed could often be at odds with each other.

Moser hurriedly closed a desk drawer just as Simon crossed through the doorway and took the seat Moser gestured toward. "Herr Barre."

The wireless in the corner played a piece Simon knew as a favorite of Sophie's: Beethoven. With the music's crescendo Simon leaned across the desk. "Why did you invite me here? What is it you wanted me to see?"

"You are a man of taste and class."

"You don't need to sell your city to me." Simon swept his gaze around the room and spotted a chessboard near the window. "Do you ever play without a board, Herr Moser?"

"I like the feel of the pieces in my hand."

"During the war, I know several men took to using descriptive notation in letters. Perhaps even sending codes."

The music faded and Moser shifted. "Men will do anything to stretch their brains in a time of war, will they not?"

The pieces Simon chose to display were as evasive as his smile. They invited one in . . . to a point. "Stretching. Perhaps the same could be said of lectures stretched to include professors from across the Atlantic."

"The world is opening."

"So this is how you'll close out Communism? With midterms? Behind lecterns?"

Moser inclined his chin so slightly Simon couldn't tell if it was an affirmative. "I would like to go about the next era of my city in a more dignified way than what some of the Red zones are planning."

As quickly as he began talking, Moser stopped, leaving Simon to either fill the silence or use it. "A very interesting group of men at the exhibition today." Simon adjusted his tie. "Americans."

"Giving carte blanche and easy access to Soviet agendas in London and beyond? Don't look so surprised. Any man of means and influence is aware, has been approached. Are you familiar with the Morgenthau Plan?"

"An American plan to demilitarize Germany. Regardless of cost." From Simon's brief notes from MI6 a few years back, it would have allowed for twenty-five million Germans to starve to death in pursuit of assuring Germany never had the opportunity to rise to power again.

Simon had trouble seeing the end of the game, instead distinguishing from each individual piece in this instance. He would never justify that death toll.

"There are rumblings of something new from across the ocean: a less drastic approach," Moser said. "Why not anticipate an approach?"

"Hence why you are suddenly interested in adding Americans to your faculty roster?" Hard to starve out a revolution like the Hofers and other men with manifests if there was a far more powerful force at play.

"I want to know what the plans for my country are and at what expense. The powerful men in my sphere view architecture—like the plans you saw in those displays—and artifacts as a rallying cry."

At what expense?

Simon used the frigid walk from the square to the Sacher considering the cost exacted for his being there. He even stopped just outside Julius Meinl to revisit a letter from his chess opponent tucked long ago into his pocket:

> Nothing is by accident. You have two choices. You can either play to your opponent's whim, surprised at every turn. Or you can let yourself off the hook for interpreting every move and movement and moment as having potential meaning. This doesn't make you daft. A wrong turn is still a strong turn. Because at least you put everything into it. But it should at least inspire you to keep your eyes peeled before you cross the road.

Easy for an anonymous chess note to boast. *"Put everything into it."* But what if Simon put everything into the wrong thing?

CHAPTER 23

February 1947
Neuer Markt, Vienna

It had taken Sophie some time for her to steady herself from Sidorov's threat as she waited for the boarding call at Wilsonovo nádraží. It had been a smooth train ride from Prague. At Hauptbahnhof she hailed a taxi and proceeded to Seilergasse and the Pfandhaus.

At Müller's, bolstered by the *Der Messias* treasure under her arm, she accepted her hatbox and case from the driver and transferred them so the folder at her side was within easy access.

The chime over the door jangled as she angled herself in the doorway and set her cases behind an old lawyer's cabinet with a few Meissen porcelain statuettes on display. From the direction of the office, she heard his soft voice in clipped responses as he finished a phone call.

"Herr Müller?"

He joined her amid the displays with a smile. "A long-lost starling."

She followed him to the back and watched as he opened the folder she'd handed him. "Novak said it's safer with me," she said in response to a raised eyebrow she'd interpreted as his wondering why she had it at all.

"Lots of markings here." He moved his magnifying glass over the bars, measures, and lines and squinted.

"Is something wrong with the manuscript? I truly thought it just showed signs of wear." What had Novak seen in it and why, especially, did he want Herr Müller to verify its provenance?

"It does. It is a myth that our composer was able to write with no corrections, is it not? Look at the blot here."

Sophie strained her eyes to detect it.

"Leave it with me for further study and I will see that you have your authentication."

She gave a single nod and tucked the manuscript back into the folder. "Thank you again." She riffled in her purse and set down an envelope. "See that it gets to Frau Wagner, will you?"

Even without opening the envelope, his smile stretched at the weight. "Novak pays you well."

She finalized some business with him and provided Novak's payment for Herr Müller's services. She leaned over behind the lawyer's cabinet to retrieve her cases. Odd. She was certain she had left her hatbox at a slight diagonal. Was she imagining things? If someone had been in the shop, the bell would have jangled.

Sophie blamed her imagination, the train trip, and a long day. She quickly started to walk the few blocks to her flat to drop off her cases and report to Novak via telephone that she had seen Müller as per his instructions.

Prague had settled over her shoulders comfortably, but Vienna still held her heart. The inherent beauty in the structures and bordering the rooftops, not in their war-blazoned imperfections but what grandeur they would soon be again.

Just then a man with a long gait intercepted her from the direction of the Michaelerplatz. "Villiers!" Simon's face was grim but lightened when he saw her. "When did you get back?"

Sophie tugged at the brim of her hat. "Today." Why had he used *that* name? He could have called her *Sophie* or *Sophia*. Even *darling*. *Villiers* was his default when they were at Bletchley. Now it seemed forced.

He didn't look much better than she supposed she did. There was a film over his eyes and dark circles under them. His cheekbones were more pronounced in a thinner face. Did he ever eat anything?

He studied her for a moment. "Are you all right? Let me take you to dinner. When did you eat last?"

She could have laughed at how they rode the same mental train. "This is not a social visit, Simon. I wasn't expecting to see you at all."

They fell into step. Simon's brow creased. "I don't like you crossing back and forth between Vienna and Prague. The Czech border guards are taking people off the trains for interrogation, to try to gain some control."

"What could I possibly have that would make them drag me off a train?"

"I don't know, Villiers, you tell me." His voice was short, almost snappish.

That name again. As if he was trying to impose distance between them. But he seemed to catch himself. "I'm sorry. Truly. I've been worried. I hated the way we left things."

She couldn't blame him. She felt it strongly too. They walked a few steps in a silence more pronounced because it didn't reverberate with their usual camaraderie.

They spun around at a sound behind them: a pulse or echo like a gunshot. Simon pulled Sophie close beside him.

"You're jumpy," she said when it turned out to be a tailpipe backfiring. But she didn't move away. She liked his warmth beside her. She had missed Simon.

"Just worried about you," he said after a moment.

Church bells tolled from nearby Peterskirche, noting the hour as they approached Stephansplatz. "There's a man in Prague who has the same book as you." Was he pleased she was thinking about him?

"Which one?"

"Chess philosophy. Hearing his passion when he spoke of it—the difference between chess and war—was like hearing *you* talk for a moment."

Simon stopped. "Was this at a pawn shop? Or for a client of Starling's?"

This time when Sophie heard a *pop* and a *bang* and Simon pulled her down, she knew it wasn't a car.

———⋄⋄⋄⋄———

The wind left Sophie's lungs as she got her bearings and registered the shock of being squashed under Simon. He had driven her to the ground the moment the shot cracked. She frantically wriggled from under his weight and turned him over.

Eyes closed. Breath light. Her heart tore. He couldn't be. What would she do if—? "Simon! No!"

He grunted and shifted.

"No. No. No." She panicked. "Simon! Can you hear me?" She ran her hand over his arm and across his chest, trying to assess any injury in the darkness. "Simon!"

He eased open his eyes. "I'm fine." He slowly sat up and wiped at his trousers.

Sophie's breath returned in an avalanche, slamming so hard her torso was on fire. She cursed the whimper that expelled with her first inhale.

He scanned her face. "Are you all right?"

She pounded his chest. "I hate you, Simon Barrington!"

"Ah." A smile ticked his right cheek and he got his bearings . . . and his glasses. Surprisingly unscratched. He fixed them onto his nose. "You're fine." He extended his hand and pulled her to her feet so they were facing off. Nearly the same height. Breath moving at the same pace.

What would she have done if he were injured? Or worse?

"Never do that again!" She pounded his arm. "Never."

"Take a bullet for you?" He brushed at his overcoat. "Well, *almost* take a bullet for you." He peered over one shoulder. She assumed he was searching for where the projectile had ended up.

His face was whiter than it had been when he punched his brother at Camden. It was as if the ground shifted and everything was off-balance. She took his proffered arm and they continued their stroll.

"Were they shooting at you?" he asked, solemnly.

"I don't know. Were they shooting at you?"

"I don't know." He waited a few strides, then leaned in and impulsively touched her cheek with the crook of his index finger. "But I will say our Soviet friend at the Hofburg hasn't even glanced at me since that last night we were in the Volksgarten."

Simon didn't lean away once they were far enough from the altercation. Their shoulders brushed and she kept a tight hand on his forearm.

When she thought Simon had been shot—or dead—her world had drained.

Sophie tucked her fingers into her palm. "Simon." She shuddered, his reassuring touch now felt like a singe.

And as the adrenaline of the night waned and the day wore like an unraveled thread . . . Sophie felt *married*. Not just in font and ink, a piece of paper, but in the still, sure way Simon filled up the space beside her. In the way he breathed. In his smell and sense and stride.

In the way he had thrown himself in front of danger to preserve her safety.

For the moment, with his breath on her neck and his presence driving one foot in front of the other, she was home.

The sound of the gunshot hit Simon with a far more potent blast than he anticipated. A blast that had stirred him into action. Nothing like near death to bring his protectiveness to the forefront. His chest constricted. Was Moser or Adameck responsible?

"I think that . . . ," Sophie said in a hoarse voice.

Simon pressed his finger to her lips. "Shh . . . Sophie."

Another step and then another closer to her. The first steps he now recognized as a part of a complicated dance. The next . . . he assumed she was falling into his rhythm. Uncertain but thankfully willing to pursue the next phrase.

He held her still. "Did you hear the shooter leave?" Simon took in the perimeter frantically, jogged on a diagonal and peered down Habsburgergasse from a distance. A prickle skittered up the back of his neck. For all of his weaving in and out of Vienna, he had never been shot at before. Not boldly in the open like that.

Something had shifted. The only varying element was Sophie.

Simon stole a hand out reflexively and tucked her fingers into his own.

She didn't pull away and he felt her shiver beside him. He instinctively tightened his hold. He drew her in the direction of her flat, feeling her pulse buzz through her fingers as they reached her block.

She pulled her key from her purse without disengaging from him and turned to the front door. She only slipped her fingers from his as they maneuvered into the stairwell in its stale chill.

He studied her and beheld the same grace she had wielded at Ashton or Camden, when her fingers flew over the keys of a Bösendorfer, the same dramatic tilt of her head when she was speaking of Mozart's starling, his muse, in a cage.

They both noticed that the door to her flat was slightly ajar. Simon instinctively tucked her behind him and surveyed the landing. She followed him closely, reaching for her handgun. He reached into his trench pocket for his Webley MkVI revolver. Moonlight streamed through the blinds, creating shadowy stripes in the sitting room.

Sophie flicked on the lamp on the side table and incandescent light washed over her ransacked apartment. "Oh," she said dryly, though her voice was still tightly wired. "Well, that settles it. I'll get the rest of my things together and move out permanently in the morning. Diana will store some of it, I'm sure."

With his gun at the ready, he moved through the flat, looking in other doors. He moved out of the kitchen and bathroom to her bedroom. "Open window!" he called from inside the room. "No one's here." The street traffic below made a racket: a rumbling lorry passing by and a siren blaring.

Sophie stepped into the door frame and glanced around. "Nothing taken. If I had been here, I would have set up my touch points."

They both knew her reference.

"First time for everything, isn't there? I've never had this happen before. Not that I know of. If someone other than yourself, Gabe, or Diana have been here, they've not disturbed any of my touch points at all."

"You're scared and startled." He looked at her kindly when she turned and met his gaze. "You can tell me anything. Because . . . you *know* that I'll ensure it's all right."

Her shoulders settled as she fixed drinks from the side table where she usually kept her marriage certificate. But she didn't answer him.

"What were you doing in Prague, Sophie? Truly."

She swiped a strand of mahogany hair that escaped from her pinned updo, then reached for her sherry. "A contact I met there has a connection here and I wanted to see it through." She swirled the amber liquid in her glass. "It's not my story to tell, Simon. Otherwise . . ." She took a sip to finish her sentence, leaving behind a red lipstick stain on the crystal rim.

"If the connection is Adameck, you should tell me. Dangerous things are happening here." And he was just beginning to put the pieces together. He knew far more about Moser at this point.

Silence fell between them. "Well, you're not staying here."

"Oh, where shall I stay then? Do the Somervilles have a hideaway bed?"

"You could stay with me."

"Your voice is a little hoarse. Here." She sloshed a few more fingers in his glass, then moved to flick on the wireless. The "Lacrimosa," the opening movement of Mozart's Requiem Mass in D Minor, matched the somber mood and the moody sky out the flat window. She tugged the drapes closed.

Mozart played on. A requiem for a city dead and waiting just beyond her blinds.

"You could stay with me." He accepted the refill. She folded herself onto the sofa and crossed her legs. "At Sacher's. We're married, not that anyone would care. It's safer there." He settled his eyes on the certificate on the bar.

Sophie sipped through a laugh. "You seem to forget, darling, that I was in Vienna for long spurts of time alone." She set her glass down, as did he.

She truly did look pale even in the warmth of the flat. Simon removed a match from his pocket, struck it on the side of the mantel, and set the few logs in the fireplace to a slow burn. "You must be connected to something very valuable."

Sophie smoothed a corner of the rug with the toe of her shoe, and opened her mouth. "I didn't expect to see you tonight."

"Apparently."

"And I don't know if I should . . ."

"Should what?"

It took nothing for him to jump in front of her to thwart danger if need be. That was as natural a reaction as breathing. But it was the few seconds in the span of that breath that shook him: when he was left wondering if his world would be deprived of her.

"How many times have we *almost* had a conversation like this?" she asked. "You know something and you can't tell me or won't tell me and I stand there gaping at you, *waiting* for you to realize there is no one truly on your side but me!"

He knew she wasn't talking about a gunshot in the dark any more than she was speaking to the invasion of her space. Perhaps she thought it was safer to argue than to address any of the mounting tension between them. "You have *no* idea what you're doing. We just have another war to wander around in. I can take care of myself."

He stared at his glass. She was being defensive because she was startled. Frightened, even. Once he saw that flash of vulnerability cross her face, he wouldn't defensively question her; she'd just retreat.

He lowered his tone in a different approach. "You know what I never forget? That you married me. It's not just seeing that certificate either. Whether you're here or in Prague, I always remember." He watched for a reaction.

"I am here for Herr Müller to appraise fragments of a Mozart manuscript. *Der Messias.*"

He studied her a moment. She was telling the truth, at least about her visit to Müller.

She sipped her drink, her eyes never settling on him. But she was clearly concealing something.

He tested the waters. "You can trust me, Sophie."

"I know, Simon."

But it was becoming harder to believe her the longer she held back.

CHAPTER 24

February 1941
Bletchley Park, Buckinghamshire

The telegram about Julius came on a long afternoon. Everyone was hunched over their desks in the crowded hut. Fisher and Diana were intercepting wireless communications from a corner by the window. Simon's own work space had a basket overflowing with translated ciphers and cillies he was accustomed to, determining coordinates and enemy positions.

One of the messages brought to him was quite different from the usual decrypted codes. It was an impersonal telegram about the death of his half brother. The man shared his blood. His mother had loved him. And Simon loved her. It was at least a starting point for a semblance of mourning.

Simon was given leave for the funeral, and he retrieved the car he had billeted at a neighboring garage. There was an opulent wake and reception, though Julius's remains would forever be interred in France.

When Simon arrived at Camden, he had to part a sea of mourners until he found his father, wearing a mourning band in the manner of old tradition. He barely looked Simon in the eye, though his solicitor took Simon's elbow and told him, in no uncertain terms, that they needed to talk.

"And you won't even look at me," Simon said the next afternoon, sipping a brand of brandy he had missed while imbibing watery pints at a Bletchley pub.

"I won't look a coward in the eye." Charles Barrington glowered. "Pushing papers behind a desk while real men give their life's blood."

Simon stiffened. He had signed up to fight a war that used his brain and logic and hunches. The experience removed him from the collective consciousness. He would forever be an outsider.

"Do you remember one night when you were very little and had been ill? You told your mother that you loved her. You had your weak, sentimental moments, didn't you?" Charles's eyes were red, whether from whiskey or tears or both, Simon wasn't sure. "And she didn't say it back. I *forbid* her to say it back. You were her punishment for a stupid mistake. So she was to publicly raise a cold shoulder to you." Charles took a moment. "But I know that you love this house out of the same weak sentimentality. You'd commit to preserving her memory here. I would wager that your love for her memory outweighs your hatred of me."

Simon wanted to tell him right then and there that perhaps Margaret had never said it in front of Charles, but she had said it.

What was the use of bringing it up now?

A new butler, Davis, appeared with a refill on a silver tray.

"Look at you attempting to retain some semblance of the old ways," Simon said coolly.

"How do you know that?" Charles didn't even raise his glass in Simon's direction.

"Because you are trying to preserve Camden! And you've been spending far more than Camden earned long before Hitler invaded Poland. Now wings are closed off and taken over for convalescing soldiers returned from the front. Furniture is spread under white sheets like ghosts to tuck away Camden's previous grandeur. Your tenants are impoverished or deserting you altogether."

"We are at *war*," Barrington said.

"Camden has been falling into ruin for years before the war, *Father*." Simon inclined his glass to a chipped painting above the mantel.

"Well, my solicitor will want to speak to you tomorrow. Julius's death made me consider my future. My legacy."

"Camden will be my legacy now that Julius is gone."

"Your legacy? You don't even have a father."

Simon buried his hurt. Or was it even hurt? At this point he couldn't tell.

"You are the natural-born son of nobody. But I know despite your feeble attempts to hide it, you were fond of your mother."

Heat sizzled in Simon's wrists and snaked up his arms until the anger settled in his suddenly dry throat.

"If you want to preserve any part of your history with her," Barrington said, "then you can talk to my solicitor about the new addendum in my will."

The next morning, Simon found his father's new solicitor, Finchley, perusing the side table. Breakfast at Camden, despite rations, was still an elaborate affair.

Simon tucked in to the dining room table and requested coffee.

Finchley slid his spectacles up on his nose. He was older than Methuselah, and his wiry fingers could do little but hold a fork that stabbed at one kidney at a time. Simon might have reasoned that his father's change of attorney had a lot to do with the war and the men depleted in the field on account of their service. But he knew better. Charles Barrington chose a man with one foot in the grave purposefully so Simon couldn't drag the affair out. Charles might hate him, but at least he recognized Simon's shrewd intelligence.

"Why are you doing all of this?" Simon said to Barrington. "I stay out of your way. I have never threatened to take what you wanted for Julius."

"I want to make your life as challenging as she made mine."

"Mother always sided with you. She shoved me aside for you and Julius. I was *never* in the way."

"Is that what you think? Your mother, Simon, was a bloody Communist," Barrington said in front of Finchley, a disclosure his father never would have shared before outside of the family.

Something more than Charles's threats had changed.

Charles smirked. "Oh yes, I had the house appraised before the trust moved in. And look what I exhumed from the guesthouse? Behind the shelves of gilded-edged pages of Dickens and Agatha Christie, as it turned out."

A library that concealed a tome shared between Simon's mother and his nameless father. Straight, unfamiliar handwriting contributed to the margins. A history of a philosophy and Red Marxism.

It felt a tad like betrayal and a bit of longing. But betrayal at what? Simon's idyllic memories and perceived perfection? Memories owed him nothing. Yet he longed to know why his mother was so moved by something Simon hated.

Perhaps she was just curious. Perhaps he should loathe his real father beyond a mixture of abandonment for possibly introducing her to this ideology. Perhaps it was a secret kept as tightly as the one Simon and his mother had shared over chess games and stolen hands of cards and crosswords passed underneath a locked door.

"There could be a perfectly reasonable explanation. Why sully her reputation like that? In front of someone outside of our family! In the middle of a war! When her son has just been killed!"

He had another line of questioning that had to do with his mother's relationship to Barrington, but Simon tucked his questions into the smooth lines of his Savile Row suit and played with his lapel.

"If you want to honor your mother's legacy, you will marry a woman of equal or greater circumstance to Camden," Barrington said.

It was dirty pool and a sneaky hand. It was the movement of

significance on the board that changed the game. Simon dug his fingers into his palm. "Or else?"

"Finchley! Spell out the details for him." Charles's eyes stayed on Simon.

With Charles Barrington's gamble, he shoved Simon in the direction of a trap not unlike the one that found Barrington ensnared to a woman he did not love to save the estate in the first place. To save his mother's estate, Simon had to be kept in the world he loathed forever. Had to marry a woman of equal or greater circumstance. "Who's to say I want it at all?"

Simon stared at the portrait of his mother hanging over the mantel and then at the cold font and ink of the addendum. She was in the walls and in the way her floral scent would precede her entrance into a room. In the loving look she would slide him across the table even as Simon built up his protective walls and kept to himself. Even as she tried to protect the secret that allowed her to privately acknowledge him yet publicly side with Barrington.

"Someday you'll understand more clearly," she had said not long before her death.

Simon wouldn't give away Camden until he had surveyed every last crevice in hopes of turning every last page of his mother's story there. If Barrington could produce a Communist pamphlet to destroy Margaret Barrington's reputation, then Simon would retaliate by accepting what his stepfather anticipated he would refuse.

He scrawled his signature where Finchley told him to sign. Angrily, he had Davis arrange for his car and his luggage to be brought round.

Simon left the estate that had only been home in a few stolen moments.

"Rest in peace, Mother."

—◦◦◦◦◦—

It wasn't hard to find Sophie at her usual table in the pub near Bletchley. His face must have betrayed his haste to get to her because not only did she sit up at attention, she pushed away from the table, even as her male companion still held to her hand.

"Villiers," her companion said.

"My sincere apologies, Pete." Sophie drained the last of her drink and nodded. "Thank you for the sherry."

She followed Simon out of the crowd and into the night. Spring was nipping at winter's heels, but frost still glazed the grass, and the pond where he took her gleamed. She smoothed her skirt beneath her and sat on a bench adjacent to him. "Well, nothing like leaving a perfectly lovely companion and a hearth and drink to sit out here in the cold with you." Her words were belied by a teasing tone.

"I've just been at Camden."

She blew a strand of hair away from her face. "Oh."

"Julius is dead. I got a letter from my father so I went there for the funeral."

The appropriate reaction was something about condolences or apologies. Sophie merely let out a long breath.

"I'm the coward, of course. The traitor."

"That's rubbish and you know it."

"Well, that's the way it is to him. His son died. He probably wishes it had been me."

Sophie grabbed Simon's hand. "No."

They wouldn't be able to stay here for long. Crowds were spilling out of the pubs to head to whatever entertainment was on at the main manor house.

"But it gets worse. There's been an addendum to his will. A provision." Simon took a moment.

"What kind of provision?"

"He now stipulates that to keep the estate—I must marry a woman of equal or greater wealth by the time of Charles's death, or he will leave Camden to the National Trust in his will. Preserve England's great history."

"That sounds like something out of a Jane Austen novel. He can't be serious."

"Don't you see? This archaic amendment is the perfect way to get back at me. For all he hates me, I think on some level he can gamble. He knows that while I loathe Camden, I will honor her legacy."

"You have too much integrity to marry someone simply for the opportunity of saving your estate. You would hate binding a woman to you for that reason. Simon, you cannot let them have Camden."

It was a long moment before Simon nodded. "And I have another life now, don't I? There are far more important things than the estate. But, Villiers, in a way he's throwing me a bone. I'm the illegitimate child of a woman who never loved him. I'm the last man who should stand to inherit."

Simon clenched his jaw. The severity of his circumstance dawned on him. He swerved and looked at her. "I should let it go. No one ever wanted me there anyway."

She gripped his kneecap. "Stop talking, Simon." Sophie raised her hand. "Your blasted father. He wants you to relinquish the estate."

"Well, wouldn't you?" He pushed his gold-rimmed glasses up the bridge of his nose.

"I won't let your *lout* of a father give it away. Your mother loved it, and I know she cared for you in her own way, and that's enough to put her far above the rest of your abhorrent family."

She took a breath. "Marry me."

— ◦◦◦◦◦ —

"Villiers . . ."

"Stubbornness doesn't become you, Simon. Marry me. I am of equal or greater circumstance."

"I don't measure you that way."

"Posh. Whatever nonsense you're about to spew out, I do fit the will's stipulation!"

"But you don't love me."

"We are the British aristocracy." She chuckled. "Love rarely comes into play."

"I won't play with your future, Sophia."

"You're my friend and this is my duty. And I want to spite Charles Barrington for being an oaf." She slid off the bench and got down on one knee. "You are the dearest person in my life."

When he didn't immediately answer, she continued. "It's not exactly Rhett and Scarlett at the burning of Atlanta, but we're still operating under wartime measures here."

"It wouldn't be fair."

"What's fair? War? This wretched place and its wretched coffee? Your father and his horrid conditions?"

"I would never ask you for this reason."

"I am asking *you*." She met his gaze straight on. "Don't leave a lady waiting, dearest. This is an awfully unflattering position."

He touched her shoulder to motion her up. "My mother married for money and your parents did and they are not happy. I won't ruin what we have. Friendship. Alliance. Rapport."

"Nonsense, Simon, we will do this for your mother."

"You didn't even know my mother."

Sophie slowly rose. "I have evaded marriage so far. As you know, my parents tried to shove me into matrimony before"—she smoothed his tie, then tugged at his lapels, gripping them to keep him in place—"and it didn't work. After all, I turned you down. Twice."

She raised her eyes to his and waited until she saw the tease in her own reflected in his. "But know this, whatever side you are on, Simon Barre, that's *my* side."

"But love." He raised his hand and stroked her cheek with his thumb. "You should marry someone you love."

"I wasn't conditioned to love, Simon. I was conditioned to excel, to marry well, to hold a polished teaspoon at an acceptable angle. But that just means that when I give any affection at all, it's because it is earned and not instilled."

He raked his hands through his black hair. "We can't just divorce."

"Have a few lovers lined up? What about Mary from Hut Six? Diana Foyle?"

He spun around and faced her. "No. But you deserve a family. And there's the very real matter of my illegitimacy."

Sophie made a sound that might have been a word if she could have funneled it into identifiable vowels. "I never want to hear you talk about legitimacy again! There is nothing about you that isn't true and honest. I am not falling on a sword here. Your horror of a step-father conjured up some Dickensian addendum to a will that rivals the Jarndyce case in *Bleak House*." She placed a hand on Simon's forearm. "This is about ironing out a wrinkle and righting a wrong. It's too perfect."

"How do you mean?"

"Charles loathes me. So we can revel in how angry this will make him. Simon, this is an emergency. And it isn't like the moment I step home my parents won't have a queue full of useless men they want to help *my* inheritance. Our union will get them off my back." She looked up at him through her lashes. "And I would be landing the fourth most eligible bachelor."

"Sixth." His mouth moved into the ghost of a smile. "It will have to be in a church. Out of respect for my mother."

Sophie nodded. "Done."

So they found a vicar of a neighboring church to perform a quick civilian ceremony. A few awkward words muttered in a small sanctuary and a slight brush of the lips, that was nothing. Well, almost nothing. Too much of *something*. And a realization that their lives, though united, could always go separate ways.

Even though there was no rice tossed in the air or canapés and champagne on the lawn, even though the witnesses were a church warden and an organist, the day meant something to her. Deep inside a strong, invisible line connected and weighted them with the commitment they had spoken despite the circumstances surrounding it.

She would choose to stay in Simon's orbit.

Marriage was a piece of paper. That was all.

After she parted ways with Simon and returned to her billet house, she had retreated to her room with the certificate burning in her pocket. She tucked it behind her crystal sherry decanter. Next to her pearls the paper was the most precious item in her possession. And her history—*their* history—became as hidden as the names they had shed.

CHAPTER 25

Simon met the mounting awkwardness between them with an uncustomary gesture. He shrugged out of his coat, tugged at his collar, and rolled up his sleeves. Simon Barrington of the perfect cuff links Sophie had given him at their fake wedding and the Savile Row shirts had rolled up his sleeves as he assessed the circumference of her living room.

The casual, definitive movement shook her. He was letting down his guard. Just as he had at Mayfair House.

With each fold of the fabric, Sophie was too aware of his forearms. He was stronger, and his long arms featured sinewy muscle more defined than his usual attire would betray. This was a far more intimate gesture than might be expected.

With a little bit of leftover adrenaline from the bullet aimed at them, her arm, it seemed, had a mind of its own. She placed her hand on his shoulder, then moved it to the curve of his neck. While she had avoided any type of intimacy before in a moment of self-preservation, she sensed she wouldn't get far with the same tactic tonight. Or know if she even wanted to.

She was playing out a relationship at the most inopportune time with a man whose name and future was bound to hers. For better or worse.

In measures and in bars.

"You scared me tonight." His voice wavered on an exasperated sigh.

"Thought you'd have to live without me?" She could make out the tension under his fingertips as if he meant to draw back. But he didn't move an inch. And neither did she.

Their breath met in the middle. She was incapable of moving out of his orbit. She had only felt this way once before: when his eyes glistened with tears and his father's denouncement echoed out of the estate door and into the trees where Simon escaped from an argument. Now she wanted to press him close to remind herself that he was alive, but the look in his eyes clanged through their silence.

"What is it about Prague? Is it about showing me what you're capable of?" His eyes were blue fire. "Or is there something of personal interest?"

The last time they had been in each other's vicinity she had staked her ground by claiming she owned a corner of the world without him.

"Mozart owned Prague." She offered while her mind churned. *"Meine Prager verstehen mich."*

"My Praguers understand me?" Simon translated the German.

"Here in Vienna they tossed him into a pauper's grave, but in Prague thousands attended the Requiem Mass in his honor. There I can feel that I am on the verge of becoming myself. Just a shadow now."

She warmed to the illustration. "You should see the way the city courts shadows. No wonder Mozart was inspired. Sometimes on the bridge I hold my fingers up as if I am taking a photograph and . . ."

"I can't let you go back to Prague. Not after tonight. For Mozart or for whatever reason."

"Because we—*you*—were shot at? I don't think you can *let* me go anywhere."

He edged closer. "Sophie! If you would just—" One hand massaged the back of his neck for a moment. "Fine." His eyes leveled on hers. "Go to Mayfair House. Either that or Camden. Oh, don't give me that look. You can't stay here."

He moved closer still.

"Can't I?" Sophie wasn't satisfied with the touch of their shoes, so she grabbed his lapel. "I've been a million places without you, Simon."

Right now, she was too close and she was reading between their lines anyway. So it seemed rather a waste for her lips not to be on his.

Simon kissed her back for a moment, then she felt his growl through her. "Are you *kissing* me to get your way?"

"I'm kissing you because I want to. Because you . . . you almost died. Or . . . something in that vein."

I'm kissing you because I lo—It was better if the word were left to singe the tip of her tongue.

She was dizzy by his restraint and empowered by his persistence. His scent and the slight sheen of perspiration on his forehead. Yet it had taken a war and a marriage for the safety of his estate for the blinders to come off and her to realize she was dangerously close to breaking the unofficial promise she had made to her grandmother.

Simon took the lead. His kiss was different now than at Camden or even on the park bench in the Volksgarten playacting for a Soviet soldier. In the slow crescendo of passion, in his intention and her reciprocation, in their collective anticipation, she felt a . . . a *vow*. A promise in the soft way his fingers tangled in her hair and his movement and pressure offered.

"Ugh." He disentangled himself and stepped away. It was Antarctica without him. "You run so hot and cold, Sophie. I won't allow you to break my heart."

"So you'll just break mine?" Sophie felt the warmth drain the farther he stepped back.

"I didn't think I had the power to do that."

"Where are you going?" Her eyes were wild on his.

"To pack your cases." The flash in his eyes, his unkempt black hair, and his rolled-up sleeves showed her he was as prepared to turn the next page of their story as she was.

But she *deserved* him—for all of their stops and starts. And the longer she was in his vicinity, the more she desired him.

"Simon!" She had *no* clue what was happening or who she was supposed to be in the here and now—only that the man standing—*fuming*—across from her was becoming more disheveled by the moment.

She was unraveling him and the power she wielded scared her. Because she felt more than a little off-kilter herself.

———◦◦◦◦◦———

Simon had often calculated how this romantic showdown might play out. Reality was a different game of chess altogether. And what was he trying to win? Her heart? Perhaps. Their argument? Most certainly. But not *this* argument. Sophie was here, brown eyes wide, leaning up and toward him. He could so easily take her into his arms.

A task would see him on course. Of course, Simon had no idea how to pack a woman's things. He found a case in the closet and began throwing clothes into it from hangers above it. He absently opened a few drawers, then when confronted with a delicate negligee, he turned to find her watching in the doorway.

"Finish this, would you?" He stepped out to the sitting room and rang for a taxi. His nerves were already frayed from their tense meeting.

"Can I help you?" he asked in a strained voice a moment later, attempting to be the gentleman he knew was several paces behind where the evening was heading.

She shook her head.

He helped take her cases to the cab and shoved them in the trunk. Then he watched her turn the lock on the outer entrance of her flat. He exhaled when she was safe next to him in the leather seat, the taxi swerving out by a line of broken buildings as it pulled away from the curb.

More than once he opened his mouth hoping words would spill out. Beautiful, eloquent, rational words.

They didn't.

Not long after a silent car ride, the valet at the hotel took his keys and saw to Sophie's trunks being moved to his suite.

Sophie was behind him, walking by the red-papered walls and over the ornate patterns on the plush carpet. Their ride on the gilded lift was silent, intruded by the bellboy who rocked forward a little on his spit-shined shoes.

Finally, they were within Simon's suite, with the broad window overlooking the Staatsoper and the span of the Albertinaplatz swathed by the moon. The attendant asked if Sophie needed help unpacking, but Simon didn't fancy anyone else in the room. They clearly needed to finish what they had started.

Simon watched her. Her fingers weren't running a line along her thigh as if it were a piano keyboard. He took the absence of her nervous habit as positive sign.

"Why did you agree to come with me?" Simon tossed his fedora on the bedspread and wriggled out of his overcoat.

"We weren't finished with our argument. You took all of my possessions and shoved them in cases that *you* saw to the door and to a cab."

"You kissed me," he said bluntly. "That is why we didn't finish our discussion." He was exhausted, but it did little to drain the heightened atmosphere between them.

She took the room in stride, owning it as if she had always belonged. And whatever he said—or didn't say—turned her toward him to pick up where they had left off.

Simon remembered back at Mayfair House over six years ago, how vulnerable she had looked when she'd slept, her hand tucked under her chin. He had been a gentleman then, tiptoeing out of her room. But now there was a piece of paper uniting their names. He was kissing his very real *wife*.

"Please stop," he said against her mouth.

She made a sound of disappointment and he gently stilled her with his hand, which took every last reserve of strength buzzing through him.

Sophie caught her breath. "You certainly know how to make a lady feel wanted."

Simon panted a moment and adjusted the glasses askew on his nose before he removed them completely to fold into his breast pocket. "You fogged up my glasses."

Sophie laughed. "What a crime." Her face was full of vulnerable expectation.

He was pressed against her still, and his mounting heartbeat matched the pace of her own. It felt *right*. She felt *right*.

He wanted to be kissing her. He *needed* to be kissing her. But he didn't know what *she* needed.

In his head a chessboard presented itself: squares and lines. A move here and a pocket of a player there. He shoved it away. She needed him right here and present, and he couldn't afford to fall back on his usual method of overthinking. But he was very close to a precipice.

Simon would have to do something for which his life at Camden had prepared him, in secret smiles with his mother and buried childhood treasures tucked in a chest and away from Julius: compartmentalize.

CHAPTER 26

Sophie moved her hand over his cheek and into the curve of his collarbone and then fiddled with his button. Their breath met over the fabric and Simon instinctively reached up to refasten his collar. *Compartmentalize*, he told himself.

Sophie tossed her hat and overcoat onto the bed.

For several ticks of the mantel clock, there was a silence that clanged loudly.

Simon thought of filling it with whatever nonsense came in his head, but Sophie beat him to it. "There is a very good reason, darling, that I need to go back to Prague. Do you trust me?"

"Not when you kiss me like that."

"I don't want to have a row with you."

Her mixed signals were as crossed as the wires on a stormy night in Hut Three. "We have to row, Sophie. We have to row or I have to kiss you senseless. I think you'd prefer it, too, wouldn't you? There is no in-between here. We've been like a string of dynamite burning for years and it's finally reached the end of its fuse."

Sophie rolled up her sleeves. The casual tilt of her head seemed an almost rehearsed movement. Then she clicked on the wireless near the window and tuned the dial to a somewhat familiar piece. The last bars a whirl of violins speeding into a turbulent Strauss waltz.

Simon reached to loosen the tie he wasn't wearing and wondered whether the chaise longue or the bathtub would be more comfortable for the span of a night that found her comfortably asleep in his bed, her hair across the pillow probably catching the moonlight.

"I'll get you a blanket for the chaise longue."

"Oh, so I take that brocade monstrosity in the corner?"

"Yes. I am too fond of the sheets. Silk, you know. I went four years of the war without silk sheets." He was rattling nonsense to keep from saying something . . . anything. *He was just kissing her.* Or was she just kissing him?

"Rotten, wasn't it?" Sophie said. "All that scratchy regulation cotton. Even worse material for stockings. I could go to a bar at Claridge's and have them painted on—"

He erased the rest of her sentence with his mouth.

Simon paused, gulping for air. The look she gave him was at once full of desire and yet achingly vulnerable.

She moved to her suitcase, a gesture that almost suggested the opposite of her earlier determination to go back to Prague. It was strangely intimate to hear the wire clothes hangers scrape over the bar in the closet and then her silks as she hung up her garments. He studied the cutoff point of her brown hair past her swan-like neck.

"Why are you doing that?"

"Because for as long as I am here, I want to feel I am rooted somewhere." She surveyed a few blouses, smoothed the line of a sleeve.

Her task completed, she sighed and took in the room, then settled her eyes on his chessboard, black and white pieces standing at attention.

"What's this? Playing chess with yourself or a ghost?"

A whisper. "A sort of ghost. Don't move anything, please," he said when she had reached to touch one of the pieces.

She stepped back, still mulling over the board, a sly smile on her lips. "I just thought . . ." She picked up a black bishop, inspected it, then returned it to its spot.

"Thought what?"

"That maybe it was time we started to think about . . ." She kicked out of her shoes and began rolling down her stockings. "That I am reckless enough to be here with you." Sophie dug her toes into the plush carpet. She pulled her blouse out from her waistband and moved her hand to the bottom buttons.

He tried to turn away. He *willed* himself to turn away.

Sophie unfastened the last of her blouse buttons and wriggled out of the top. He watched her a moment before turning his eyes in the opposite direction to an arranged plastic plant on the table, a rather remarkably boring map of the Hofburg above the bureau, and finally to the heavily mustached portrait of Franz Josef. He stared at it until his eyes burned.

"Oh splendid!" Her voice was genuine as Beethoven funneled through the wireless. "The *Pathétique*." She stepped out of her skirt.

He could see it from his peripheral vision, and a current jolted through him and with it three little words tripping at the end of his tongue. Too close, considering how intimate their situation. He focused on the nice, safe emperor again.

"You are not undressing in front of me, Sophie." He knew she wouldn't willfully use him, so he forced himself to read in her body language what she wouldn't form in words.

"I don't see you leaving the room." She cast him a coy smile. *"Husband." That* drew his attention. She smoothed out the wrinkles in her slip.

Simon observed the slightest tremor in the movement that belied the confidence in her voice. She was asserting her own brand of bravery, not manipulation. Her tone said one thing, her body language another.

She was choosing to be vulnerable with him, but in unrolled stockings and an unbuttoned collar. And he would hold on to the trust she asserted even as she evaded his questions.

"I merely think that . . ." He nudged his glasses up the bridge of his nose. It was just a chessboard. She was just an opponent. Or, alternatively, a message in need of decryption. *Compartmentalize, Simon!*

"I merely think that—Sophie! How . . . ? Why . . . ? What do you expect me to do?" The slip was alluring. What was *in* the slip even more so. It was right. It was fair. He would never look at or feel about another woman the way he did her. He had bound himself to her with the hasty ring and the hasty words that slipped out in that small church.

She kicked a stocking away. The gesture drew his attention to one shapely calf.

"And I, darling, was fashioned to keep that conversation as light and inconsequential as a meringue." She blinked up at him.

Simon folded his glasses and set them next to the plant.

"And now you're all flustered."

"Yes! In the course of an evening I've been shot at, we've fought, we've kissed, and you've undressed in front of me and . . ." Simon stopped, poured a drink, and considered asking how she was *not* flustered. But then he remembered that she was and was just playing through it in a different way than he was. "We just lived the same night."

"Being shot at." Sophie sighed and fell onto the sofa.

"Your flat was ransacked," he said softly. "Sophie, what do you have in your possession? You must have something that you're returning to Prague for."

She shook her head, then her gaze shifted to study the carpet. "But that near-death experience. It jolted something, didn't it? Sickness and health and all of it?"

"All of it?"

"All of it," she repeated casually, but a hint of uncertainty simmered under the surface that smoothed his mirth away. "Can it be enough that I'm here?" Her natural smile emerged, not one put on by expectation or the night.

"I miss what we were. Regret that I said daft things to you before you went to Prague." He pressed to keep them on course. "I miss my beautiful, desirable friend." *Blast!* There was no rule book. There was no play. He couldn't merely view her as a chess piece like the ones strewn across the squares of his board. For one thing, she was his *wife*. He liked that name better than the ones they had given each other over the chessboard at Camden.

Somewhere in the recesses of his mind, he recalled how she had forbidden him from stringing four letters together. The ones blasting him at the speed of his heart. He liked the way those letters felt on his tongue.

Liked them enough to surrender.

The *Pathétique*, second movement. Sophie could still feel the notes buzzing in her fingertips from playing the grand Bösendorfer at Ashton and the upright at Simon's Mayfair house. Now, through Beethoven's city, she focused on it in a waning attempt to keep control of her emotions that were quickly rising to match the intensity in Simon's blue eyes as they roamed her face and stopped on her mouth. She liked this Simon, no longer content to conceal the words she often figured were in the clench of his jaw.

He leaned forward. She gave the slightest nod and the dip of her chin, aware that he hovered in wait of permission.

His lips touched hers, tentatively at first. She knew then that the song she was hearing for the thousandth time would never sound the same.

The kiss was different now. With this kiss he pursued a conversation stronger than words, one that assured her he meant to live every last vow he had muttered during their rapid-fire ceremony at Bletchley.

Her confidant. Her barrier. Gold-rimmed glasses removed, collar undone. And she knew that she meant to live every last vow back . . .

except for a *few* omissions as to where she had come from and what she was doing there.

A magnetic field drew her so strongly toward him, she had little control over where the bounds of friendship and their long-promised alliance ended and this new stirring began.

"I meant every word, Sophie," he said against her lips. "In the church. I know you were doing it to help me secure Camden, but I meant it."

She wasn't sure she could bear the weight of his honesty. While he held her close, her heart thrummed with the reminder of her grandmother's rebellion.

But this wasn't entrapment. This was *Simon*.

The longer she stayed in his arms, the more she realized how little they needed that word—or any other—at all.

As long as she didn't hear it, could she show it?

CHAPTER 27

L ater, with Sophie asleep beside him, Simon was overcome with a strange intuition that their lovemaking was just another undeniable proof. She had defended him to his father. She had married him. She had gone to Vienna for him, and now she had shown him a part of herself no other person on the planet knew.

She *loved* him. She had to love him. Every instance proved she did.

No. He couldn't measure his certainty of her love by past actions, so why was he determined to do so now?

Other than *every* last thing had changed.

"Touch has a memory." Simon had been forced to memorize the Keats poem in school, never knowing that the words would someday be made manifest in more than a flick of a match on a cigarette, or his hold on a sherry decanter, or his fingers framing the curve of her cheek. *Better than the other senses*, he refined the poem.

He didn't know how she was still sleeping when he wanted to bottle every moment inside.

Sure, a few thoughts barreled through his brain once they had finally exhausted every variation and she had retreated warm and supple right next to him. If he had been too hasty or if he had said something while distracted or if he had lost control, he led with his heart. And with every touch and progression of their night together, he had committed to her more deeply, sewn himself into her.

Simon flicked on the bedside light before he reached for his cigarettes and lighter. He struck a light and pressed the cigarette to his lips. A long moment later, the sheets rustled beside him and Sophie blinked up at him, shading her eyes.

"Pass that over then," she said sleepily, by way of greeting, and shifted up so they were shoulder to shoulder against the headboard.

"This is all I want for the rest of my life." He handed her the cigarette. It was a motion familiar to their friendship and banter, yet brand new here.

"Smoking in bed? Rather dull." But her smile was incandescent. Her cigarette was poised at the same angle as her head, thoughtfully inclined.

Was she remembering? Did she have regrets? She had been shy at first, then completely trusting. She allowed him to take the lead, and he would never find an appropriate way—in shared smoke or words—to express how grateful he was for that trust.

She handed him the cigarette nub, and he took a final puff, then extinguished it into an empty tumbler on the side table. "Are you all right?"

"Perfectly all right." She pressed her nose to his shoulder. She was pliant and he hoped happy. Their being together was a certainty, wasn't it? An eventuality.

With her ease and her trust, Simon felt in many ways that he was meeting himself for the first time. The Simon who truly had Sophie. His shoulders settled. On one hand it was blasted irony that he would choose to finally pursue their love story at this moment when he couldn't see the hand she might be playing.

No. If he analyzed it, he might pull away, build a wall, and barricade his heart before she could break it.

He swallowed down the clump of words that had been a companion to him for far longer than he had sense to recognize them. Sophie was playing her left fingers over the coverlet. He stole her hand and she didn't stop, mimicking notes up his forearm instead.

"I don't want you to go back to Prague." But this time it had nothing to do with what she might or might not be doing there and all to do with wanting to rise beside her and hear her breath before he drifted to sleep.

She shook her head. "It's too important."

"What is it you're searching for? Adameck? That's the man who found you."

"His boss. Overseer?" Her head leaning against the headboard turned toward Simon. "He is the one I am working for in Prague."

"And?"

"Simon, is this night just so you can lure secrets from me?" And while the question was light, he interpreted the slight uncertainty in her voice.

His heartbeat quickened. "No." But he could understand how she went there: tit for tat. It was how he was raised. If you doled out a favor, your name was scrawled on an invisible ledger for later.

He searched her eyes: curious and shaded. "I've arranged a key." He could give this much to her. "I've encrypted it with anything . . . untoward. Diana helped me."

He didn't want to be whispering these secrets in the half-light. He'd rather share terms of endearment, soft and certain, like Charles Boyer to Hedy Lamarr in the moonlight in *Algiers*. Instead, Simon said, "It allows me to encrypt places and names of men who are bartering illegally, using the Soviets to starve out the Austrians for their own gain. Wielding political power." He didn't imagine her stiffening beside him. "Starling." He took Sophie's hand and spread it over the coverlet.

Too many words were running through his brain like too many notes crammed into a Mozart libretto presented to the emperor.

"And what is the key, Simon? You always have a key."

Concerto no. 17 in G Major. *Sophie's concerto.*

"K. 453." His work in Vienna, everything he never spoke of, culminated in the Starling Concerto.

She was the answer.

Sophie stretched her arms behind her head and stared at the ceiling above the bed. In a few hours the bells outside would toll and the delicious smell of the dense yet sweet Wiener *Brot* she loved would trip over the tiles and she would leave.

"Sophie," he said softly. "If there is something you want to tell me?"

Sophie froze. "Don't do that, Simon."

His expression evened out. "I love you! I always have, and I was too much of a coward to defy your stupid wish never to say it." He leaned up on his elbow. "I bottled it into friendship and needing you to run all over Vienna for me and share cigarettes at Bletchley Park and outshoot me. But I have since that party at Ashton, and I will forever. And you love me. I know you do! You show it in a thousand and one ways."

Sophie stilled. His assertion hit her like an anvil. He said it. They had *promised*. The word triggered the recollection of her grandmother's scent wafting as she strolled across the polished marble and waxed floors of Ashton. Sophie supposed it was inevitable he *might* say it.

But he said it so evenly. Strongly. No irony.

The sheet hadn't been torn from her, but it might as well have been. "You weren't supposed to say that."

"Oh blast, Sophie."

"You shouldn't have said that, Simon."

His eyes bored into hers. "You're the part of myself that always adds up, that I don't need to justify." He touched her cheek. "Don't you see?"

She saw the strength it took him to forge the words. "Then . . ." She only *just* kept her voice from a whimper. What else would he exact from her with those words? She could explore their meaning in a touch or a caress, much like she could interpret a complicated musical phrase.

Would he demand she stay at his side? Certainly he had done so when concerned about her safety. What about when their mission was over? When life took them back to England? Back at Camden with silver tea sets catching the light and a dinner menu to consult with the cook.

"Then *what*?" His voice was gentle, coaxing. "Then it breaks your rule? The one you made me agree to before we were married? That we can share a kiss now and then, that I can take a bullet for you if needed, but we can never say what we feel? I showed you what I feel and you showed me too. Curse it, Sophie, we just spent—" Simon rose a little higher up the headboard and seemed to fight for control. "I thought we just acknowledged that our relationship ran a bit deeper."

An understatement.

She had a million and one memories from their night together. Was this it then? Could she be reckless to a point? Give way to a point?

"Is it something I did, Sophie?"

How could she not be ready? Even with him? She was just as responsible for their tempo, for the rise and variance of their movement. She was willing to throw her heart into the pace he set.

It was so easy to express her passion into leaning over the piano keyboard and feeling the press of the keys through the long lines of her fingers. This night was of a similar timbre. But words? She had been taught to fashion words into a defense.

"Our parents are *not* what love is. My *father* was not what love is," he said. "You're only scared of it because you think you know what it is. But I do." He nodded. "I do because I love you. It's my fault that you didn't know it. That I turned you into a barometer for my other relationships. It was *my* poor attempt at self-preservation that led us here. If I did anything tonight to push you away . . ."

He shook his head. "*No.* I won't apologize for telling you what you *deserve* to know. I've only said those words to one other human in the whole of my lifetime. That used to make me sad, make me feel that I was something less, but now I know why. It was for *this*. Because those words were only—always—meant for you."

Sophie pulled the sheet up to her chin. His touch chilled on her skin now, even as his words burned. He grabbed her hand, but she pulled it back and looked into his eyes—to watch his heart break.

The man who truly cherished her would recognize how the realm he cast them into would startle her. No. That wasn't fair. Or was that just an excuse? She was willing to follow him through every tempo he set . . . until the medium changed.

"There's a grace in this, Sophie. In accepting the way I feel about you. The way you feel about me too."

She slid out of the bed and anchored herself to connecting points around the room to regain control: the moonlight filling the window, the clothes unfurled out of her case and those carefully hung over the wardrobe bar. The contrast between what was in her head and the part of her heart still thrilling toward him. "I should think about getting to the station."

She could catch the train before the first bells chimed and their entire nearly perfect night had come full circle. "You broke your word." Sophie tried to keep the tremor from her lips and failed.

"I only broke my word if I offered it to you to secure you or to bind you to my estate. I only broke my word if I said it and didn't mean it. I love you."

My how easily he said it. She envied him that. When she tried to open her mouth to speak, no words emerged. Part of her *wanted* to say it. She didn't regret what was shared between them—in action, at least. But in words? She still felt betrayed by it. That he had pinned her with it.

Certainly last night would spin over and over in Sophie's head but would always end with him saying what she asked him *not* to. And the movement would stop without a coda or refrain. An unfinished line like the chaos of Shostakovich or the rising crescendo of a Beethoven symphony. In music she found romance and surety in incompletion; here it made her feel foolish.

"You know how important it was to me," she whispered.

"That I lie?"

Her heart accelerated several beats. With the certainty that her time with Novak was not at its end and that Simon—with his spoken vows and acknowledged love—would hold her fast, she needed to *run*.

By running away she would certainly shatter his heart; by staying she would twist her own until she regretted it. She could trust him . . . to a point. Give in . . . to a point. But he was requiring full surrender.

"You can trust me," Simon reminded her.

It was cowardly to collect her things, to slide her clothes off the hangers in the wardrobe and move them to her case. Cowardly to turn to the window and avert her gaze before he could meet it. But oh, how her mind transformed both into an act of bravery.

The last time his voice had wavered to this degree were their last moments at Camden. She had pledged her loyalty to him. But then her independence wasn't at risk. She would always need a contingency plan.

Which made it even more difficult, if not impossible, when she finished collecting her things and turned away.

CHAPTER 28

If Sophie was able to compose herself enough to walk away after the night they had shared, then all of Simon's certainty was for naught. Yet he had been so *sure* she loved him.

Simon fell back against a pristine coverlet, the wireless melding into crackly Mozart: a blend of perfect harp and flute. It had been only a matter of hours since she shut him out and averted her gaze. But in the incessant tick of the clock, it was a lifetime. And in the strands of music funneling through the airwaves, it was a constant reminder that settled with the deft grace of an anvil.

While the room and music were uncomfortably pristine, everything else tasted stale. He was insatiable for her. Like a newlywed lost in the haze of leftover passion from a honeymoon. It should have been his honeymoon: Sophie in his arms and as close as his breath, feeling the same way, meeting him halfway and dispelling his uncertainty.

He loved her for all of those reasons certainly. Their marriage, now, was complete. It had terrified and exhilarated him until every small piece of his life fit together. And he felt—no, he *knew*—she reciprocated. Until she didn't.

She was ripped from him, and yet her shadow was still impressed on his side. Worse still, she had *chosen* to be ripped from him. She was bound by what he interpreted as a fear of love. Well, it wasn't as if he was conditioned or prepared for it either, but he was no longer terrified by it. Doubtless she was. Yet, her leaving was a step too far.

The unbearable silence drove him to the wireless where he fell into the cautious, careful rhythm. German voices preceding a long concerto that just made him conjure Sophie's long fingers dancing on the keys, chasing the next movement or signature change.

He hadn't realized he had fallen asleep until the *brrrring* of the phone on the bureau startled him. As he was blinking awake, he noticed the sun at its zenith out the window. "Yes?" Simon's heart constricted. If it was Sophie . . .

But the voice was British. Finchley. His father's solicitor. Simon cursed that he had left the Sacher's forwarding address on the table of the Mayfair flat, soothing his conscience enough just to know if the right person needed to find him in an emergency, they'd put two and two together.

"Your father wants to speak to you. He's very ill." Finchley paused a moment. "Sir, I should warn you. He's fading fast."

Simon didn't realize Charles Barrington was fading, let alone fast. He adjusted the receiver just in time to hear his father's voice rasped with pain and a long bout of coughing.

"I'm here to remind you of the addendum to my will," Barrington said.

"Wonderful timing," Simon muttered. That addendum led to his marriage, to Sophie looking up expectantly at him in a rapid proposal and then, wondrously, when said marriage became truth.

"I am reminding you of how determined I am, lest you squander my estate."

Simon shoved his glasses up his nose. If Charles Barrington was truly ill, Simon would conjure a sense of propriety at least. A man like Barrington would give in to temper. Simon would not. "I didn't realize you were ill," Simon said as his father fought for a breath.

"I want you to live the rest of your life knowing that my final thought was of how you are not a Barrington." His father wheezed. "That you were unloved. That you were responsible for Julius dying for a pencil-pushing bureaucrat at the Foreign Office while he shed blood for our country." Barrington coughed again.

His so-called father used his last breaths to tell Simon he was an unloved failure. The last reserves of his energy to add another demoralizing brick to a solid wall of resentment.

"I married Sophia Huntington-Villiers years ago," Simon said blandly. Though his heart pulsed. Had it truly been years ago or only the previous night? "I have met your conditions. Camden is rightfully mine. My *wife* is of equal or greater consequence."

He waited for Barrington to interrupt. "My mother loved me. She just couldn't show it in your presence." He cleared the emotion from his throat. "I will take care of the estate my mother cherished. Moreover, I will continue to care for the welfare of our tenants and ensure the grounds are kept to your high standards."

Simon sounded like he was reciting Latin verbs in first form. He didn't care about anything *less* than Camden in the moment, and yet it ironically bound him to her.

And even as the bitter recognition that Barrington's last painful breaths were reserved for him, Simon was oddly numb to it.

The line went silent. Doubtless Barrington had heard every last abhorrent word. But then the man's voice sputtered through again: "Don't make your mother a saint, Simon. I didn't. I knew she was going to . . . she said that . . . Bloody feudal system. Then it was easy to use what I knew against her. The same thing—"

"Pardon?"

The reception crackled. ". . . made her ill. And I had had enough."

Simon waited. *Had enough?* Made her ill? Was Barrington rambling, or was he using his last breaths for a purpose?

"Enough," Barrington repeated, though his timbre now sounded faint and faraway. "Of her scholar. Of her Communism. Of . . ." Barrington trailed into a mélange of mutterings Simon couldn't decipher beyond his own interpretation.

After several moments of gently calling Charles's name and gradually raising his voice, Simon gaped at the receiver. He would hear no more slander against his mother or himself. No more.

Numb, he turned to the window to watch the pedestrian traffic on the Albertinaplatz below. Women holding shopping bags and coffee cups, with resoled shoes and heavy hearts.

"Lord Barrington." Finchley's voice was muffled through the receiver. "Lord Barrington," he repeated.

Simon didn't need to hear this. Barrington clearly was slipping away while his solicitor still spoke to him. On the third repetition, Simon said, "Yes."

"Your father is gone, my lord."

The title. Another name. Another label. The one he had married Sophie to secure. He was the eighth earl of Camden. "Mr. Barre is just fine."

"Sir."

"Finchley . . ." Simon swallowed. "H-how . . . when did—?"

"His lungs, sir. Raging cough. He wouldn't see the doctor."

Too proud, perhaps. Or too stubborn.

"Thank you, Finchley." But the startled tremor in his voice was hard to contain. "I didn't know he was ill or I . . ." What would he have done if he *had* known?

"He didn't want you to know."

Of course not. Then Simon might have had the upper hand. Would the man ever had spoken of Margaret's death if not for being a few breaths from his own demise?

"My lord, there's a lot of paperwork here."

"There always is, isn't there?" Simon hung up the receiver.

Stunned.

His brain was a crowded attic to begin with, notwithstanding the information barging in. Was his father lucid?

Was Charles Barrington responsible for her demise?

Rubbish. He was getting too emotional after a near sleepless night and Sophie walking out on him. Simon pressed his eyes shut a moment. *Compartmentalize.* First, paperwork.

Much like the paperwork resulting from the last time he had seen his father. Not his father. Barrington. His real father seemed farther away somehow, now that Barrington wouldn't expose a secret much like the one about his mother's Communist enthusiasm.

Barrington had rambled on the phone. But it only drew a starker line between their last face-to-face conversation and the information Simon read between his father's staggered breaths. His mother was a Communist. Simon had pretended not to care in the moment of the revelation—even as it pervaded every step he had taken since the war and beyond.

His stepfather had seen to her demise.

He would keep his assessment clinical. His mother had threatened to leave with her lover and Barrington had an ultimatum.

Simon's childhood was that ultimatum.

Even as he tried to block the dagger in Barrington's voice that day at Camden after Julius died. Even as Simon tried to blur the same ornate panels and portraits that had witnessed his half brother's cruelty to Sophie. Barrington was dead and Simon wanted to know more.

He lifted the receiver. To acknowledge the worst of your history was to shove your reputation down a few pegs. It didn't matter here if he was Barrington or Barre. Rather, that he was the man uncertain enough in stitches that had sewn up his history that he would ask a favor.

Gabe, thankfully, was in his office when Simon rang. "This request is a long shot." But Gabe had a way around archives and connections as well.

"That just makes it more interesting," Gabe replied. "Eternity?"

"No. A matter of personal interest."

Simon spoke of a historian who would have been at the estate of

Charles Barrington—Camden, Sussex—about thirty years earlier. He could hear the scrape and pressure of Gabe's pencil on the other end. "He was researching the feudal system and had strong Communist affiliations." He trusted Gabe.

Simon rang off, tenting his fingers on his temples. Then he retrieved his fedora from the side stand and studied the lining. *This is good. This is what you want.* A play. A cipher. His real father. The words about his mother that hovered between a deathbed confession and an insult.

A *distraction*. As long as he was thinking about Barrington, he wasn't thinking about Sophie.

Until he was.

The life he had pledged to her beyond perceived obligation to his mother and Camden. The name he took *because* of her. The marriage in name and paper forged to combat his father and yet all too conveniently echoing through his brain and heart.

Sophie was still here. In the room. Around him. Even as he attempted to grapple with the magnitude of Barrington's passing. Of Simon's new name.

He compartmentalized as best he could when someone knocked on his door. He crossed to open it and a bellhop stood there. "Message for you, sir."

Simon fumbled in his pocket for a coin and accepted the small slip of paper.

A chess move.

Simon raked his fingers through his hair. The last thing he wanted to do was screw his brain on straight and attempt to find a pattern, not only in the moves he was playing but in the erratic patterns of Das Flüstern's communication with him.

Simon took out the previous note: the one that mentioned looking both ways before crossing the street. Did it have something to do with Simon and Sophie being shot at even though the man was in Prague?

Simon let out a long breath and turned to the chessboard. "I'm getting sick of this." He cursed at the board. A slow game that wouldn't end. And he wasn't getting any further in identifying the double agent playing it.

I'm raising the stakes, the message accompanying the play read.

Simon picked up the white pawn and moved it by proxy to d3 for his phantom player. It was an oddly familiar move, and one that took him close to Simon's remaining queen and knight.

Simon retreated to the bureau and took out his book on chess philosophy and flipped pages to the passage he sought.

If a player makes a surprising and unanticipated move, the player may interpret it as intentional to spark a reactive move.

Simon stalled with the piece in his hand. He was close to instinctively making a move. He almost smiled. The board looked rather like the one spread before him when he won his first national championship—just before his mother died and he left for Cambridge. He remembered everyone asking if he was nervous. And yet he never was when faced with the chessboard. It was always familiar. A safe and logical friend.

But now the board meant something different with a faceless nemesis in the city Villiers had retreated to.

Simon tucked his discarded black piece from Das Flüstern's move into his pocket. The phone rang again, and he had half a mind to ignore it. "Yes!" he nearly barked into the receiver a moment later.

Brent Somerville.

"What is it Somerville?" Simon was too tired to squelch the curt tone of his voice.

"I'm at Moser's office. He's dead."

CHAPTER 29

Simon froze. Moser couldn't be dead.

"You have a gun with you?" Simon asked, pressing his fingers to his temple.

Brent sighed. "You know exactly how good I am with those."

"Brent! I don't have time for your sarc—"

"Yes, I have a gun."

"Stay put. I'll come to you."

It didn't take Simon more than twenty minutes in a taxicab outside the Sacher to be deposited at the university and the block with Moser's office.

Brent sat on the corner of the desk, his gun aimed at Simon the moment he entered.

Simon held up his hands in mock surrender.

Brent slid off the desk and tucked the gun into his pocket. "I should have called the medics or the police, but my finger kept dialing Sacher's."

Simon took a quick peek around the shadows. Papers were scattered everywhere and the phone was off the hook. It was the same office he had visited before, across the hall from Brent Somerville's own and yet not remotely the same. Simon didn't look at the body, just made out a pair of shoes and a rolled crystal glass. The decanter near the wireless was open.

"I heard something. I was on my way out. He must have . . . see . . ."

Moser had taken a side table and lamp down with him. Simon swept his gaze over the desk while Brent was occupied with something on the floor near the leg of the desk.

"Simon." His voice was urgent. "Look at this."

A piece of paper lay next to the body, and the words scrawled in Gabriel Langer's bold print startled him:

STARLING TURNED.

Simon took a moment to try to squeeze the breath out of his chest. Why would Gabe have left a note like that? And why was he delivering it to Moser? Or . . . Simon flicked a look at the decanter and in the direction of Moser's body.

No. It was his mind playing tricks on him. "We can't stay here," he said a moment later. The words in Langer's handwriting were blazoned on his mind. He half-shoved Brent out of the door and quickly tucked the note in his pocket. Who else had seen it?

"Did you see Langer in the university offices today?"

"No."

Simon didn't know if the killer was around, nor did he care to find out. His mind traveled on a singular track. "Walk."

"Simon . . ."

"Walk, Somerville!"

Brent continued forward. Simon stayed half a step behind. "We should call someone."

"We'll call someone once we get you home." Simon didn't want to be stuck in endless interrogation, and he had a sixth sense that saw him wanting to see Brent safely to his flat as soon as possible.

Starling turned.

Simon trusted Langer. He and Sophie had worked closely together. If Langer had suspicions, if Sophie *had* turned, then Langer would know. But why did he tell Moser instead of Simon?

He felt his throat close. Starling *turned*. She was in Prague where Brighton and his team were narrowing in on Das Flüstern, and there was a chapter of her life Simon hadn't deciphered. What could she have taken from him the night they had spent together? He rotated his cuff link at an alarming pace.

No. She *wouldn't* have . . .

He racked his brain, thinking of what she might have taken. Other than his trust and his vulnerability.

Simon swallowed hard to become the Simon the world expected— eyes glaring ahead and clipped voice in perfect control.

Brent theorized a mile a minute: "Did it have something to do with Moser's wanting to hire the men we saw at the exhibit? Was it who Moser was connected with politically? Or perhaps the antiquity pieces of value in his office?"

Simon remained silently in stride beside Brent until they neared the Ring and hailed a taxi. Simon wasn't sure if he cared enough about himself in the moment to discover what happened to Langer or even to look to his own self-preservation.

He fixed his jaw and focused his eyes ahead so intently at the night zooming by the car window that he almost forgot Brent was next to him. He remained completely silent as they wound through the streets to Domgasse.

And in the long, silent beats, Simon felt something shifting.

And that included the Somervilles.

He was becoming accustomed to wading in the dark for an answer, but he also assumed when he had invited them to Vienna, he would have a surer sense of control. With that faltering, Brent was wading into unnecessary risk.

They rounded the narrow cobblestones of Mozart's street. The taxi stopped and they exited. There was a small cobbled walkway, slick from the earlier rain, that glistened on the precipice of a sudden freeze.

Simon followed Brent on the ascent two flights up to Brent and

Diana's flat, feeling more than hearing Brent's expression of panic. He stiffened, then sprinted inside after they reached the second floor.

"Diana!" Brent shouted.

Silence. A burnt smell wafting from the kitchen, mismatched cushions on the sofa, a slow stream from the wireless. Then . . . an overturned bureau and desk. Papers strewn on the carpet.

Simon's chest constricted. He was responsible for Brent and Diana.

The window was open just enough so the breeze could tickle the lace curtains. He tossed his fedora onto the table and ran his palm over his mouth and down his neck. The room had been ransacked.

"Diana!" Brent's voice was louder now.

They spun at the sound of footsteps in the hallway, Simon's hand instinctively reached for his gun.

A long exhale unwound his shoulders and spiraled through his fingers the moment she stepped into view. "Diana, are you all right?"

"Look at this place," she said breathlessly. "I went down to see if the doorman had seen anyone come in or out. I was at the market when it happened."

Brent gripped her elbow, surveying the damage, and Diana shook her head. He shuffled his wife inside, settled her into a chair, then saw to the kettle.

Simon strolled to the bureau and looked through the chaos of up-turned drawers. But it was more a show for Brent than anything.

"What do you think he was looking for?" Brent's voice teetered between annoyance and incredulity.

Brent was wavering. He had just found a dead body, and Simon had kept him from reporting it. Then he found his wife amid scattered papers and a careful upset of their daily existence.

Diana held up the small revolver. "You will both be happy to know I had this at the ready." But Brent wasn't able to see her determined expression.

"Whoever did this took quite the look around," Simon observed sourly. A similar frantic upheaval to the one in Moser's office.

Diana moved to stand. "I should clean that up."

"No you should not." Brent handed her a cup of tea.

Something about the easy and eager way she accepted her tea and the slight wrinkle of her nose in thought tugged him back to a time when all he had was her loyalty and complete trust, and it set him off-balance and just proved how tired and overwrought he was.

"Simon." She was watching him. "Maybe you should be sitting down."

He gathered up the papers first, putting them into a semblance of order. Then he ran his hand over his face. He could read her worry, but he knew it wasn't for herself.

She was still watching him. "Brent, get him a drink, would you?"

Simon scratched at his unshaved jaw. He accepted a glass from Brent and stared at it a long moment. His ears were buzzing and his heart was racing. "Well." Simon took a sip of his scotch, struck a match on the side table, and lit a cigarette. "Now you can tell me where Sophie is."

"Excuse me?" Diana said.

"I don't like your tone, Barre," Brent added.

"Give us a moment, darling," Diana said with a smile.

Brent looked at Simon a moment before he acquiesced. "Just don't snap at her."

Simon looked around the flat: run-down, compared to his suite at the Sacher, with wallpaper peeling in the corners and a radiator that announced its presence if you stepped on an uneven board the wrong way. Simon always felt the room was comforting. Right now, it suffocated him.

She wrinkled her brow. "I wouldn't lie to you, Simon. I know how important she is to you." She let out a long breath, her eyes shining with anger. Helpless anger, perhaps, but anger nonetheless. "Tell me what is going on."

Simon's pride held him like a vise. He didn't want to admit Sophie had left him. Even if Diana couldn't comprehend the depth of what her leaving actually meant. Nonetheless, he slowly loosened his grip on the armrests. Langer's note burned a hole in his pocket.

"I don't know where she is. It must be . . . serious then."

The catch in her voice tamed the tempest raging inside him. Simon fell back in his chair a moment and released the tension in his jaw. His eyes glared so intensely on her they began to burn. "I'm sorry, Diana."

"I hope since he didn't find what he was looking for, he won't come back," she said hopefully. "I'll never tell a soul about your key, Simon."

K. 453.

Simon opened his mouth but no words came out. It had been a secret between him and Diana and now Sophie. He had told Sophie about the encryption the night before. He stretched his arms a moment and with the movement came an idea.

"You and Sophie left the city last month. You took my car and went to an abbey. Tell me about that meeting."

Diana nodded. "A man named Tomas Adameck. I didn't hear what they spoke of though. Sophie was completely silent about it."

"She's completely silent about many things." Simon kept the bitterness from his tone.

Evening light was mellowing and the dust motes near the window were more pronounced over the radiator.

Brent reappeared with his empty teacup and Simon rose to meet him. "I'll take care of what happened this evening." He left Brent to fill in the blanks to Diana. Brent hadn't pressed Simon on the note about Sophie and Simon was grateful.

CHAPTER 30

With every step, every sputtering streetlight, and every toll from Peterskirche's bells, Simon's heartbeat mounted at a fevered pace. He had Gabe's note in his pocket.

He became increasingly aware of a slight footfall behind him, then an incessant tapping of what he soon determined to be a rifle butt belonging to a man in Soviet garb with a face Simon recognized.

He gave him a furtive look before continuing, but the tapping continued louder.

His fingers flexed, ready to grab his own weapon or lunge into an attack.

The soldier seemed to read the intensity in Simon's eyes. Yes, he was wielding a service-issue rifle but flinched when Simon produced his gun and aimed it at him. Perhaps he was so used to threatening people with his rifle, and how few retaliated.

"You're too dedicated to your job." Simon seethed. "There's being conscientious and then there's being insufferable. Too insufferable." Simon leaned in, with sudden realization. "The kind of insufferable someone pays for." Simon steadied the gun.

The soldier relaxed his stance and fell back a step. Simon recalled that the man had hurt Diana and followed Sophie. Simon now had the upper hand, and it was worth more to find out what the man wanted rather than assert dominance.

Simon loosened his grip on his gun and tucked it back into his coat. *Take a different approach.*

The soldier glanced around. Simon noticed how lean he was and how pronounced his cheekbones. Simon retrieved his cigarette case and offered him one. The kid took it greedily. While he was blowing on his fingers and rubbing the cigarette in his palms, Simon procured a lighter.

The soldier's bright eyes stared at Simon a long moment. "Why would I talk to you?"

"Other than the cigarette and the clearly effective threat?" Simon reached back in his pocket and produced a wad of Austrian schillings. "Because I'm interesting," Simon said sardonically. "You should be relieved I am so accommodating."

"He told me to watch for a"—he stumbled on the words—"a tall woman."

Simon pieced together the parts of Sophie's life he was barred from: her work in Prague, for one. Perhaps he should have kept a sharper eye on her. But he wasn't a watchdog. Even now, knowing the treacherous men who had orbited around her made him feel as if he was at the center of a secret he wasn't supposed to be keeping: about Adameck, about Sophie.

All of this new perspective because Simon had said the forbidden word that drove her away.

What would it be like standing here attempting to extract secrets if she hadn't dashed out of his life when he told her he loved her?

There were other similarly dressed guards, sure. This portion of the city was always well guarded. But on this particular night, they were straight as the columns on the Theseus Temple nearby.

"Did he pay you?" Simon asked and was met with the slightest shift. The young man's eyes widened again and Simon straightened his shoulders.

"Yes. For the tall woman."

"And the flat in Domgasse?" Simon narrowed his blue eyes. "And to follow her to a pawnshop?"

The soldier stiffened. "I won't give you a name!"

Simon gave a curt nod. He already had an idea. Sidorov. He didn't know the extent to which Sophie was connected, but she was. The man had tried to attack Simon trying to find Starling.

"You attacked a blonde woman outside a Pfandhaus in the Neuer Markt. Why?"

"Will you give me money? As you said, he can pay me. Then you can pay me."

Simon rolled his eyes, reached into his pocket, and extracted a few bills. "Why did you attack a blonde woman outside a Pfandhaus? Clearly you're more accustomed to wandering around trying to scare people."

"Because he said I could, if it meant scaring the tall one."

"Well, it backfired, didn't it? She wasn't scared."

The soldier nodded. "Maybe not yet."

The bells tolled and Simon put his gun away. The soldier took off quickly through the Innere Stadt as Simon crossed the Graben, passing the large gold-tinted Plague Column designed to ward off illness and disease, and sidestepped blockades en route to Seilergasse.

The Pfandhaus Sophie frequented was tucked into the Neuer Market where *Pensions* boarded the lucky residents who had found housing in the torn city, where jewelers and tailors awaited better times amid boarded-up windows and sandbags in turrets and crevices. Men visible in the windows of cafés sipped the last of their coffee before they set off into the fast-falling night.

Simon approached the awning with *Müller* etched in a bold, bright font. He peered through the darkness, then removed a metal file from his pocket and picked the lock. He glanced up and noticed the bell above the door.

After hearing the first toll warm from nearby Kapuzinerkirche, he decided to wait until they warmed to full chime before he pushed the door open completely. He called out a quick, "*Gruss Gott.*" Silence.

Flecks of dust motes settled on books and statuettes. Simon cast a furtive look to the door before he walked past a tall Baroque-era chest and through a small hallway where a slice of light bled through a slightly open door.

He waited. Then took a step forward. The office was empty and in a perfect disarray of cluttered organization. He let out a long exhale, then narrowed in on the desk and a piece of musical manuscript worn and smudged by thumbprints and time. A name and an address in Kampa Island were written on the side of the folder. *Jan Novak.*

At a slight rustle, Simon moved back but kept his index finger on the manuscript.

"Who are you?" the proprietor asked. A hint of recognition flickered in the man's intense gaze.

"I'm a friend of Starling's."

Müller looked weary, the fine lines around his eyes and forehead more haggard as he stepped into the light.

"Put that down." There was a slight, almost undetectable quiver in the man's voice as he focused on Simon's careful handling of the paper. "I rent a flat above the shop. I can always tell when someone is in my shop."

Simon smoothed a page of the manuscript while focusing intently on its bars and signature. "I'm no musician, but it doesn't seem like there's a full piece here."

Müller shook his head, walked by Simon, and lowered himself gingerly into his chair, easing the folder and its contents in his direction. His shoulders raised in a rigid hunch. For seconds he was still as a statue, no movement, but his breath permeated the air.

Simon didn't know why Sophie had left, and he didn't understand why *Starling turned*, but he wanted to complete the last pieces of her puzzle.

Müller's eyes sought Simon's. "He says that he loves Mozart. He says that he is working for an important client and Starling believes him. *Špaček*. That's what he calls her."

It was clear as soon as the words fell from his mouth that Müller regretted them. "But I need proof that you are on her side."

"Proof?" Simon took a breath. Played a new move and steadied his gun. "Let's try a different conversation."

To his credit Müller's light gray eyes were filled not with fear but with curiosity. "I remember the first day I met her." His eyes sparkled a little. "Moser introduced us. I was thinking I had never seen a woman so tall before. And then she looks around my shop, appraising it as if she is measuring all of the wonders by their worth. She has a gift, you see. She sees the potential of things." He studied Simon. "And what do *you* see?" He didn't wait for Simon's answer. "I need proof that you will help her. That you will help here."

"As you can see, I am the one exacting demands." Simon gestured with his gun.

And whatever was reflected on Simon's face, in his slight responses, must have betrayed him because Müller wasn't frightened. He waited for Simon to follow his gaze. But all Simon saw were eighth notes and careful rests—the whole of a message she would tap out over her left knee in a language he never fully understood beyond her interpretation of it at the keyboard.

"What does Starling prize more than anything in the world?" Müller asked.

Simon had to give it to the man. He wasn't sure how he had factored into Sophie's leaving or the message in Gabe's handwriting, but these questions were a certain way to garner trust.

"Her pearls," Simon said with a dispassion he didn't feel. "They belonged to her grandmother."

"The manuscript is Mozart's German version of Handel's *Messiah: Der Messias*," Müller explained, clearly satisfied with Simon's answer.

"At least it *will* be. Starling has been charged, from what I gather, with bringing the pieces scattered in Prague together." He leaned over the notes and lines. "It looks like it could be from Mozart's era, but it is doubtless a copy. It cannot be the original."

Simon could feel the press of the man's gaze. "Musical pieces that scattered throughout the war have seen some wear."

"Indeed they have."

There was more to what Müller had in his possession than notes and bars. Simon waved his gun slightly. "Tell me about this one."

Müller reached into his pocket for a small magnifying glass. He held it up in surrender and Simon merely nodded.

"See here?" Müller motioned to the folder to an address in Kampa Island, Prague. "There is a man there named Jan Novak. He has been interested in myriad pieces for years. Anything rare. Sometimes he seemed more interested in the value than specifics." He shook his head. "Most men want to focus on one artist or field. It's odd that he's taken to musical fragments. Long before I had met Starling, he was known to me. Not unlike her, either."

"How is he not unlike her?"

"The way Starling can make people trust her and confide in her is remarkable. With no more than a word." He studied Simon a moment and seemed appeased enough to continue. "And what Novak did was remarkable too. Wanting to reunite treasures to their rightful place. Always seeming to know where something would turn up before it did. He had a sense."

Sophie had spoken about artifacts scattered across Europe as quickly as the thud of encroaching jackboots and the descent of the Nazis. This Novak, it seemed, did the same. And preternaturally so.

Müller had turned the pages on the Sophie Simon didn't know. "And Starling?"

The pawnshop owner was silent. Simon casually motioned toward the man with his gun. Judging by his calm manner, Müller clearly doubted Simon would fire it.

"An untrained eye would think this fragment was worth a fortune," Müller evaded the question about Sophie, "but there are small inconsistencies." He pointed the end of his magnifying glass at it. "Just above the signature here." He held the glass out to Simon, who set the gun on the desk a moment and accepted it.

Simon knew enough to decipher a clef in the time signature, but this was a slightly misshapen one. He held the glass back a moment and then again, trying to see the manuscript as Sophie would have. Without the aid of the magnifying glass—alongside his glasses—he wouldn't have noticed it unless he squinted.

But wouldn't she have known she was passing a message? Whatever it was, anything could be seen as a calculated risk.

"I may not read people well," Müller continued, "but I suspect Starling was either a remarkable actress or genuinely had no idea she was passing information at all. Hours perusing this piece has shown me it is more than meets the eye."

An infinity symbol for one. Simon set down the magnifying glass. "Were you expecting a message?"

"No. As I said, it was only recently that Novak was interested in music at all. And Starling must have been distracted or else she would have noticed this. And given her perception of its worth, I doubt she would want to be seen carefully scrutinizing it on a crowded train." He clicked his tongue.

Simon looked at the fragment again. Away from Müller it might wield even more secrets.

Simon tucked his revolver back into his jacket. "I know it's a lot to ask, but would you let me take the manuscript fragment?" He extended his wrist. "My wristwatch as collateral? Or money?"

Müller handed the folder to him with a curt nod. "Starling. Bring her back safely."

"Starling sure is going to a lot of trouble for something of such little value, then." Simon theorized.

"Ah, but that is where you are wrong. I can appraise based on the metrics of my trade. But that means I am halfway blind, ja? To Herr Novak, the piece is valuable as a sort of message. To my countrymen and to Herr Novak's countrymen, Mozart is a beloved son. You cannot determine the worth of something merely by assessing its perceived limitations."

———◦◦◦◦◦———

During the war, Sophie had once told Simon she supposed he had a greater capacity to love than most. "On account of your having experienced so little of it." Her voice was pragmatic as she flicked the ashes from her cigarette. "But it might be dangerous for you, darling. Because you like having your head screwed on straight. And maybe someday it will fog up those glasses of yours and blur the lines of your chessboard."

Simon treated the folder Müller had given him with utmost care as he crossed the short distance to his hotel room. Part of him ached for the previous night, when his worried edges and lines had been smoothed by Sophie's presence.

Now Simon's room buzzed with static, the usual perfumed corners stale.

He laid out the puzzle: Was this Novak Das Flüstern? He clearly had influence and access to the world of art through Müller.

But then there was Adameck. In his imaginative ledger and in the encrypted book he kept, Adameck was a far likelier candidate: One, the man met Sophie at an abbey. Two, he was well connected in Prague and Budapest with men familiar to both Gabe and Sophie. Three, he was somehow connected to many pieces of Simon's world in Vienna—and in far too many ways to be coincidental. But more blatantly—he was a registered member of the National Socialist Party and had tried to run Simon over.

Simon flicked on the lamp and revisited the manuscript. He didn't have Müller's eyes, but then Müller was looking for something completely different.

He stared at it until his eyes crossed, then put in a call to Tab Martin, whose voice finally patched through. Simon told him about Moser's dead body at his university office and how Brent Somerville had found it. Simon wasn't sure how, but he assumed Martin would have a way of ensuring it was taken care of. For all Simon knew, a caretaker would discover Moser as if Simon and Brent had never been there.

"Anything else?" Martin asked.

Starling turned was pressed into his pocket and seared his brain. Simon wouldn't offer that crucial information. Not yet.

"And you?" Martin asked. "Simon?"

But Simon was distracted by a knock at the door. "Hold on."

He answered and accepted the message, then ripped open the cream envelope with the hotel's insignia in hopes it was news about Sophie.

Ironically, it was from Gabe: *A Czech scholar named Jan Novak can be traced back to Sussex in the time period you had specified.*

Simon's eyes only flickered over the rest. He picked up the telephone handset.

"All right there, Barre?" Tab said.

Simon flexed his fingers to fight off the tremor beginning in them. He should tell Tab about Sophie. Even if he left out his theories about Brighton, Starling was a peripheral part of this operation.

But when Simon spoke it was as if through a tunnel. "I have somewhere to be."

CHAPTER 31

Wilsonovo Nádraží Station, Prague

The Vienna skyline was long behind Sophie when she noticed an absence above her collarbone. She jolted forward a moment. *Her pearls.* She wouldn't have left them purposely. And yet, when had she ever been without them? She reached for them so instinctively.

She sighed and fell back against the headrest. She knew exactly where the pearls were: on the side table at the Hotel Sacher next to the cuff links she had given Simon.

She trailed her finger down the raindrops on the windowpane as she smoothed away the prickles of guilt. Guilt if she had led him on just to leave. Yet how could she have led him on when she had felt every moment of the night as deeply as he did?

He overwhelmed her until she wanted to rail against him and run so far away that he couldn't hold her to say she loved him back. She told herself she was strong, acting of her own volition, protecting her heart and interests. But she knew she was just a coward hopping a border to get away.

As soon as the train skidded under one of the double-arched terminals into Wilsonovo nádraží station, Sophie called Novak from a booth in the station, letting him know she had arrived. The telephone line fizzled and crackled as she waited for his response.

It was a long while in coming. "Successful?"

"Herr Müller has what you asked me to give him."

"I have another errand for you." He mentioned a *zastavarna* across from St. Giles Church. Then he rang off, seemingly satisfied.

Sophie quickly found a taxicab in the queue outside the Wilsonovo nádraží. She had the driver detour so she could drop off her hastily packed luggage before proceeding to the pawnshop whose name Novak had given her.

She supposed it was the phone call from Sidorov before she had left for Vienna or the blast of the bullet that had propelled Simon to tackle her to the ground that kept her head turned slightly over her shoulder and her eyes panning out the window of the car.

When she reached her destination, a chill whispered over the back of her neck and shadowed her steps through a dark fairy tale of steeples and cobbles, where markets had spread for centuries and the martyrs enshrined in the statues stood sentry on the bridges and quarters. She found Husova Street: an uneven swerve of buildings shaped like a bass clef and hosting the Baroque church of St. Giles, now as familiar to her as a pawnshop snug between a haberdashery and a tailor.

After she exited the taxicab, Sophie tilted her hat, pursed her lips, and opened the door so the chime—not unlike the one at Müller's—rang out at her arrival.

Sophie gave Novak's name and presented the koruna he had given her along with a black leather folder she opened in order to safely tuck inside the piece of manuscript the shopkeeper had presented her.

The transaction was quick, with the shopkeeper barely looking up at her from the counter separating them. Though he did place pince-nez eyeglasses on his nose and inspect the manuscript carefully.

"You should tell him," the shopkeeper said in hesitant English. "As per his directive, someone came in and I turned him away. He had sought out two pieces of *Der Messias*. 'Let All the Angels of God Worship Him' and 'Though Art Gone Up High.' He will want nothing to do with the man." The curt nod of the shop owner made Sophie believe she would understand why.

In response, she focused on a crest stamped on the folder and then on the manuscript itself to buy time to decrypt why Novak would want nothing to do with those pieces. She squinted and peered closer, narrowing in on a perceived smudge of a line. Whether worn by time or circumstance, or perhaps even interference, she did not know.

Then it came to her. Neither of the songs mentioned were included in K. 572: Mozart's *Der Messias*. Rather, from Handel's original version. Whatever message Novak was trying to send was drawn from Mozart only.

"But everything else is in order?" she said.

He tapped his index finger on the manuscript, and she saw the same fine lines and delicate notes as the other pieces. Yet this time with a small note and address. Another meeting place.

———◦◦◦◦———

The street map Sophie had acquired not long after her arrival in Prague offered a confusing crisscross of names she couldn't read let alone pronounce, so she used the river and the steeples as her guide. Karlův most, guarded by saints and statues, stretched over the Vltava River. She took her time when she reached the medieval bridge and maneuvered over stones still slick with the freezing temperature. Above her the clouds hung low and heavy with snow that had only just begun to fall.

Her destination in Hradčany was a fortress compound that towered over the bank from the Malá Strana side of the river and surrounded its magnificent center: St. Vitus Cathedral, whose steeples sharply stabbed the wintry sky. Sophie was breathless by the time she reached the broad cathedral doors. The opening gate had been guarded by stern-faced officials.

Wenceslas, entombed therein, was the modest contradiction to the jewels tucked into stone shrouds, the priceless art etched in the windows and tucked into the arched frames and vaulted ceilings of the cathedral, the sculpture and art surrounding the High Altar.

Sophie proceeded to the place the note mentioned: a grille separating the Lady Chapel from the sanctuary. Just beyond her the ornamented tomb of St. John Nepomuk, bohemian martyr, stood witness.

Sophie had Brent Somerville's voice in her ear again. She could never precisely recall the exact scripture, but she knew it mentioned something resembling *store not your treasures on earth where moth and dust doth corrupt.*

Yet Sophie saw the treasures too often in the opulent buildings with gold embellishment and grand marble columns overrun by delicate veins described in delicate precision in Diana's lengthy architectural tomes.

"Everything is of great value when you are straining to rub two coins together," a clipped British voice said behind her. "Starling."

"Brighton," Sophie breathed out in recognition.

His mouth slid into a snide smile. "Care for a stroll?"

CHAPTER 32

Marcus Brighton's voice still made her stand at attention. Much like it had when he had first approached her to join his Special Operatives Executive team and assumed she might amount to something. She was tall and indomitable, he had said. She recalled how easily she had fallen into his plan for her to carry messages into France. Then, when that had failed, to be repurposed into a hut at Bletchley Park.

Sophie followed Brighton across the palace grounds. Soon the opulent facades and carefully consecrated bricks of the magnificent church were replaced by a row of squat, suffocating wall-to-wall shacks that might once have been houses.

The Golden Lane was anything but luminous even as Brighton expounded on its history. Named such because it was rumored to have once housed alchemists.

Brighton looked up to a turreted tower that shadowed the sloping roofs. "Castle guards would live here and then perform their duties to protect the city or see prisoners to the dungeon. The city can't just stomp history out like an anthill."

A shiver rippled down her spine. "I don't understand why you're telling me . . ."

"Prague has had few reasons to celebrate for several years, but when Reinhard Heydrich was assassinated during Operation

Anthropoid, celebrations arose. People still pray at the St. Cyril and St. Methodius Cathedral to honor the men who saw to the Butcher of Prague's demise."

"Well, that war was won at least." In music she was trained to hear a sharp or flat note or a poorly perceived shift in octave or tone. It taught her to read between the lines. The more Brighton spoke, the more intently she tuned in to hear what was in phrases and complicated lines. He was leading her to something, but she didn't know what. "Rather morbid place."

"Just as Wenceslas Square is a stone's throw from the former Gestapo headquarters. Not so far as the dungeon just there." He inclined his head. "It is where they held their interrogations."

She studied the gravel under her shoes. "I assume you didn't find me to give me a history lesson."

"Maybe of one sort. Did you find the death mask yet?"

Sophie stiffened. She hadn't mentioned the mask to him. There was little, it seemed, Brighton did not know. Which put her in the position of feeling like she was long being used.

"That must be one of Novak's Mozart pages under your arm?"

She didn't expect him to know about Novak. Then again she wasn't expecting to see him at all.

"I have something *far* more interesting," he said. "Why don't you give me your folder and I'll give you mine?"

Novak was a current client, but Brighton was part of her history— and Simon's. She didn't want to betray Novak's trust, but she also had little choice. She knew the way Brighton worked. And she knew how she had once disappointed him when her name and face from the society pages gave her away. So she slowly gave in.

With the exchange she was met with stationery from another lifetime. Embossed in gold with the Barrington crest. As if by instinct, she pressed her fingers to her bare collarbone.

Brighton's man in Vienna is a man named Barre. He's actually some upper-crust Brit named Barrington. He hasn't hidden his identity well. I've earned more than what you gave me. He has a few allies in the city. A man named Langer. A theology professor named Somerville and a woman who goes by the name of Starling.

—A.

"What's this?" Sophie's voice wavered.

Brighton merely folded his arms and coaxed her onward with a raised eyebrow as she discovered a wad of papers behind the note. In the margins was writing in a hand unfamiliar to her.

My husband and eldest son are returning to our Mayfair estate on business. Camden is in need of a visiting historian to loan credence to its tenure since the time of the serfs and feudal days. It is a long shot, but I assumed I could find a way to legitimately recommend you. My husband trusts me.

It didn't take long for her to piece together that she was reading the hand of Margaret Barrington. She carefully rearranged the letters she had read and continued.

I do not trust Barrington to give Simon his inheritance, so I will wait as promised. But he is starting his Cambridge term soon. He will not mind leaving this behind. I know that about him. And perhaps someday I will tell him that I have met someone who was the other half of me. Who understood me.

Her hand shook as she scanned the documents until her eyes settled on something of import.

I know you think I am too trusting by staying here, but Simon deserves to come into part of his inheritance. He'll have the Mayfair house and a trust when he reaches his majority. I don't trust Charles not to take that from him. So while I appreciate your concern, I have to hold fast. I confess that Charles has been unbalanced and his temper is higher than usual. I don't know if it is the state of the world or the estate's affairs. Simon always set him off, but he agreed to be civil for my sake.

Sophie wanted to know more, but what might it mean for her or Novak or Simon? She carefully arranged the letters into the order in which he had handed them to her, save for the one about Simon's inheritance, which she surreptitiously tucked into her pocket.

"You are working for Jan Novak," Brighton continued. "The same man to whom these letters were addressed. Doubtless you have come to your own conclusions about the sender."

When Sophie didn't respond, Brighton continued. "Don't look so shocked. I am affiliated with the same man."

"Why?"

"Because after the war, in Vienna the Communist Party enjoyed a spike in the vote. Since then some men have alienated whole blocks of potential voters. Prague is in the midst of a chapter that could see drastic political change. Even more than Vienna. For years, I have known of Novak. Even met the man once at Camden. I knew he and Simon would be of use to me one day." He appraised her. "And now I have you too."

"*Tell me a secret,*" Sophie had once whispered to Simon. Now, in the course of a mere day, she had one he would kill to know.

CHAPTER 33

Innere Stadt, Vienna

Simon hadn't turned off the wireless after Sophie departed his hotel room, and so he was stabbed with several variations of her in a musical program recorded at the Musikverein. And as in all things Vienna, it found its way back to Mozart.

Amadeus. "God's beloved." If Simon ascribed to the philosophy of Charles Barrington, then God's love was withheld for those like the composer: blessed with prodigious talent and validated by a father who placed him on a piano stool and in front of royalty and demanded perfection. Likely there was little left for an illegitimate son of a Communist sympathizer.

Simon drowned his thoughts with the sounds of Hotel Sacher: the frenetic *ticks* and *clicks* of the journalists' telex machine receiving bulletins in the rooms a floor below.

Someone tapped on the other side of his heavy wood door. It had been less than half an hour since he had telephoned Gabe at his office, demanding he come see Simon as soon as possible, so he was surprised at how soon Gabe arrived.

Judging by Gabe's frown, Simon's loosened collar and matted hair was noticed.

"Are you all right?" The man was clearly as tired as Simon and didn't stand on ceremony as he crossed over the red carpet into the room.

"Worried about Starling," Simon hoped Gabe might expound on the note in his handwriting.

Gabe folded into a chair by the window and fixed his ice-blue eyes out it. "The light here is different from anywhere else."

Simon followed Gabe's sight line over Albertinaplatz. The sun melted low over the steeples and what was left of the roof at the Staatsoper. It was truly beautiful.

"My city is being used as your plaything. Not just *your* plaything. The Russians, the Americans, the French." Gabe shook his head.

"Is that why you delivered that message?" Simon hoped he had kept his voice in check. Dispassionate. He retrieved the piece of paper. *Starling turned.* "Is she a traitor?"

"That message was my taking dictation from a man who was adamant I deliver it to Moser. Moser's door was locked, and he didn't respond so I slid it under the doorway."

"Who?"

"A phone call. I didn't recognize the voice. Russian though. If Starling and I were carefully watched, it made sense that someone linked us together. I was given no trouble." Gabe shook his head again. "I told you Starling was becoming a little too interested in certain pieces. I assumed it had something to do with that."

"Or perhaps you were just noticing it more because you are starting to turn sour at all we're doing here," Simon translated ruminatively.

"Do you blame me?"

Simon knew then he wouldn't get anything actionable out of Gabe, and Simon felt a bit deflated at the loss of that lead. At least as far as Sophie was concerned. "So is this why Moser was killed, do you think? This arrangement with the Russian? Or the men he wanted to teach at his podium?"

"I was just delivering a message, Simon."

Simon showed him the manuscript piece Müller had given him.

"My family was in possession of something similar." Gabe's

heritage was affluent. At least it *had* been before the war drained all but Gabe's attempts to assume a noble poise that drew wandering eyes from his frayed sleeves and collar.

"Most of our estate, as you know, was lost. Or at least . . . scattered. Perhaps it's another similar situation."

Simon nodded. "But of what interest is this piece? Is it that this Novak fellow wants to get it back to you and use some philanthropy at the same time? Return these artifacts and pieces in a roundabout way while also relaying messages?" Simon raised his shoulder.

The *Der Messias* manuscript was in fragments. Pages: a few truncated bars. Notes slightly ripped or frayed so that supposed eighth notes gave way to air. Entire songs of the Oratorio missing altogether.

"I'm not daft enough to think that Eternity has dissolved and everything changes, Gabe."

"I know. *Der Messias* is an odd choice, be it for messages or otherwise. It's a valuable arrangement, certainly, due to its age and its association both with Handel and Mozart. But Handel is the genius in this case, and Mozart's rendition doesn't hold up to most musical enthusiasts. Is its value about the piece, or is it a message about the selection of this particular Mozart? Many priceless Mozart manuscripts went missing during the Anschluss."

An inference. A composition within the realm of genius but scraping up second best. Simon pushed his glasses up on his nose. "And about the other thing I requested?"

"There is every reason to believe that a man named Novak was a visiting scholar in Sussex Downs during the time period you had mentioned. He wrote chess pamphlets. I skimmed one. Rather like Machiavelli meeting *The Art of War*. Some, I believe, would be of great financial value."

Simon felt his heartbeat in his fingertips. "How so?"

"Because I am certain they will end up on the Schwarzmarkt soon enough."

Was Simon close to finding the answer he had searched for his entire life through the realization of this connection?

The blood drained from his face, and he slightly turned from Gabe a moment under the guise of polishing his glasses.

"My contact sent a small passage to me," Gabe said, "from the man behind the pamphlet. I asked for verification. A fib, of course. I had so little to go on."

"My fault."

"I want my city back and of course you want Sophie. The philosophy was that 'a sacrifice of a play meant that the game trumped everything else. A true game was marred by thought for peripheral pieces.'"

"Winning is more important than letting anything get in your way," Simon translated, shoving his now shaking hand into his pocket.

"Yes." Gabe stood and moved toward the doorway.

If Gabe's findings were correct, then this ruthless method of winning was in Simon's lineage and bloodstream. The hypothesis made it easy for him to excuse moments when he had pursued winning over anything. Even at the prospective cost of friendship: for Sophie. For Diana, even.

Simon shut the door after Gabe departed. Simon's past and his present were colliding. Gabriel didn't need to provide any more information for Simon to realize that his world had more to do with Eternity than he would have preferred. After all, the spy ring had brought him to Vienna but yielded now that there was a bigger force at play.

And Jan Novak was his father. Gabe's information was too coincidental otherwise.

Simon turned to the chessboard. His next move meant more now, because fewer pieces were left on his side as he was close to being captured. He had been too busy to fully comprehend or feel resentment over how he was losing the game.

Simon was truly a champion when he had something to prove,

which did little to account for why he was losing. In any other game his next move would propel him to sacrifice a piece or two on his end. Simon hated even the semblance of relinquishing any part of the board even if said sacrifice was vital to victory.

His opponent—his father—if as meticulous as Simon supposed, anticipated Simon being caught off his guard. He mulled over his next move. Now fully aware this was the most important game of his life, he went to find a monogrammed pen and pad near the dressing table.

He opened the locked desk drawer where he kept the previous messages and moves and looked at the first one, then the most recent.

Simon sank into the desk chair and leaned his chin on his hand a moment. He couldn't for the life of him figure out what the plays could mean. He had tried a city map, for one. Every code he could think of from Playfair to a Vigenere Square Cipher to an algebraic equation.

Simon pushed the papers back when something winking from the dressing table caught his eye in a slit of sunlight streaming through the blinds. Just near his gold cuff links and cologne and under a card bearing the insignia of the famed Sacher *S*, he noticed a glimmer of white.

The Villiers pearls.

Sophie wore them as a symbol of her freedom. It was the first glimpse of herself she had truly shown him back during their momentous first chess game.

He twined them around his fingers, then carefully folded them into a silk handkerchief and into his pocket. She had left her independence with him.

He smoothed a piece of monogrammed stationery and pressed the pen nib to paper in careful choreography: no wavering line, no quick, illegible cursive. Rather in the elegant hand of Lord Barrington, not Simon Barre.

I will meet you on the Staré Město side of the Charles Bridge tomorrow evening. Doubtless you'll be wanting to head to Prague anyway. I hear there is something of great value to you here.

Das Flüstern might care little for the pieces lost collaterally as he dominated the board. In his game, pieces would be sacrificed in the pursuit of reckless and sure victory. It was a familiar strategy that taught Simon that for all the satisfaction of a sure win, he shouldn't play the same move.

As much as he wanted to speed out of the Sacher and head to Prague, he refused to sacrifice pieces without accounting for their loss. Even as a part of him wanted to live up to the phantom expectations he had set against his idea of a man now close at hand.

Doubtless the chess master he supposed D. F. to be would mark such careful detail a loss. But Simon didn't know how to play any other way.

"You're going home," Simon told Diana through ruddy reception of the telephone.

"Pardon?"

"You and Brent are going home to London."

"Why now? We've done *dangerous* before! And we have nowhere to go. Our former landlord has let the Clerkenwell flat."

"You should have left long ago," Simon said gently. "You can have my Mayfair house. For as long as you wish."

"We can't afford to rent a house in Mayfair."

"But I can. It's yours."

"You're not even discussing this?" Diana's voice cracked. "Even when we came to Vienna, you *discussed* it with us."

"But this is what I do, Diana!" He had never raised his voice to her before. Not truly.

"*Simon.*"

"I'll arrange for a car tomorrow morning at 9:00 a.m. Leave the key under the front mat. I'll wire someone in London to pick you up and help with directions. Anything you need, just ask."

Diana huffed. "I won't do it. I will not lose you, Simon. I need you to . . ."

Simon ran his hand through his black hair. "I won't have you on my conscience." Something in the tremor in her voice harkened him back to their time at Bletchley Park. When he had bartered information about her wounded husband in exchange for her helping him. Explaining that that was how Simon knew how to do the right thing. That friendship was a currency in exchanged favors.

Yet Diana had told him she might have unconditionally done what he asked anyway. Because she valued and cared for him. Even as Simon was conditioned to look for the bargaining chip.

If Starling truly had turned, then his bargaining chip would be as safe as houses in London. He could keep *one* card and not show a full hand.

"I used you once, Diana, and it was the worst thing I have ever done."

He remembered all too clearly Charles Barrington's voice in his head. "*A Barrington does not waver, does not justify how he exacts what he needs. Rather, just demands it. Reparation can easily be found later.*"

"But you had your reasons. I've learned that. You told me then it was how you knew how to do the right thing. What is the right thing now, Simon?"

Pursuing Sophie and accepting what he would find, whether she had turned on him or not, was the right thing. Breaking through his own wall, turning his heart over, and showing it to another person was the right thing. He could give Diana this. "I'm madly in love with her, you know."

Diana took a long breath. "I've known for years."

The *Starling turned* message still burned a hole in his breast pocket. "The right thing is her." He ended the call.

Simon shoved every last Das Flüstern letter into his case, not that the plays added up to anything. He could squint and strain all he liked. The game had never been about the moves or notation but in the identity of the opponent.

CHAPTER 34

February 1947
Prague Castle, Hradčany

Simon was Brighton's pawn. Clearly Simon was unaware of the information Sophie now held. But wouldn't Brighton assume, given the intensity of their relationship, that she would break and run to tell him? Sophie scrambled to find the upper hand.

"Simon and I had a row."

"Inconsequential." Brighton waved a dismissive hand.

"The kind that leads to a complete falling-out." She trained her eyes forward. "He's nothing to me now. If you're showing me this to get something from him, then you should know I am more interested in the work I am doing for Novak."

They walked in silence several paces, Brighton scrutinizing her through the heat of his eyes on her profile. Certain he was judging her reaction, she straightened her shoulders as they maneuvered beyond the castle grounds, retracing the slope she had earlier made up to the castle.

After a few steps in sync, he casually said, "You're married. Rows are expected."

Of *course* he knew about their marriage. He was tapped into a network not unlike a spiderweb—weaving translucent lines into a complicated pattern.

"Why are you unloading all of this on me now?"

They were nearly at the arch: Charles Bridge spreading across the rippled river. Sophie knew a quick path to Novak's Kampa Island house. The path she meant to take without Brighton at her heels.

"I want Novak, Sophie. I want him to work for me. Fortunately, we have a card to play. Simon." He looked her over. "You are Simon's breaking point. And Simon is Novak's." His eyes were keen on her face before he fell back a step. "I hadn't meant to tell you. Hadn't wanted to seek you out. But I'm running out of time here and this is an easy fix."

"Dragging out Simon's heritage is an *easy fix*?"

"It's not enough to have Simon in Vienna anymore. This isn't personal."

Not personal to you. Sophie had left Simon with a chill on her skin and a muddled mind, but she couldn't temper the loyalty she felt for him or how this man had betrayed him far more deeply than her turning away, crossing to the lift, and exiting the Sacher.

Sophie felt the pang of expectation and the wince of a secret kept much as she supposed Simon would feel if he knew what she had done.

The words she planned to tell him warmed through her fingers and up her arms, smoothed over her shoulders.

"Thoughtful, aren't you? Just like you were when you used to play piano at Camden. Margaret Barrington *loved* the piano. Almost as much as she loved some of the new Communist propaganda circling around the high academic set."

Sophie bristled. She wanted to ask what had happened to her, but Brighton's bread crumbs were clearly intentionally cast, and some held in reserve.

"As I said." She spoke slowly. "We've had a falling-out."

Sophie read as much in Brighton's body language as his words. He must have known she would never use this part of Simon's history.

For any reason.

"How long do you suppose your falling-out will last?" They had reached *ulice* Na Kampě, a street just swerving from Novak's town house now in clear view.

"If Simon is Novak's breaking point, then there is nothing you can get me to do."

"Novak knows more about you than you do him. He wants Simon. Get Simon here on amiable terms."

They had slowed and the breeze whipped Sophie's hair and ruffled the collar of her coat.

"If you don't, I will. This is your chance, Sophie."

"I won't manipulate him."

"You are Simon's weakness. Don't think I don't know how to use that to my advantage." Brighton studied her intensely. "History doesn't matter right now. Don't give in to some moral high ground. Tell me you'll get him."

Sophie didn't answer.

"This is where I leave you then. I tried. But I will get him here. I need him more than I need you." Brighton walked away.

"*Špaček.*" The name prickled over Sophie's spine in Sidorov's voice.

Brighton had left her to a wolf. His convenient absence as she stood alone outside of Novak's house was as intentional as his withholding what he knew about her relationship to Simon. He must have known of her transaction with Sidorov.

Of course he did. *Spider's web.*

Novak's house was dark, all light extinguished. She set her case down at the edge of the door frame. A few candle flickers from neighboring houses compensated as best they could for the pitch-black winter night.

She smoothed out her grimace and slowly turned on her heel, looking up under the brim of her hat. "Pardon me," she said coolly.

Sidorov's fingers dug into Sophie's arm.

"I am well aware to whom you were speaking at Prague Castle." He seethed. "Herr Brighton. I hired you for something and you work with other men to get it. And yet Mozart's death mask still hasn't been found." Sidorov cocked his head.

Her nerves were strung like the wire on a garrote, with Sidorov as the handle on one end and Brighton on the other.

"You've met with people all over Vienna," he gritted through his teeth. "At Minoritenkirche. In the Volksgarten. But I hired and *trusted* you." He raked his gaze over her face. "And you've taken too long."

She straightened her spine. "Surely I cannot be the only reason you are here." Was he responsible for the bullet that nearly killed her and Simon in Vienna? She was filling in the gaps as quickly as she could, now that she knew far more than an artifact was at stake.

They faced off long enough for her to notice a resonant darkness overtake his stare. Her fingertips prickled.

Sophie instinctively moved, reaching for the revolver in her waistband. But he was faster.

Sophie abandoned her pursuit of the gun and immediately sprang into her training: his throat, his abdomen, his groin. She gained ground with surprise and frantic force, emphasized by the sheer annoyance at how this interlude was keeping her from the information she was still processing.

Simon's father was an enemy. But not so much of an enemy Brighton wouldn't sell Sophie out. Which meant Brighton wanted his enemy.

She twisted both into a fury that manifested in her digging her elbow into Sidorov's side. But any agency and upper hand she had diminished with his size. He wrenched her left arm behind her back and twisted until she cried out.

Sophie attempted to slip out of his grasp using a slight conjure of strength to try to escape him, but he was faster. The cold steel of his gun pressing into her back rendered her own weapon useless. He kicked it to the side.

Brighton had truly abandoned her. Sidorov's grip showed little mercy, a foreshadow of the means he would use to extract answers still parading in blanks across her mind.

Back then, her SOE training seemed awfully like a crude dress rehearsal: Amateurs brushed up and prepared as quickly as possible before they were shoved in over their head. Rife with possibility and the slow, snaking burn of a world war about to ignite. Now, her war had a face and a name. This was about Simon . . . *her* Simon. Brighton made that abundantly clear.

She had no control as Sidorov led her away from Novak's house before near shoving her in the back of a Škoda she hadn't noticed a half block away.

Sidorov backed the car out from the narrow street and made a sharp turn in the direction of the hill she and Brighton had only just descended. Sophie quickly studied the perimeter through the passenger seat before she jiggled the door handle.

"Not a chance." Sidorov shoved the gun in her face with the hand not holding the steering wheel.

Sophie had to have something to give him. To bargain. She was nauseated at the prospect of finessing a need for him to keep her alive. The prospect of the mask might not be enough, she reasoned as she pressed her forehead to the window glass. But she could improvise.

What she *wouldn't* give him was of equal importance.

Sidorov swerved into the castle complex Sophie had just abandoned.

She wouldn't give him Novak's past nor his connection to Simon. Sophie could only hope this was enough.

———◦◦◦◦———

Simon's knuckles whitened on the steering wheel as the miles tucked Vienna behind him. The peace of the Austrian countryside was free of flak towers and Soviet patrols, even as occasional barbed wire bordered otherwise serene villages. Men and women in traditional garb coaxed goats to pasture, clashing with checkpoint officers with guns and cold eyes controlling the transit of people across the border.

As Simon neared Prague, bored soldiers stood at attention at the blockades as his car inched toward the horizontal metal bar. He answered their questions in nonchalant monosyllables. He was rich and very important. Couldn't they tell from his handsome demeanor and polished car?

And even though the landscape and terrain bore similar traits to Austria, Simon sensed something pulse in the atmosphere. He gripped the steering wheel in response.

Prague announced itself in draped gray. The spires of St. Vitus and Our Lady before Týn were easily recognizable from the two quarters—old and new—flanking the Gothic bridge over the Vltava River. The cobbled streets were crooked and slick with wintry glaze.

Simon steadied the steering wheel and carefully maneuvered until he turned his Bentley to the Alcron Hotel just off Wenceslas Square. A valet saw to his keys immediately upon his exit. Simon strode through the ornate front doors and left his cases with the bellboy.

The concierge smiled, expecting him after an earlier phone call arranged at Sacher's. Simon pulled out his new title to great aplomb and immediate subservience.

Once the door to his room was opened, Simon was met with a musky, smoky smell. He jangled the chain on the bedside lamp to illuminate the suite and retreated into the WC. He met his blurry blue eyes in the mirror and ran his hand over the shadow on his chin. Before when he had studied his reflection, it was impassively, ensuring his hair was slicked back and his gold-rimmed glasses straight.

Now he wondered if he would see something different.

He had spent countless parties behind a veneer of a painted smile and blank stare. The true test would be if he could fashion both when satisfying his curiosity about Novak. He suspected his heart was being held together by quickly dissolving threads.

Unlike the Sacher, his room was devoid of Count Basie or Benny Goodman. Just penetrating silence greeted him. Simon straightened and flexed his fingers as he had so often preceding the tap of the chess clock not far from his elbow to begin the game.

He had never wanted anything more in his life than this moment, every harsh word that had fallen from Charles Barrington's lips, every moment that Julius had tormented him, every glance or look from his mother before she had retreated behind an aloof mask that kept him at a safe distance for his own good. He had once told Sophie he would give his life to know the truth about his heritage. Odd that it warred for secondary dominance in a mind filled with worry as to her whereabouts and loyalties.

Still, one move at a time.

Simon smoothed his suppositions as neatly as he smoothed his tie and tugged the intensity of Gabe Langer's findings with determination. Twisted the very real fact that this man was irrevocably linked to his past while rotating his cuff links.

Finally, he retrieved his gold-rimmed specs from his pocket and settled them on his nose. And with the last of his armor in place, he tried to justify meeting his father before he banged down every door and wove in and out of every street in pursuit of Sophie.

CHAPTER 35

Simon approached the bridge just beyond Křížovnické Square. Moonlight painted the city's arches in an eerie spotlight. Music was inherent in Prague's architecture, and it marked his steps: in the crackling of ice near the river's rim and in the soft sweep of snow underfoot. For a moment, with the crystalline frost on the river and the dark banks bordering it, he almost forgot the city was in the aftermath of war.

He pressed his lips into a firm line, kept his eyes in a relaxed show of nonchalance. Then he shoved his hand deep into the pocket of his overcoat, feeling for the outline of his Webley MkVI revolver.

Jan Novak. His father. On the bridge before him. He couldn't foresee an ending that would match the one he had sketched in his head with vague lines. So he played it as best he could.

He stepped around the last pedestrian stragglers on the calm night, the *clip-clops* from a horse-drawn cart—still warring with fast automobiles for right of way—in a connection of old and new. Just like the two towns flanking either side of the river.

Novak studied him so intently, Simon couldn't help but raise his eyes to meet the man before him. Bright, intelligent blue eyes searching his own. Simon affected a casual disinterest he hoped read in his loose shoulders and relaxed countenance. His heart thrummed as he clenched his jaw and furtively reached into his pocket to secure his gun. "Where's Starling?"

Novak lit a cigarette and took a slow drag. He leaned over the railing of Karlův most, staring out to the ripples of the pitch-black Vltava below. The moonlight reflected off it a little just before it was blotted out by the shadow of the castle on the hill. He offered a smoke to Simon, who held up his hand in refusal.

"I got a note. *Starling turned*," Simon continued. "I need to know where she is."

There was a luxurious melancholy to Prague: rich in its statues and spires while its dark, bloody history tripped at its heels. As luxurious as the library at Camden where his mother sat across from this man's unflinching blue eyes. Novak suited this luxury well. Even in the darkness, Simon could make out the tailored cut of his collar and the square dice-shaped cuff links that glimmered in the streetlight.

Simon removed his fedora and stared into its brim a moment while Novak flicked ashes from his cigarette, then tossed the butt in the river.

Simon sensed Novak watching him, but he wouldn't look up and give him the satisfaction of knowing he rattled him. Simon just hoped that the heartbeat thrumming through his shirt wasn't detectable.

"You do such a poor job of feigning disinterest." The wind picked up and the frost made Novak's breath fog against the pitch black.

"I am disinterested in anything but Starling." Simon lied.

"Quite keen, that one," Novak said.

Simon twisted his cuff link. He anticipated a level of distrust, a wall of uncertainty. But Novak was intently interested in him, had *studied* him, had wanted to meet him. He couldn't interpret his way out of this situation. In fact, the man's body language and his cryptic alignment of words made Simon wonder if they had hit a wall. Should he be flattered or angry? Suspicious? The latter, certainly, when it came to Sophie.

Simon needed to get closer, needed to read the man as he would an opponent. He kept one hand in his pocket and blinked his eyes into focus.

Simon had spent his whole life imagining what he might say to his father, what he might ask. Was his right hook in the gentleman's boxing league inherited skill? Whatever quirk and habit inherent in him and ruled out against his study of his mother, he ascribed to this man.

A few shadows passed. Soldiers that had perhaps maneuvered down from the broad castle above them, high atop the sentry hill.

Novak wasn't about to broach the subject of Simon's parentage, so Simon wouldn't give in. "You hired a woman to find and trade for fragments of Mozart's arrangement of Handel's *Messiah*. Why?"

"Because beautiful things must find completion."

"Nonsense. There were inscriptions on the manuscript. Messages, perhaps. Who were you communicating with? Das Flüstern?"

"My cause is different from the one you are suggesting," Novak said easily. "Das Flüstern isn't a man so much as an idea."

"You. You're this *idea*."

They walked a few steps, presumably in the direction of Novak's house, and Novak hummed, filling the silence between them. Simon found he knew the symphonic poem by Bedřich Smetana. Even in the man's rough voice Simon heard the lap and ripple of the water reflected in the clear notes. Sophie had told him it was about the Moldau River and that the Nazis had banned it from being played.

The bridge had doubtless seen many similar scenarios: whispered with tense moments and men falling to their deaths. While Simon had remained as noncommittal as he could, considering his worry for Sophie, Novak's casual and calm manner—his *humming* of a song— merely shoved Sophie's absence through Simon again.

He no longer cared about Brighton or decorum or the mystery of Das Flüstern or Eternity or the whole lot of it. He wanted Sophie.

Using his free hand, Simon gripped Novak's collar and put all of his weight into driving Novak into the stone barrier. The surprise initially caught his father, though a small choked laugh was followed by an attempted nod. "You clearly know who I am, Simon."

The physical resemblance became clearer the more Simon looked for it. Until there was no shadow of a doubt.

Simon maneuvered them into shadow and removed the revolver from the inner pocket of his coat. "Why do you need me now?"

"Brighton said I can do an awful lot if I have you." Novak watched with an amused expression, clearly aware that his mention of Brighton's name was a revelation to Simon.

Simon processed it slowly until every nerve was taut. He pressed his lips in a hard line and narrowed his eyes to look just past Novak's shoulder.

How long had he been a pawn?

"Brighton assured me what a wunderkind you *could* be."

Could be. *Almost.* Simon had been an *almost* all his life.

He wanted what was offered in this man's appearance so badly, it hurt his throat and caught in his chest. Every answer was right here. *"She doesn't want you anyway."* He could hear Charles Barrington's voice. *"She can take care of herself. She left you. You have waited your entire life to meet your father."*

Ironic that the sentiments ascribed to his mother in memory so perfectly suited his uncertainty about Sophie. For every sting of his stepfather's backhand, for every slight that Julius had paid him, for every whisper of Simon's illegitimacy amid the silk and satin of his father's soirees, for every moment his mother looked wistfully at him before turning away. And he wanted to ask Novak a million questions until a million answers were wrung out, resulting in his legacy. His affirmation.

But he made a vow to put Sophie above every last thing in his existence.

He could choose his history and every last question, or he could choose the other half of his heart. So he gave up the one thing he had always wanted more than anything: belonging.

Simon pressed the gun to his father's temple with a swift, startling movement. "Where is she?"

CHAPTER 36

The next sting on Sophie's cheek wasn't as painful as her anticipation. She didn't know where Mozart's death mask was. She did know the tether that bound Simon to Novak, but not to completion. Not insofar as that connection related to Brighton passing her over. Indeed, as her eyes blurred on the grimy wall, she entertained the thought that she was here as a plaything. But how could that be when his questions were so incessant?

At the speed of them Sophie's mind turned like the rotors in a Bletchley hut: turning, turning, then clicking to a stop. Even as her brain fizzed and faltered, her heart anchored and stood fast to him. Even if she couldn't utter the words that fell so easily from Simon's tongue. He loved her and she ran. She loved *him*. So she stayed.

And deflected as long as she could.

Sidorov worked in dramatic pauses, Sophie had quickly learned. It not only punctuated the jack-in-the-box uncertainty of his next assault but stripped away his sense of urgency. He wasn't using her as Brighton was—in quick solution to a problem. No. She was a slow, lazy semicolon to play with so he could assert authority while hopefully still getting what he wanted.

"I know how to break people." He kicked a metal chair out and shoved her into it.

"And I know how to be broken," she said with little tremor in her voice.

He allowed her one of his dramatic pauses then, and she took in the rickety radiator in the corner and the gray walls that contrasted the opulence of St. Vitus, which, with her poor geography, she assumed wasn't but a stone's throw away.

"*Store not your treasures on earth,*" she recalled Brent's voice and held on to it fast.

"Why did you bring me to Hradčany?"

"I am an important man here. Will be more so when I have the mask. Das Flüstern promised me. Even promised to meet me if I had something worth giving him." He inclined his head at her.

Sophie laughed.

"What?"

"Other men are out there hoping to further the Communist agenda and wanting the mask to purchase some sort of Austrian national pride and you . . ." Sophie shook her head. *You're not supposed to bait him unless you have an escape. A plan.* She had no escape. No plan. "You just want to show that you have it."

And this time when he struck her cheek, it went numb.

She knew what Brighton knew, but she didn't know what Sidorov knew, and she wasn't about to tell. The mask was one thing, the *Der Messias* fragments one thing, but Simon was another. She was toeing a precarious line here: Another sting. Sophie realized she would need a game plan.

For now it included biting the first consonant of Simon's name on her tongue.

Her breath quickened. *You're not scared. You're a Huntington-Villiers. You're a . . . Barrington.*

The name came with a hiccuped gasp. And with it, everything changed.

All of the moments of insecurities and ripples of rebellion before culminated in this opportunity to prove she was more than she had believed possible.

"Novak," Sidorov said. "He is the key to the mask, is he not?" He looked at her fingers with his slate eyes. "He is a competitor. For the object I want."

"There are several antiques that are far easier to acquire. I can give you a list! Do you fancy Klimt?"

Sidorov raised his arm but didn't strike. "We had an agreement."

"If it's money you want . . ." Sophie hedged.

"What is Novak's connection to Simon Barre? Don't tell me you do not know. I've seen you both in Vienna together."

Sidorov had encountered Diana and Sophie in Vienna. She thought about the soldier who had attacked Diana at the Pfandhaus. Then of the same soldier who she had encountered the night Simon pressed his lips to hers near the Theseus Temple in that dark garden.

Was Sidorov watching her through a guard? One who watched her cross from Michaelerplatz as the remaining streetlights sputtered? As Simon tucked her into his side.

"I know nothing about Novak." Sophie ironed her voice until she was little but an automaton. "And I have fallen out with Simon Barre." Sophie smoothed her face into a stern mask. It was one thing to protect a mask. But tucked under the soiled shirt now sticking to her was the thrum of something far closer to her.

"I sense that if I know Simon Barre, I will find the key to Novak. And then I will have my mask that you have not found."

"This is a lot of trouble for a mask." Sophie licked at the blood at the corner of her lip. His backhands were surprisingly powerful. Under her coat she had tucked Margaret's letter to Novak. And if Sidorov found it, he could turn and twist Simon much as he was doing her.

"Tell me a secret, Simon," she had whispered, so close she could taste the toothpowder on his breath and feel the smile in his eyes.

Start small. A pinpoint. If she allowed her mind to cast farther, she might drown with what he might eventually wring from her: Müller's Pfandhaus. Diana and Eternity. Simon and his code system of people and places and artifacts in a careful grid cracked with a Mozart catalogue.

She'd protect the letters first. *Margaret and Novak.*

The night dropped like ice outside the small window, and frost clung to the pane.

A light buzzed overhead. The surrounding four walls were petrifying but not unexpected. Not when she saw her present through the film of her prospects as a Special Operatives Executive. Sophie naively imagined withstanding the worst in pursuit of heroism. Anything for her country and cause. Now . . .

During her training, she had been drilled like a soldier to withstand torture: commands she transposed into the staccato phrase of a concerto to keep fear at bay. But that was before her heart was involved.

When Sidorov *truly* started in on her—beyond his barking and his backhands across her face—she had felt the mounting fear start in the acceleration of her heartbeat and the dots of perspiration at her temples. Could her courage live up to her imagination?

The country and cause bit was long gone. But perhaps she could still redeem herself in her own sure, still way. Because . . . *love.* She had learned to love in a hundred different ways without ever knowing. In the ruminative steps of a first waltz and pressing her lips to Simon's to erase Julius's force.

In the pull of their preternatural ability to find each other in the midst of chaos.

In the rubble of beautiful Vienna: her lips meeting Simon's in a ruse to deceive a soldier.

Then in the kiss they had shared in her flat and at the Sacher, when words were diminished and better suited to touch and mingled breath.

"I will kill you, you know."

"You won't." Sophie heard a voice scratch like nails on a chalkboard. *Hers.* "Or else you would have done so already."

The more he interrogated her, the more she resisted. At first on account of his assumption that she knew more than she did, but then because she had little to lose. And most significantly—because she met each incessant question and barrage of pain as a vow.

I won't give up a secret before Simon knows it.

It had almost seemed possible to keep that secret until Sidorov grabbed her right hand. He held it a moment, then dropped it only to retrieve pliers from his pocket on the opposite side of the table.

Sophie dizzied. The thought of never playing the *Appassionata* again. Or the low, languorous notes of the *Pathétique.* Or the bars inspired by a caged starling in possession of a prodigious composer she felt as strongly here as she did in Vienna.

With the first rise of bile in her throat, she knew that she might leave with her life but not with her passion. Not with the way he kept nudging his pliers in her face. Her playing had become the form of rebellion she lived in notes and tempo when the constraints of her upbringing were prison bars around the slight moments she tried to live up to her grandmother's wisdom.

The knowledge of Margaret's letters burned a hole in her pocket with intense secrecy. Her hand was a distraction. Even if she loved playing more than . . .

The thing she loved most.

The thing she *had* loved most.

Sophie Villiers might not have been able to conjure the words when pliant in Simon's arms, but Sophie Barrington could and would *live* them. To every last letter and syllable. To every last motion. Beyond every last cowardly thought that drove her from his side.

You have my loyalty, Simon Barrington, she thought defiantly, much as she had promised a long wartime ago.

Sophie Barrington silently dared Sidorov to do his worst.

CHAPTER 37

I don't know where she is," Novak repeated.

With or without the press of the gun against Novak's temple, Simon knew the man wouldn't run away. He had that card in his favor. Novak was as interested in meeting Simon as Simon was him.

But Simon buried this knowledge and kept the revolver poised. "Why use Starling? For these . . . manuscripts. Eternity? Are you working for the Eternity ring?"

"A tall woman. Regal. Word gets around. Many of my contacts in Vienna have used her. To use her was to prove that you cared not a thought for money. She worked with far more than just the old flotsam and jetsam that the war coughed up." Novak's eyes narrowed shrewdly on Simon a moment.

"Surely you know that she never keeps her own cut for any of the transactions she brokers. She gives it away. It endeared me to her when Müller first mentioned her. I can appreciate Sophie Huntington-Villiers just as I can appreciate Brighton promising me a meeting with you. He knew that he couldn't pay me with something as trivial as *koruna*."

He studied Simon so intently. Still, if one of them faltered, it wouldn't be Simon. He had an entire childhood of Barrington parties that had trained him for this moment.

"If you're not going to shoot me," Novak said, "it is getting cold."

Simon looked left and right—over the city spliced through with a river like a dull knife.

"It is one thing for men like me to ensure that the Communist philosophy is spread over the country. It is quite another to have it threatened by men late of Hitler's regime. We were your *allies* against them, and now they can prove quite useful."

"So, you want to use men like Adameck?"

"I have a far wider influence than Adameck. Leftover Nazis are crawling under many floorboards, so why not dig a few out to round up men who would as sure as hide in a new political affiliation rather than be run out on the rails for an old one?"

Novak twisted his cuff link. "Because I have been working on building my reputation for years. With men like Brighton, for example. Brighton didn't remember me, but I remembered him from one of Charles Barrington's parties just before I left Camden." Novak took a beat, perhaps to let the information settle in. "There was no way I could have known that our paths would cross again. But I am glad for a long memory. When every meeting has the prospective to mean something, you take close account of it, wouldn't you say?"

This meeting was supposed to mean something to Simon, given the countless nights he had stared at the ceiling at Camden imagining it. And to a faceless man.

"You see the world the same way I do," Novak continued. "Through a chessboard. So that's how I communicated with you." Novak talked easily. "And it is how I carefully meted out my place here."

Meted. In Novak's Czech accent it was drawn out with too many syllables. Like a coat that didn't quite fit over his shoulders. The man was trying and not coming up to snuff, in spite of the effort.

Simon raised his shoulder. It was a hunch to measure this man's pride. A precarious one considering all Simon desired to know of him.

Novak had led them to a house tucked into a uniform row. "Everyone needs a place, Herr Barre. A sense of belonging. And if the world doesn't naturally give it to you, you make it up." Novak reached into his pocket for a key he clearly didn't need as the door was slightly ajar.

A small case sat at a peculiar angle at the doorstep. Sophie's. Novak clearly didn't notice it yet. He was too concentrated on surveying the front of his house. Could Simon possibly retract it without Novak seeing?

He followed Novak inside but not before kicking the case slightly to the side of a straggle of branches that in spring might qualify as a shrub.

Simon had discovered what evaded him with Eternity—Novak had a network far more impressive piggybacking off the former and sewn into the fabric of the next war with just enough threads connecting to the last one. Novak became what he needed to be: a rallying cry for the merits of Communism in the Viennese political sphere, a man who believed that a cultural masterpiece would remind two cities of the homelands worth fighting for through an ideology.

He was magnificent and everything Simon was *not* as he faltered through this world of espionage.

Brighton had wanted Simon, it seemed, but only until he had the real thing. A dangerous double agent Das Flüstern certainly was, but not if Brighton lured him with Simon first.

How ironic to be so incredibly valuable, and yet not for what he could accomplish but for who he was. It was a feeling Simon had starved for his entire life, and it was a cruel twist that it was offered here.

"The chess game was Brighton's idea. I had approached him about you. Your name kept reappearing, and then you changed it from Barrington, as if it would make a difference to those interested in you."

"I am not a Barrington," Simon said.

"Still, you had had *everything* that mattered. The best education. The best clothes and experiences. Just *look* at you."

"I had *nothing*. You took everything from me. My identity. My mother's affection, even. She had to hide it her entire life."

"We could work together."

"I will not be Brighton's pawn. Or yours."

"Oh, Simon. How I *know* you."

"You don't know me at all."

"Society pages. The papers." Novak waved a hand. "It's not hard when I think of your mother to imagine how you would turn out. A bit of a romantic in there, I would say. Beyond those fancy glasses and clothes. And Charles Barrington to ensure you were well bred." Novak tilted his chin in appraisal.

"Is it monetary compensation you're after?" Simon tempered his curiosity.

"Not a lot of money in this war."

"Indeed. Well, at least not in Vienna," Simon said pragmatically. "The Soviets seem to starve those they'd liberated from the war, making POWs build that wretched statue of one of their soldiers off the Ring, withholding rations, electricity . . ." He left a string off the sentence, hoping Novak would tug.

"Some of us want to fund it. Someone like me needed a war to finally find some value. I have made a lot of money." Novak looked pointedly at Simon's shoes. "You're polished down to the footwear."

Simon's eyes burned as he attempted to find approval in Novak's stare. A natural instinct. He couldn't help but seek validation nonetheless.

"Money's a rather clichéd reason for switching sides."

"I suppose when you have it, it would be," Novak said as they crossed to the parlor. "You can't start a war without two korunas to rub together." Novak looked pointedly at him. "It started there. I could never afford the pieces I had studied, but I could appraise them."

The chessboard on the side table near the bookcase lured Simon. He looked up and around. Marble lines and Baroque pieces. A game as familiar as the one near the window at Sacher's.

The board, like his own, was in midplay.

Novak watched Simon's careful study. "And I have an idea that Brighton underestimated your connection with Špaček. But I didn't."

Simon retrieved the note from Langer and held it across the board. "So, what is this, Das Flüstern?"

Novak clucked his tongue. "Besides melodrama? Bait, perhaps. *Starling turned*. Believe me, no one cares if Špaček turns left or right."

He stretched his arms over the board. "It's rather like your Eternity, isn't it?" Novak smiled. "That's the name of a group of men using churches and passing notes to infiltrate every city after the war. Child's play. There's a much larger game at stake here. The enemy of your enemy is your friend." He let out a low laugh. "If I had listened to Brighton, I wouldn't be nearly as forthcoming in telling you this."

"Brighton said you were a dangerous double agent."

"Only because he would fashion me to be. I don't go around ripping out fingernails and pushing corpses into the river. That's for men like Sidorov. For Adameck. But I will work whatever side I have to. I'm seen as dangerous for the information I possess and wield. But more so because I have people willing to do things for me. Detestable things.

"Right now I am working for the Soviets because they want to devise a plan that matches what the other Allies intend to do in terms of rebuilding. Brighton said you have a similar wealth of knowledge. Of Vienna."

Simon wasn't sure if the slight rise at the end of Novak's statement posited a threat. "What about *Der Messias*?" Simon said evasively.

"It was scattered during the war and a good place to start consideration of how art and history could be used to further a second ideology, so to speak. As an emblem." He stopped for an emphatic beat. But Simon didn't buy it. He'd left something out. Something in Novak's eyes had gone dead.

"There was Mozart: prodigy of the world, and he usurps a masterpiece. The critics hated it. Sometimes genius begets genius. He added wind instruments and a garish trombone section; he imparted the

Italian structures he loved. To his credit he acknowledged it shouldn't have been taken as an improvement. It was a replica. A copy."

Novak shook his head. "I could easily tell which men shared my ideology by those who knew the difference between the musical numbers in the Mozart piece and those in the Handel. If they had just heard about *Messiah* and thought they could use that to get near me, I added an extra layer. They would have to know that Mozart's version had omitted some of Handel's pieces. And a hope that whatever is lost in the original can be found, if varied, in a second try."

He was evading the question with an almost-rehearsed spiel. "Not the original."

"And to many keen ears, not legitimate." Novak continued. "But it kept Starling busy and it allowed me to expand my influence."

Novak left a silence open, but Simon wasn't about to fill it. He smoothed his expression into a bored look. "Why Starling?"

"Because to be seen using Starling to the Viennese is a boon, is it not? It helped my reputation. She is renowned for her taste and discretion. Besides, she is the favorite of Herr Müller's. Müller has nothing left to lose, you know. I chose him not only because his name has been well known to me in Vienna long before the war, but because he lost his entire family during it. His son was a prisoner of war. His wife died in a bombing while visiting her sister. He repurposed his familial love to a love for preserving Vienna."

Novak paused, his bright blue eyes locked on Simon's, clearly in hopes of eliciting a response. "So I sent Adameck and learned that you and Lady Sophia Huntington-Villiers were more than just acquaintances. Two birds. One stone."

Simon reached for his gun again.

"This game is rather dull now, Simon. Put your gun away."

This man was behind every moment Barrington tattooed his anger on the side of Simon's face, to the corners of his mother's heart barred from him. But if Simon put his worth into the hands of this flawed and susceptible man, he would never know his own value. His father was fallible. A traitor.

If he expected this man to be the answer for all of the questions Simon had about who he was, he'd be wrapping his entire identity up in a lie. But he had to put his faith in something.

Fortunately, the phone rang and Simon was given a few moments to steady himself. Every sinew and line and nerve was a tightening wire as he fought to maintain a casual air. He closed his eyes to block out the moment he had imagined hundreds of times and was now playing out before him.

"Who was it?" Simon demanded when Novak hung up the receiver.

Novak's voice was grated. "It seems like I've found Starling. This man Sidorov feels like he can use her as a lure for me. Imagine that."

"Is that a challenge?"

Novak kept his low-lidded eyes downturned. "Do you want it to be?"

"If you know where Sophie is—"

"And what about our game?" Novak nodded to the perfectly formed chessboard. A sense of longing lingered behind the question.

Simon swept the back of his arm across the board, dispersing the pieces.

Simon saw a flash in Novak's eyes. At first glance he thought it was anger. But the longer he held the man's gaze, the more uncertain Simon became.

He shoved his glasses up his nose. "You know where Sophie is and that is all I care about."

"You lie. A madman named Sidorov is holding Sophie hostage. He's violent. He doesn't care about any glorious cause; he has no need to spread one ideology to usurp another. He just wants to succeed. Wants to prove he has the upper hand."

Novak shook his head. "Shame, really. She doesn't deserve his cruelty."

Simon's heart lurched. Sophie was with this monster. "I endured Adameck trying to run me over in the street," he said casually.

"Did you not hear me? I won't directly impede anything you are trying to do. You want to bring down Eternity? Stop these little traitorous rings from popping up here and there? Fine. But I want Vienna."

"Why?"

"Because I can grow what I've been doing here. And you can help me."

Simon pondered his proposition. To hell with Brighton and Moser and a sequence of music and a new war Simon understood even less than the last one. His yearning to meet his father predated the moment Sophia Huntington-Villiers entered his life. A few hasty marriage vows for an estate, a few caresses, and a passionate night he could mark on the map of his memory as he moved on.

Did Simon really care about stomping out Communism, or did he just need another war to keep from retreating back to Camden?

"If you know so much about Sophie's captor, then you know where she is!" And this time when he retrieved his gun, his aim was steady enough and his purpose sure enough to see the threat through.

"You'd choose her?" He did little to keep the surprise from his voice.

Simon held the barrel steady as Novak gave him an address in the Hradčany castle grounds.

It took every nerve ending to steady his hold, and he blinked stinging perspiration from his eyes. It wasn't enough that Simon rise in Brighton's estimation: he would never feel he had met it. And chasing the approval of his father with his chess moves and his long luring of Simon was as fruitless as hoping he would make Barrington proud.

Simon could try and fail to live up to the expectation of a man he had waited his whole life to meet and who even now wanted to barter for what Simon offered. Or he could suture the cracks Sophie had made in his heart when she ran, leaving behind the memory of

how she had once pledged her loyalty to him as he turned his back on
Barrington and Camden.

Forsaking all others.

Odd, his fingers were steady now.

Simon cocked the hammer.

CHAPTER 38

W hy do you want the mask so badly?" Sophie asked. For the first several questions, Sidorov had slapped her a few times. But there was an air of showmanship that allowed her to recover from the sting of his backhand and keep herself in check.

"There is the very real possibility that this artifact does not exist at all. Or is a copy or a fake."

Perhaps he wanted it because everyone else did. Few things more valuable than an object rumored to be greatly desired. "I do not have the information you need."

She blinked to stay awake as Sidorov's questions continued. He showed little interest in tempering his violence. When the ringing in her ears from his backhand desisted, her brain cleared enough to pull back and find a safe point . . .

To Simon.

"If I have done such a poor job, why not just sack me and find someone better able to assist you?"

Her stomach turned at the appearance of Sidorov's pliers. Sophie had heard this was a popular interrogation technique. Rip out fingernails one by one in a slow, rotating agony. How long would her will hold out?

"It has to be you. For more reasons than just you breaking your word." He rapped the makeshift weapon on the table separating them, then grabbed her right hand, his pliers poised to wreak pain. No more showmanship. He started with her thumbnail.

She railed against the agony, ramming her weight into the rim of the metal table and grappling with the last hook holding her determination.

"Jan Novak," Sidorov said. "You work for him. I have a close contact with him, but he has had little time for me. Not for you, though."

Sophie's ears buzzed and her eyes blurred. There was no reason for his cruel ministrations at this point other than the power he wielded.

She remembered Brighton's ultimatum. She needn't be here on the precipice of losing something she so deeply loved: the feel of her fingers on piano keys, the swell of Mozart or Beethoven when she heard the first notes she created.

The questions melded into those she *could* but *would* not answer.

Sophie *could* quantify the memory of Simon's breath on her neck and his voice in her ear and the still, sure regret that drove her to claim her corner of the world again. She *could* verify that Simon was drawn by Brighton and Novak because he was Das Flüstern's son. But she wouldn't give this information to a man who so easily ripped at her fingernails.

Give him enough to know you are needed. Sophie licked parched lips, tasting the salt at the top of her perspiring mouth. "Novak is not unlike any other man in pursuit of money."

"It's more than money!" Sidorov spat out, taking his censure against her answer in a twist of her finger into further agony.

If she stayed in the present, she would go mad. So she drew on what dregs of strength she had through past troubles. She hadn't been able to tell Simon she loved him because she had run away at his uttering of those three words. But the power of the letters in the case still sitting at the front of Novak's town house? They made her think of Diana going on incessantly about the many Greek forms of love Brent had written to her about during the war.

Maybe Sophie ran away because she couldn't speak of love in one language, but she had given her loyalty. And the more she resisted

Sidorov's torture inspired her to think—in her case—that loyalty and love might be one and the same.

Her once-manicured nails were now cracked. In the case of the first and second nails of her right hand, they were removed altogether. Sidorov had been persistent. He seemed to know how to build from one question to another.

A slight *thud* sounded through the paper-thin walls and Sidorov's voice bled through, having a one-sided conversation. Must be on the telephone.

She wasn't sure where she was, only that it was within the fortressed Hradčany grounds. She could sit here as useless as the pawn they had made Simon—or she could prick her ears to hear the words against the backdrop of a mournful Shostakovich concerto on a muffled wireless radio. That composer wrote a symphony in captivity. They called it a Symphony for the City of the Dead. She felt its minor chords far more than any Mozart in this moment.

She focused on the words she could make out. *Esterházy,* she heard through the drips and soft echoes. Then something about Hungary.

There was a palace in Esterházy. It once belonged to a prince when the Habsburg Empire was a jewel and Vienna was ivory and cream and not soot stained. It was where Mozart had first performed his arrangement of *Der Messias.*

That bloody manuscript.

Sidorov's voice trailed off, then he returned with fresh determination from whatever information he had received. "I have been remiss." The corners of his mouth tugged down in a patronizing frown. "You may well be telling the truth about the mask. But I believe you know how Simon Barre keeps his information."

Fingers throbbing, she said, "Simon and I had a falling-out."

Sidorov removed his gun, and Sophie swallowed what was left of the chalk in her mouth.

Was the location woven into Simon's coding system? Inspired by the Köchel Catalogue? *Focus on something succinct and precise.*

Simon had encoded vital information that extended far beyond her grasp of the world he had created in Vienna. What she held in the value of art and history, he had impounded into a secret language. One she knew.

K. 453: the Starling Concerto.

The secret he had told her in a voice so endearingly vulnerable. The heart of his current work entwined in an anecdote she had told him long ago about her music tutor and a caged bird. With it, she might have spared her mangled right hand.

"I don't know." She lied. The price of her answer was the last fingernail on her right hand. Each now involuntarily curled into her palm.

Sidorov removed the clamps holding her arms down. "Get to your feet."

Sophie complied, recalling what she could of the Villiers' bearing while her weight favored falling in the direction of her hurt hand. She unevenly countered it with her will.

Time counted out a slow and uncertain measure. The incessant tick of the clock was replaced by Sophie's bleary acknowledgment of a slate-gray sky. The middling sun haloing the rooftops might have coaxed spring to one observer, but to Sophie it merely concluded a day melting into another.

She followed Sidorov over the sleek cobblestones to the awaiting car. Her heart was racing. She could feel the pulse down to her fingertips, every stab into her tortured right hand was a needle prick. Sophie's steps were uneven from exhaustion, and she stumbled on her T-strap heels.

As a girl she assumed that a castle was a fairy tale-in-motion with turrets and moats. In this melancholy city it was a compound of buildings erected in a grand history around the central focus of the cathedral with the premises appropriated by the Nazis for interrogations.

The way Sidorov opened the passenger door, grabbed her arm, and pulled her trembling form across the cobbles was a gesture of superiority.

"What is this then?" Her teeth clacked, but at least the crisp air revived her a little. "Trying to impress me by showing me off in a short tour of the castle compound?" She hugged her frame against the bracing cold.

"We're here to do a transaction, Starling. Your specialty. You chose Novak over me, so you can face him now. And get me what I want."

"I didn't choose him. I never promised I wouldn't . . ." But she let the words fall on the pavement. Sidorov hadn't listened before.

She raised her left, whole hand to her bare neck. Where her pearls should be. Then she smoothed her matted hair and tugged at the blouse and trousers she had been wearing, asleep and awake, for a day and a half since Sidorov had shoved her inside the heavy wooden doors.

They drove past St. Vitus—magnanimous in its marriage of scalloped structure and stone—and farther into the mazed and medieval compound of palaces and buildings, a prison, and a golden alley of squat, tumbling houses like children's building blocks. He swerved to the curb and she carefully unfolded from the passenger seat.

She hadn't yet pieced together how Sidorov was connected to Adameck or to Novak. Just that Sidorov had found her and maimed her. Now he pushed her into a small, squat building that doubtless was as old as the others surrounding it. The arched windows and long corridors gave her the impression of a chapel. It was a carefully planned but poorly executed interrogation.

She fell forward, only just stopping herself before her forehead hit the table.

"And Novak?"

Sophie was on the last fraying tether of rope but a few fibers and fraying threads asserted the possibility that the rope would hold. She had been stretched so far, she could rally just enough of an intake of breath and a slight raise of her shoulders.

But would she sacrifice the last of her strength to a man who was grasping at straws?

"Simon Barre and I had a falling-out," she repeated.

"Prove it," Sidorov said.

And on her life, Sophie would.

CHAPTER 39

*I*t's not what you do, but what you can make others believe *you have done.* Sophie had paraphrased the quote from one of her father's beloved leather-bound Sherlock Holmes volumes a half-dozen times in her own work. It suited here.

Perhaps Novak was the legitimate one with the influence that swayed other men to do his bidding. To secure the transaction of artifacts in Vienna and Prague. Whatever Novak asserted, he did so boldly.

Sidorov hadn't touched her for several moments, so she fixed her eyes on a smudge of light in the corner and waited. Judging by Sidorov's swift curse, it was clear he wasn't expecting the tall figure darkening the entrance. Sidorov stood from his place across the table from Sophie and approached the door. "You are not Jan Novak."

"Good eye." Simon smirked. "Especially considering we have met before."

"I spoke to Herr Novak. He was to be here, and we were to work out an arrangement. For Starling." Sidorov moved closer to Simon.

"The arrangement has changed." Simon's intense blue eyes focused on her.

Sophie tucked her battered hand behind her back. She wouldn't give Sidorov the satisfaction of being right. Of connecting their dots and sussing out the veracity of Simon's and her relationship. Especially because she had survived so much to avoid it.

She couldn't *read* Simon. She thought she knew his tells: the pulse pounding in his temples, the tightening of his jaw muscles, adjusting his cuff links. She knew them as well as she knew where to strike an attacker for the most effectiveness.

But Simon wasn't moving. Wasn't shoving Sidorov into the wall. And part of her—the hurt part that had conjured his face and dreamed of his rescuing her a thousand times over—felt betrayed by his inaction.

Yet her logical part reassured her that Simon always swore to fight for her, just as she had pledged her loyalty to him, despite the circumstances of their parting.

Sidorov's eyes narrowed and his chin raised slightly. Even during his interrogation of Sophie, he spoke of Simon in vague terms, as if he didn't know *how* the man before him fit into the world he inhabited: the world of Novak, of Mozart's death mask. But judging by his refrain from reactive violence, his curiosity was piqued. He also hadn't fired his firearm the moment her husband walked into the room.

Husband. Sophie flushed to her ears. The word that had been used so casually in banter now manifested in the way her heart stirred and her blood pulsed.

"Novak couldn't make your meeting because when I left him, he was *indisposed.*" There was no mistaking the grave tone in Simon's voice.

Sophie gasped. The man was dead. If Simon had met him, then maybe he knew Novak's identity and his own connection to him. Maybe, too, he assumed that Sophie had kept that secret from him as recently as the night she had coldly left him.

Simon gave her a subtle look. He was bluffing, but Sidorov didn't know that. Simon furtively surveyed the small room. The slight movement of Simon's arms tucked behind his back belied his statue-still stance. His revolver must not be at the front of his waistband of his trousers but the back.

The tension crackled through the room, but Sidorov did not move from her side, watching Simon almost as intently as she had been. Now, he was waiting for a move.

Simon glanced at Sophie, a subtle flash in his bright eyes, before he lowered his eyelashes.

I should get down.

After his warning, Simon swiftly drew his gun.

Sidorov drew his own firearm, and rather than turn it on her, he aimed it at Simon.

They stood locked in a standoff. Sophie could almost *feel* the tenacity in his resolve. He had the height advantage, but she had borne the brunt of his opponent's reckless rage. Simon would never fire without provocation. Sidorov was hotheaded and impatient. Simon was more proficient but Sidorov was equally dangerous.

"Why was she so determined to protect your connection with Novak?" Sidorov spat out.

Simon's response was unflinching. "Starling is often on retainer for many clients for many different reasons. Perhaps she had a conversation with Novak that has left me in the dark."

"I didn't get much out of her." Sidorov employed a new technique. "But perhaps you might have. Despite your *falling-out*." He hissed the last words for Sophie's benefit, perhaps sensing the taut connection between them.

Simon leveled his gun.

"I can recommend her left hand, Herr Barre. The right is completely mangled. Nasty business removing fingernails." He centered the gun directly in line with her thumping heart.

"But I assume she'd talk more if you take the use of both hands altogether. Pity, isn't it? I had heard she was a great pianist."

And with the first admission of the extent of Sophie's injuries, Simon wavered a moment and his aim slightly faltered.

Sidorov took advantage of Simon's distraction. Despite the

struggle, Simon removed his index finger from the trigger. He wouldn't risk it firing when he had little control. Not when it might shoot in her direction.

She wanted to leap over and protect him, help him, shove Sidorov into the wall behind him. But any movement on her part would distract Simon further.

Simon drove a swift elbow to the man's stomach, and Sidorov dropped his gun. Simon kicked the weapon away from his assailant toward Sophie's direction.

She grabbed it and raised it just as Sidorov pressed Simon's weapon against his temple.

Sidorov chuckled. Perhaps any man would, seeing the state of her right hand. Especially a man who didn't know what Simon did: Sophie was ambidextrous, as she had proven a half-dozen times at one of her father's shooting weekends.

Sidorov flexed his thumb and cocked the hammer.

Sophie widened her eyes at Simon, trying to read *anything* in his face. Perhaps fear that her ordeal might throw her usual aim off course. After all, the pain in her damaged right fingers put her at a disadvantage.

If she *missed* . . . If Sidorov was *faster* . . . She slid her injured fingers over the unfamiliar revolver. She had accomplished far greater feats with a partridge and a fallen tree in the Ashton woods. But she held Simon's life in her hands.

Sophie licked her lips, reeled herself in, cocked her head, and narrowed her eyes in line with Sidorov's shoulder.

She blinked the stinging perspiration from her tired eyes. A tremble moved over her, and she tightened every muscle and sinew into place. With the next move she was likely to kill a man: either the one who took her passion or the one who ignited it.

Sophie locked eyes with Simon's—seeing just a flash, a light, a *challenge*—and it was in this glance she fired.

———◆◆◆———

Simon had closed his eyes just as she pulled the trigger. Now, slowly opening them, he turned to survey Sidorov on the ground beside him. The gun that might have shot Simon through the head lay under the man's outstretched arm. Sophie truly was an astounding shot. She had barely missed him.

Simon surveyed the bruises on Sophie's temple, the cut on her lip, the right hand she rubbed furiously. He didn't know how to assess the extent of her injuries. Immediately, he was more concerned by her pallor and the tremor in her shoulders.

Her eyes on his were wild before they fell to Sidorov. "I killed him . . ."

Simon slowly and carefully moved the man, closed his eyes, and blocked the worst of the blood trail from Sophie's perspective. A moment later, he walked toward her as she frantically looked over his shoulder.

The gun hung from her hand. "I killed him." She raised the gun in question, and Simon gingerly took it from her fingers. The slightest touch and she winced.

Simon's eyes steadied her, and finally she drew a deep breath. Only to pursue another line of thought altogether. "There's a rumor about Mozart's death mask, Simon. It's what I came to Prague for. Novak, but I didn't know then that he was your father." The words came out in a rush the moment he approached her. "Did you know that Novak . . . ?"

"Not now, Sophia." He had to map out the rest of the night. Balancing his concern for her with his abandoning his conversation with Novak—the last key to his past—took some careful cartography.

He flicked a side glance at her. "Shoulders back," he commanded. "Straighten your spine." He lengthened his own. "Breathe in." His own breath caught in his windpipe. "Eyes on me."

"Just like when we were dancing," she said on an exhale. "Sidorov's dead."

"We'll tell Brighton. Or Tab Martin. They'll know what to do." He felt her tremble slightly through the steadying hand he held under her elbow as he led them out of the castle compound over slick cobbles and past sputtering streetlamps.

Doubtless the eyes of the sporadically lit windows peering from the dungeon, castle, and through the stained glass of St. Vitus had witnessed countless similar deaths. "Why did he bring you here?" he asked.

"Brighton told me the Gestapo used the grounds to torture prisoners."

Simon nodded. "Perhaps just showing off." He steered her in the direction of his Bentley behind the Gothic cathedral.

He'd earlier had the foresight to hail a cab from the base of Kampa Island to retrieve his motorcar at the Alcron. It bit into the time it took to pursue her, but it was a necessity. And still where he'd parked it.

Simon opened the passenger side for her. The sooner they were tucked behind the tinted windows, the better.

Several silent moments followed as he put the car in reverse. Silence still as he paid off the guard near the barrier arm separating the hilled castle grounds from Malá Strana below.

While she studied the wintry streets through the passenger window, he took the opportunity to look at her right hand—raw, twisted, and bleeding in her lap. It made him sick, and a fierce anger burned, imagining what she had suffered. Her chestnut hair was slightly parted, and he made out a circular-shaped welt on the side of her neck.

Sophie noticed him watching her. "Not my dominant hand anymore."

"You had the upper hand, even under the circumstances." Simon was breaking, but he would never let her know. "And I can only begin to imagine what the past two days have been like for you. But you can draw strength from how you concluded them."

Simon would have driven faster if not for the uneven, winding streets, the erratic streetlights, and the black patches of ice. He would have challenged her too. After all, despite the night's revelations, he still had his pride. Her leaving prickled under his collar. But her injured fingers and matted hair drove the last of his irritation away. For now, he would reason aloud: it calmed him and inched them closer to their destination.

"Novak is your father, Simon." She formed the sentence he had been unable to say outright.

"Right now, Novak is only a piece of a puzzle Brighton charged me with. When I see Novak again face-to-face, that might change. But he had to become momentarily incapacitated so I could find you."

"Momentarily . . ."

"He's alive. Just injured." Simon felt more than heard Sophie's exhale beside him.

"Sidorov was interested in your connection with Novak," Sophie said. "Brighton knew everything and I didn't know what he knew." Her tired voice fortified. "But I didn't tell him anything. You had my loyalty the whole time."

Simon stared at her face in the shadow of the streetlights.

"I'm fine," she said softly.

She wasn't fine, but neither was he. "I don't believe the mask is what's important here, Sophie. It's what it represents." Simon turned on the blinkers and navigated over the slick cobblestones to avoid a swerving car. "I have no doubt there is a mask—a fake one—in Prague." It was still speculation, but he supposed the men with a fragment of *Der Messias* accomplished much of what he had done.

"I think Novak's been luring collectors here with his Das Flüstern identity to divert them from the scent, and the real mask is safely tucked in Vienna."

"Where?"

"That's what we're going to find out."

Sophie turned back to the window. "You left your father to find me. You once told me you'd give your very life for that information."

"In sickness and health," he said simply.

He turned off the ignition close to Novak's house. He'd left the man with a nasty hit to the head and an unfinished conversation and chess game. Judging by the mellow light through the window, Simon's instinct was correct.

Novak wouldn't go anywhere until he had finished what he started.

CHAPTER 40

Simon had parked a few houses down from Novak's door. But while he turned the car off, he didn't immediately get out.

"If there is anything you learned in your work for Novak about this blasted mask, I need you to tell me. I don't care whose story it is to tell or if you are keeping someone's secret." His voice was weary but determined.

Sophie had no desire to keep secrets under lock and key. She had withstood two days under Sidorov's interrogation and torture to finally feel down to her bones the gift of Simon telling her that he loved her. It wasn't until she truly lost something that she recognized how much he had risked in saying it. He had laid himself open in a way she hadn't been able to. Now she wished she could spare him the hurt of betrayal by the two men so integral to his life.

"I heard part of a conversation with Sidorov. I don't know where the mask is. But he mentioned Esterházy. I was . . . *distracted*, but not so much that I would mistake that." She shook her head. "Esterházy is where Haydn lived. Under the patronage of the Esterházy family. The first performance of Mozart's *Messiah* arrangement took place there."

"And?"

"Churches and Pfandhauses, culture and art and soirees. These esoteric fragments of a little-known piece. I thought . . . perhaps Das Flüstern's—Novak's—organization wasn't unlike the Eternity ring in London. Painting his propaganda through a city's higher echelons. Promising something that high-ranking officials and academics and artists might . . ." She stopped. Her head was buzzing at the pain in her hand.

"The Americans are planning a European Assistance Program to see to the economic stability and rebuilding of Allied-occupied countries. The Communists have something similar. In retaliation. I believe Novak is at the heart of that." Simon looked left and right before running his hand over his knee. "So much of the assistance will focus on restoring culture."

Sophie took the shift in his voice's timbre. "Simon, if you're angry with me because of how we parted, I understand. But whatever you decide is your next step, it's mine too."

"Sophie." His breath left a cloud of condensation on the car window. "One move at a time."

She swallowed her hurt. He didn't want to hear it yet. "Whatever you need," she conceded.

Simon opened the driver's-side door and stepped out.

She smoothed her hair with her left hand. Her right was shaking. The slow walk from the Bentley to Novak's door was a long one.

"I had left my satchel here. When Sidorov abducted me. I should have told you back there and—" She pressed her trembling lips and took a breath. "There's a lot of valuable material in it." Not only some of the *Der Messias* fragments but the correspondence from his mother that Brighton had given her.

"I found it when I was here earlier. It's in the trunk of the Bentley," Simon said easily. He eased open the unlocked front door.

Sophie made out a crisp British voice in the front room, followed by Novak's soft Czech accent. Simon's head was turned in the direction of the men's conversation.

"And for a moment I thought you had the best offer," Novak said. "As long as you were willing to give me what I wanted, I would happily offer you crumbs: a Nazi sympathizer here, a few high-ranking of-ficials there. You had very good leverage when you brought Simon Barrington into view."

"You're the one who wanted to lure him out. *You* said he would be much more willing to accept the truth that we were working together if he felt that he was a part of it."

"The man knocked me out with his gun, Brighton. Clearly I was wrong. Which means I am not the only one at a loss here. He has learned as much of the truth about you as he has me."

"Why didn't you restrain him?" Brighton said. "He's not a violent man, and knowing you're his father should have been enough to keep him here."

"You clearly underestimated the depth of his connection to her."

"I've always known that she was his Achilles' heel. Anytime he has wavered in his duty, it has been more because of her than these hunches he follows."

"He's feeling around in the dark. You told me that."

"She said they had a falling-out."

"And you believed her?" Novak said.

"Wouldn't you? You're the one who wanted to work with her." Brighton sighed. "You of all people should know about doomed love affairs. Betrayal. Many have waded through those darkened waters. It does little good if Simon Barre dove after her."

Simon was still as stone. Though the flash in his eyes was a melding of surprise and annoyance, she knew he was weighing his next move.

"He had the element of surprise," Novak said. "But *you* didn't fol-low through on your promise."

"But at least Simon's *here*."

"Here in Prague, yes. But he did *not* act as you led me to believe he would."

"Which was what?" Brighton said.

"You said you had influence over him. Which is why I needed you. More and more I am seeing that I overestimated your powers."

"Only because I won't let you demand how much information I give you." Brighton cursed. "I wanted your talent, your connections, and I suppose it serves me right that you turned out to be Amateur Hour on the BBC! But if you have this artifact half of Vienna is up in arms about, then we're even. I can't say I understand *why* it's important, just that it was enough to lure Sophie Villiers here. And I have to respect a man who would toy with two cities truly believing an antique is auspicious enough to tip the political scales."

"A people's composer belongs to everyone," Novak said. "Accessible to peasants and kings."

Had Sophie been led on a wild-goose chase for something already in Novak's possession?

"Then I can leave with the mask and you can find Simon," Brighton said.

Sophie's waiting for Simon's reaction made her nearly forget the throb in her fingers. He must be wondering why two men supposedly so adept in this shadow world they had forged failed to notice Simon and her eavesdropping in the front hallway.

But rather than barge in, Simon merely stepped into the sitting room and cleared his throat. Perhaps they were half-expecting their visitors, because when Simon started to move past her, Brighton's tone was more subtle annoyance than surprise.

"Ah. Simon."

Sophie held on to Simon's forearm, and he covered her hand with his. They were a team. He wouldn't let her go. He would keep her at his side but also upright. She leaned into him a little as they crossed through to the sitting room.

Simon inclined his head toward the sofa, but she couldn't seem to move. He met her eyes a moment.

"Sophie shot Sidorov back at Hradčany," Simon told Brighton, then turned to Novak. "No doubt you surmised I would come back and here I am. Not sure what you had to do with the Russian, but he's not part of whatever this is anymore."

Simon motioned both Brighton and Novak to sit. Brighton did so immediately. Novak took a moment.

Simon coolly reached into his jacket pocket and produced his revolver. Doubtless Brighton and Novak were armed, but neither seemed too threatened by the weapon at first—until Simon leveled it at Novak with a glare that hardened his blue eyes to ice.

Novak lowered into a chair adjacent to Brighton. Sophie chose the settee just behind Simon's left shoulder.

"So this is your dangerous double agent?" Simon directed to Brighton while studying Novak. "Someone you've probably known far longer than those chess plays you showed me in Vienna."

Brighton shifted. "I came here to see how Novak was attempting to make sure the Communists had a stronger political showing in Prague. Except I didn't know it *was* Novak at first. He was using that Das Flüstern moniker."

"Money is crass," Novak interjected. "Brighton here believes politics are acted out in parliament, but here they are secured in refinement. Soon the Americans will be in Vienna with their Assistance Program, which will not only see to the financial reconstruction but the *ideological* one. The starving, sad people will be given art and culture. I am merely trying to inspire something similar."

Simon hadn't lowered his gun but he wasn't holding it so tightly.

"There's rising tension," Novak continued. "President Beneš is not a capable leader, and for all of its cracks, Prague has been my home since I was a scholar. I need the Communist Party to win because I won't allow certain men to get ahead while others drag behind."

Simon turned to Brighton. "And that's why you used me? For this man's access to swaying political powers?"

THE *Mozart* CODE

"It wasn't personal, Simon."

Not personal that Brighton had taken what Simon had spent his whole life trying to find and used it as a bargaining chip? Not personal that he let Sidorov torture her so brutally as answer to her refusing to lure Simon per his request ? To show she was of little consequence other than as a means to the bargaining chip of Novak's mask? Doubtless he had put together her maze of finding and trading relics. Or perhaps even as a comeuppance for years before. A woman who couldn't even cross the border. Judging by his long pursuit of Simon, Brighton took pride and root in those he weeded for his use. Sophie failed. Twice.

"No? What isn't personal about capitalizing on someone's breaking point?" Simon said. "But you and I are alike in that we overestimate human capability, Brighton. Instead of this grand and mysterious enemy, Eternity was really a bunch of men trying to find new ways to pass pamphlets to like-minded people and map their way to safe houses."

Simon turned to glare at Novak, whose eyes blazed right back. "But truly . . . they're just men grasping at straws to ensure their worldview spreads before history takes its course. The loudest voice can convince *anyone* that it is in the right."

"Simon," Novak warned. "You are made for this work. You don't want another war like the one we just fought. You don't want to see people starving while rich men like Charles Barrington trod on the lower classes. Margaret didn't want that."

"Don't say her name." Simon's voice raised several decibels. Then he addressed Brighton. "You set me up in Vienna. That first meeting."

"No."

"Fine, you merely withheld key information: you knew I would be intrigued enough to play the game." Simon shook his head. "This is mad."

"No more mad than any other Allied country showing up and

assuming that just because they drove the Nazis out, they could start driving their own agenda," Novak said.

Sophie watched Simon survey the room: the impressive mahogany bookshelves and then the chessboard he approached with a determined stride.

Next to it was a nondescript open box with blue lining.

Simon cast a quick look at her, and as she joined him, he lowered his gun.

While three men watched her every move, Sophie studied what was in the box. It was almost *too* perfect. Her breath caught in her chest. A mask.

Simon gingerly peeled back the box's lining and checked behind the velvet-covered lid. He even inspected the clasps.

The visage of the composer was worn to a shine, the grooves and wear too likely to mimic an original. Sophie had only seen the mask in detailed illustration in books and sketches. It was artful, much like *Der Messias*.

She smoothed the box with her good hand to see if she could find a secret compartment, a folded paper with certification of authenticity. Another man's etching on a masterpiece might well be its own brand of beauty and innovation, but . . . "This is a fake, Simon."

"Novak!" Brighton spat. "You said nothing about it being fake."

"You have the chance to write your own story, Simon," Novak said. "Here and now. You and I can influence what comes next. Not in broad strokes perhaps but in slight adjustments."

"You cannot *possibly* think I would align myself with you now."

A large clock in the corner ticked in the ensuing silence like an ominous metronome, and the air in the room grew thick. Everyone was standing now. Brighton stood closest to the door. Simon was positioned at the apex of both men with Sophie to his side.

She and Simon would need a contingency plan to redeem this blasted mess. There was no real mask in Prague, perhaps, but Novak so easily got her to take manuscript pages over the border. And Adameck was always traveling between the two cities. Novak played this card well. Sophie was torn between lunging in defense and Simon keeping control.

Simon's eyes were electric despite his exhaustion. Brighton was still . . . too still.

Novak took a long time to speak. "You are not what I expected, Simon."

"Next time you have a hankering to meet your heir and lure him into a stupid, elaborate game to help you meet with men of a different league . . . try sending a telegram."

The chill in Simon's voice pricked Sophie.

Novak's face darkened. He had doubtless imagined the scene would play out much differently.

Brighton's patience was faltering and he drew his gun. And aimed it at Novak. Sophie was overwhelmed by the need to protect Simon's father. With Simon and Sophie here and no concrete information to barter for, Novak was now useless to Brighton.

She lunged in an attempt to retrieve the weapon with a quick slice to Brighton's windpipe and an elbow to his torso.

Brighton was undeterred in his attempt to fight her off.

In her exhaustion and pain Sophie sensed more than felt Novak intervene: whether to defend her or settle his own score with Brighton, she couldn't be sure. But the ensuing seconds accelerated her heartbeat.

She imagined Simon as she heard his shot crack: fierce and precise.

Simon fell back a little. He had taken the brunt of Brighton's answering fire. Clearly he was as determined to save Novak as Simon was to protect Sophie.

Her lip trembled and then her hand and then the whole of her until Simon's attention shifted from Novak back to her. "I'll live, Sophia."

"Simon." His name in her voice was a plea.

"I'll live," he repeated.

But Novak wouldn't on account of Simon's shot. Novak had fallen, a long ribbon of blood marking the carpet.

Simon didn't kneel, nor did he panic. He used the last few moments of a man's life as an opportunity for himself. "Did you love her?" Simon's anguished voice was almost unrecognizable to Sophie. "Did you love my mother?"

"I . . ." Novak looked around, startled but lucid.

"Did you *love* her?"

Simon hadn't seen the letters Brighton had bartered with.

Novak took his time before speaking. "She was the answer to a question. A comrade. An ally . . . I knew that under the right influence . . . she could have imagined and lived . . . a glorious life."

"But did you *love* her?"

Sophie wasn't certain she had ever heard anything as mournful as the question shrouded in Simon's attempt to maintain control. He would allow himself this one moment of personal vulnerability even as his father's life drained away.

Sophie looked to both men before settling on Simon. If only time and unspoken words had been gobbled up before tempers could mount and break. But the senseless end was no different from many similar during the war.

While she might have been Simon's breaking point, and Novak's the prospect of meeting his son, Brighton chose violence over anything else. It was a stark contrast to the Brighton she had known years before. And while it pained her deeply, she reluctantly saw how it could be a useful weapon in this new war.

When Simon finally addressed Brighton, it was in a cold voice. "Did you arrange for a message that told me she was a traitor to find me? *Starling turned?*"

"The elections are not so far off, Simon," Brighton said calmly. "And in our world everything might seem to move at a glacial pace. I needed to get you here. Believe me, if Sidorov hadn't used Sophie as a weapon, Novak eventually would have. You killed a dangerous enemy because he had nothing more to lose than a misguided sense of loyalty to a cause that helped him reconcile why he could never fit into your mother's world."

"I asked you a question."

"Yes. Simon, I know you well enough to know that you will find what Novak has hidden. But remember, *I* saw you kill him. If you are going to obliterate me, then you will need to have a *very* good plan."

It didn't matter what Sophie and Simon did. It didn't matter that Sidorov was dead in Hradčany and Novak here at their feet. Men like Brighton could finesse actions into sacrifices and accidents into combative standoffs for the good of a greater cause.

Simon's protection of her was nowhere near as magnanimous; it was primal.

After a few moments in which Simon was still, he turned to her, eyes wide and questioning—needing to find an answer in her own. Sophie took in the room, whose silence was as sonorous as a requiem. She tugged at Simon's sleeve and shot him a questioning look. What would they do about Brighton? But as Simon led her away from him, she knew it didn't matter if they left him there.

"We don't need either of them," she whispered as he led her out the door, feeling the same jolt of confidence that stretched through her fingers when they pressed the keys of her favorite Bösendorfer. A fake mask and this dissonant meeting between a trio of men unsure of their next move. But Sophie knew. The satchel in the trunk of Simon's Bentley had most of the sheets of K. 572 she had been charged with finding.

"Simon," she whispered.

"Not now, Sophia." His eyes scanned the room, gun held tightly in his slightly shaking hand.

As he attempted to carve order from chaos, she wanted to love him for herself, yes, but also for all of the people in his life that should have . . . and didn't. And it gave her enough strength to grab his elbow and await his next move.

"Ready to play medic, Villiers?" Simon's voice held a challenge.

The answer to the question he had spent his life pursuing must have left him as confused and riled as she was. And yet, he was holding on. The least she could do was see him out the door before shattering into pieces. "I will try."

"I can't drive to Vienna like this." He winced, assessing his shoulder wound. "So you'll have to play Florence Nightingale before we set out." He winked at her wearily. "We're going on a treasure hunt."

"And what about"—Sophie gestured to Novak—"all of this?"

"Brighton's right. It would be my word against his. But we have a new board, Sophie. We have a Pfandhaus in Vienna and we have Gabe Langer. We've got the pieces. I just need to figure out how to play them."

CHAPTER 41

"Y ou will need a very good plan."

Brighton's words tripped on Simon's heels as they left the town house. He couldn't give the man the upper hand until he had some concrete evidence.

The walk from the door to the Bentley was made longer by Sophie's slow pace, as if trudging through gelatin. He wouldn't let her crumble because he loved her, but also because the distraction allowed him to focus on something other than the consequence of his pulling the trigger.

On his father.

He cupped her chin. "Sophie! Keep your eyes on me." Watching her, he just might be able to still his breath and slow his mounting heartbeat.

The snow was filling up the street too quickly, gathering in small hills on the windshield. Simon pressed his hand to where the bullet had hit his shoulder and led her out the way they came.

Once they were settled inside his car, Sophie turned on the ignition and blew her hair from her face. They needed to find somewhere safe, far from Brighton or the haunted castle compound. Simon directed her to drive over Karlův most, where the saints that had overseen his first meeting with Novak now seemed to leer under misshapen webs of snow.

Sophie's left knuckles were white on the wheel while her right arm lay motionless and merely balanced as she steered. Her arm strained in defiance of the slippery ground beneath the tires.

"I trusted you back there, Sophie. That you knew where the mask is." If he kept talking, he would keep from drifting. The throb in his left shoulder remained steady but bearable.

"It wasn't a bluff. I wouldn't lie in such a moment. I knew what was at stake. It's a hunch but a good one."

Sophie swerved the Bentley onto the narrow street that, like a tentacle, sprawled out from the famous old square to be straddled by the Prašná brána, the medieval Powder Gate Tower sectioning the old town from the new.

In a dark alley tucked away from Our Lady before Týn church, she turned off the ignition and winced at the sudden movement as pain rippled through her injured hand.

"I keep medical supplies in the trunk." Perspiration dotted his forehead, despite the time of year. Here, they were in a safe nook, close enough to find help in Staré Město if needed but tucked into the shadow of the same. After a few hours' sleep and recovery, he might be able to steal his wife out of the city. "As I said, I need a medic."

She gestured at his shoulder. "We need to sew that up."

It was a minor wound in the grand scheme of things. Nevertheless, he was holding on by a thread, waylaying the shock and pain, determined to find a way to close the gap he felt between them.

She returned with the supplies, and he saw how difficult it was for her to finagle them given her injured hand.

"Surprised you trust me at all after how I had treated you in Vienna." The words might have been conjured in defiance, but her tone was unmistakably unsure.

She shook her head, and tears that hadn't fallen before were a small tidal wave. "Why aren't you angry with me? After all you've learned tonight? After my blindly working for this man for weeks and stalling everything?"

"We have the rest of our lives to argue." He was hoping to coax a smile, but even though she was turned from him, her rigid posture spoke volumes.

Her breath fogged the driver's window as she surveyed the side of the church. "Why stop here?"

Torchlight mingled with the streetlights still sputtering. Don Giovanni's licentious behavior was performed at the Stavovské divadlo opera house blocks away from their location. She was nervous to be near him too. "This light is as good as any. And isn't there a law of sanctuary? It's safe to know there's someplace we can hide at a moment's notice."

He didn't know what Brighton's next move would be. More still, was Sidorov just one man desperate to find something that would elevate his situation, or did he have people working for him?

They needed to get back to Vienna.

"Here." She handed him the bottle of vodka that rounded out his emergency supplies.

Simon glugged it, grimacing. Simon hated vodka.

"Simon." His name caught in her breath.

"Don't."

Sophie undid the top button of his soiled shirt. It stuck to him where the blood had dried. She carefully peeled back the fabric over the wound and smoothed her good palm over his shoulder. "It's clean through." She helped him wrestle out of his shirt. "This is going to sting." She sloshed vodka on a cleaner part of his shirt before pressing it into the wound.

Simon grunted as the alcohol spread. "How can you see what you're doing?" he hissed.

"I can't." She only had one good hand on the torch and its aim was floundering at best.

She swallowed, trembled, and started again. "S-Simon . . . I'm sorry." She struck a match and pressed the flame to the end of the needle. Then she worked the thread through the eye.

He knew she wasn't apologizing for her makeshift surgical skills. So he rewarded her by letting her into the next play. "Moser curated an exhibition back in Vienna. And I saw fingerprints. On the glass of a particular exhibit. Lots of them. As if people were focused on a certain building in Wallnerstrasse. At first I second-guessed myself."

He swallowed hard at the first stab of the thread into his skin. For several moments he watched her face in concentration and contoured by shadows. He desperately wanted to know the extent of her injuries beyond her beautiful damaged hand. "You mentioned Esterházy earlier. It's a palace in Eisenstadt but also in Vienna. Though the Viennese one isn't as grand, of course. Is that what you were trying to let me know? Back there?"

Sophie nodded. Finally, the wound was stitched and clean enough until they could find a doctor in Vienna. His shoulder stretched uncomfortably and they needed to go, but he wasn't willing to relinquish the moment with her until they found a bit of their old footing. He needed it more than ever now that he'd traded his past for his future.

"Sophie, what are you thinking? I know you feel guilty but I need you."

"I am only ever unequivocally yours." She was so different from the Sophie who had left him alone at the Sacher Hotel and yet so very much the same. "I didn't know who Novak was, and I didn't know who I was until you were in the balance."

He was pleasantly surprised when she leaned over, cupped his chin, and emphasized her words with a slow pursuit of his mouth. Here in the shadows, with the last mournful bells of the evening tolling over the statues and stones, he had her completely. With matted hair and head resting on his shoulder, her stale breath a whisper from his chin—there was no moment for pretense and he could take her exactly as she was.

CHAPTER 42

Prague's first bells tolled bright. The streets slick with ice and flecks of snow: a world enchanted.

She cherished this Simon: out of sorts. Allowing himself to be human just as she had chided him to be years ago. At some point of weary conversation just before he fell asleep, he softly told her that Barrington had died and that he would step into the titles their fake marriage had procured.

The estate he didn't want beyond the memory of his mother.

The irony pinged her as she studied him in repose.

His pallor only made the blood on his stained shirt more pronounced, but Sophie's stitching job had held up through the short hours they rested.

"Enough sleep to see us through?" he asked groggily, blinking.

It had been little over an hour. "Just enough, I suppose."

"Well, it will have to do."

Sophie leaned forward and threw her arms around his neck with a fervor that had been building since the evening before. "Now it's *my* turn to be strong, Simon."

At his slight wince, she backed up a little on account of his shoulder. "Keep your eyes on me." She pressed her lips to his, and he met her mouth freely, tender and strong.

His hands framed her face with a possession that might have sent Sophia Huntington-Villiers into retreat. But Sophie Barrington recognized the gesture, not as one claiming but as proof of his ardent feelings. His trying to be gentle meant so much, considering her hand hurt worse upon waking.

He tasted like sleep and stale vodka and sadness, if the latter had a taste. And she didn't care. What they'd made together was sewn up of far more than a night of confessions. He had given *everything* for her, was excising his grief by pouring every last breath into her, and the least she could do was offer the dregs of her exhausted self.

It was only when she tasted the salt of her tears on her cracked lips that she disengaged to gulp icy air.

"How's your hand?"

"One is functioning perfectly."

Simon nodded. "We'll swap driving halfway."

The wintry sun flickered over the statues of martyred saints lining the bridge, reminding Sophie of wax melted under candle wicks. And as they left Prague behind, she felt she was turning a page. Simon, cognizant of any other traffic on the motorways, sometimes looked around. Never quite at ease.

But Austria in its rhythm of green and gold soon stretched beyond the blockades and checkpoints of Czechoslovakia, and she could see it steady him.

A cerulean sky framed majestic alps with frosted tips: clean and fresh as the edelweiss just beginning to yawn into the sunlight as the last snow melted. Sheep and cows dotted the pastures flanking the small, winding road through which Simon navigated. Sophie attempted to keep her eyes open.

"Sidorov was right in what he told you." Sophie trailed her right index finger over the window. "I'll never play the piano again," she said after a long silence.

"I've no great hankering to sit behind a chessboard anytime soon." Simon's tenor was tired but even. "So I'll play chess again when you play piano again."

He had lost more than one sense of purpose. *For her.* It was almost a stronger vow than the words she had whispered at their fake marriage.

Midway through as they switched their driving journey, Simon retrieved Sophie's satchel from the trunk, and she shifted the letters Brighton had given her to gingerly extract the pieces of *Der Messias*. Simon contributed with the page Müller had given him.

Sophie aligned the score on the closed trunk. Simon glanced around to ensure there was nothing near the curb but the wired ribbon of a fence and a field of sheep.

"See, they're almost all intact."

"Did Novak plan on selling this?" Simon raked his fingers through his hair. "He was so evasive when we talked to him. When I was at Müller's trying to find you, there were markings on the piece. I thought it devalued it."

"Some of the pieces are certainly from Mozart's time, but others are not. Some I found dated to 1884. Still valuable as a first printing but not nearly as much." She pointed to the top of the page. "Mozart used the Italian instead of the English to denote the movements and parts. See?"

She followed Simon's sight line. *Parte Seconda.* "The movement numbering here is from the Franz edition of the piece in the late nineteenth century. Novak had me focused on three pieces from the second part of *Messiah*. And it didn't matter if they were from Mozart's time or from the nineteenth century. It wasn't so much completing a piece . . ."

"As completing a message," Simon finished.

"And there were a few odd interactions. From men who were interested in acquiring or selling a piece of music but from the pieces of Mozart's version cut from Handel's oratorio."

"What do you mean 'cut'?"

"Omitted. He didn't include every piece—or song—that was in Handel's original oratorio. So those who knew what Novak was pursuing or the men he wanted to work with would know that it was the arrangement and not the original." Sophie recalled the man afraid at St. Vitus Cathedral, pointing out Novak's power. Then she recalled Sidorov trying—and failing—to procure the mask for himself. Perhaps not even knowing the true extent of its value. Then Adameck...

Adameck.

Novak's intermediary.

Sophie looked at the piece again, nodding in answer just as Simon made out a lorry far ahead. "Come," he said.

Several hours later, finally Vienna announced itself in its restoration—cranes and craters amid the backdrop of steeples and spires against the steel gray of the sky. She wove the Bentley in the direction of Esterházy with the premonition that her time in the city was drawing to a close. If not by her own volition, then Simon's.

Wallnerstrasse was prime for construction. Signage marked the palace's gates and Baroque windows and facades for temporary leasing. Only the gold coat of arms bearing a crowned griffin was an insignia of the past.

Her parking job on the side of the narrow curb left a lot to be desired, but she followed Simon up the stone path. The palace wasn't grand like Schloss Schönbrunn or Belvedere: singular estates with manicured grounds. Rather, this palace's facade fell into line with the buildings rimming the street's thoroughfare.

As they strode up the deserted street, a portentous feeling crept over her, and she cast it off.

The broad double door of Palais Esterházy took little effort for Sophie to open, and their shoes echoed over tile worn from years of patrons and musicians, diplomats and spies strolling over it. The opulence surrounding her left her feeling exposed. But also as if she was falling back into her rhythm with Simon.

The interior was as empty as the street outside. But both Sophie's and Simon's hunches had aligned this location with Novak's plan to hide the mask, so she had to believe in their instincts.

Art and music exuded from the etches and lines of its architecture and in its many rooms: the grand foyer and salons exposed through broad, arched French doors. It didn't boast the same grandeur of the ballrooms and painted rafters of its namesake in Eisenstadt, but the tarnished and subdued Esterházy Palace still radiated its regal lines.

Sophie peered in and around the rooms one by one, assuming in their bare, absent-of-furniture state what function they might have served in Mozart's time. A library, a salon, a place for men to puff on cigars and roll brandy over their tongues.

And in a narrow ivory room with a window peering over a *Hof,* or courtyard, she was drawn to an upright Bösendorfer piano. She slid her finger through its veil of dust and admired the plaster garlands that draped across the ceiling that must once have held a chandelier given its gaping center.

Sophie peered beyond the piano as the sun streamed over the pocked, unvarnished wooden floor and spotted a box. Nondescript and just at the edge of heavy, drooping curtains.

"I didn't suppose it would be so easy to find," Sophie said, hearing Simon's footfalls behind her.

There was no lid and in its stead a sheath of black silk was only slightly indented to fit the shape of the object inside.

Strange. To most, the composer was preserved in oil paintings and sketches. His untimely death meant his youth was immortalized, sacred, and perhaps even heightened by those wishing to reflect his influence in a preserved visage.

What would she find? An eerie countenance? The pockmarks so familiar to those who had withstood the travails of the time? That whole Victorian-era notion of the circumference and size of the brain denoting genius?

From poverty and chaos he had fashioned genius. His music still throbbed under the mangled nails of her right hand as surely as if she heard it by heart just *being* in the city that inspired it.

Mozart.

A prominent nose and full mouth almost tipped up in a smile. Serene. Peaceful. Not handsome and not prepossessing. She imagined the plaster being poured over his just-chilled face. The mold curving over his cheekbones and the sockets of his eyes. There was a stark sadness to it. The warmth leaving a human. The light and flicker of creativity gone.

Simon scratched at his unshaven jaw. He gingerly ran his fingers over the interior silk, the careful contours and grooves of the case made for its precious cargo. Whatever fragments she had pieced together in the *Der Messias* manuscript were made whole here. Doubtless, men under Novak's influence were still grabbing at pieces and messages and codes in hopes of finding what they had: the genius of the piece made manifest in the visage of the man here.

"What are we going to do with it? I don't fancy it becoming a rallying cry or symbol for Novak's Communist agenda."

Simon took a moment. "And I already have the albatross of a lordship hanging over my name, I won't be responsible for sneaking this out of the country."

"It belongs in Austria," Sophie decided. "He was born there."

"Yes, but didn't Prague give him the wonderful send-off? They appreciated him."

"But Austria created him."

Simon's smile was just a flicker but still it sparked his eyes. He was slowly coming back into himself and she loved it. "It's your call of course, Sophie. You did what Haas and that fiend Sidorov asked you to do. You're the one here with it."

"I don't think we should keep it or even leave it hidden away in here. Someone else might come after it. For the wrong reasons."

"No?" Simon raised an eyebrow. "We'll think of something. Sometimes the best place to conceal is in plain sight."

CHAPTER 43

Simon took it all in. This palace in Wallnerstrasse that bore the fingerprints of academic men studying it in miniature at the exhibition. Perhaps not even knowing the extent of its significance or the treasure it hid when they moved around Moser's world. Simon was used to secrets unfurled at parties or in grand salons but at a pace as languorous and arduous and slow to find its rhythm as the longest chess game.

He didn't understand the significance of Mozart's arrangement of *Der Messias,* but he did appreciate it, especially if it was a bread crumb leading to his greater understanding of the man. Sophie had told him that Mozart had arranged *Messiah* specifically for performances in Vienna. Diana had often told him that stained glass was artfully inserted into churches so illiterate populations could internalize the Scripture spoken from the pulpit in a visual language they would understand.

Perhaps Mozart's function was a similar one.

But after the bounty had been excavated, Simon felt oddly disappointed. Novak's life had already ended. The symbol of mortality before him reminded Simon of what he was trying so hard to compartmentalize: that the puzzle he tried to complete in learning about his history—his very belief that the revelation of his natural father would help him understand his limitations and strength—led him to disappointment. What he didn't find in Barrington's estimation, he certainly wouldn't find in Novak's legacy.

Simon stilled beside her. Perhaps the grief was manifest in the contours of Simon's face. Perhaps etched so deeply they would change his countenance like the contours of Mozart's face.

God's beloved was human, buried in a pauper's grave and penniless at the last. His glorious requiem was finished by an unknown. His *Der Messias* was not fit for Handel's heavens to many listeners. A visage unremarkably human.

"Do you regret your choice?" Sophie's whisper surprised him. Something about the hallowed moment, so reverent to her upbringing and passion, prompted her to need to hear he would choose her, even if her heart had sewn up the certainty before he put it in words.

"No," he said without beat or breath. "But that doesn't mean I don't wish that things were different."

For a moment she looked at him, her wide eyes full and glistening.

Sophie focused on the mask, and her study matched the serious attention of Herr Müller. He supposed Sophie had a gift Simon had underestimated, so focused on drafting his way through his time in Vienna pursuing Eternity. But it became more complicated as it stretched beyond Britain. Where Communists no longer had to hide.

Simon merely nodded and carefully lifted the visage from its resting place.

Sophie drew a steadying breath and accepted the mask from its resting place. There was also a page of the manuscript she had pursued. Sophie studied it solemnly.

"I guess he wanted a piece for himself. Another part of his safety net. So no one would ever put the entire manuscript together. 'Brecht entzwei die Ketten,'" she read the title. It was this that widened Sophie's eyes as she returned the mask to the box's safekeeping.

"*Break the chains in two,*" he translated.

When Simon first determined footsteps in the vacant palace hallway, he supposed he was hearing things. Even so, he instinctively reached for his gun, though the movement tightened Sophie's stitching job across his shoulder. Simon winced and motioned her behind him as he slowly stood, outstretching his right hand.

"Adameck." Sophie addressed the man before Simon could speak.

"What are you doing here?" Adameck seemed as perplexed to see Sophie and Simon as Simon was to see him.

Nonetheless he reached into his pocket—presumably to draw his weapon but thought better of it when Simon clicked the trigger of his own.

Simon didn't want to shoot anyone else, even if this man deserved it after killing David Moser at Novak's command. Simon wasn't sure if he could. He certainly didn't want Sophie to. So that left this man like a gnat: unwanted, yes, but hovering nonetheless.

Before Simon could answer him, Adameck spoke. "I hadn't heard from Pan Novak in days." His cold tone faltered.

Perhaps it was punishment enough that Adameck slink off to find another leader. Simon didn't have any crucial evidence that he was a murderer. Previously, he would turn to Brighton for that, but he sensed his former supervisor would be sweeping a lot under carpets using the defense of this spreading new war.

Novak clearly trusted this man, but Simon didn't know on what grounds. Fortunately, Simon's intense glare and his gun kept him talking.

"No one's been here. It's been empty as a tomb. Novak only let a few trusted men know what was here. He said it made the information communal."

Simon turned to Sophie with a slight nod.

"He was planning on coming here." Adameck stepped near the mask.

"He's dead," Sophie said.

Simon wasn't sure how she anticipated how difficult it would be for him to utter those words, but he appreciated her assistance.

Adameck was far from threatening. He was just as confused and exhausted as Sophie and Simon were. Without Novak, he had lost his compass.

"Why did you try to kill me?" Simon asked.

"I had seen you with Marcus Brighton, and Novak told me I should trust him as far as I could throw him. I never meant to *kill* you. I just meant to threaten you. Novak told me you had established territory in Vienna. I bought off a few men to prove that we had too."

Novak had mentioned he used men who wanted to hide themselves into a new war when the old one didn't go their way. Adameck was perhaps acting more out of desperation than any conviction. And Simon was desperate to end this part of the game. But what if it led back to Brighton, who might wield his power to keep Adameck in his pocket?

No. It was best if Adameck was far away. Simon doled out his own justice now.

And ironically it required becoming a Barrington. "If you promise to leave Vienna, I can pay you off."

CHAPTER 44

This was his heritage, Simon gathered after Adameck had accepted his payoff and promised to disappear far from Vienna or Prague. More than the green span of Camden or his father's provisional wills. Simon was the product of a union that met in the middle of a philosophy he railed against. His mother's pamphlets. His father's slow, steady control of Prague using artifacts and music, and Simon's belief that he could respond to the wealthy world that shunned him by fighting a cold war.

Perhaps Orwell coined said term because so many of the men involved in it never got farther than a waiting freeze. Hoping intelligence collected crystalized into something to help them gain an advantage over their enemy.

But Simon had enough to trust Gabriel Langer and Müller to see where the next piece of music would lead while he and Sophie stepped into the shadows of his new lordship. The latter had been an afterthought since Finchley's telephone call. Buried under his need to find Sophie, his revelation about Novak, and the very real fact that both of them had pulled the triggers.

While the demises of Sidorov and Novak were justified in their saving of each other, and while the result of his gunshot bore a far deeper emotional resonance, Sophie would also bear the weight of pulling the trigger. Her killing of Sidorov would certainly rouse her from sleep and cause her to run her left hand with its still-strong fingers over her kneecap.

Simon was scribbling on a small piece of paper extracted from his disheveled coat when Sophie drew his attention the third time she said his name.

"Do you think that you understand Novak?" she asked.

She didn't finish the sentence, but he knew what she wondered. If he could *think* like Novak, he might be able to do something with the bounty before them.

He could have easily answered her in broad strokes, but instead he read the depth of her question and answered in turn. "I don't have the luxury of processing Novak now. Not beyond what we have here. I killed my father. When I finally stop to think of it, then the dam will break perhaps. In most important instances of my life, I have had to compartmentalize. My mother. My suddenly being the Camden heir." He reached out and stroked her cheek. "Our wedding night as well. Our *true* wedding night. And now. But in both instances, I had you."

Her gaze lowered to study the scuffed floor, and he shifted and rebalanced his weight as a sharp pain stabbed his shoulder. Simon winced, then made out a strange weight in his inner pocket.

A quick pat of his jacket and he knew exactly what it was.

He reached in and extracted the pearl necklace he had tucked inside. The clasp had broken. He hadn't previously noticed, and perhaps that was just as well. He might have seen it as an omen as he set out to find Sophie.

"Here." Simon held out the necklace to her. "Didn't you once tell me this was your safety net? A sure way to find your independence if you needed it?"

Sophie's fingers met the beads with familiar affection. "Yes."

He put his hand over hers and drew it over the silk case of the death mask. "Novak needed his own safety net."

———◦◦◦◦◦———

Judging by the look on the doorman's face, the rotating gold doors of the Sacher Hotel had seldom seen worse than an injured man and woman seeking the russet halls and the guarded opulence of his expensive suite.

When they finally reached his room, Sophie opened the curtains and peered out with an exhale at her temporary home.

No wonder Mozart played to the rafters and settled over the patched stones of each church. He was desired for his music and accepted by his father, Leopold, who so greatly saw the span of his talent as he paraded him through every palace and salon in Europe. When Simon pursued the same acceptance, it was not through talent but succession. Yet how similar were the expectations impressed on both?

Sophie moved the mask to the wardrobe while the hotel doctor saw to a much better treatment of Simon's shoulder.

Simon wondered how interconnected Brighton was with Novak. He supposed as the election grew closer and the American plan became more transparent to Brighton, he panicked as to how to secure his influence. And Novak—or at least the magnanimous reputation preceding him—required Brighton to alter his usual code of conduct. That was why Novak had insisted they play. So he could prepare Simon for the world he wanted him to infiltrate.

"Brighton's not the enemy," Simon said absently but loud enough that Sophie looked up from the manuscript pages of the three intact movements from the second part of the oratorio.

"Perhaps not. Many men have creative ways of fashioning their conscience to get what they want." But where did that leave the rest?

There were still some he could trust.

Gabe Langer was more than fit to continue what Simon had started. He'd give him his encrypted information and the key that would unravel it: K. 453. It would most likely lead him back to men whose shoulders he had brushed at soirees and whose lectures had filled the classrooms at the university Brent Somerville had just vacated.

When Simon called him to mention that a former Nazi sympathizer with a distinctive car and a glass eye had just walked away with some of Simon's fortune, Gabe knew exactly how to put justice in motion.

"He'll be rich," Langer had said. "But it won't do him much good." There were Nazi hunters in Prague and Vienna. It wouldn't take them long to find Adameck.

Simon adopted a greater purpose. In this new era, what men valued might change as quickly as day to night. So he imagined a new scenario. Herr Müller drawing back black silk so a face etched with genius met him, and the man falling into his chair, a slow smile stretching. Müller would never hear from Starling again. And the mask would find its home among dusty antiques and artifacts that, like so many, were just trying to find their way home.

Try as he might to convince himself he could remain objective, Simon would be far better suited far away from Brighton's world and MI6. If his heart hadn't been in the job before, it certainly wasn't now. He couldn't be certain of Brighton's allegiance, but he knew his own.

Camden.

If he couldn't set wrong to right on a large scale, why not start with his corner of the world? He studied the mask for one last languorous moment.

Warming to his plan, he turned to Sophie. "We'll hide it in plain sight."

CHAPTER 45

Summer 1947
Camden, Sussex

A nd even though I know that there is little chance I will see you again, I was going to go with you."

His mother wrote her love story across an imagined rendezvous much as Simon had his own across two wars. But she had stayed at Camden. For Simon, on grounds now swallowing him in manicured bushes and cushioned lawns, he tried to see the estate through her eyes.

Sophie and Simon had come full circle. Back to the oil paintings his mother had loved, the Meissen porcelain, the Beidermeier chessboard unplayed like the Bösendorfer that Simon had recalled from Ashton. He wasn't on friendly terms with Sophie's parents, but he was on monetary terms, and he was learning swiftly that the latter secured a far more lasting bond.

Still, he never found the closure he always assumed would accompany the final play and the revelation of his father. Perhaps Simon and Tab Martin and Gabe Langer were all pawns who made one move or another and propelled the final game a little bit forward. It was hard to see how his own participation would contribute to halt the spread of his father's Communism. But hadn't Diana often spoken of the stonemasons who had worked piece by piece on the great cathedrals, knowing they would never see its completion in their lifetimes?

Sophie and I are just one brick.

THE *Mozart* CODE

His looking for an ending merely kept him from their beginning.

He felt more committed to Sophie in the moments that colored their every day. When he saw her grumpy after a sleepless night or held her when sleep was interrupted by a nightmare recalling Sidorov's questioning.

Simon had heard Sophie's left hand run a scale or two, and he had been reading of a man who had found great success in using exercises and therapy to improve the lives of wounded veterans. Simon would lift a chess piece again when she pressed her right fingers to the keys. Though she had lost her fingernails, they had stalled the ability of her nerves to regenerate and heal. As if her fingers were tucked tightly into her palm in compensation of memory and must be held close. Additionally, there was a ghost of a painful impression that kept her fingertips from achieving the easy dexterity she had enjoyed before.

But until then, he found his mother's heartbeat in the grand halls and marble arches. She had died for love. Barrington could not live with his wife acquiring passion beyond their careful match. He resented her and finally disposed of her—even as her memory and taste pervaded the hallways and grounds Simon was becoming accustomed to viewing, not as the illegitimate heir but lord and master.

So he would redeem the estate. They'd start by consolidating Sophie's interests at Ashton with Simon's insistence that his own inheritance—especially as it pertained to the men who had relied on Barrington for their family estates and investments—be well cared for. Slowly, surely, Simon put the misdirected faith he had in his father and Barrington and even Brighton into a future with her.

The furniture in the new wing looked like slouched ghosts, with their protective white sheets and covers. Sophie saw to the retrieval of her favorite pieces of art from Ashton and a few of the new horses too.

Evening darkened the window, and he caught his reflection and straightened his bow tie before narrowing his gaze on the cut of his cheekbones and the curve of his chin. The turn of his mouth that when smiling or in a rigid line of concentrated thought featured brackets on either side just like his mother. His blue eyes belonged to his father: the same eyes looking back at him as Novak's life drained away.

A moment later, Simon stepped out of the second-floor suite and peered over the banister of the open gallery overlooking the party in the grand ballroom, where ladies' silk spilled over the sheened tiles like liquid, and laughter from men his father knew rumbled over crystal-cut decanters.

For a moment he froze. Felt every nerve and sinew up through his forearm. He couldn't do it. He couldn't straighten his spine and command the room as he had at Schloss Schönbrunn so many months ago. He couldn't find that strength. Hadn't he left the last of it in Prague?

The grand staircase he descended had always reminded Simon of a comma, but to Sophie it swerved like a bass clef. It was one of the first things she had remarked on as they began grafting their life together. Now, at its base, Simon accepted a glass of champagne from a passing server and forced his lips into a smile, then moved in and around dignitaries and earls in a complicated waltz.

"Here, darling. Snagged you a little something from the serving staff." Sophie appeared at his arm with a plate of oysters on the half shell. Her brown eyes were as carefully lined as her red lips.

"Those could kill me, you know."

"You've made it this far." She leaned up and kissed his cheek. "But keep your shucking knife with you at all times. Just in case."

She took a slow sip of champagne as the musicians in the corner warmed to Mozart. "K. 428. String Quartet no. 16 in E-flat Major," Sophie recited.

Would every Mozart piece be a possible equation thereafter? He lifted her damaged hand to his lips. Simon traced Sophie's shoulder blade and farther down with his fingertip.

"There are guests," she reminded him.

"Then you shouldn't have worn that dress." It was emerald, of the same color palette as the dress she had worn the first night he truly met her. It was only devoid of one thing: the pearls he had seen mended with a new clasp currently situated in his right pocket. They had hosted some parties together, but this one was particularly auspicious on account of its guest list, and Simon wanted to mark it with a memorable moment.

"Simon!" she chided as he pulled her tight to his side.

The grand ballroom was strewn with acquaintances and almost-friends—lined like garlands sparkling with pretentious titles and dripping with jewels that snagged the chandelier's light.

Sophie's hand in his was a barometer of his ease as they approached different sets, nodding and standing on ceremony. Playing a role. He read the slightest emotion: a laugh or a wink or a smile in the pressure of her palm against his, their fingers intertwined.

"You're made for this, Simon."

"Well, some guests are more palatable than others." He let go of her hand but only to extend it to Brent and Diana Somerville.

"I come bearing gifts!" Brent Somerville handed Sophie a newspaper while keeping one arm tightly in Diana's.

"'Death Mask Rumored to Belong to Wolfgang Amadeus Mozart Found in Vienna Pawnshop.'" Sophie's voice held a grin as she read the headline.

"Imagine something so priceless being found in a pawnshop!" Diana said, eyes wide at Simon.

"Priceless things are being found everywhere nowadays." Sophie sipped her champagne, her gaze meeting Simon's. "Wouldn't you say, darling?"

———◦◦◦◦———

With Simon's hosting alchemy, the guests were appeased. Even her parents were impressed. *Mostly* impressed, Sophie decided. Every corner of the evening was lightened once Diana confirmed she and Brent were starting a family, and talk of christenings sparkled with the champagne and music.

Simon immediately promised to provide a new pony.

"If it's a boy, we'll call him Peter." Diana sparkled. "For you." She looked to Simon with a smile.

Simon ducked his head and a smile spread. "Simon called Peter." Peter who was the scriptural rock on which the churches she loved were inspired.

"You'll be his godparents," Brent added.

"He must have riding lessons." Simon warmed. "His education! Any school. Anywhere in the country. Or abroad. Do they still do grand tours, my love?"

Sophie loved the smile that was just starting to come back. It was full-on and bright as a light bulb, most likely with the realization that the place that had so long been an albatross on his self-worth and memory was somewhere he could host friends and create new memories with her. Nonetheless, Brent cleared his throat uncomfortably at Simon's generosity.

The more she saw Simon's smile the weeks after Prague, the more she felt burdened to restore him. Not to the Simon straining to find purpose or legacy, but rather the Simon underneath his pin-striped armor and crisp collars. Kind and smart and so willing to love.

She wished she could have accepted that love much earlier. But she settled for the way it filled her now.

Now it led her to follow him outside as the manicured grounds stretched perfectly before them. As they did now while the party buzzed behind them.

Lights winked over the garden, and the fragrance of freshly bloomed buds and grass met her nose. Sure, the weight of his inheritance settled around them in marble and stone, even as he interlaced their fingers and drew her marred hand to his lips as gently as the breeze stirring the cloths on the high tables through the French doors and a few bars trilled from a violin.

Le Nozze di Figaro. "The Marriage of Figaro."

Simon often had the hired musicians play her favorite pieces as a surprise. So that in the interim of her feeling Mozart beneath her fingers, she could make him out in the corners of their estate. That way he was always there.

"Ah tutti contenti saremo cosi." She recited the missing lyrics the violinist played by heart. "Then let us all be happy."

For now she was happy, holding tightly to Simon. But it might not always be so. Happiness might hide under a spat or be buried under the expectations of a world whose key and tempo might change as quickly as the war they had survived. Happiness might hide under his pillow on the nights when she felt him jolt awake in memory of the chapter of his history he closed.

The violin's refrain started the aria's motif again as Simon retrieved his cigarette case from his cummerbund. He struck a match against the veranda. She read a promise in the movement of his pressing his lit cigarette to hers and eternity in the smoke shared in subsequent silence.

"Happy, Sophie?" His question sat in a halo of smoke.

"I love you, Simon Barrington." She dropped her head to his shoulder. "I love you. I love you." It was remarkable how easy three words came now. Perhaps not so remarkable considering they had been there all along.

With little space between them, she felt more than heard the rumble of his laughter.

"See?" He flicked the last ashes of his cigarette. "That wasn't so hard."

ACKNOWLEDGMENTS

It usually takes a village for a book to find its way into the world. But throughout the isolation and lockdowns and unprecedented anxiety of life in Toronto during a global pandemic, it took a massive metropolis.

Throughout my chipping through the ice of this book to thaw it into completion, I was met with the most incredible compassion and support. Indeed, I can safely say that this book of my heart would never have found its path to the page without the influence, patience, intelligence, and encouragement of many. A community that became a much-needed raft.

Kim Carlton: From late-night text chats during the most severe days of lockdown through drafts and drafts where you believed that this story was capable of things I couldn't envision myself achieving, you were not only my book whisperer but a dear, dear friend. My respect and admiration for you as an editor and friend knows no bounds. I am truly blessed to know you, and I aspire to employ your patience, integrity, and compassion. My books have benefited greatly from your influence. I have benefited greatly from your wisdom and patience.

Julee Schwarzburg: Your name deserves to be on this book as much as my own. Not only did you sacrifice days and nights and holidays for my *London Restoration*, you gave your all (and more) to Sophie and Simon's love story, and I am awed by your devotion to it. I so respect your talent. You have made me not only a better writer but also a better person. May I strive to put my all into everything the way you put your all into the manuscripts in your care.

Amanda, Becky, Caitlin, Kerri, Savannah, and Margaret: It is an honor to work for a community of book lovers who treasure integrity as well as challenge me to be a better version of myself. I love being a part of the team.

Bill Jensen: my agent, colleague, and friend. I was so delighted to express our shared passion for Mozart and *The Messiah* in this book of mine. I appreciate and admire you so much, and I continue to learn from your example.

To Susan Elia MacNeal, Ashley Weaver, and Anna Lee Huber: You provided joy and support constantly during a very bleak hurdle of my life. How fortunate am I that women I respect so much have shown immense grace in uplifting me through challenging creative moments.

Kate Quinn: You inspire me to go back to my book love first and know that my own rambly words will find their way. I am privileged to know you.

Mimi Matthews: You are truly a kindred spirit both on and off the page. Your steadfast resilience is a constant inspiration to me. Thank you for being a constant listening ear.

J'Nell Ciesielski and Aimie Runyan-Vetter: I am honored to have you as colleagues and friends, and I am so happy that we are throwing our creative lots in together.

To my guinea pig readers Courtney and Renee . . . I am so, so thankful for you. You inspire and encourage me at every corner. Simon loves you, and so do I!

To Linton and the crew at Union Social in Toronto: You don't know what you've got 'til it's gone. Oh, how I needed my space there during the harshest days of the pandemic. Luckily, there was light at the end of that dark tunnel. My books are so often passport-stamped by amazing writing sessions in my corner there.

Elaine Choi and Lori Diaz: Those magnificent lectures on Handel's *Messiah* helped fuel my passion for the theology behind *Messiah* as well as its many incarnations. Thank you.

To Patti Callahan: Thank you for always being in my corner, for encouraging and inspiring me.

Allison Pittman: I will never *not* move you to the top of my text chats. Forever and ever. You're my jam. You're the first person I want to share news with and the last person I want to share a snarky comment with before I go to sleep. We are BOGO!

Sonja Spaetzel: I have no idea what to say. So I just hope—as per always—you read between my lines. My life is so much richer because you are in it. And I am blessed that you are so invested in me. You're my lifeline, Spaetzel.

Annette Gilbert: Of course, a book that features Mozart wouldn't exist without you. When I was a kid and you showed me *Amadeus*, I cherished how you let me into your world. So often when I put pen to paper, I think "I hope Annette will like this." I love you, AOMH.

To Jared and Tobin, Leah and Ken: Thank you. From care packages and phone calls, books about embracing myself and pandemic-inspired home-made wines labelled for Sophie Villiers, I will never ever forget your kindness and belief. I am so fortunate that I not only *like* my family—but also consider them friends.

Gerald and Kathleen McMillan: You believe in me more than I ever will believe in myself. I know the greatest way I can honor you is to attempt to live by your example in whatever poor and faltering way your anxious and imaginative daughter can. So I could attempt to fashion the sacrifices and unending support you've given me into a paragraph, or I could tell you that the threads of Matthew 6:19–20 sewn into the tapestry of this poor and wavering book offering of mine are my way of acknowledging your example. Every part of my life and my work is imprinted by your unfailing faith in me, yes, but also (and most significantly) your unfailing faith.

With special thanks to Eva Ibbotson, Patrick O'Brian, and John Murphy.

Wien—mein Herz—you always make me feel as if a little part of me has always belonged to you. And I wouldn't want it any other way. Before my time my Oma found and fell for you and much, much later, I learned I inherited her passion. I cherish and keep that close . . . and always will.

DISCUSSION QUESTIONS

1. When we first meet Simon Barrington in *The Mozart Code*, we learn that he has left his real name with his favorite revolver back at his family's estate. How did this information shape your first impression of him and how much you trusted him?

2. *The Mozart Code* is not a traditional spy story, but rather a love story. For one, it is more interested in the slow pace of the onset of the Cold War through Simon's chess game with Das Flüstern and Sophie's pursuit of invaluable and misplaced relics. But the ultimate purpose is to bring Sophie and Simon together. In what way was *The Mozart Code* a unique experience from some of the other espionage-driven stories familiar to you through movies, TV, and books?

3. When Sophie's first (and only) mission for the fledgling Baker Street Irregulars goes awry, she allows herself to be truly vulnerable with Simon for the first time at the Mayfair House. Likewise, when Simon's father and brother reveal his illegitimacy to Sophie at Camden, Sophie confesses she likes it when Simon allows himself to be vulnerable and human in front of her. How does their finally revealing their vulnerable sides begin to fortify their love story?

4. Simon is able to express his love for Sophie in words, whereas Sophie proves her love for Simon in action and what she is willing to do for him. Are you someone who finds it easier to express emotions in words or in gestures?

5. In several instances, we are shown that Sophie sees the world through music, whereas Simon sees it as a chess board, and yet the longer they spend together and the deeper their relationship, the more these lines of art and logic blur. What are some other ways that Sophie and Simon complement and influence each other the more we learn about their history and growing love story?

6. Sophie never truly recovers from her perceived failure when she is recognized on her first SOE mission. Indeed, not only is Sophie's self-perception greatly influenced, but also her growing desire to find a life far from her recognizable heritage. Is there a mistake in your past that has shaped some of your decisions and life choices? How have you worked toward forgiving yourself and moving forward?

7. Mozart's influence is prominent throughout *The Mozart Code*: from Sophie's enthusiasm for the composer through the rumored death mask and as emblemized in two cities precariously threatened by the fall of the Iron Curtain who lay claim to the composer. When it comes to the restitution of the Mozart mask and Sophie and Simon's decision as to where it truly belongs, did you agree with their choice? Why?

8. When Sophie first encounters Simon in adulthood, she feels an immediate rapport with him. Likewise, Simon is able to open up to her when they share a silent moment on the veranda. Can you think of a time when you felt an immediate affinity with someone? How did it influence the relationship you have with them now?

9. Sophie and Simon both end up giving the thing they love most (Sophie, the piano; Simon, his sense of long-pursued belonging) for each other. Can you think of a time you put something—or someone—else above what you wanted most? How has that sacrifice influenced you to this day?

10. With Novak, Sophie begins to believe that cities had chosen "human portals through which to whisper their secrets." Can you think of a place that whispered its story to you?

11. Though Simon and Sophie try their utmost to escape into one war (through their work at Bletchley Park) and then another (in early Cold War Vienna), they are never far from its shadow on their heels. Can you think of an inopportune moment when your background or past presented itself?

12. Names are a major part of Sophie and Simon's journey to finding new belonging with each other: the names they give each other at their first chess match at Camden; Sophie's moniker "Starling"; Simon's embracing of the name Barre; and Sophie's using the barometer of Simon's use of "Villiers," "Sophie," or "Sophia" to gauge how he is feeling toward her. Why do you think names are important? Is there someone significant in your life who calls you a term of endearment or nickname when you are away from everyone else?

ABOUT THE AUTHOR

Photo by Agnieszka Smyrska

Rachel McMillan is the author of The Herringford and Watts Mysteries, The Van Buren and DeLuca Mysteries, and The Three Quarter Time series of contemporary Viennese romances. She is also the author of *Dream, Plan, Go: A Travel Guide to Inspire Independent Adventure* and *The London Restoration*. Rachel lives in Toronto, Canada.